I0817616

More Praise for

KILL DICK

"*Kill Dick* is a love letter to LA's darkness and light."
—*USA Today*

"If this book were any better, I'd cut my own head off."
—Ottessa Moshfegh, author of *Lapvona* and *My Year of Rest and Relaxation*

"Finally, a book brave enough to say what we've all been thinking: Dick has got to go."
—Lukas Gage, author of *I Wrote This for Attention*

"*Kill Dick* is a fever dream. Luke Goebel perfectly captures the consciousness of a certain kind of woman—raw, lonely, desperate, and cinematic. Full of grief and longing, it's got some of the most unforgettable sentences I've ever read. This book makes me want to write a crime novel, move to LA, or maybe just become a killer. Goebel is something else."
—Harriet Armstrong, author of *To Rest Our Minds* and *Bodies*

"Stunning. Part noir thriller, part searing social commentary, *Kill Dick* follows a young artist-turned-addict through the dark, unforgiving, and stratified streets of Los Angeles as she confronts her father's complicity in the opioid epidemic. In bleak, beautiful prose, Luke Goebel weaves together a narrative that exposes the savage heart of privilege and power, raising questions about truth, memory, and the nature of storytelling itself. With haunting descriptions of a city literally and metaphorically aflame, *Kill Dick* captures the burning zeitgeist of our time."
—Kimberly King Parsons, author of *Black Light* and *We Were the Universe*

"For lovers of Bret Easton Ellis, Luke Goebel's *Kill Dick* renders a pop-infused and murderous portrait of an iconic Los Angeles on fire—complete with pools, pills, ennui, murders, and a cacophony of brands. But this novel has a timely pulse, and Goebel—with his gorgeous sentences and imagistic prowess—pulls off one of the hardest tricks of all: making morality fun."
—Melissa Broder, author of *So Sad Today* and *Death Valley*

"Engrossing, fanatical, full of private grief, and yet charismatic, tender, and intrepid—aglow with more spirit than most Americans have the right to wield."
—Blake Butler, author of *There Is No Year* and *300,000,000*

"From Brentwood to Thai Town, West Adams to Skid Row, Luke Goebel's irresistible *Kill Dick* draws a deranged—and yet curiously, charmingly relaxed—map of Los Angeles, coming off like a sun-dappled, shaggy cousin of *The Shards*. Like Eve Babitz before him, he seems to love and understand the city as few do, but Goebel's eye, his sly metafictive wit, and—above all—his language, are entirely his own."
—Matthew Specktor, author of *Always Crashing in the Same Car* and *The Golden Hour*

"Luke Goebel's delirious debut novel festers in the sun-sick, dissociative Southern California of Joan Didion and Bret Easton Ellis. In *Kill Dick*, Los Angeles is hell, and Susie Vogelman is its most reluctant angel: vacant, brilliant, heartbreaking."
—Anna Dorn, author of *Perfume and Pain* and *American Spirits*

"Luke Goebel's *Kill Dick* is a hypnotic descent into wealth, chaos, and the deranged art of self-destruction. It's like if Joan Didion and Hunter S. Thompson had a love child raised on Oxy and existential dread—impossible to look away from. The prose moves like stolen cash; the world is decadent and rotting at the edges. Honestly, if you're not reading this book, what are you doing? Probably something dull and unpaid. Consider this your invitation to the party—just don't expect to leave unscathed."
—Anna Delvey

"Someone I think I can trust."
—Giancarlo DiTrapano, founder of *The New York Tyrant* and Tyrant Books

"One of the last few geniuses we have left in this life. I mean that."
—Scott McClanahan, author of *Crapalachia* and *Hill William*

"I'm in love with language again because Luke B. Goebel is not afraid to take us back through the gullet of loss into the chaos of words. Beyond ego, beautiful, and look: there's an American dreamscape left. There's a reason to go on."
—Lidia Yuknavitch, author of *The Chronology of Water* and *The Book of Joan*

KILL DICK

A Novel

* * *

LUKE B. GOEBEL

Red Hen Press | *Pasadena, CA*

Kill Dick

Book layout by Ava Morgan

Library of Congress Cataloging-in-Publication Data

Names: Goebel, Luke B., 1980– author
Title: Kill Dick: a novel / Luke B. Goebel.
Description: First edition. | Pasadena, CA: Red Hen Press, 2026.
Identifiers: LCCN 2025021035 (print) | LCCN 2025021036 (ebook) | ISBN 9781636284651 hardback | ISBN 9781636284668 ebook
Subjects: LCGFT: Thrillers (Fiction) | Fiction | Novels
Classification: LCC PS3607.O333 K55 2026 (print) | LCC PS3607.O333 (ebook) | DDC 813/.6—dc23/eng/20250515
LC record available at https://lccn.loc.gov/2025021035
LC ebook record available at https://lccn.loc.gov/2025021036

The National Endowment for the Arts, the Los Angeles County Arts Commission, the Ahmanson Foundation, the Dwight Stuart Youth Fund, the Max Factor Family Foundation, the Pasadena Tournament of Roses Foundation, the Pasadena Arts & Culture Commission and the City of Pasadena Cultural Affairs Division, the City of Los Angeles Department of Cultural Affairs, the Audrey & Sydney Irmas Charitable Foundation, the Meta & George Rosenberg Foundation, the Albert and Elaine Borchard Foundation, the Adams Family Foundation, Amazon Literary Partnership, the Sam Francis Foundation, and the Mara W. Breech Foundation partially support Red Hen Press.

First Edition
Published by Red Hen Press
www.redhen.org

For Ottessa

"And now my beauties, something with poison in it I think, with poison in it, but attractive to the eye and soothing to the smell . . . poppies, poppies, poppies will put them to sleep."

—The Wicked Witch of the West, *The Wizard of Oz*

"The smell of the flowers is killing us all."

—*The Wonderful Wizard of Oz*

"They carried the sleeping girl to a pretty spot beside the river, far enough from the poppy field to prevent her breathing any more of the poison of the flowers, and here they laid her gently on the soft grass and waited for the fresh breeze to waken her."

—*The Wonderful Wizard of Oz*

1

In Brentwood Circle, Los Angeles . . .

Here they came again, the winds, blowing through Hollywood, up and around the hills—dry and hot—roaming across Mulholland into Sherman Oaks and onto Burbank, or whooshing Laurel Canyon and down Beverly Glen, sifting buttermilk-pancake dust up through Beverly Hills and Bel Air—rustling clusters of pines and palms, sun-lashed sycamore and coastal redwood, rows of Italian Cypress, sun-hot oranges and lemons—before finally touching down in Brentwood, where Susie Vogelman lay stoned on a chaise longue by the swimming pool in her backyard, wiggling her toes indifferently in the rushing air.

She'd be sober in two weeks and a couple of boys would be dead at her hands, but she had no idea what to do now, plastered to the upholstered chair in her mother's La Perla bathrobe. That fall was full of drama, but Susie wasn't paying too much attention. Not to the coming election, or "the killings," or the orange haze of doom that loomed on the horizon. Her mind was on the winds that carried the tawny dust from all over Los Angeles. She listened to the howling, slurped some drool. Her skin was burning through her tanning oil, but that was okay. Back in New York, she'd always stayed so pale. She'd been home since she'd dropped out of NYU about, what—a year, year and a half ago? Who could keep track of all that time? She'd spent most of it snoozing by the pool, feeling nothing, high. Dried cornflakes on her chin stuck like glue. She was safe. This was Brentwood. The barbarians at the gate didn't know the guards in the entrance pavilion.

A neighbor's yard wafted charred death into range, disturbingly seductive, warm animal flesh. Though she'd given up eating meat years ago, it was making her mouth water. The meal was likely being tended to by some interchangeable house staff, who from the smell of things was sneaking a cigarette. She knew cigarettes had been tested on lab beagles. Susie was pro-animal rights, anti-vivisection, anti-liberal, anti-conservative, anti-end-stage-capitalist—even as a child of fortune—but mostly she was anti-labels, anti-gravity, stoned as she had to stay upon the chaise by the water in order to tolerate her still life. The usual birds flitted and hummed in the pale air, fighting the autumnal gusts by the pool's teal surface. They landed in her trees in the backyard—hiding out with Susie from the terrible fates that were coming that miserable fall.

* * *

This version of things begins with me windswept and stoned on the chaise, completely unaware of the changes that would drop me into the light of the platinum city and the world of "the killings" which would come to define this season in Los Angeles. I didn't know it then, bombed on Oxy, the drug that was killing the world, but my young life was about to come rushing at me like a murderer. Everything was fate, like the wind, and blew past me unnoticed. I barely caught mention of "the killings" on the news, which I avoided at least so much as I could help it. When I had, on rare occasions, seen news of the deaths on TV of a few fellow junkies hanging from hooks by their skulls or with zip ties slipped around their throats, dead in motels across Hollywood, they only registered as random bodies mutilated in bad hotels. There were other, more compelling horrors capturing the attention of the nation in those months during the fall of my nineteenth year. Early victims of "the killings" were simply addicts who had overdosed and had their hair cut off—hard to say in which order—and then it was parlor tricks of nipples severed and glued to eyelids, all that loud dross attention-getting by some Los Angeles sicko who wanted to be Charles Manson . . . or maybe they lived in Upland, or out in The Valley. No one I'd ever know.

I turned it into art—that's what this novelization is about, this *roman à clef*: how protest was created, and how I, both an enfant terrible and an ingénue, was subjected to so much horror and engaged with it all. As a learning tool, or a study, a dead body is not new. I was the first to use the form as a medium for artistic protest. Or I became known as the first, which of course I wasn't. It incurred plenty of hatred in the public sphere, but I stay out of the public sphere, like anyone with half a brain. I am a private person, but all I went through had a cinematic quality, an artistic sense of public drama appropriate for these commercial times.

I, of course, learned that the first "murder," which had occurred a year before, was a young woman I knew. I later became convinced "the killer" was someone very, very close to me. As the writer of this piece, I don't want to be in relationship to confession. I'm not carving a statue of myself. In court, where you first heard from me, I was left having to account for myself after the events unfolded and often in ways that weren't entirely fulfilling. So much cannot be fully accounted for by myself or anyone else, now that they're gone: the victims. In order to craft this, I need to include multiple points of view, inviting the characters into the story, wrestling with their metaphysics as best I can. I'll slip back into my role of third person narrator, where I'm more comfortable, rejoining those terrible winds.

* * *

Susie Vogelman scratched the lapel of her mother's bathrobe, marred with breakfast cereal—the downers made it hard to keep her mouth closed while chewing—or, she wondered, was she just lazy? Her hair was a mess, but she figured she looked fine in her white Eres triangle bikini. Inside she felt like a late Picasso, one of those portraits of his wife Jacqueline that made Susie giggle at LACMA and MoMA. The open misogyny of it was funny from such a playful genius. Women *were* freaks.

Life in Manhattan had been a shock of stress after living in the slow town of LA; her sharp, Franco-Jewish features drew too much male attention. She looked like Mélanie Laurent from *Inglourious Basterds*. They had the same placid nose and cheekbones, which Susie believed hid her own inner landscape of chaos, her *Jacqueline*. She looked friendlier than she really was, which meant she had to act meaner than she was to rebuff those who thought they saw an opening, which was annoying—to have to play the bitch.

She was a bottle blonde but dark at the roots now. She knew she was pretty—not Hollywood pretty, but New York pretty, a shade too bony in the shoulders and hips for waist trainers and Brazilian butt lifts. *Fuck it.*

"You look French," the men in New York had said to her. "You look like a Parisian teenager." Sometimes she wore a scarf over her throat to hide the scar on her neck, not because she thought the scar was ugly, but because it was hers, like a private part, and men liked to point and say, "You have a scar," as though she didn't know that. As though she'd never even noticed the scar before. As if a scar could appear out of nowhere. As if the scratch hadn't even hurt. She'd been struck by a ricochet she'd caught the first time her father had taken her to a shooting range, when some idiot with a handgun shot a metal post. She clutched her bleeding windpipe while troglodytes with American flag hats and gun shirts stared blankly, not even half a hero in the bunch.

It was one of the most terrifying experiences of her life up to that point. While the injury was utterly superficial, superficiality was one of the defining characteristics of preteens on the West Side. So, no, she didn't want to hear about it from losers in New York; as if men in Manhattan could come up with anything original to say to anyone, nonetheless to a genius.

From professors to brokers to meatheads in the West Village, shitheads in the Meatpacking District, they said the corniest lines. "Are you a student? What's your major? What are you into? You look like that girl from *Inglourious Basterds*." From Washington Square Park to the Bowery. SoHo. Chinatown. The city had become a bad trip, one long night of partying that resulted in eyes crusted over with sleep and mascara, pockets full of snotted cocktail napkins from bars she couldn't remember going to, names and numbers scrawled in ballpoint pen—"Lovely to meet you." "I'm staying at the Standard. 317." "To my little French coquette." And her mind had slid out from underneath her. She'd failed her classes, all but the easiest one: it was an English course taught by Professor Krolik.

Susie was hungry, wondered if she needed another pill, then smelled the meat next door, and glanced at her body stretched below, almost transparent but leaden, like tanned solid glass. Peeking from the cups of Mom's Eres swimwear, she could say she didn't like her upward-turned breasts, nipples the color of pink carnations, the cheapest flowers, but she loved all flowers. She resented her body, like a friend she reluctantly took around, who solicited unwanted attention and was probably likewise annoyed with Susie for her lack of passion. She appeared like glass, transparent, fragile, invisible. She felt like lead at the deep end of the swimming pool.

Lying out by the water in the late sun, she was hoping to feel something special unfurling and curling around her finger, a new unseen mystical feeling beckoned like a gift from the chemical romance she could purchase in pill form and be close to, as it took *this* and gave *that* in exchange for her time, money, and selfhood. Living at Mommy and Daddy's was a mirror of self-hatred. She was a failed attempt at form at nineteen. An outline. A blob. But she took comfort in being blobby until the wind blew the blob into worse memories.

Finding her NYU roommate dead on their gray dorm room carpet hadn't helped her state of mind, with campus police swarming, a body bag, all of the questions. The roommate had OD'd while on prescription drugs—downers and OTC antihistamines; she was allergic to the city dust, or she had a heart condition—Susie never knew the whole story. There were inconsistencies, an investigation. The pills were never found. The girl's dark hair had been cut off in uneven hunks.

Susie had palmed the pills before campus security could get to them. Maybe she'd grabbed them to protect her roommate's privacy, although the pills showed up on the toxicology report. Maybe it was a proprietary sense of guilt, since Susie's own father was in the business of pain management. Maybe it was her karma. Or fate. Maybe she was just doing what her mother had done before her, reaching for pills, leaning into a void. Susie checked into The Carlyle Hotel, where she ordered truffle-dusted French fries and bottles of Veuve Clicquot, took the girl's Oxy, kept the TV on mute, hung the "Do Not Disturb" sign, skipped the funeral.

Susie thought of her old friend Faia after her roommate's death. Faia had stalked Susie for a time after high school, the summer before heading off to their respective colleges. Had Faia been watching her in New York? Hanging around Third North? Or the Village East while Susie caught the opening credits of an afternoon matinee before she passed out, drooling on her Moschino hoodie? No. Faia was back in Palo Alto, learning to be a robot. Susie hadn't even known her roommate was using Oxy.

She had turned her cell phone off, let her parents flip out with worry from across the country. She stared at the hotel walls remembering colors, no, not colors, but sensations, memories of an LA childhood that could make her sob, but she didn't sob—the downers. The times.

She felt like she had spiritually nuked herself now. An amoeba, by the water's edge. That's basically what one candidate was offering, the happy end of all compromise. Fascistic annihilation of all doubt and remorse. Susie took her annihilation in pill form.

In New York, the art students Susie knew were either wealthy or hustling to strike it rich, or else they were screaming and throwing their shit against a wall, passing it off as performance art. If anyone was looking, it was only to dismiss them as anonymous rats who wouldn't be any competition. They wouldn't be a target either, though. Fucking rats, they'd outlive us all. They had no ego, running the rails in ratty fur coats. The next day they were gone.

When she was accepted to NYU, her parents ordered her a cake with a mock copy of *The New Yorker* on it displaying Susie's face. God, it was humiliating. The magazine was a pitiful cunt rag of stupid snippets in response to lame art, tidbits of idiocy from people whose opinions were as tight-assed as their screwed-up faces. New Yorkers were mostly stupid and pretentious, practically glued to the guardrail of commercial groupthink and liberal brainwashing. In LA at least people didn't dare expose themselves. They smiled and ate the blinis and risked nothing, waiting to be entertained, talking about who they knew or what they'd seen or who they collected.

Upstairs, her mother clicked around on high heels and came down in a gust of perfume meant for a younger woman that smelled like a million flowers mixed with what—battery acid? Exhaust off the 101? Dior or Nina Ricci. Both trash. Her mother's Botox and fillers and facelifts. Her constantly rotating wardrobe of size six, thousand-dollar shift dresses. Her taut, freckled arms. Her mother whooshing in and out of wherever. She was like that flower whose name Susie couldn't remember—a vase of whatevers on the mahogany table in the foyer that the housekeeper kept replacing and replacing the minute they started to wither. An obligatory beauty. What were the flowers on the kitchen island called? She had painted them in elementary school. Bleeding hearts? No. Never in this house.

"I'm off," she'd say now, jangling her keys, leaving Susie to pant by the pool. No conversation. No air kiss. Just the lingering sting of mom's perfume, which was, Susie knew, distilled from a flower called *Disappointment*. She remembered her father from when she was a kid, and the Russian nanny who cared for her and had driven her back and forth to Marlborough. All her friends went there. She remembered the doodles she drew on the knees of her jeans. The housekeeper always scrubbed them out, erasing her art. The giant Flemish rabbit in the laundry room, the old pool, and the summer light on the pool—its shallow shimmer, the kind that doesn't settle, just keeps flickering, each ripple catching the light, holding it for a split second before it slides away, indifferently, into the next moment, and the next. The new pool was shaped like a kidney. Was Oxy bad for your kidneys? She could find out but she didn't care.

She'd returned home to this garden of her own after NYU, while the flowers of fascism threatened to bloom and her dad became more and more in love with talking about Nazis, like the character from the DeLillo novel he read every time the family went on vacation, along with *Inside the Third Reich*, *The Origins of Totalitarianism*, *Becoming Hitler*, *The Plot Against America*, *Hitlers zweites Buch*, and *Hitler: Downfall* as well as Wilhelm Reich and the rest of the basterds. The skull pin on a Nazi hat gracing the all-too-visible covers as he read by the beach. It was embarrassing.

On their last family trip to Thailand months ago—a five-star resort on an island that smelled faintly of lemongrass and chlorine—Susie developed a ritual. Each morning, before the sun had properly decided whether to scorch or seduce, she would retrieve her striped hotel towel and stake out a new lounger, always a few chairs farther from her family than the day before. In one hand, her sunglasses; in the other, a dense black slab of philosophical provocation: *Fanged Noumena: Collected Writings 1987–2007*, by Nick Land.

Her father, sweating rosé and still clinging to a TED Talk accent he'd adopted in the last few years, held court beneath a pretentious umbrella. That morning's lecture: the psychological taxonomy of men obsessed with World War II. "There's the romantic fatalists, the hardware fetishists, the alt-history fantasists . . ."—he had categories.

Susie, barefoot and unreadable behind mirrored lenses, was already gone, halfway down the beach to a less chaotic patch of sand. She dropped her towel, cracked open the book, and attempted—for the fifteenth time—to make sense of "Art as Insurrection," the essay her old English professor had cryptically recommended with the words: *You'll know when you're ready.* She wasn't sure she ever would be. A waiter passed by. "Another coconut water, miss?"

"Sure," she said, without looking up. "With rum."

Susie didn't have any friends now that she'd returned to her childhood bedroom with matching bedding and brocaded drapes decorated with flowers, her neat closet full of clothing hung and folded, smelling of the family detergent, which smelled like what? Like the house. Like the housekeeper. And sure, some fuckboys texted her but she ignored them. People invited her on social media to attend things and do things she'd never do.

Life went on. Barely.

What were those flowers on the kitchen island called? She could see them and not see them. No shape and color, but the shadow they made. By the pool now, grown up, mostly, she could still go all the way back to her childhood and to the laundry room and feel the rabbit against her ankle, Susie reaching down to clutch it against her, to hug it like a pussycat, its strange fast heart beating against hers, thinking, "I love you, pretty rabbit," just a moment before it scratched her across the neck and leapt out of her arms and back into the manicured yard.

Her father killed her bunny.

Dad—try to remember him from back then, she told herself, blinking her eyes away from the sun. She reached for her Ray Bans. Was someone watching her? She pulled her robe closed across her chest, then got hot and untied it and let it splay open. These were Garrett Leights. *Idiot.* She was safe. The house and grounds were safe. This was a gated community with a wall and a guard shack and another gate just to drive into their driveway. Her mother used to trip the alarms—*what's that fucking code?* She'd tap the buttons with sirens blaring after a Sunday out for Froyo and mani-pedis when Susie was young. Her mother always called her father. "What's the fucking code, David?" Acted cute when the security guards came, performing grandiose bewilderment.

He was always changing the code, paranoid, talking in secret languages over the telephone, project names that sounded like he was in the CIA. *Flamenco. Tango.* He *should* be worried, Susie thought. Her father was the attorney to the Sicklers, the billionaire manufacturers of Oxy, poison that killed hundreds of people on the daily. The fate of her family and her own life were inextricably bound to the Sicklers. It was bad karma. With her dad's help, they had intentionally targeted blue-collar communities of West Virginia. They hooked coal miners and poverty slaves on tablets of heroin. Eventually, their aggressively marketed pain relievers created a new world of pill-popping moms and dads with back pain and ergonomic office chairs. Then they'd taken the underground, turning counter-culture kids into opiate fiends who soon went straight to heroin that cut their throats, so to speak. Their pills were up and down Sunset, across fly-over nation, everywhere, dropping bodies. Susie wouldn't die, though. She knew when to chill with the pills. Six days on, one day off to clear the system. Her father's discipline had not been for nothing.

She remembered him coming home early from work one time, ranting about some kids who got tasered at UCLA and student uprisings, the threat of revolution, and the dark sides of human history. That was the day he took the Heckler & Koch HK416 from the safe—a short-stroke gas-piston rifle, fitted with a 30-round STANAG magazine—and let her cradle it. It felt clinical and inevitable, a bright-lined instrument meant to finish arguments.

"There are two kinds of people that matter," he glared at her. "And they both have guns like this. Everyone else has opted out of the conversation and is now irrelevant."

He taught her how to release the safety, take off the butt stock, take the gun apart and clean it. When she was able to do it without thinking, instinctually, adeptly, a soldier in her dad's army, he was satisfied and patted her on the head.

She was mortified now at the thought . . . Assault rifles were for racists, backwoods Confederate-flag-waving assholes. No one was coming up the hill to fight in Brentwood. Brentwood was not ripe for the revolution.

One morning while Susie ate her cornflakes, her father told the housekeeper to go mop somewhere else and explained to Susie that her mother would never be able to protect herself; that she didn't have it in her to grip the assault weapon with her long pretty gel-polished fingertips. Race wars festered under the surface, he told her. *The country isn't stable. Our people should be armed, us Jews. It's insane Jews don't all arm themselves. Criminals. Nazis. Radical socialists. Epstein. Blood libel is returning. Know how to shoot to kill. Head and heart.* Now that Susie knew how to use the gun, it would be up to her to defend the house if her father wasn't home, should the big one hit, if riots began, when they began. He told her about Rodney King, O.J., Manson, even SDS's "Days of Rage." The United Federated Forces of the Symbionese Liberation Army. The Altamont Free Concert and the Hells Angels stabbing a man to death from the stage while Jagger sang "Under My Thumb."

"Yes, Daddy." She was almost eleven. Honestly, it all sounded cool now.

That was her first *daddy* before men told her to call them that on Myspace, Facebook, in texts, on dating apps.

"Yes, Daddy. Yes! Yes! Daddy!" *As if!*

Who knew how much money her father made as a crooked attorney? Her father, always lumbering in and out of rooms, suit jacket an inch floppy under the armpits. She wondered if any of his money was in her name yet, now that she was of legal age, not a kid anymore.

Where was her father now? If she got up and picked some flowers, would she find him dead, too, on a blue-gray carpet inside the house? Could things work that way? Maybe, maybe. Susie didn't have the energy to get up and pick any flowers. She wasn't passionate enough in general, she thought. *A failure*, her parents would call her. *Stupid bitch.*

It's why she'd left the art program at NYU. She didn't have the fervor to compete with fellow students clamoring for internships at the Met or PS1. She dismissed them all as petty climbers, seducing married men who gave them Louis Vuitton Richard Prince collaboration handbags and Apple computers and took them to dinners or to the Hamptons, everything like an MTV reality show competition, immune to the coming tsunami swells of social change. All important art is born out of war and privilege. The great artists are the mild sufferers, because the real sufferers die. Who cares? Everyone sucked now.

"Just wait," Susie thought, glaring at those kids in class. "Your day will come. We are always *at war.*" Though her dad believed the tides of change would work against him, Susie believed they would work in her favor, redeem her. One day she would be resurrected, would reign supreme, the artistic genius of the new millennium, having put up with enough bullshit. She picked up her phone to post a photo of her armpit on Instagram—there was gritty ingrown hair growing among pilly dots of yesterday's antiperspirant. Isn't that the world right now? The unkempt armpit of the spoiled and suffering? She was a genius. She tried to take the selfie but the phone slipped through her fingers—the tanning oil.

In college, she had taken drawing classes and painting classes, and had studied art theory and art history, and for a while it felt right. She knew she was good at it. She painted still life oils of food and flowers. Her flowers were incredible—like Dutch painters from the 1600s. Such flowers. Such light.

No one liked her work. Her teachers tried to encourage her to leave still life in the past, and to be *relevant*—at least paint human models. Could she put a dead fetus in the fruit basket, her peers asked in critique, snickering. Maybe a severed penis in a bouquet of flowers, they laughed. But she didn't want to paint humans. "Humans are tacky," she told them. When pressed, she explained why: technology had perverted the human form. Vanity had overtaken the possibility of true beauty. People were used to looking at themselves on screens, and selfies had completely ruined portraiture. "Eventually the art world will max out on high concept and tech, return to texture, away from external fabricators. Flowers are the future. I like truth."

She could tolerate Cézanne's still lifes, but hated his portraits. She didn't like Egon Schiele, although she appreciated the waxy malleability of his subjects. At least they were honest. Everyone's face and body had been objectified on Facebook and Instagram from birth. Flowers were interesting. People thought they were small nothings, but Susie knew the flower had been miscast all of its life, mistaken for delicate when it was actually a kind of trap. A siren call for attention. *Look at me.* No—*really* look. Try to live in beauty, and in so doing, reject everything else.

What did Susie want out of her art? "What do you want to say?" her professors asked during critique. The very question was total condemnation and condescension.

"What do I want to say? Are you kidding? I want to say, 'Look at this fucking flower.'" She was already taking more pills.

A girl in the back of the class sneezed. "Sorry. Some of us have allergies."

The professor, in her forties and fading, crossed her legs and tilted her head.

"Flowers are losing their scent due to pollution. It's killing the bees, etcetera. So maybe you could make art about the environment. Take it out of the object and make it more abstract, so it has a deeper meaning. Save the bees, or something. *Glyphosate.* Clean the oceans."

"There's no deeper meaning," she grumbled.

"Have you ever thought about just being a florist? Cut out the middle man?" her teacher quipped. *Bitch.*

Susie stopped going to classes, used her ID card to access the NYU art studios in the Barney Building. She loved the feeling of painting high, and painted at night when no one else was there. She painted in her underwear in her dorm room alone when no one filled her roommate's place. She painted on downers. Then she painted less and took more pills. Then less and more and more. She roamed the dorm in a permanent bathrobe and a bad attitude and said "fuck you" when her RA knocked on a wellness check. "I'm dead." She was painting a mutilated rabbit next to an order of Peking Duck, smoking a Marlboro like Marla Singer.

She stayed at The Carlyle whenever the gray carpet got to be too much. One of her teachers, Phil Krolik, who believed in her as an artist, was in a different discipline, the English Department, and taught mostly about environmental issues, animal rights, plastic, like some washed up activist from the '90s. Susie didn't care about his affirmation. She liked his face. It was studly, and neurotic, which softened the jagged nose and jaw with a kind of skewed beauty, like a sick flower. Something that had bloomed too late. He responded to her with eagerness, solicitation of approval from her that made her feel seen and powerful, like she was the one grading him. She invited the professor to The Carlyle. They didn't have sex. She just painted him and they talked on pills.

Looking back, Susie was pretty sure he was gay. She'd seen it in the way he dressed, weirdly pristine, pants a little too short, and how his gaze never rested on her lips or her breasts or exposed midriff, but over in the corner of the room as though an invisible man were standing there. She kind of missed The Carlyle. The TV in her room had been impossible to navigate, so she'd just left it on a channel of sunsets and elevator music. It made everything seem okay for a while.

That was before she had "the break," as her mother had taken to calling it, which wasn't a "break" at all but simply a letter sent to her parents' address, from the dean, alerting them of Susie's failure to thrive at New York University, which her mother opened.

"So, you're having a nervous breakdown," she said coldly on the phone. But really, Susie had been very, very calm. (The Oxy was working.) She asked her hotel professor to call her mom and explain she was doing fine in his class. He'd obliged, saving her mother's number and later calling with a favorable report under the pretense that Susie had won some award for an essay she'd never even turned in.

By the pool now, Susie's mind was blooming very, very slowly. Words in her head were watery, and she sloshed them around, and the words dissolved, came undone. "Ooh ooh, ah ah!" She should call someone, she thought. She wished she had some friends in the neighborhood. She never had any true friends. Just Faia Sickler, the opioid heiress-to-be, who betrayed her in the end with kisses, then stalked her. Plus a loose quorum of uncaring socialites with whom her mother had forced her to associate as a teen. Artists didn't *need* friends, right? But they needed money and introductions. Works that looked like luxury items. Faia would have plenty of money and influence from the spoils of the opioid epidemic. They weren't friends anymore. Things had gotten weird after she'd kissed Susie at a party one night in the Bird Streets, feeling Susie up and forcing her down onto a bed.

Faia had been acting strangely back then, looking at Susie in a new light. It felt like another one of those mind games that Faia was perpetually playing. More and more since she'd gotten into prescription stimulants, cocaine, Valium, and Xanax. Faia was high that night on speedy coke, pulling Susie up the stairs of the three-story contemporary into a privacy bedroom with glass louvered windows and a mirror cut with lines. Ironically, Susie had been worried about her best friend's drug use back then. The Cure's "Pictures of You" played in the room and it felt like a Robert Downey scene in some '80s flick from back when Los Angeles was a glamorous empire, before the sun began to sink for good into the west, dropping into the sea like a departing god. That old song marked the moment she lost Faia and their friendship, as if the song had been a premonition for all that she was going to miss. Faia's family hated Susie all along, thought she was a hanger-on, an employee's daughter who didn't measure up. To them Susie was negligible as glass, and they looked right through her to the more rewarding scenery beyond.

The week after Susie pushed Faia away, Faia stole the boy Susie had been crushing on all throughout high school. Rod was anorexic-bulimic, had high cheekbones and a turned-up button nose with rabbit creases and flushed cheeks. He was Susie's only high school crush, a quiet drama-boy type who wore clothes like a male Audrey Hepburn, turtlenecks and boxy blazers with the crest and who rarely spoke; good boyfriend material. She'd wanted to finger his asshole. Suck his rod. Then Faia began following Susie and having her followed when Susie stopped talking to her, refusing to let Faia back in. By the time Susie was ready to make up, Faia refused.

"Helllloooo?"

Los Angeles was out there, right here, surrounding her. Maybe she should take one of her father's fast cars and go down to get a drink at a hotel bar, see what happened. The Polo Lounge or Hotel Bel-Air—*somewhere pink*—and do, what: stare at photos of Steven Tyler, Steve Jobs, or Joni Mitchell? A wave of nausea crept up her arms. She couldn't drive like this. *Stay put, Susie.* You're in the right place. Look at it, the bougainvillea crawling across the ten-foot walls, the flowers, look at them! She would grow up to be an important artist, oh yes. Maybe her painting teacher was right. Forget paint, focus on concepts.

After Faia stole Rod and turned him into her temporary lover, Susie realized all men were either too hard or too soft, too fickle or too stupid to know how to choose who to stay with, like in old Woody Allen movies she used to watch with Faia in the theater at the Sickler estate. She preferred to focus on herself as an artist until such time as she could meet a man or woman or whatever on her own terms, from a position of power, not end up like her idiot mother, or most of the other morons around the world who entered relationships without being aware they would end in misery or one of the many other forms of self-destruction and death.

Maybe she should have just kept her friend and put out and been happy. But the wet nature of Faia's jungly body and the way she felt absent inside Susie's mouth gave her the creeps. It was as if colonialists had already come to the overgrown habitat and stolen the resources, leaving behind a cursed sadness, a vacant coked-up pain Susie didn't want to feel spread as it slid against her leg. The automatic nature of

Faia's body in its movements made Susie feel alone. Maybe she was just a prude, inexperienced, afraid. She wanted her friend's love, not just some ass.

The cornflakes in the bowl had gone mushy. She dropped the spoon she'd been absentmindedly holding onto the hot grass. It was cool. She felt languid. *Oxy or Midazolam?* She couldn't remember. Midazolam prevented memories from being formed. The water on the pool was diamonds in clear velvet, waving at the sun. Her mother or father would be home soon. What was the pool water? *Diamonds on velvet.* She'd taken a green pill, she remembered. She'd been buying them from a kid she'd met online named Royal-Lee. The name Royal-Lee sounded like a guy from a boarding school in Connecticut, not a kid selling pills. She was suddenly feeling woozy.

What about the flowers?

The ones growing on this property, tended to by men in green landscaping company uniforms with jugs of poison on their backs? Would she and her parents get cancer from the tending of the flowers?

Which were the ones she loved most? The little purple flowers on lavender hubs, bursting like the thinnest glass, with sugar-crystalline-hairs, almost like salvia with tiger lines? Or, Dwarf sungolds? Red hot pokers? No, these were not the best. Parrot tulips. Showerheads like mons pubis. Veronicas. Wax flowers. Coral ginger. The impossible-to-replicate lilac—with the smell of memories. Certain smelling flowers: apple-scented roses, gardenias, jasmine, and gladiolas, sweet hydrangeas, fuchsia after rainstorms, woodland peonies. Mums. She wasn't getting to the best ones. Bluebells. Ranunculus. Pansies. Morning glories. Belladonna. Spider gerberas. Banksia. Milkweed. Phlox. Puya. Poppies. She thought of old Disney films in their plastic cases from her childhood. Singing flowers. *Alice in Wonderland. You really could learn a lot from the flowers.* What?

She'd always hated gerberas. Too neat. Too cheerful. Like the kind of flower you'd get from someone who didn't know you. Someone who smiled at you while you were backing slowly out of the room. Georgia O'Keeffe said nobody really sees a flower, not really—and maybe she was right. Because when Susie stared at the gerbera in the glass vase on the breakfast table, it didn't look happy. It looked weaponized. Engineered for appeal. That round, perfect face—too symmetrical to trust.

People read their own lives into flowers. That's what O'Keeffe meant. Sex, sorrow, cheap joy. Gerberas didn't mean any of that. They were just standing there, all color and geometry, waiting to be misinterpreted. Is that all she was?

She heard the door creak open and shut. She felt sad and at home and thought she heard him, her father. Was she asleep? Was she dreaming? Had she drowned in the pool? Was she a total drug addict now?

"Honey?"

"Daddy?" she heard in her mind.

"Susie."

"Daadyyyy?" Had she said anything? Out loud? Fuck, was he going to get mad again? Threaten to throw all her stuff out if she didn't find a job? Take away her cards and spending money? Trash her room? Beat her?

Was she supposed to be feeling so underwater?

"Honey!"

He came out of the glass door beside the bougainvillea with a Bud Light. She closed her eyes and envisioned her dad, a little tall, a little fat, still lumbering. Wearing a Dodgers hat and a loosened tie. Feigning concern. Then he was over her, looking down. A gangster with a bad poker face. Ready for the next Holocaust. There were gold bars buried under the flowering plum.

She blinked. His face was blurry and sweaty.

"Honey, it's time for you to cut this shit out. Get a grip. Seriously. Waketh my love. To slumber from th'asp fall not, tis not yet eve, and Los Angeles is the West!"

She laughed. Or she choked. Was she so high? Was she dreaming?

"You think you're being sexy with your bathrobe hanging open? Look at you. In your mother's robe. It's Tuesday!" He sounded like Jon Hamm. "When was the last time you washed yourself? What's that smell? The end of the world is coming."

"Daddy . . ." She groaned again inside her mind, eyes closed.

"Are you sick?"

"I'm tired," she said in someone else's voice. Could he smell her pussy?

"You're fucking tired? You have no job, no life, no responsibilities, and no interests."

She felt her eyes roll back. Sleep.

"Ooooh, Daddy . . ."

"Wake up!"

A slap across the face knocked her Garrett Leights off onto the grass. He was a brute. He frightened her. The glasses were Chloe, actually, she saw now.

"I'm fine, Dad," she heard herself saying, opening her eyes. "Chill out."

2

Cecil Hotel, Los Angeles . . .

It wasn't long after I dropped out of NYU that "the killings" began in motels in Los Angeles. I hadn't really "dropped out." My parents had yanked me. The first victim's name was Ashley, or Asher, or Ash, depending on when you knew her. She had gone to Marlborough School with me and Faia Sickler, was a couple years older than we were, and was an addict at the time of her death, according to the news. Oxy tablets were scattered across her nightstand at the Cecil Hotel. Her head was covered in blood where she lay on the floor of the shower, the water on, mostly missing her gashed skull, as a stream of pink ran to the drain away from where blood pooled and met the water's edge. Sections of foil and several segments of a straw littered the nightstand next to the low, unmade bed. It was unclear if she had been killed or if it was an accident. The police speculated. The news reported mostly because of the hotel's dark history.

I remember watching her once, riding up Arden Boulevard on a bicycle while Faia and I walked the two blocks toward Melrose. She headed up in the sunshine, probably to the Wilshire Country Club; I recall she stood on the pedals to pump the bicycle just a bit faster and she looked sort of free, in that way that we all looked back then from time to time, in the right circumstances, in our private, privileged gated high school in the sun. Her hair was cut so the wind took it back in a few chestnut sections from her plain face. Perhaps she was a member of the country club. Lots of students were because of the proximity to campus. Neither my family nor Faia's would ever join as it was not a prestige club. Like I said, I barely knew her. We were in different circles. I don't want to sound spoiled, but it's true. My dad drove a Porsche. Her dad drove a Nissan.

She was twenty-one when they found her body. Maybe she'd just OD'd on her way to the shower. But her hair was cut from her scalp and scattered around the room. Young hair is so pretty. Knowing what I know now, of course she was a victim of "the killer," his first one, and it was political. I had seen her before. I never told the police or the courts or the news, but that winter we had used together. I thought of her more over the months that followed, as the scenes of "the killings" repeated in motel rooms around our city. At first, I managed to skirt the whole issue of her death and the question of murder, mostly because I kept myself so high. I don't know if she had stayed more than once at the Cecil Hotel or not, but it would be easy to find out. For a long time I couldn't remember what day we had used there together but of course it must've been close to the time that she died.

Had I not been so stoned when the story broke, it would have freaked me out further, hurt me, a second death in my life that year, another girl I knew who died while living under strangely proximate circumstances to my own. The whole issue of her death and her hair lying around the room, draped over the arm of a chair, and on the carpet . . . it was almost scary. It brought Oxy into the news in Los Angeles, and eventually the world. Like I said, that first killing really just got attention because of the black history of the Cecil Hotel.

As the papers reported, this was the same hotel where Richard Ramirez stayed for weeks while planning his invasions crime spree, and where the Black Dahlia had been seen, in the hotel bar, before her murder—before she'd been cut in half. There had been multiple suicides over the years, and obscene deaths in the establishment: a woman with her head wrapped in telephone cables fell to her end from her window, and another woman was robbed, raped, and strangled in her room. Several men jumped on the roofs of nearby buildings and died; another jumper landed on a man on the sidewalk below and both died. Someone else shot himself in the head in the hotel, and another serial killer had once stayed there. Police were investigating this death as a possible murder, but nobody knew what it was, and as I said, I had begun to wonder if it was connected to me.

3

In New York City . . . More Than a Year Ago . . .

My former professor would play a major role in the events that got me sober that fall and in "the killings" in Los Angeles. At the time, I didn't know Professor Krolik had come to town. Back at NYU, he'd taught me a core-curriculum composition course, as I've already relayed, in the discipline of English, which he'd ever-so-concisely named *Philology in Contemporary Culture: A Key to Understanding Numbness from Representational Media Overload.* Come one and all NYU first-year idiots and geniuses.

I was his favorite student, even though I never turned in a single composition. Maybe it was lust, or sexism, or projection, or seeing something punk rock in my increasingly drugged posture sitting in my chair-desk at the front of class, even when I was falling asleep, once landing on the floor with a thud. Maybe it was self-hatred, knowing I could see through his attempts to point the finger of blame and tell the youth to rise up and rob banks while he attended faculty meetings—that all his insistence to fight the system was an attempt to cover up the fact he had grown into a privileged cis white man in a sport coat applying retinol to the loose flesh and stretch marks that ran down both sets of his cheeks, which he probably studied way too often in the mirror of his tiny, smelly bathroom, holding onto the last flickers of his thirties. He was a vain man, with a feral look in his eyes—a look that knew beauty was the only skill he really possessed, and once it faded, he would be entirely redundant to society, unless he reinvented himself, which he wouldn't know how to do, since he'd always rested on the charm of his rakish good looks. Like a golden coyote who knew someday he'd turn into a pale possum and have to play dead.

Like most lecturers of his time, he taught students who were interested in fields he'd never heard of: dermatological AI, influencer poetics, and fashion-forward pharmacology. He bitched to me about the measly pay, inadequate recompense for the constant threat of being accused of politically incorrect language, sexual harassment, or any inappropriate sexual connections with the students—all the liberal threats against white men of which he bemoaned the coming of before everyone else because they happened in academia first. Of course, he *was* guilty of all those offenses—but, in the end, none of them got him in trouble. For all his passionate rhetoric and speech-making, no one actually cared. No one cared about him.

Professor Krolik, as he called himself, regardless of his actual title of "lecturer," was an underachiever hanging on to a career he'd mostly failed at, just as he had mostly failed as an activist in his youth. The one time he'd been successfully arrested at a protest, he was bailed out and brought to Sherri's diner for ice-cream sundaes by his mother. This was before he'd begun his vegan phase as an ALF supporter back in the early '90s of *Goodfellas* and GigaPets, CDs for a penny, and the Timothy McVeigh bombing inspired by the Waco standoff. He'd rather liked it, he'd told me, when things got real with the torching of ski lodges, car bombings of vivisectionists, and he'd been fascinated by the first World Trade Center bombing, the rise of Al-Qaeda, and their plot to blow up LAX. He wasn't for terror, per se, but he wasn't for Clinton getting his dick sucked in the Oval Office either, talking about what *is* is. *Fuck everything*, he'd say to himself while smoking a joint, then land home to stare at the walls and feel empty in America. The '90s were my nostalgic era, a time I lived through as a baby but didn't experience with full understanding. He couldn't give me access to that era of my childhood, but something of it remained in his belief in idealism. He had slashed a logging truck's tires in high school back in Portland. He blew up a mailbox, while on acid, using a homemade bomb, but it turned out to be the wrong mailbox and it mostly just fizzed and melted the aluminum shell. He had been abused by his father, neglected by his mother, and suffered multiple traumatic brain injuries as a child—mostly from neglect—and had never been quite right in his mind, plus he'd indulged heavily in addictive behaviors as a young man—coffee shops where you could smoke inside, pot and beer and porn. He was a good teacher; knew how to play to the crowd and command an audience with his rage. Although out of place in our era, the rage was compelling—a flashback to a time we sensed growing up, even from the west side of LA. Professor Hamlet performing in Manhattan.

He'd told me he would have liked to do something more than talk at the front of the classroom, but it was hard to throw himself against the gears and levers with so much privilege, especially when it would make him the lone voice of a generation. He *did* admit he'd figured he'd someday attain the status of someone like David Foster Wallace or at least be the male Joan Didion. I believe he was often flatulent in class and would wrinkle his nose at the front row, cocking his head searching for a patsy. The other students would collectively gripe and shake their heads to whatever degree their relationship with privilege afforded them outrage.

Professor Krolik, class was supposed to be over ten minutes ago. What's that smell?

He'd taught thousands of students like me, lecturing in blank white classrooms, like airport terminals, but with projectors and desks. He thought he deserved to be surrounded by baroque-framed oil paintings of picturesque landscapes like professors at Bennington. Most classrooms he taught in didn't even have windows. His students were being overcharged and underserved. Slouchy, hung-over brats stared at him as he spoke, sizing him up like you'd size up a waiter or a salesman. A few precocious over-achievers took notes, hanging on his every word, and laughed at all his jokes. I was in neither camp, of course. I was different, I guess; I was actually interesting, a real artist in the making. I sat in the first row and looked at him as if I were the only one in the room. Professor Krolik probably hammed it up a bit more than usual when I was there. But how could I know? How could I know anything? I am certain his classes fell under Steinhardt's calling to give BFA students a "broad base in the humanities, social sciences and sciences, which complements the art-making process and provides students with opportunities to interpret the meaning of their artworks."

We had laughed reading it off the website while smoking a spliff in my room at The Carlyle. "It's just so arrogant," I scoffed. "Boomer torture language." I had been painting Professor Krolik in a signature "The Carlyle" terry cloth robe that was supposedly good enough for the Duke and Duchess of Cambridge, as he sat in the high-backed chair in décor designed by Dorothy Draper. The second housekeeping call of the day came and I sent them away, dedicated to my work at the easel, feeling important and anxious as I painted him as a big blurry white cloud with a crown, à la the *Rape of Proserpina*, with me as the nude woman with the great hair.

I stopped when he said his neck hurt. "Try one of these," I had said.

Then we both lay on the poofy luminous bedding and Sferra white goose-down duvet with percale cover, which, okay, wasn't vegan but we were high on my pills.

"They're nice," I'd said. "They make everything seem easier."

He said he didn't associate Oxy with ease, but heartache. He was trying the opioid for only the second time, telling himself that maybe this little pill would help him understand the drug that his twin brother was hooked on, enslaved to for life, and for which he seemed destined to be institutionalized until death, in and out of rehabs, a guest at the Twin Towers (the downtown jail by the 101) and on the streets of LA unable to be found for months at a time on the opposite side of the country, in the city they'd known as children for making movies with Patrick Swayze, Molly Ringwald, Eddie Murphy, and Sharon Stone; he must be a full-blown junkie by now. Why had his brother always been so far away?

In LA you could sleep on the street in the sunshine, he figured. And his parents wouldn't look for him there. His poor brother, out all alone. In the last six months, his father had cut his brother off financially, so he couldn't go to any more fancy Malibu rehabs, and he'd become permanently homeless. Did Oxy make it easier to be so down and out? He hoped so.

In his old apartment on W. 103rd, Phil would look down at his knees and think of his twin brother's knees, or the large mole on his brother's face, or his hairline—some sweet and adorable detail of his physical body—and then he'd imagine his brother's cremation someday, and feel a stabbing, storming emptiness. He went back through their texts, voicemails, searching through photos of the two of them on Facebook: his brother somewhat dead-eyed in his dress blues, with a cropped flattop above his larger forehead and thicker neck, otherwise it was like looking in the mirror. His twin brother on a motorcycle.

He and his brother as boys holding one another, their tiny limbs flung however they went at that moment of sleep, a brother's arms stiff down his bodyline, Peter's own arm up flamboyantly over his head, their sleeping faces close enough to kiss. That photo was like a blueprint for their grown-up selves, although he didn't know if the blueprints really held plans for the men they'd become, or if he was just projecting now onto the little boys they'd once been.

His brother's masculine boy head was deployed fully to the mission of sleep. His own face was feminine with pursed lips, sleeping on his side, in flamenco pose, eyelids feathered with delicate lashes. It was a shame what this world did to little boys, although that was something you couldn't say anymore. No one cared. What happened to time? *Their time? Men's time?*

During his tenure at NYU, Professor Krolik pretended to be just another bleeding-heart liberal who found fault and conspiracy in America and lectured on it—from Bernays to Blackwater, he railed at the atrocities of capitalist society, the melting ice caps, and the increasingly blasé yet gutted feeling everyone shared that the world was hopelessly doomed, to eighteen-year-olds who were on their phones posting selfies, sending nudes, close-ups of their assholes or a perfectly angled dick pic, GIFs and memes about the Illuminati, while he taught about global warming. He asked the students what the word *Shakespeare* connoted, or *MILF, DILF, GILF, FILF, SILF, BILF, PILF, TILF, CILF, NILF.* Did anyone care about nurdles, turtles, fertilizer runoff, eutrophication, groundwater contamination, soil degradation, ocean dead zones, algae blooms, feedback loops, soil acidification, pollinators, heavy metals, endangered species, indigenous communities, or the world of activism that had once tried to stop complete corporate takeover? Had anyone ever heard of René Girard, Naomi Klein, Emma Goldman, David Graeber, Mark Fisher, Peter Singer, Derrick Jensen—*have you fuckers heard of anyone?* Teaching was so self-indulgent, like running a boring talk show. Nobody was listening. Except maybe me, but my listening was *ironic* as I was obviously high.

Besides, why was he doing this? He came from money, too. His affluent grandparents and parents had promised greater fortunes later in life, and a series of small trusts to access in the meanwhile, as long as he stayed employed. So, he'd gone off to work as an educator to appease them until the inheritance came through, and in doing so he found he hated who he had become: an under-motivated, aging, privileged, "straight" white male who never actually was cool. His personhood had melted in the limbo, while he waited to get rich. It was depressing. He had waves of greed—they usually occurred after phone calls with his beloved grandmother, where he fantasized buying cars he didn't need, acquiring real estate on the Upper East Side that he couldn't afford to buy and that he would hate living in, and couldn't keep without paying more; traps of luxury that would keep him enslaved to the money however it was doled out—it was a fantasy of being stupid, he guessed. He was too intelligent to know what to do with his life. He was slightly envious of his twin brother, who had gone out so brazenly to join the Marines, and then undertook the life project of being a gutter junkie with such dedication. By contrast, Professor Krolik changed his tie twenty times in the mirror before leaving his apartment, which was barely furnished because—God help him—buying furniture was too much of a commitment.

So, he was trying to access his brother somehow via me and my (dead) roommate's Oxy in my room at The Carlyle: trying to get back to his twin, the only person who had ever made any sense to him. Because they were twins, when his brother spoke, Krolik could imagine that he was his brother, talking to himself, without feeling threatened. And so the Oxy did make things easier. He felt at ease. Until the next day, when he worried about his job and texted me to make sure I wouldn't say anything about whatever we'd done. Not that we'd *done* anything.

I think he just loved being with me, escaping into my identity. Imagining himself as young and girlish, too. The simple taboo excitement of being with a young mind and body. He missed being newly adult in the world, the low stakes and high anxiety. Once he'd fooled himself into thinking he was alpha, large, animated, a well-endowed professor, ready to stand up for himself against the slings and arrows of outrageous fortune, but he'd realized with me, I think, that he was much more beta, more deferential to watching a woman work, more interested in disappearing, maybe wishing other men would take his place and he could watch, or be photographed, humiliated, shamed, or dominated. His hairline was receding. He'd started shaving his earlobes. He admitted was okay with all of it, the Rogaine and the teeth whitener, the zeitgeist away from masculinity, the social programming to be sub. Pursue deep fetish. It turned him on. A basketball up his ass and a bicycle pump in his mouth. Why not? Professor Krolik would die someday, the very thing capitalism was always trying to keep from his awareness, and everyone's awareness. But they wouldn't fool him. He knew it was soon going to be over, as his era receded and he went over the hill, having never really lived a day on the mountaintop with the sun beaming on his face like Moses or even Charlton Heston, him more of a Sisyphus or just a sissy or a simpleton. So few people ever actually understood themselves, while the masses got more confused, and he feared he was among the latter, one more subject under attack in an endlessly advancing mental illness called society.

He shared with me that whenever a real professor (at a holiday party or academic ceremony) asked him what discipline he taught in, he'd say he was in the Observational Humor Department, and they'd leave him alone. I came to office hours and pursued him, which at first confused and then enchanted him, and later became among the several reasons for dismissal from NYU.

Not that I had tattled on him. No. It was just that he'd started showing up late and disheveled to faculty meetings in wrinkled suit coats, missing due dates for grades, taking naps during office hours. Those nights at The Carlyle had meant more than any line on his CV or measly lecturer pay, because now he understood the siren power of the pain drug that had eaten his brother, and all else was pointless.

Except me, but I withdrew from school. At The Carlyle for the last time, the night beyond the windows was a blanket of light pollution and the sky-heat hovered below the higher atmospheric cold of winter. My legs glowed from under the light of the hotel desk lamp. I lived well for a failing freshman.

"You know, Phil, in LA, there's a whole world of people who just drive around their neighborhoods drinking fresh juice and dreaming up whatever world they think they're living in," I'd said to Professor Krolik. "They all make up reality on the fly and pretend like there's no history, no expectations. Everyone gets to be somewhat important, even if they're all just losers who'll never make anything out of their stupid lives. You could teach college by showing Netflix and having students write essays about their haircuts. In New York, if you're not famous or fancy rich by thirty, you're a total loser. You're not made for New York. You're not a true intellectual. You're a dreamer like me. Trust me, LA is just so much easier."

In the end, he lost his job, cashed in his trust fund, told his parents he was taking a research sabbatical, and went West—no one showed up to give the final. He gave everyone an A+, uploading the grades through Boing Boing on his first-class flight to LAX, not yet realizing that the Burbank Airport was so much closer to the east side and less crowded, a far better choice for people with money. But he was new in town. The *professor* had become the student. He was new to my city and he landed just in time to change the world for better or worse . . . in a way that would forever terrify the heads of corporations like Dick Sickler.

4

In West Adams, Los Angeles . . .

"Peter Holiday" was the fictitious name Lecturer Phil Krolik took for himself once he reached California. He'd used his trust fund to buy a turnkey operation under his brother's name, *Peter Krolik*, a state-funded, fully subsidized drug rehab center run out of a rental apartment building in West Adams, on the opposite side of West Adams Boulevard from Exposition Park. He would use the rehab as his base to find and help rehabilitate his brother, he told himself, thinking—not entirely incorrectly—*if I build it, he will come.*

It's hard to keep track all of these names, Phil Krolik and Peter Krolik (and Peter Holiday, who was really Phil Krolik). It was a constant thorn in the side of the proceedings in court. Even Judge Tlothitckh had a difficult time of it, keeping track of the twins and their names and Phil's alter ego, as Susie would spend hours giving answers on the stand, on the ninth floor of the downtown courthouse . . . after "the killings" of the unhoused or homeless in Los Angeles.

People had once called West Adams the ghetto because you bought drinks and cigarettes through the bulletproof windows at the gas stations at night, and there had been violence during the Rodney King riots—whose beating had been filmed by George Holliday (no relation to Peter Holiday)—but West Adams was never a ghetto. It had once been a land of lords and colonizers in the early days of LA. The palms still stood tall and mature as evidence.

In the activist world, people used aliases all the time to avoid detection from the authorities. *Peter* was his brother's name, and *Holiday* had tradition and a jejune flamboyance. It was a name he could actually stand to deliver without flinching, practicing in the mirror with his hand out. *Krolik* was over. Phil Krolik was misery, his past misuse of time spent in neglect of his own soul. He was new now, on the frontier of culture and storytelling. His old self was withering back in New York, a wan coward begging for pittance. He didn't want to be that self anymore. As Mr. Holiday, he was tan and virulent. The charming romance of the name "Holiday" complemented the seriousness and heft of "Peter's" large face and crooked nostrils and was a perfect marriage of opposites, he thought. Like something momentous that deserved to be celebrated: *a holiday*—but an important one.

He'd used his brother's name (Peter Krolik) on all the documents and accounts concerning the rehab, showing his brother's identification documents, which had been given to him for safekeeping by the family attorney. This allowed "Peter" to collect unemployment from New York while running the crooked business in LA, and if he made any mistakes, broke any laws, or if, God forbid, anyone died, the cops could go find his brother and hold *him* legally accountable; his brother would be safer in prison, anyhow, maybe. The family attorney told him that their parents wanted nothing to do with his brother until he got sober. It was too painful for them.

The "rehab" was a dilapidated cube of Spanish-colonial architecture, 6,800 square feet, with twelve bedrooms and eight baths, four discrete addresses and mailboxes, iron-railed balconies from nine-foot wooden doors that opened like heavenly gates onto the hot sun. The building had a turret, two double garages, and overgrown, night-blooming cacti that rose toward the sloped clay tile roof that was missing a third of its tiles. Temporary cyclone fencing hid the front of the property as though it were perpetually under renovation. *Closed for repairs,* it suggested. As were the people inside. He kept the rehab's name, *The Villa*. It was, in fact, a shithole, although his brother might not think so.

Inside was a mess of old floors with missing jags of wood and giant peeling walls, picture moldings half torn off, a staircase with broken steps, shredded curtains, peeling water-damaged plaster, and a stage just big enough for one. The residents had decorated their rooms with flotsam dragged with them off the streets: blue tarps and sleeping bags, milk crates of junk, broken VCRs and outdated electronics. The

VCR was an emblem of a bygone era, the world of Miramax films and dream of empire that was now burning to the ground. Out in the streets, friends of the unhoused residents were soon to be hunted by "the killer," someone who preyed upon individuals with tangled hair, mismatched clothes, sunburns and worn-out shoes, carrying their belongings upon their broken backs, stinking of dehydrated piss and fecal incontinence, soon sliced apart with their blood splattering the walls of motels.

Ash, Susie's old classmate, was the first—once from money, though not really; she'd slipped through the cracks and ended up prey. "The killer" chose those without homes, the addicted, and abandoned—*his people*, he called them—and the cops never understood why but the news speculated: was he playing savior to them, offering some warped salvation from all the other killers in suits and offices? Pill-makers, lobbyists, insurers, bankers—his notes left behind in those bad motels claimed he saw these desk jockeys as the actors behind the curtain, a velvet-draped stage backed by a brick wall. Democracy was a vaudeville act that hid the truth he was "working" to expose, before the entire theater went up in smoke, with all the exits sealed,

The bedroom walls at the Villa were covered in tear-outs from magazines, the vision boards of people who wanted to be other people. Phil began his work as "Peter" in good faith, thinking the residents were there to get sober, and he'd have no trouble keeping them that way with curfews and sandwiches and whatever pre-existing programs he inherited with the operation: AA, meditation, group talks, DBT workbooks, the DSM-4. He'd been a professor. He knew how to talk to people, and he liked visiting the residents scattered throughout the chaotic rooms. Giving lectures had once been his end goal, but now they were a means to another end, inspiring the indigents to search for his brother, while giving hope to the hopeless.

He was exploiting the system, sure, but the system was so exploitative to begin with—the richest nation with only the forty-second-highest life expectancy and the most expensive healthcare—and the residents needed someone to love them even if they *were* addicts, not because they weren't addicted anymore. He could guide them through their hell toward salvation. An existentialist wrote: "Hell is other people." A Russian novelist countered: "Hell is not loving other people." From growing up in church, he knew the only heaven to be found on earth was in love. He would love them until they were ready to recover. Those thoughts justified his small gaming of the system and made it all okay, one day at a time. Having graduated out of the deep vice of educational institutions and abandoned the impotent rage he'd once held as the loser he was, he was now master of his domain, a leader of indigents who had sorted themselves into groups by the drugs they were addicted to.

Team Speed was moody and unpredictable, prone to freak-outs. They were using meth, after all. Team Opioids were into analgesics, of course, and they were the vast majority at the Villa, just as they were the majority of the drug problem in America. There were those, too, who abused more recreational drugs: crack, MDMA, bath salts, DMT, LSD, and malt liquor. The members of every team were so addicted, Peter felt free to be even sloppier in his reasoning than he had been as a professor. No one was taking notes. There would be no final exam. If you failed, you died. Everyone else got an A. Peter wanted them all to get A+'s.

At the Villa, yellow finches flew into the hot yard in the morning and he threw Nyjer seed from the pockets of his Tom Ford silk cashmere kimono, and then lay in bed and felt sunshine pressing on his bare thighs where the robe parted.

It was hot that fall, so hot the addicts were often almost buck-naked in the house. Sometimes they were fully nude, even in mixed company. AC units whirred only through Peter's suite and fans rotated in the Villa downstairs where walls had been partly knocked down to studs to form a larger open space. The house smelled of sweat, trash and body odor, urine and mildew and citrus, and the earthy smell of peppermint soap mixed with shit.

Peter's closest house member was Royal-Lee, a handsome twenty-year-old just starting to explore the complicated terrain of gender questioning, and who was possibly ethnically diverse—his, or maybe, rather, *their,* mother was white and sounded awful, and Royal-Lee's father was unknown. Royal-Lee was on the payroll, off the books, and helped Peter deal with the often-terrifyingly addicted house members they both sometimes jokingly referred to as "Surlies." The patients would not stop using and became more dangerous when they tried to get them sober. So, with Royal-Lee's help, at the advice of the addicts, they began collecting more pills from state healthcare prescribed to the house addicts and then selling the extra Xanax for profit. After a cut for Royal-Lee, Peter kept the profits and subsidies for the care of his previously homeless patients.

For the housing of his addicts, Peter received state checks by mail each month. The only problem was the payments didn't begin to cover expenses, especially if he wanted to provide cruelty-free deli meats, organic whole grain breads, non-GMO produce, prebiotics, and fresh salves for their cuts and scrapes, ointments, pills and appointments when they got sick.

As he settled into running the place, he tried playing them classical music and promising spiritual rewards. Of course it was all nonsense—Tchaikovsky and Schubert wouldn't save them from Fentanyl—and he didn't know anything about how to get people to do things, not without the artificial pressure of *grades*. It was easier to let them keep using and to give lectures while they were drugged and willing to listen, which was the only thing he had any experience doing. The inertia of opioid users and that of captive audiences in traditional collegial learning environments was not dissimilar.

Peter began to have doubts about the altruistic organization he was running.

He had doubts that he could make it in LA, even though Susie had assured him it was "so much easier" than NY. So, he'd joined another "altruistic" organization. It was a secret society that promised to help people harness their inner potential, manifest the important spiritual work that each singular soul was destined to deliver into their world.

He hoped they would help him figure out a way to make the Villa work, now that all of his money was invested. So, he reshuffled his hand, so to speak, using his operation to get multiple scripts for analgesics prescribed through a network of doctors orchestrated by a psychiatrist,

Dr. Morris Delray, who was a Diplomat of the American Board of Psychiatry and Neurology and a total pushover for anyone with money, located in Beverly Hills on Bedford Drive. He was also in the secret organization Peter had joined, "The Church of White Illumination," as was the former owner of the rehab as well. As was Dick Sickler. As were countless powerful men in Los Angeles.

Peter had a growing feeling he might be hunting Dick Sickler. He didn't know what he wanted from the man yet. He knew Sickler was connected to Susie, at least partially responsible for his brother's addiction, and was someone who needed to be handled. It was Susie's mother who found Peter the turnkey operation in the first place. He'd reached out to her weeks before moving to town, and she had appreciated the support he'd shown for her daughter. She was very gracious when he asked for career advice over the phone. *She was the one who started him on the path that would lead to Susie's trial.*

"I'm sorry, what is your first name, professor?"

"Peter," he lied. "Peter Krolik."

Within a few days, she'd arranged for the documents to be prepared for the sale of the rehab. She knew the selling party, an old connection from her world of LA charities. The former owner, after negotiating the shifting landscape of substance abuse for decades, found himself unable to keep up with the increasingly dangerous world of addiction and dereliction. If he'd stayed another day, he'd told him when they met, the addicts would've kicked him down the stairs and eaten him to survive.

The papers were ready by the time he had called from the airport. So, Phil had signed his brother Peter's name on all the dotted lines. Even though he had some misgivings—Susie's mom hadn't shown up to the signing, and he would never meet her, he supposed, didn't even know what she looked like—in the end he made the purchase, and got on with the business of saving lives.

At the Villa, he received a call one day while drinking an iced coffee with sweet foam that Royal-Lee had brought him. An agent from The Church asked him a series of questions about his income level, professional position, personal beliefs, dream life, ambitions, sexual desires, fears, matters of guilt, and mental and physical health history, as well as a list of each member of his family. He answered her questions more or less honestly.

"Entrepreneur—Catholic—dreams of driving and can't see the road or apply the brakes—encounters with androgynous lovers who shape-shift sexes and scenes of humiliation and domination, feminization—fear of death and failure—guilt over addicted missing twin—hypo-manic hypochondriac—and smoker. Mom and Dad live in Oregon. My brother, he is currently at large."

He was lonely in the new city and appreciated her attention. She had the kind of concern for him as a man that he appreciated from a woman on the telephone. She said he would be invited to an annual meet-and-greet at the Bel-Air campus, but first the woman would need proof of funds that he could afford to join. He used the files from his brother's trust—a trust his brother couldn't use while *using heroin.*

* * *

The Church headquarters in Bel-Air were opulent. Gardens fore-grounded pink buildings. The campus's grandeur and geometric forms invoked the power of Masonic Halls and the Gardens of Versailles. There was a neoclassical lodge, a mortuary, and pink sparkling mau-soleums, guest cabanas and hammam, and private stucco bungalows, all meticulously kempt across a massive campus dotted with tennis courts and fountains. The manicured grounds smelled like chlorine and fresh clipped grass. It felt like a college campus for grown men who wanted to fuck the world like it was a young co-ed.

A tour guide spoke to them.

"You'll have access to this all. If you become one of us. It's really not that difficult. You just have to fit in."

The guide wore a skinny-collar suit, a thin tie, a radio clipped to his belt. Not a hair out of place. He'd just finished puberty. He had that attractive nervousness laced with optimism, eager to show his teeth when he smiled, ready to be fucked by everyone. Like his teeth were made of solid cocaine.

Something about being here made Peter feel young. He felt like a sapling, a tadpole, or what was before that . . . an egg? A jelly mass? A cluster floating on the surface? Would the older men find him attractive, give him money, feel him up in the steam room?

He was offered a walking tour of the campus, during which the tour guide explained that they reprogrammed the subconscious of their members through enacted performances.

"We wear costumes and act in plays," the guide said. "The sets depict archetypal scenes like 'Ancient Egypt,' the 'Stone Age,' the 'Crash of the Stock Market.' We dissemble popular paradigms of limiting beliefs by sharing the keys of true knowledge, surpassing iconography and thus understanding the power of the soul of man. We also tell you who's really running shit."

"Great," Peter smiled from behind his sunglasses. He had taken a Valium. A man walked across the campus with his arm around the shoulders of a preppy-looking boy around the age of fifteen. Peter could imagine himself here. He lit a cigarette.

"At the higher echelons, scenarios are enacted in the real world, meant to shape so-called consensual reality. They're just bigger plays, but important. We're working on the election this year. This man is very interesting. It's a new world. How will you change it? We're working on drug addiction, dereliction, disinformation, democracy. We're going to Mars."

The guide spoke of all things as though the organization was certain of the outcome, but Peter couldn't tell what the outcomes to anything in his own life would be, much less the tides of the wind, or the fate of the future of the free world. Of course, the world was only free if you never had to look at the price tags, which was how he'd grown up, but things had changed. He'd never felt 100 percent certain about anything. Especially not lately, in such strange times.

The old world is dying and the new world struggles to be born.

The main lodge was a ten-thousand-square-foot windowless building. Outer walls held high-relief sculptures of double-headed eagles with sharp crested wings spread at the center of low-relief stone backgrounds. There were huge brass-cauldron-like fire pit urns at the base of the walls, each about the size of twelve people. On a wall in tile mosaics were symbols of scales, a key, a pyramid, a lion, the masonic square and compass, the Coptic cross, and the words *Liberty, Equality, Fraternity, Devotion*. Underneath each word was a short passage about the value the word represented. *Fraternity: behold how good and how pleasant it is for brethren to dwell together in unity.* Maybe men's stuff was making a comeback: confident bold brotherhood and fraternal love for the modern era.

Peter wasn't a man's man, per se. He'd mostly had sexual experiences with women, but enjoyed a private world of homoerotic fantasy and self-exploration. He'd gotten four fingers up his ass once with the help of some strawberry-flavored lube. Maybe Peter should try to embrace brotherhood now that he was in The Church. He liked male dogs, male animals, as much as female animals, especially male birds, which had the prettiest colors. He knew this probably wasn't the kind of masculinity The Church was interested in fostering. Or maybe it was . . . maybe rich men were more sexually . . . open? Of course they were. Was there even such a thing as brotherhood? In the Kantian sense? Or did that just lead to Hitler, Mussolini, Hideki Tojo, and the Orange Candidate?

One week later, he'd received his formal invitation to join. As part of his orientation, he performed in a play called *War in Heaven*. He'd gotten the lead as God. It was instructional, not egotistical, but Peter couldn't help himself. They didn't call it the lead, but what else could it be? What was more of a lead role than God?

They were given gold scripts, old dusty wigs, and fake beards, musty with time, smelling like the lining of an old woman's purse—or his grandmother's drapes he used to hide in as a kid, giggling like a drunken Polonius. On stage, Peter sat on a gold throne, naked except for a long, thick white merkin. Naked children danced around. Or maybe they were little people. Men in masks worshiped a bull. Elders knelt and prayed and flittered around each initiate, as though each was the center of "Ring Around the Rosie," all in perfect silence. A bell rang. "So Young" featuring Veronica by the Ronettes played. Moroccan mint tea was served.

Was he God? Ever since, whenever he had to appear in front of people, whether it was at the Villa or The Church, Peter wore the disguise of the beard and wig he'd stolen from *War in Heaven*. It made him feel more like "himself," more like Peter Holiday. He had to dress well. "The appearance of power is powerful," The Church taught. "Success is just telling yourself and everyone else *I win* all the time." When he met Richard Sickler, what would all this playing God and belonging to The Church bring? How would living in Paradise City change him?

He was taking notes from all their rituals and indoctrinations, texts and methodologies, for the small fortune it took to join. They preached "spiritual capitalism." There was power to be gained through the Eleusinian, Dionysian, Delphic, knightly, and masonic traditions. It was essentially the same bullshit Peter was trying to sell the Surlies. *Mind over matter. Compounding interest.* Except he was networking with the billionaire members and millionaire pledges, instead of other addicts; it suited him. He felt like Richard Gere in a 450SL, listening to Blondie.

* * *

At night, Peter locked himself and Royal-Lee in the upstairs suite. He was scared of the Surlies. And afraid of an FBI bust. The cops. Detectives. He was pretty sure he could jump off the balcony without breaking both legs if he needed to escape fire, invasions from within, mutiny, police, et al. He'd bought a vintage Continental with the suicide doors in cash and didn't change the registration, kept it in the garage along with a Super Beetle from 1973, with the longer nose and curved windshield, that he'd bought for Royal-Lee. If they had to escape one night, they'd grab the keys and run for the hills, except the hills were always on fire. They said the Santa Ana winds picked up the red spark of a cigarette tossed out of a car window and the entire mountain erupted into flames, but it was always either neglect by the power company or some crazy fucker driven insane to the point of arson. Either way, it was glorious from afar, as the sky filled with high smoke and made the California sunshine all the more orange and weirdly vivid, light pink and yellow tulles of the day and orange fire in smoky bolts of velvet below at dusk.

Peter was working on a new lecture to explain the importance of manifestation. Life was whatever you thought of it. Positive thinking, right? He had trouble believing in this concept. If it were so simple, Peter would manifest his twin brother at the door right now, the real Peter Krolik. He tried. He listened for a knock. Nothing. He tried again, scrunching his face. He felt Los Angeles out there and the heat of late summer and the paradise of flowers in the city. He tried to send a message telepathically to him, wherever he was. "NYC vs. LA." Nothing.

His brother ironically was worth more than two-and-a-half-million dollars, the lawyer told him, since he'd never been eligible to touch his trusts. If he were dead, the money was his. *No thanks. He would find him. He had to.* His brother was why he'd moved to West Adams. If he'd had his druthers, if his brother were not out there to bounty hunt and resurrect—his twin! Oh, how he loved him!—he would have moved to the mountains of Malibu instead of West Adams, learned to surf, found a blonde girlfriend or something, and gone lame that way in the shallows. Picked up another teaching job.

He sat at his vanity, puffing a hand-rolled cigarette, patting sweat off his face with a Gucci bee-pattern silk pocket square, squinching his face in the cracked, rusted iron-framed vanity. He opened and closed his eyes, then lips, clenching his jaw muscles, smiling. Sweat loosened his beard wig, so he dabbed the corner near his mouth with spirit gum. The smell of the glue reminded him of gasoline, sickly sweet and heady. *That* reminded him of anal beads, sex shops, and his teenhood spent drooling over magazines, going to sex stores in Portland, underage, and hitting tanning booths, stoned, in his mother's pink bikini underwear with a bow and pearl on the front. He was a weird kid. Thank goodness. At least he'd stayed off heroin, unlike his brother. His face reflected it all: pretty, slightly criminal, troubled by consciousness, overly determined and a touch dense. He looked like a figure in a Modigliani painting. He looked like a madman.

It had been hard to make friends back in Portland. Other environmental activists thought Peter took everything too literally. They wanted to talk, not kill someone or blow up a lumber mill. They were in *high school.* These people would turn into loser liberals, distracted by race, gender, sexuality—any category of victimhood the DNC could weaponize—while the party kept dodging holding pharma responsible, ending genocidal war, poison food, its leaders stuffing their faces with veal and pills.

He took a drag and exhaled into the fan nearby, wig and beard blowing in the mirror. With the beard securely glued, and once his glasses were placed on his nose, and the bee scarf tied into an ascot, with strings of prayer beads hung around his neck, he'd look older and wiser than the trust-fund brat he knew that he really was. Could you be a brat at almost forty?

In Los Angeles, you could be a brat forever and *triumph.* Just look at Brad Pitt, Johnny Depp, and the Kardashians. When he'd come to LA, he had expected to find something beneath the façade. The essence of LA was still an effusive, unnamable mystery. Or else it was completely empty. On the east side there was the reshuffling of the past, cycled a million times through thrift shops. People in Los Feliz ate thirty-dollar organic grain bowls for lunch while working on laptops. On the West Side, they spoke quietly, but if you got close enough, you heard they were still talking about money. There was a great embarrassment of riches in LA, just as in New York, but in LA the dream was something that could never be held: fame and talent, instead of money and class. It was like Edward Said argued: One couldn't skip the crucial steps of struggle and self-development. Unfortunately, Peter hadn't self-actualized, kneecapped by the promise of generational wealth and the narcissism he'd inherited from his society.

If only he were truly free—the thought had occurred to him more than once—he would join the homeless out on the street. Then he'd be with his brother, at least in spirit; as the truth was, he wasn't a real intellectual, or a real addiction specialist, or a real anything. Of course, it was a problematic line of thinking, appropriative of the true agonies of the unhoused.

He approached the balcony's threshold and smelled jasmine as he watched bad cars driving up the hot road. Outside were these palms, a city, eight million humans, countless flowers and bottlebrush shrubs, papaya trees, jade and bamboo, roses and jacaranda, coral ginger and giant birds of paradise rising high, with enormous white and blue and orange waxy flowers: a tropical reality in a silver screen dreamland. If only he were famous, or talented, or passionate about anything other than his mostly poorly articulated outrage, his disgust for champagne socialism as well as rising fascism that was bubbling up everywhere.

The Villa was minutes from Skid Row, where homeless souls lived by the hundreds in tent communities. You couldn't drive down their streets between Fifth and Sixth without them wandering in front of your car, asserting their laws from within an empire of trash, pushing twin-shopping-cart-tanks with tarpaulins stretched overtop, their homes on the sidewalks, addicts wandering like psychotic zombies or inmates just released from prison, which many were. They were fucking miserable. But they seemed more human than the humans. They hadn't become technology like everyone else. Edward Said would fight for them. So would Dean Spade, and many other theorists, if they ever left the library. He might not be able to articulate himself as well as these theorists, but he could perform direct action and provide direct assistance.

Still, Peter had gone only once with the Surlies to Skid Row to look for his brother. After that, he let them go alone, because while he felt drawn to the search, he also felt his age and status, and knew he didn't belong. He preferred to let the Surlies invite the homeless to his place for today's open sermon, later this afternoon. It was a good way to network and spread the word about his search for his only brother. He didn't know when they would begin to show up exactly.

Sometimes the Surlies went and handed out sandwiches at night—tuna salad, ham and cheese, hummus in pita for the vegetarian vagrants. You had to respect everyone; that was the gist. Wrapped between layers of cling-wrap was a picture of his brother's face and the number to call. Today, they were out asking for leads, networking locally, inviting people for the afternoon's big sermon. There'd be free Oxy, they whispered. The vagrants didn't give a shit about free sandwiches. They wanted drugs.

He thought of the portraits Susie had painted of him at The Carlyle. She said she hated painting people, which is why she'd painted him as a white blob, like that marshmallow guy in *Ghost Busters*. He got up from the vanity and lay down on the floor. He did fifty pushups. Next, his thirty-pound dumbbell curls. He would die someday. He was aging. In seriousness, he'd been bored all his life by heteronormativity and hurt by toxic society. It wasn't that he was trans, but hadn't he once been young with skinny limbs and nipples that could have been for breastfeeding? Dressing in women's clothes? Panties and bra? Were there not sides to his personality that didn't exist for most men? Yes or no?

He could never know other men. He'd always felt they were all afraid to admit they had desires for more than women, some ancient Grecian truth. He believed every man must want access to the pretty, the pink, the sensual and the sensational, and to be free, and allowed to flower. To bloom from behind. He'd felt this. He'd worn a dress to class in college once to show how he felt. Not as the professor of course, *but then again, if he had*, he probably couldn't have been fired. Now you could be whatever you dared. No one in this Villa even knew his true name; no one in the city knew him except Susie and his brother, and neither of them knew he was here. Maybe he should fall in love with Royal-Lee? Sure, he could perhaps be called out for bringing up the rear, so to speak, but he *was* finally free to explore himself as never before.

5

Off to Bedford Drive . . .

Perhaps I'd hate the old me, too, if I hadn't been *me* all along. I hated the old me enough to drug her and hold her hostage at her parents' house, but hating yourself is wasting yourself, and I knew that even when my seemingly unattainable mission was to become the first artistic genius who bridged the worlds of pure art and activism into pop. Few people truly understand pop. It's about being popular. Few people are exceptional. Few people don't completely hate themselves. People who hate themselves almost never succeed—except as fascists. I didn't want to stay a slave to the preciousness of making irrelevant art anymore, failure being a kind of self-imposed fascism of its own.

We know I forced myself into the public sphere, or was forced into it; but even before, I was searching for a way to capture the schizophrenic meaninglessness of our overly media-inundated lives.

I thought of painting Osama Bin Laden getting fucked by the Energizer Bunny.

Too Tala Madani? *That wasn't Tala Madani.*

Eric Prince sucking Eminem's dick?

Too Vincent Namatjira? *That wasn't Vincent Namatjira.*

I was feeling stupid that morning, and having found several Oxy tablets in a Tic Tac box, I swallowed one to slow my mind that was racing to find purpose, and drug it back into submission. I needed something that would get me to the top, a place so many men were granted easy entry, and to somehow help make the world a better place. I knew I needed conflict, the law of good art. In the realm of protest art, there was Chris Burden's event in which he had Bruce Dunlap shoot him in the arm with a .22-caliber rifle at the F-Space Gallery in Santa Ana to protest the Vietnam War. There was Andreas Sterzing's portrait of David Wojnarowicz sewing his lips closed as part of the "silence equals death" campaign in response to AIDS. No one did anything radical anymore, it was all just business.

Once you got to the top, you need something marketable and pop to mass produce, like Paul Sietsema's phones or Koons's shitty balloons. Did Koons really think those balloons were interesting? Sietsema's phones were good. Koons's greatest sculptural work was *Michael Jackson and Bubbles*, which showed the right amount of ambiguity between skewering and fully celebrating the opulence of Michael and his monkey in glossy, glazed porcelain, painted garish colors, housed at The Broad. There was something profoundly beautiful in his unwillingness to grow up, to be plastic, innocent. *Not that Michael was that innocent.* It made it better because this town was at the center of all social decay, or so all the conspiracist dorks were saying. What could I do to really strike back and provide the new female gaze? I felt I couldn't readily compete against the male-dominated paradigm of the post-Charles-Saatchi-Damien-Hirst art market. Except some women had: Marina Abramovic (Orange people were saying she was a Satanist who fed human bodies to the Female Candidate), Judy Chicago, Marilyn Minter, Cindy Sherman, Sarah Lucas . . . pedophilia in Hollywood was a big topic in this election. You had to be taboo to be included.

I looked at the Tic Tac box: two pills were blue. Thirty milligrams. Those were powerful. I yawned so hard it hurt the corners of my mouth. My brain rushed to find a way to capture the feeling I had of suffering and loss when, in the middle of sleep, I woke up to see a bird's nest flying off into the fall winds from the eaves of the roofline outside my bedroom doors. *Goodbye!* There was so much wrong in the world, so many people being blown up, so much trash in the ocean, so much destruction, so many fires, the worst always yet to come. I felt myself being blown away.

Someone was killing people downtown. I wondered if something might happen to Royal-Lee—an overdose of my dealer, maybe, the mutilation of the body. For some reason, I thought of Faia Sickler. "The killings" were bringing more attention to her family. Maybe Faia would be found next with her head cut off, placed in a motel shower, hot water running over her face for hours, until the skin peeled and bubbled from the heat and steam or just softened to disfigurement. I didn't want to think of her like that. It was too horrifying. She would never be caught *dead* dead in a motel, I thought, having no idea how on the nose this thinking would ultimately end up. Then I texted her, randomly, for the first time in years, although of course nothing is random, or else everything is; could just some things be randomized? This supposed a higher consciousness. I tried to remember theories but all I could think of was Kant and his treatise on the sublime.

Been noticing more killings. Hope ur ok.

I looked at the big square of my Venetian plaster fireplace, the Mario Bellini red-mushroom chairs and French bubble ottoman, two sets of French doors to my wraparound balcony behind clean white drapes. Luxury without power was stupid. The Female Candidate appeared on NBC, muted. Her hair looked like Doris Day on crack. The way her bronzer settled into her wrinkles made her face look like Claymation. The caption read *600 hours spent on hair/makeup this election.* I attempted some fuzzy math. Almost a full month 24/7 in dressing rooms to combat a man who didn't know how long his tie should be. Or maybe he knew *exactly* how long his necktie should be. Wasn't a tie a suggestion of one's prick? Would someone shoot one of the candidates and get it over with? Why couldn't I get over life's petty traumas? Why was success for success's sake so seductive?

The news now announced the latest "killing" of another unhoused person who was addicted to drugs. Their body was found altered in a queen-size bed at the Full Moon Inn, a cheap motel in South Los Angeles. Details were emerging. I wasn't emerging for anything but drugs. Back in those vapid days of addicted youth, I was a portrait of a young wastrel, *The Absinthe Drinker* from the Blue Period. My French mother's condemnations rang in my head.

"Oh, Susie, get a life."

I won't overly indulge my addict life back then, when my days would rest on getting more pills, then eating a Shrimp and Crab Louie at The Grill on the Alley—without the seafood, so basically greens, black olives, avocado; a vinaigrette, of course, substituted for the Thousand Island dressing—before looking at religious art, pilgrims, and aristocrats in oil at Gallery 19C. Or maybe I'd go to Gagosian and fail to feel connected to the current world legacy of art and interesting culture that I yearned to be a part of as much as I hated it.

In the alley behind ISAIA, some woman was found dead in the dumpster next to the back door of the Wolford hosiery store last week. The woman was missing two fingers, her death could not be connected to any of the other "killings" that fall, and her fingers wouldn't be found until they looked in her stomach; inside her vagina was a broken pill bottle full of Oxy. I'd have a Diet Coke when I got home, lie out by the pool, then maybe masturbate to sleep. None of this would actually happen. Simply put, I'd OD before noon.

That late morning, I woke up to the alternatingly short, sharp pinches and watery warbles of the house finch singing from the pink trumpet tree outside my room. I went scrambling to find pills before locating the Tic Tacs in the back of a drawer. I hate to talk about my addiction like this in first person. It isn't that I can't tolerate the truth about the addict I was, it's just such an oversaturated genre. Confessionalism is so cliché in this day and age, and addiction stories are limp. This is about so much more. I'm going to dip out into third person, take an asterisks break, and proceed forward in 3D.

* * *

It was another sunny day. In the dark mirror, Susie, lit from behind, looked like a vampire as she slipped on her Gentle Monster "Kurt" sunglasses. Her hair was matted. Her nose was creased. She had sheet marks all up one side of her face. Her chin was too pointy in the mirror. She requested a ride service on her phone. When she looked up, the Armenian driver was at the gate and she was outside, sitting on the curb, in front of her house. Sunlight flickered in her eyes through the midday darkness and made her feel lucky to be stoned on easy street,

Brentwood Circle, hiding behind shades in front of the bushes. How had she gotten out in front of her house?

This was one of the coolest, most terrifying aspects of being extremely high. She looked at Royal-Lee on her phone as she rode to Beverly Hills, studying photos. You found yourself like Dracula appearing a few frames further into the movie than you'd remembered. In one photo, Mariah Carey inspired low-rise jeans. She guffawed. Sure, the jaw was a little too large, nose upturned somewhere between Sam from *Bewitched* and Wilbur from *Charlotte's Web*, but it could all be cute if you looked for the more delicate features, she supposed. It was just those pants! Jennifer Aniston had a prognathous jawline, too. There were all kinds of beauty. But one still needed taste.

She scrolled through more photos and found Royal-Lee with someone who looked like her old professor, Phil Krolik, but with a bushy beard and the name *Peter H.*; different hair, kind of blurry. He looked rough around the edges. Was she too high or seeing things? Had Phil Krolik lost weight and grown a beard since NYU? She tried to click on him but his account was private.

She looked up and saw Royal-Lee standing in front of the building. Feeling mischievous, she decided to take another pill and told the driver to stop. He could let her out half a block away and she wouldn't have to take the pill in front of him. Then she realized she didn't care. These people meant nothing to her. No one who had meant anything to her even meant anything to her.

"Never mind," she said, unscrewing the cap to the bottle of Fiji and popping open the Tic Tacs. "Just circle the block." She shook out a pill. Bit it and swallowed half. Were these air-conditioned seats in the back? Or was she just cold-hearted? The driver circled. She ate a wintergreen Lifesaver from a bag strapped to the passenger seat. She hadn't brushed her teeth. Or her hair. She smelled her armpit. Grapefruit and piss.

Susie made a fart sound with her lips.

"Excuse me?"

"No, I didn't fart. That was a lip sound from my mouth."

Could he smell her? She thought she might be getting a UTI.

Royal-Lee finished a joint on the front steps of the office, smoke swirling in the sunlit breeze. She'd swallowed her pill like a Boomer in a CVS parking lot. There was nothing ritualistic about her drug use. She told herself she wasn't a real addict, but someday, perhaps, she'd try other methods of ingesting the dope. Drugs weren't fun anymore. They came from cartels instead of mystics. They came from her dad and Dick. Fuck them both. She needed both dickheads to get money and pills. She could always get Oxy prescribed from some pain management clinic but Royal-Lee was too convenient. She should get some coke.

She thought about Royal-Lee, who had probably been the skinny loner in high school. As much as they were afraid of the violence on the streets where they grew up, she thought—and then thought maybe that was logistically racist—the other students at Crenshaw were probably all aware that, statistically speaking, as the social outcast who was ostracized for not being a jock, Royal-Lee was most likely to come in carrying an AR-15. Susie could fuck with that. Everyone she knew was a total conformist.

School shootings were something her old professor used to talk about in class. He said the rise in mass shootings, especially by young people, was a response to hyperreality. Phil used to preach about Baudrillard, the exchange symbols of consumerism, and it reinforced her faith in art back then, even though the art world had become a hyperreal monster of its own, in bed with fashion and celebrity and billionaires. Krolik preached that capitalism replaced truth with empty symbolic gestures. Such were the vicissitudes of whatever shit went on, she supposed. There were probably shooting drills at Crenshaw, where Royal-Lee had graduated. They didn't have them at Marlborough. *Smart.* Because whoever might shoot up the school just went to the same training exercises as the other students. Wouldn't they know the protocols and exploit them? If anyone went to hide in the storage closet, bingo, wouldn't the kid who had sat in the exact same drills open the closet door, pointing a gun barrel in their faces? *Blam.* She felt self-satisfied, then imagined blood and brains everywhere. The mop in the bucket on wheels. The yellow plastic signs of piso mojado/wet floor. Kids screaming. Corpses on the floor like dummies with the weird look of death, sleep without dreaming. *Shakespeare*. She'd seen it on her roommate, that animatronic death look. It was uncanny. Maybe it would have been different if there'd been blood, bullet wounds, teeth, anything to exhibit the violent reality of her unnatural death. Gun violence was upsetting, but pills had killed way more people. Pills were a choice. Still, society was fucked. These rehearsals for catastrophe were part of every era—a way to negotiate terror. Air raid drills, mass shootings, and then when the old world gets lost, and we can't return to it, we idealize it. Maybe the key was to stop complaining about the world we live in?

"Is this good? Can I drop you here?" The driver had circled. Was he making this weird? Why? She yanked the handle, surprised as it opened fast, and she almost fell out of his fucking car, draped her body around what, *air*, and sort of folded herself into the grass and watched Royal-Lee, feeling closer to him somehow, like friends, their drugs in her system, Royal-Lee just a few hundred feet away from her, totally unaware. A hedge of hibiscus partly blocked the view across the yard.

Time and space were funny. She could just hide. Is that how "the killings" happened? Someone hid behind a bush or a wall by the ice machine, then slipped into a room behind the victim. Could she imagine being "the killer" and sneaking behind someone with a knife? It was egotistical to think it had anything to do with her. But, of course, it *did*. Royal-Lee had said to meet in the garage. She couldn't buy drugs out in the open on the front steps of a medical office building, right? The building was for people to buy drugs *inside* of. It was so stupid she couldn't just get drugs from her dad. It was like he worked for Hershey's and she couldn't ask for a candy bar.

Was she really trying to reach *him* through the pills? Was this love? *Pieces of You?* All his wealth and all this privilege and she just wanted to melt into soft repose. *How stupid*. Was she stupid? She wasn't David fucking Hockney, king of swimming pool scenes, heir to the Bay Area Figurative Movement's light and leisure. Her teachers insisted you had to make robots that twerked or were racially offensive, walls of televisions blaring a message of white-male-identity rage while witchy sex dolls performed the futility of female existence. *Real abuse*. Fuck you, Jordan Wolfson. Or was he cool? Of course he was! He had managed to succeed in the current market, and he was unabashedly leaning into his own internalized antisemitism and misogyny. Where was her rage? The creative anger that David Lynch talked about? The pills were robbing her impetus. Also, there was the rise of previously underrepresented identities to contend with that didn't help her much. She was under the spell of Dick's opiates. To what movement could she ever be heir apparent while drugged into incoherence? She refocused on Royal-Lee and let her mind drift, making up a story on the fly. She did the voice-over like it was some afterschool special: *If only those losers from Crenshaw High School could see me now . . .*

Royal-Lee bragged about being mostly raw-vegan in their first conversation. Vegans. Always have to tell you. It was true. He had a classic eating disorder look. An orthorexic health fanatic with 3 percent body fat. *Was beauty enough to base a life on? Yes, of course it was; this was LA. So, that was all the boxes, as long as they kept checking them and improving, like everyone else on the Internet. It was a lot of pressure.*

Now wearing Gucci, Valentino, Celine—a fashion tourist in a city of natives, wanting to feel beautiful. A perfect specimen of Millennial looks. Nice full lips, long legs and a high waist, flat tummy, a smooth flawless chest, and the curves of a juicy butt, if their back was arched slightly, like in those low-rise jeans in that Mariah photo. She didn't care. As long as she got Oxy. Susie loved everybody. Or she hated everybody. It was all the same. It was a totality of feeling reaching beyond tautology, ad infinitum, fuck all, Warhol, et al.

Royal-Lee probably never had a real boyfriend before, and maybe had been fucked with. Who cared? Thick brown wavy hair, high cheekbones and almond-shaped Aramaic eyes, slender arms and wrists. A string was worn around the waist to make sure too much food was not ingested—and if that happened, whenever that happened—a finger was forced down the throat. Bulimia was not just for rich cis girls. She forced herself to get up, slumped through the yard and into the parking garage, regretting her decision to not just get hooked up on the steps. She was looking for the cream-colored vintage cabriolet Royal-Lee drove.

Her eyelids felt so heavy and decadent, like cakes sitting atop the ionic columns of her cheekbones. She couldn't find the Beetle. She checked her phone and saw the address. Suite letter P. She would go up and through the lobby and check the front steps. If not there, she'd go to the suite. This was taking too long. She needed her pills. She felt happy, like she had a secret, and was a different person, a delicious derelict on a covert mission, but she'd better not lose Royal-Lee. She better not fuck this up. She was getting higher by the moment. She was getting way too high.

6

Out Front of Doctor Delray's, Beverly Hills . . .

Royal-Lee was taking a risk at work, smoking a joint on the front steps of the doctor's fancy-looking office building, rather than getting high in the underground parking garage, because he wanted to watch the beautiful cars rolling by—Porsches, McLarens, BMWs, and Range Rovers—being handled by beautiful people. Maybe someday, somebody would handle him, whisk him away to his new life in the hills, rubbing oil on the belly of a multi-millionaire, making smoothies and getting them off before breakfast. Maybe someone would want Royal-Lee. No one offered a second look.

Maybe it was because Royal-Lee was wearing a camo Supreme fanny pack (holding ten thousand in cash) and an oversized Alexander Wang cropped pocket tee and Diesel leather shorts that no one stopped to talk to him. Was this outfit too stylish for so far west? Showing too much leg? At least they got to wear this to work. He liked having a job. It kept him busy and offered a sense of purpose.

According to Peter, one of the deepest ironies of life was that people who worked for others were the freest, while the leisure classes were often enslaved to greed or negativity. It was Hegel's "Master-Slave Dialectic," Peter had explained, looking at his phone, and then up to Royal-Lee, like the only person he wanted to explain anything to ever.

"Although the strict translation of German's *Herrschaft und Knechtschaft* to English," Peter went on, "is 'Lordship and Bondage.' Royal-Lee, German is full of subordinate clauses. *Dass, Weil, Wenn, Ob, Obwohl.*"

Royal-Lee could never remember any of these words.

While unsure about Peter's classist ideology, that BDSM title, from the lordship's mouth, had turned Royal-Lee on. He would like to be a subordinate clause bonded to Peter. Flights of lust triggered a much deeper anxiety in Royal-Lee. Even if free from the Kingdom Hall, there was a lot of indoctrinated shame and trauma around *man*-sex. Peter being older and handsome and patient and kind helped—he was part of the adult world and not something frivolous and disposable—not like some kid you'd meet at a club. Not that there was anything wrong with that—frivolous lust among kids. It beat them shooting up schools. Dancing and clubbing seemed fun.

It was just that if Royal-Lee was personally going to commit such a consummate act, it should be for something approximate to love, with someone trusted. A *real* man. Royal-Lee imagined silk sheets, a set of lacey lingerie, corset, garter, g-string, bralette, and sometimes they strolled into shops on the West Side, imagining wearing the fine pieces they sold, negligees and thousands of dollars of French silk or lace. *Peach. Wine. Mint. Lavender.* Silk sounded delicious. They wanted to wear nude, gold, silver, and black with Peter, who said that everyone was responsible for determining what was good and bad, holy and unholy, sexy and not sexy. It was all about personal freedom. Each person was responsible for coming up with their own personal conception of a Higher Power, too. In fact, Peter claimed, you were responsible for all reality, because you either determined it somehow, or you were in control of how you responded to it. Reality had always been big in LA, at least among the elite—the ultimate show.

Most of the house called Royal-Lee "he," and Peter did, too—at first. But that started to shift, especially in moments as Royal-Lee leaned into their own beauty, when they moved through the house in short shorts or vintage silk, radiating a kind of untouchable clarity. There were days Royal-Lee liked "they," but sometimes "she" almost seemed to fit just right, like when the light caught their lashes or they slipped into some other ethereal frequency. It wasn't a transition so much as a performance—a fluid self unfurling in real time. Peter watched it all without asking, which was, somehow, the right response.

There'd been another "killing" in the papers, in the news, across the media. Did Royal-Lee know the victim? Had they seen her before, somewhere? Maybe on Skid Row? Maybe downtown? Had she been at the Villa in the first days after he went to work for Peter, six months ago, just after Peter bought the Villa? The unhoused addicts bled together like monsters in a B-horror movie about brain-eating zombies. Royal-Lee didn't like horror. Life was scary enough. In a town of tawdry stories, horror was big show business, but no one cared about the monstrousness out on the streets.

"The killings" got to their heart. The latest was almost certainly a murder. Another dead addict found in a poor motel. She was gutted. It wasn't like Royal-Lee was involved. It wasn't like they were killing people. It wasn't like *they* were *God*. But it still got to them. The idea that one was somehow responsible for reality, or at least on the hook for how one felt about it, and what one did with it, in one's own heart, tore Royal-Lee up. Peter insisted it was the divine duty of each soul to wrestle with the notion that they were helping to direct reality with their thoughts and prayers. It triggered some OCD tendency from being raised religious, spiritually indoctrinated ever since experience could be remembered. Guilt, fear, longing for home. Thoughts were prayers, and prayers mattered. Looking up, inhaling the joint, they blew smoke into the already smoky sky.

Shirley Iko's corpse was discovered at the Full Moon Inn located in South Los Angeles. She was an addict with that darkly tanned face you see on LA street people. Too much sun had baked her skull—she looked like she'd dyed herself a dirty maroon with something like L'Oreal self-tanning mousse—sun spots and carbon monoxide dotted her skin beneath matted hair, accentuating the boniness of her face that jutted out due to drugs, malnourishment, and the harshness of outdoor life. She was a scary-looking woman even before what looked like a blood ritual was performed in her motel room.

She was discovered with tablets of Oxycontin scattered across the nightstand, her hair cut off and spread on the bed like sunrays of a disconnected halo. According to the articles, she was under a hundred pounds. She had a heavy-duty twenty-six-inch nylon zip tie around her throat and above it her neck slit open like a bloodred smile. Her hands were bound in zip-tie handcuffs behind her back and her ring finger was missing. Had Royal-Lee and God done this? Of course not. You were better off not paying attention to the horrors of the world. Not engaging with the addicts and unhoused souls of Los Angeles, besides passing them on the street on his way back to his mother's apartment with a bag of groceries, filled with ice cream and donuts. Addicts were heartbreakers. So was his mother.

Royal-Lee had panic attacks that had gotten worse since meeting Peter at the West Adam's Heritage Association. He could tell you the entire history of West Adams, having perfectly memorized the Association's laminated script: *Originally, this was a place of oil barons, mining lords, and bankers who came when the Automotive Club built their headquarters here. The papers all wrote about the neighborhood's desirability and barons posted signs NO DOGS, NO ACTORS, NO COLOREDS* . . . It was among the richest neighborhoods in LA and the most racist. Royal-Lee had performed the script as the smart, cute, proper young person everyone wanted, without street pain and anger. Beautiful cheekbones dazzled Peter as he'd nodded along to the memorized speech when he first came to the Heritage Association for a tour.

Royal-Lee told Peter, "The lords of fortune didn't want any colorful folks. But as laws changed, more diverse peoples moved in, Rosa Parks Throughway was named, and most of the rich magnates moved west to the hills, and wetter horizons." With that wetter line, their eyes locked.

The lessons from the Witnesses were nonsense. If you didn't have style, fashion, money, and looks, you weren't going to get far without being treated badly, and nobody could get through a whole life that way without messing it up, getting in trouble, and going straight to hell.

The Witnesses took everything way too seriously. They taught Royal-Lee that humans were all servants of God, walking a tightrope across the chasms of hell on earth like some kind of waiter-acrobat on *American Gladiators*. Well, Royal-Lee didn't want to be anybody's servant, except Peter's. He'd only been at the Villa a little while, half a year, but it had already changed Royal-Lee for the better.

Peter saved him from living in poverty in West Adams with his mother in a cramped two-room apartment, one serving as both her bedroom and living room, with her dingy brass bed and their little TV trays. Nights, Royal-Lee used whatever data was left on the phone to pore through Instagram, shielding the screen from her lest she rattle on against the Devil and the fags and whores in Hollywood, which Royal-Lee perceived as an accusation, although he wasn't out and had never even had a first kiss, but wasn't technically a virgin, which is something not to talk about.

He remembered putting on his mother's makeup. She caught him gingerly dabbing on cheap red lipstick in her bathroom. It had looked great. She'd slapped Royal-Lee across the face, and called her child a pervert. She wasn't even supposed to care about makeup, or accept gifts, or eat too much candy, but she stuffed whole Ho Hos in her mouth, crinkling the thin cellophane during Jay Leno's monologues at 10 p.m. Things at home had been especially dour when Royal-Lee was eleven and she'd lost her job at the Kingdom Hall for gossiping about an elder circuit overseer. She started receiving gifts from a male caller.

Royal-Lee still wanted to serve God; he knew the Jehovah's would be tripping if they saw what was going on at the Villa. They'd disfellowship Royal-Lee. They'd toss him out of the giant cult, label them a *dissenter.* Anyone who dissented or fraternized with a dissenter would be disfellowshipped and shunned. Of the seven million Jehovah's, they booted about thirty thousand a year. Of course, one could come back crawling with their tail tucked between their legs, remain silent around all ye faithful, and prove repentance. Might even get an invite back into the fold, but Royal-Lee didn't want one, had another form of tucking in mind, and had questions that needed answers. Dreams and a city in which to dream them into waking life.

He had never tried on lingerie except his mother's panties once or twice as a kid, and they were too big and brown and horrible and had to be secured with safety pins that opened and dug into the flesh of their hips, leaving nasty black piercings that bled.

Royal-Lee's entire childhood had been terrorized by the Devil, which his mother and the Witnesses constantly invoked. It was as though the Devil could appear from the cabinets under the kitchen sink with a can of Comet in its clown fangs. Or leap from the door of the crawlspace of his bedroom and bite Royal-Lee's feet off. When they pierced their ears with fake diamond studs, the Witnesses bullied and ostracized them to no end. Peter wasn't like that. He didn't chastise anyone for being honest. People could be who they needed to be. No threats, no judgments, no bullying with damnation. It was a house of love.

The resting place for Royal-Lee's soul still nagged at their mind, especially with the compromises and temptations experienced at the Villa on the daily. Peter called these doubts intrusive thoughts. Royal-Lee had always thought a lot about the afterworld, and somehow imagined it as a place, like Beverly Hills, or Bel Air, or Skid Row. Peter suggested coming up with a new conception of God and Heaven and Hell, and Royal-Lee was thinking about that lately. Was that fair or was it cheating on God?

Royal-Lee was cheating on his diet in Beverly Hills, chewing beef jerky and spitting the chewed-up wet meat pulp over the platform of the staircase onto the hot grass between drags off a joint pre-roll: a blend of Super Lemon Haze and Booger weed. He occasionally swallowed. It was animal cruelty, high sodium, GMO-processed meat. What else would Peter say about eating *Jack Links*? Eating mammals was terrible. Methane gas. Suffering. Sadness. Baby animals.

After a long hot drag off the joint, they studied the packaging, blowing smoke out through clear pink MAC Cremesheen-coated lips. Then licked them and tasted the weed, the emollient base and floral notes. The sky was smoky and the day was heating up. He was sweating a little through his La Prairie Swiss UV Protection Veil sunscreen. He stared at the trunk of a Guadalupe palm that rose to fronds above cables of yellow fruit, and got kind of mentally lost while looking at it. Was Royal-Lee a queen? Were they still vegan as long as they spit out the meat? Peter loved to recount the names of flowers and plants, teaching about local ecology and botanical wonders. Royal-Lee rubbed the botanical oils on before they slept in bed together, although Peter rarely let their bodies touch.

A faint breeze blew and they went inside, thought of other things as the elevator rose to the top floor.

Sometimes, Royal-Lee fantasized that there was a video crew

following them around, filming for a reality TV show, "Royal-Lee and Peter." He wanted to be a reality star. To be in the Turks and Caicos, in a music video. Royal-Lee and Peter on jetskis, holding hands, a flock of dolphins jumping out of the water to kiss their cheeks. If reality really were a projection of consciousness, like Peter swore, why couldn't Royal-Lee invent that? Pursed lips for the imaginary camera, just a little weed-stoned. And how come Peter couldn't someday see them on the blue waters of the sea in the tropics and say, "Wow, I just realized I'm completely in love with you!"

"Great body," Peter had once said while Royal-Lee was getting dressed, "Especially that . . . Perfect."

It's a she, Peter. It's my girl.

Everything had now slowed. There was a warm free feeling as time sunk and the weed hit and they felt aware. Susie would be in the garage later, and they felt a sudden pang of panic. The thought had been that it would be convenient, but now, stoned and nervous, they couldn't be sure meeting her here was a good idea.

At the end of the hall, a big window looked out at the sun on the city and upon the Santa Monica Mountains. Royal-Lee stood for a moment and watched Rodeo Drive sparkle, felt woozy and pressed two fingers to their neck and counted, looked at their Tudor watch and box-breathed. Was Royal-Lee about to faint? This heart was skipping all over the place. That was a side effect of purging too often, your heart jumped around. You could die.

One day, Peter had said "Royal-Lee, I'm pretty sure all human beings are attracted to their born gender."

Royal-Lee hadn't said anything about being gay or straight, or how they had a hard time with his pronouns. In his mind, he was still a *he*, but sometimes *she*, and also neither. *Ze* had been an option, too, but then Peter said it sounded too German. *Xe* . . . *Ey* . . . Royal-Lee didn't know what these last two meant. *Any/all* wasn't an option yet, but was mostly accurate. *They* was a very new thing and he wondered about it. *He* would have to do. For a bit longer. They didn't want to make trouble for anyone.

Since then, Royal-Lee had tried eyeliner here, lipstick there, women's cutoff jean shorts and a crop. It was probably safer to be fem at the Villa. If Royal-Lee didn't look like a threat, nobody would attack, right? But that wasn't enough, to adapt merely to protect oneself, to hide . . . If it were even safer at all.

Royal-Lee longed for something he didn't have access to, the right to dress with extra personality. To be from another time. When fashion wasn't merely about garments you could get from China on a shoestring budget, or Italy, if you could afford it, or Spain if you preferred Manolo Blahnik. Longing for a bold declaration of individuality and defiance against societal norms, Royal-Lee didn't have a bold identity. Didn't even know if the societal norms would stay put. They would of course remain reliably under the same pronoun for his mom, who was a hater of all things queer and questioning. A gender Nazi. But they weren't talking to her.

One didn't want to dress to conform but to express a true self, embracing some vibrant cultural identity that celebrated diversity and challenged the status quo. Was there no quo? No status but rich or poor? Nothing else? It wasn't just a matter of who one loved or how one identified, but a celebration of a way of life marked by unapologetic living that they wanted. A desire to change the world. Right?

Fashion was not supposed to be just a passing trend but a powerful form of rebellion, a declaration of identity, and a testament to resilience in the face of adversity. You couldn't even smoke in a gay bar now, although Royal-Lee didn't smoke. He'd never been in a gay bar. Had never drank in a bar. Had never been with a man, willingly. Didn't really know what to dream about wanting.

Until meeting Peter, Royal-Lee couldn't fully acknowledge the aspiration to be beautiful for beauty's sake. And never told anyone about not being into girls. Royal-Lee was not some street-style beautiful-bro trying to fit in in the old neighborhood. In alone time, walking around Rodeo Drive, staring at people who had easy money for plastic surgery and porcelain teeth—who had the wisdom sucked out of their faces and put into their asses, chin implants, Kybella, dermabrasion, filler—they were just hoping to blend in. Today's cash in the pocket was for Dr. Morris Delray. Or else shopping would have been an option, mani-pedi, lunch or laser hair removal. Delray was the head shrink, so you had to be nice to him even though he was a condescending prick who looked like he wanted to dry-fuck Royal-Lee over his desk. None of that mattered. Royal-Lee really only cared about the wad of cash that bulged out and made one hip look fat in the reflection in the window before they moved it to the camo pack.

Counting cash on Peter's bed in the thousands was a thrill. So was banding stacks of 5K while Peter punched the *Everlast* or lifted dumbbells, and through the casement French doors of the balcony, palm trees rose like lollipops in the sun. Royal-Lee imagined Delray and his wife, and the kids playing video games on tablets while eating some Whole Foods version of Cheetos, *Annie's Cheesie Smiles.* Ten G's was a lot of money for what Delray did. Which was smirk and ask stupid questions while writing new scripts and Xanax refills for existing patients. He found pain management doctors to dole out Lidocaine patches, Demerol, morphine, diazepam, Vicodin, and their bread and butter: Oxy. Royal-Lee didn't like handing over all the money, but needed to be careful not to manifest anything negative with all this . . . resentment. Peter said negativity might cause weight gain. Thoughts were prayers. *Prayer changes things*, the chalk-painted sign on its rough cord of rope declared from Mom's kitchen counter back in her putrid apartment.

Up the hall at Delray's office, there was a table with a fake orchid and a statue of Poseidon near the doorbell, doorway, and mail slot. Royal-Lee couldn't recall exactly what Peter had said about Plato's account of Atlantis. While hanging Peter's Loro Piana Madrid Sartorial jacket, Peter taught how Plato may have seen art, representation, and the divine. Plato was a trickster and you couldn't take him seriously. He broke reality in half long before the Cartesian split. Inside the office, a Muzak rendition of "Love Yourself" was being piped through the office speakers. The room smelled like dentistry. Who didn't love Justin Bieber? He was a good Christian, a beautiful man. Pink orchids bloomed on a coffee table teeming with out-of-season magazines. Susie sat stoned in the front row of chairs . . . Oh, *fuck!*

Raising their eyebrows at her, she didn't respond. Her coloring was far too pale. Her hair was disheveled, but it looked like rich girl hair, except she hadn't cared for herself and it was growing out at the roots. She had pimples, like all junkies. Was it just the nature of the poppy to gum up its users' pores? Or did she also not shower? Use pads or tonics? Medicated soaps? She was wearing a boxy tee and running shorts, and a gold boyfriend chain, ugly shades, and her legs were splayed apart. What Royal-Lee wouldn't do with her privilege and position! Get off drugs, make friends, and get tons of work done! Get a decent set of extensions, maybe? A butt lift *and everything.*

"What are you doing here?" Royal-Lee snapped his fingers at her, then he felt abusive.

She slid down from the chair and passed out on the white shag carpet. *Shit.* Royal-Lee tried to stay cool, and crouched down beside her. Her lips were blue, especially backgrounded by the white rug. She gasped in little fleeting wheezes in her throat. Foam gathered at the corners of her mouth. More came out in a belch between her lips. Royal-Lee looked around, gripped her shoulder and shook her. You were supposed to care about people. Jesus said so.

Holding her head they found the nasal spray bottle in the fanny-pack, unscrewed the cap off the Naloxone and with shaky hands, jammed the plastic nozzle up Susie's nostril, closed the other nostril with one finger, and squeezed the bottle, then waited a few seconds, and squeezed again.

"Ughh," Susie said, coming back with her eyeballs rolling, head alerting wildly. Who did she look like? *Someone.* Or was that just dying rich girl face? Her eyes went straight, whites bloodshot, glasses fallen off, nose sniffling and dripping. She was lucky. She'd live. Bringing addicts back from the dead was Royal-Lee's job and felt momentarily heroic. They were never grateful. Not a single time did one addict ever once say, "Thank you, Royal-Lee."

"What did you do?" she accused, like it was Royal-Lee who had gotten her *that* high. "You creep."

"I saved you."

She flung her hand up and hit herself in the eyebrow, like a zombie learning to move again on TV.

"Ouch," she whimpered.

"Are you okay?" Royal-Lee blushed, pretending to be her friend.

"Huh?" She was limp. "Yeah, I'm okay. Are you okay?"

"Hey, what did you take today?"

"I took one, like always. Then another, but later."

"Blue or green?"

"I don't know. Both. Yeah."

"I told you to take a *half* of a blue. How much do you even weigh?"

Dr. Delray walked into the waiting room and glared at both of them on the ground, the bottle of Narcan still in Royal-Lee's hand. He shot them an idiotic look above a sweater vest that conveyed adult feelings of male betrayal. All of his life's work, all his responsibilities, jeopardized by gender-fluid youth.

"Who's this?" the doctor asked. "Are you bringing friends here?"

Susie looked legitimately confused.

"The suite was in the text," she said.

"This is my place of business," Delray said. He didn't know how to talk to teenagers. "It's an office, not a night club."

"I'm fine," Susie said, trying to push off the floor. "I'm fine. Really. No problem."

"Stand up slowly," Royal-Lee told her. "I'll give you a ride home."

"No." She shook her head as if her life was someone else's that she was just taking care of for a while—a loaner while hers got serviced. Rich people were so full of shit.

"Both of you, get out of here. My two o'clock is going to be showing up any minute."

"I'll go, but Royal-Lee," Susie said, managing to kneel. Royal-Lee shook their head *no*, already pissed. Was she kidding?

"You have something for me?" Her voice lilted in guilt, real or pretend.

"I can't *even* breathe," Royal-Lee said.

"I was lightheaded from the heat, okay? I get low blood pressure. It won't happen again. My sodium is low."

She tugged Royal-Lee to help her stand and tucked a wad of hundreds she'd taken out of her shorts into the front pocket of Royal-Lee's Wang crop and hung on a shoulder. Could she smell the Jack Links? Royal-Lee's stomach hurt, felt *too* full. Something was twisting, like a baby inside the abdomen, a sensation they'd never know. Delray was a reverse man baby.

"Royal-Lee, our work together has come to an end. Tell Peter we're done." The man was shaking, even the skin on his face moved. *Gross.* Royal-Lee had chronophobia, couldn't stand seeing flesh age.

"The money," Delray said. "Your girlfriend OD'ing in my office?"

"I'm not his girlfriend, oh my God."

"I don't even know her," Royal-Lee lied.

"Rude," Susie said.

Royal-Lee unzipped the fanny pack and stacked the cash on the coffee table. Then stood and wondered if the money would change his mind.

"Get out," he said, taking the cash. "Tell Mr. Holiday we are done."

* * *

Susie looked annoyed and plopped down on a winged bench with red silk upholstery and French-style legs, mother of pearl inlays, and stained orange pillows, stationed by the elevator. She was glowering at him, picking a golden hair off her tanned thigh.

"Peter who?" she said, agitated. "Who's Holiday?"

Maybe they should run. Run back home to live with their mom. But why? The Villa was a refuge for Royal-Lee. Back at the apartment, there were always boxes of Jehovah's Witness pamphlets. They showed a photo of a woman holding her forehead, face in agony, and above her, the words, all caps: WILL SUFFERING EVER END? Was the woman's face on the pamphlet Shirley Iko? The most recent addicted victim without a house murdered in a motel? Had she been at the Villa? Susie had just overdosed. Were they terrible people? Or was Peter a messenger from the divine? At least they watched over the addicted as they used. Peter invited Royal-Lee to use him as a stepping stone to the other shore of faith, a land free from fear, self-hatred, and shame. *Ride on my back, my shoulders, Royal-Lee. My yoke is gentle.* On the other side, terra firma awaited, fields of flowers, Peter with his blue eyes lined with pencil, a thousand messages of peace and faith and forgiveness. Plus Peter paid an allowance. He was a rich stud.

Royal-Lee could see Susie's inner thighs were semi-taut, but had lost a bit of that firm skin glow, where they'd once been more toned as shown on Instagram. Not enough cardio, Barry's Boot Camp or hiking, and clearly too many pills. Panicking about Delray, the real and immediate threat, who'd just quit, maybe they'd better bring Peter flowers. Or bring Susie. Black-eyed Susies, with OD'd circles under her eyes.

She was squirming. She looked miserable, crawling out of her skin and sniffling. *There'd be no getting high for her for a bit.* The Naloxone had blocked her opioid receptors. That's how it worked. Royal-Lee was tired of always being such a good person, worrying about everyone else.

"Sell me those pills," she pouted. "Please?"

Flirting wasn't going to help.

"Come with me. I'll take you to my place and get you hooked up," Royal-Lee was faking compassion. "I forgot the pills. I would've told you in the office, but you overdosed."

"But I didn't." Obviously she had. She stood and stuck out her hip like a brat. He had to admit it was a weak lie, forgetting the Oxy, but it was for her sake, too.

"Show me what's in that waist pack! Supreme's a Barbara Kruger rip-off. Do your homework." She lurched for the fanny and he pivoted as the doors to the elevator opened. The lower of two frosted glass rectangles lit up a dull millennium pink. Royal-Lee got in and pressed G. She grabbed at him and managed to unzip the bum-bag, but it was empty.

"I'm going to introduce you to someone."

Her face was blank. Then she scowled. "Who is it, *Jesus*? Or *Holiday*? I am not becoming a Jehovah's Witness. Unless joining gets me all the Oxy in the world and a nice big bathroom to take a holy shit."

Royal-Lee made a disapproving face and led her into the garage toward the Beetle. When they reached the car, unlocked the door, elongating and showing off narrow sides, they stuck their ass out just a little to show the gains from HIIT booty band workouts performed off YouTube. Pamela Reif was their fitness guru. *Kiss to the camera.*

Climbing in and popping the lock to her door, Royal-Lee watched her get in. She was glaring, rubbing her face, looking out the window, rolling it down, leaning out of the frame like a dog, and then she gagged and spit. Maybe she'd fit in fine at the Villa. For the first time, Royal-Lee wondered if Peter was joking when he called his rehab "The Villa." No, Peter was a serious guy. Royal-Lee started the engine and missed the gear a few times. The grinding sound wasn't instilling any confidence in Susie, then it stalled. Maybe Peter could groom her, get her sober, and they'd fix that hair of hers. But who wanted her?

"Can we go?" she said, but seemed acquiescent. They hoped she'd be quiet on the ride to the Villa. She was fidgeting and picking at her fingers. She'd be crawling out of her skin for the twenty-minute commute. Was Peter going to be okay with bringing Susie?

"Hello?" she shouted and it echoed through the garage, then Susie softened her voice. "Who are we going to meet? Where are you taking me? Who is Peter Holiday? I think I might know that dude."

"How would you?"

"He's either my old professor or maybe his brother."

"He's not a professor. He runs a rehab."

"Oh, no. No rehabs." She went for the door, then lurched at the glove box, dropped the lid and found the orange bottle of red pills. She grabbed it.

"That helps. Bye." Susie pulled the door handle and was out, then slammed it.

Another stupid move!

Addicts always did whatever it took to get high. Royal-Lee had seen house members eat burnt sections of aluminum foil to get the residue from pills they'd already smoked, even when they knew they were going to get fresh pills in half an hour. They did way worse than that. They used every cord in the house to wrap around their arms and legs and shoot pills in their veins, jamming the needles so hard into themselves it looked like they'd tear a hole through their pathways, bruise or rip themselves open. Sometimes they'd even steal the needle out of another addict who was high enough to let them, just to see if there was anything left.

Royal-Lee looked in the vanity mirror, cringing, which made the forehead and skin between the eyebrows crease. That wasn't good to do to their face. Peter would go ballistic for losing Delray. Well, if he did, he did. It was time to face facts. Royal-Lee had fucked up again. They were only nineteen.

7

Upstairs, in the Villa's Suite . . .

You have to wonder, had I gone with Royal-Lee to the Villa the day that I OD'd in Delray's office, would everything have been different that fall? The word "villa" almost makes me chuckle. It's like calling McDonald's "American Cuisine." Although you have to wonder about everything in this novelization, as a novel is not a memoir. So far, essentially, you can trust what I've told you. It's a *wonder* I survived that year and a half after leaving NYU, while living out my fantasy underworld intoxication in my father's garden beside the pool, captive to a hell of his making, or my own. I was an addict, a victim of the opioid crisis. Although victimhood is an interesting quandary. What is the role of freedom and moral relativism in a free-market consumer society? What is the difference between apartheid and mere patriarchal domination in family systems? To what extent are we free?

Saying "you have to wonder" reminds me of that senior-year class I took back at Marlborough called "Humanities" where we read Sophocles and discussed the nature of fate versus free will. In our expensive clothes, with our futures so bright we needed shades, in our Audis and Aston Martins, Bentleys and BMWs, Range Rovers and Jaguars, rolling through it all to our palatial homes. *Sophocles, Aristotle, Hume, Nietzsche.* I often still feel slightly insecure about my lack of formal education, but then higher education is a scam and graduate school is worse. Most of the losers who go into grave debt end up leading less successful lives than if they'd skipped classes and applied themselves out in the real world, letting fate have its way with them, like I did. Not that I would have had to pay for college or could ever be in debt.

Besides, the best way to learn about art and art history is to just leave your phone on record at dinner parties with artists. Everyone they reference, you look them up the next morning. I recommend getting up around 5 a.m. if you want to be anything in this world. It's what I do, if I'm not up at 3:30 a.m., haunted by memories and images from my fall, wishing I could take a pill without breaking my sobriety, thinking of what art project I am going to start next.

Have you ever seen Pieter Fris's *Orpheus and Eurydice in the Underworld*? It's a masterpiece of playful melancholy so grim it could have been painted in opiated oils. In it, ugly souls drink and smoke either suffering from madness or delighting in it; King Hades's head is on fire, and Queen Persephone stands by looking appalled. Its point is simple: you're fucked so *why look back*. Time is an arrow and life is a story only understood in reverse. Isn't that what I'm doing? This mise-en-scène of *Orpheus and Euridice* oozes hopelessness and longing, and in it I see the realm of the addict. This is what I look back upon, even as the past dissolves in ripples of falsehood, leaving only my current reflection when the water finally stills. I fucking hate liberals.

The hell of the artist and the garden of natural delights are both archetypes of liminal experiences and as such are temporary experiential realities to inhabit, free from moralism. The artist's amoral prerogative is necessary to explore what lies within, to wrestle with whatever can help them create or destroy themselves. The gnostic *Gospel of Thomas* contains this maxim: "If you bring forth what is within, what you bring forth will save you, if you do not bring forth what is within you, what you do not bring forth will destroy you." Professor Krolik taught me about all of these things, but not at once, and not only in the classroom setting.

Americans, of course, do not understand moral relativism any more than they understand Jean Baudrillard's concepts of hyperreality, my favorite. They have no idea how manipulated they are by the exchange values of symbols and meanings based on pop ideology, paranoia politics, and symbiotic branding. The French understand all this, as they understand all things. From Foucault to Derrida to Roland Barthes to de Beauvoir, the French get freedom in a way that Americans can only dream of. Americans are much more Germanic, desperate to adhere to notions of fatherland, moral rigidity, herd mentality, and hatred. They're like my father. They're inherently fascistic, tribal, and conspiracy-minded. They are insane. Both sides. They can only understand violence. I hate fascists.

The authentic life of an artist requires the freedom to create for ourselves, fuck humanity, all for the individuation of inner psychic realities. This allows an artist to journey through the depths of alienated suffering and through the heights of insight—bridging the gap between light and dark and adding to a fuller understanding of the human condition—all things the American public would need presented to them wrapped in a cocktail napkin of political partisanship and forced groupthink. Americans hate freedom. They like product. So do I. Once I was young and felt the ache of infinity and absence of mortality in my body, in my racing mind, tormenting me at every turn, begging to be drained or drugged or to plumb the depths of my inherent inborn talent and find new rules for existing in the world on my own terms. Now, pay me.

Someone else agreed with me about the need to define your own terms. "The Pain Killer," as one letter he'd sent to the news and the police was signed, wrote that he was inventing his own rules, too.

Of course, psychopaths know if you want to be something bad enough, you have to free yourself from the brainwash. That's why they kill. For instance, when "The Pain Killer" sent the signed letters to the papers, even including a few ring fingers in one of the envelopes (a sort of marital pact with the recently deceased), he said that "killing" was the only way he could change the nature of his reality in a significant enough manner so that he was able to transcend the realm of soul-obedience and irrelevance that the world had determined for him. He chose to become a monster, which is sort of like choosing your own god, right? What did Nietzsche say? Sure, there's the whole "He who fights with monsters might take care lest he thereby become a monster. If you gaze for too long into the abyss, the abyss gazes also into you." Who isn't being gazed into by the abyss? Isn't every screen an abyss? Isn't that the state of the world these days—the constantly rotating main character as the Internet star of the week, and yourself the villainous voyeur with blood urges to be kept sated.

I prefer *this* from Nietzsche, taken from *The Gay Science*, "Only artists have given man eyes and ears to see and hear with some pleasure what each man is, experiences, desires; only they have taught us to esteem the hero that is concealed in everyday characters; only they have taught us the art of viewing ourselves . . ." The art of viewing ourselves.

To be a "killer," to be an artist, to be the Orange President, to be an influencer, that's all the same game. To take by force that which is the gift of transformation from the one-sidedness of wonder into the glory of representing it in a new light, to all. To gain freedom, by any means necessary. That *is* it. To be an artist carries no hefty responsibility. The artist plays the art world, its bizarre ultra-wealthy collectors, and still manages to liberate herself through a devout practice of exploration of both the self and the divine. If she's having fun. Or else she's just irrelevant bullshit. Explore . . . exploit . . . it all depends on what's inside. Myself, I am a mix, a velvet fist in a steel glove. What else can you be if you're going to survive this world? A knife and a sponge. A carrot and a stick: I'd just as soon beat you as reward you, like my father, I guess. I'd rather shove a carrot up someone's ass and beat them with the stick, anyone from my generation especially.

Anyhow . . . it's pretty obvious that the system controls everything. You can only rise if you work yourself to the top by working the market's rules, which requires a Faustian pact with narcissism, corruption, dishonesty, hidden violence, and hatred. *Das Kapital.*

I prefer to ride in a black car with my shades on and drive a convertible up and down the 405. I like to have my gallerist call me, to have my allergist, my therapist, my assistant, my publicists, and my lawyers on speed dial or recents or whatever.

I do interviews in glossy magazines where they style me and do my hair and makeup. I like following the rules of the spectacle. You see, I'm here to die, like everyone, and I'm not going to bow before idiotic Sigma men, the type who once quoted Nietzsche—a man who wrote about the nature of women as so disgusting that people will curse it and resort to *art* or *God* just to escape the horrible truth of menstruation and child birth—*birth parent*—and the Nazis used Nietzsche as justification to kick the weak and crippled from the ladder's rungs beneath them. Remember, eight million dead Jews. My father will never forget. And then you still have to uplift people. What is art? What can art accomplish? Boots on skulls. It has to compete.

So *anyway*, all I can do now is move forward, and create my own scenes, in hopes of participating in the ancient mystery of capturing the essence of time and freezing it into art. After all, what is a popular artist but someone with scarce enough morals to do whatever it takes to project herself into the public consciousness, to make herself important enough that others may someday ask the question of whether she had to free herself at all or if it was all fate—the stuff of true stars—because they can't imagine how anyone does it; how does one make something out of oneself? *Freedom?* What is freedom? Who can claim to be free? Popular people. People who freed themselves.

Peter was promised the false freedom that proclaimed he had no duty to anyone besides himself. He became captive to an institution that uses shame and humiliation rituals to trap members into an occultist pact that essentially strips them of personal agency. A cult. I, on the other hand, at least eventually found AA. My sponsor would later instruct me that I needed to surrender my-life-and-my-will to the care of a Higher Power, a loving God of my *own* understanding. I told her to fuck off. She smiled and nodded patiently, lifting her matcha latte from its bamboo mat to sip from the stylish ceramic cup at an annoying Japanese coffee shop.

"It's just a *Higher Power*," she said. "No big deal. Nothing to stress. It can be anything. It's just higher than you."

There was a green smudge among her unevenly edged lips, then she blotted them with a paper napkin. She wore a T-shirt with a guitar and a band name with a giant hole on one side, showing off the side of her skinny torso, above black high-rise Lycra shorties. I hated that I had to meet her at places like Maru. Actually, I often hate her, wherever we're meeting. It's important I keep clean, though, although I hate that term—clean. She didn't look *clean*, she looked like trash. *Babe*,

I want to say to her, *you're not still fucked up. Why do you look like shit? Why don't you get a real job instead of working with sponsees on weekdays, drinking eight-dollar lattes?* Why should I care enough to hate her? She's weak. What kind of person believes in something and says it's nothing? She acts like she has some spiritual wisdom, that wry distressed surrender to the facts of life that so many people like me are going to die, while people like her have found the illusive secret of giving up in order to survive. I won't give up that easily. I do maybe need to stay sober, and I guess I can't do it on my own, though, and somehow, with her, or AA, as much as I hate to admit it, it's working.

"Try the ocean," she giggles. "Or, you know, G.O.D. can mean Group of Drunks," she said on our last meeting. "Good Orderly Direction."

She'd heard of someone who made a tree outside their apartment building into their Higher Power but then the tree got struck by lightning. Then the tree died. Then it fell on their car while they were preparing to back out of their driveway and they died. I want to tell her that I have narrowly avoided several cults already at my young age, and I'm not about to fall for the lame logic of the lamest cult in the world, especially not because of a stupid story about a tree.

"What kind of tree?" I smirked, reflecting her smirk, which I can only assume sits there because she's so satisfied with the ironic justice of someone not following the "program" with enough dedication and thus, dying, as the just result of their obduracy, and a fallen tree.

"Oh, I don't know. Some tree. It's not like I knew them," she scoffs.

"Exactly," I said. "There's *no* tree. That's my Higher Power. No tree. You telling me that stupid lie. People making shit up. Imagination."

"Huh?"

That's what I hate about her. She lacks imagination. She has that look like life is sucking her into it. Maybe the whole point of the world is to not fall back into the scenery. Maybe that means working with her, and not falling back into my addiction. Maybe I do need to invent my Higher Power. Then I can forgive myself for the things I did that fall. I need to fashion my own God. Maybe it loves me, and my art, and this crazy fucked up world. I don't know. I really don't know. I'm not into bullshit.

* * *

Susie didn't need anything but her own determination to rise. She did things beyond what the average person would ever let themselves do. Maybe this was because she was in the grips of a *Lower Power*, as her sponsor would later tell her. Drugs *were* a low frequency. She was low. Low life. It felt good to be low.

Phil as "Peter" was trying to raise his frequency at the Church of White Illumination. But rather than trying to find his own Higher Power, they were teaching him that he *was his own Higher Power*. They offered him worship of extreme wealth, luxury, and self-determination in their often "misunderstood and maligned organization" that was filled with some of the most powerful and influential souls on the planet.

They taught him that all you had to do is forget the value of anyone else in the world in order to self-actualize. Why live except to fly? What was there to realize except the self? He had always been interested in higher things. They were saying that his relationship with himself as the divine was all that mattered. That and masquerade balls, long black and red cloaks, masks of birds and planets, naked women, watching your brethren in orgiastic rituals, and really getting to know each other.

As a little kid, he would often sit in his room and try to levitate books with his mind. He knew he *could* lift them if he really put his mind to it; there were worlds of feeling inside him that had nothing to do with school logic. His convictions had been planted and had grown out of religious stories his parents taught him about Jesus Christ, verses about moving mountains with perfect faith and voice commands, and the miracles of Moses and Aaron. He'd felt God talking to him and he'd tried to keep his heart clean, confessing his sins in his nightly prayers, and asking to be made a better boy, although he never felt particularly male, or even human. He floated a lot into the heavenly realms of euphoria, and then dropped down into crippling despair. Often he was his own only friend. Something was wrong with him, something was going to get him—and he was alone—because his brother didn't love him enough. His brother was always saying how annoying he was.

He *was* annoying. Always buttoning the top button of the dress shirts he wore, wearing shades and polo shirts with the collars popped, hanging out alone because no one wanted to be his friend. He was basically a traumatized weirdo, watching *Amadeus*, hating himself for not being a genius, and for his love of music, and his lack of greatness; he'd stopped taking piano lessons despite wanting to be a classical music genius, because his teacher was mean.

It hadn't helped that his parents had met in a cult disguised as an Old Testament Bible study run and controlled by religious leader Dr. Wierwille on a farm in New Knoxville, Ohio. Their parents' only friends were members of the same cult. They'd all been indoctrinated to believe that letters from their family members might actually be from the Devil, so they burned the letters before reading them. It was a very isolated community, but not entirely joyless, as the commune members took acid, danced around the fire, and, except for those who disappeared off the "funny farm," remained best friends after partner swapping. Their parents and their parents' friends taught the twins about God.

So, he'd deeply believed in God, and in the righteousness of the beatitudes and the kingdom of heaven and the rottenness of mainstream culture—and the rottenness of himself, too. His parents shouted and his father hit him, then left him to stare at the walls or listen to his Walkman and experience God's love alone. For some reason, his twin didn't get as much abuse. The Abel to his Cain. He was the better brother, and so he didn't get hit or strangled or verbally berated, abused, or blamed for the misery of his parents. He felt jealous and vengeful that his father treated his brother so much better, but did being jealous and vengeful mean he really was bad and thus deserved the beatings? It seemed each twin was concerned with the spiritual world in equal parts to the amount of physical abuse they received. Perhaps that was the root of all faith. Abuse, fear, and PTSD fostered loyalty and dedication. Wilhelm Reich spent decades critiquing this. Maybe his dedication to God could still equal redemption. Maybe he could earn God's favor by caring for his brother and finding him? Not falling for liberal bullshit. Maybe he could become more of a true believer, a martyr, a miracle worker? Maybe it wasn't too late. Maybe he could use The Church to pull himself back closer to the true God. Maybe he'd made up all the bad shit that happened to him.

There was an appeal to joining a cult that engaged in the ancient search for meaning. He still wanted to connect to God. He missed living in a nonsecular society. America once had a spiritual center he agreed with. He didn't exactly want to be Republican, but he didn't want to be a liberal. It wasn't like he was joining the Illuminati, right? It was just a secret society. Maybe it was a cult, but a cult with pedigree. Or *was* it the Illuminati? And those values he once agreed with, weren't they just a false morality bunting while at the true center was Roy Cohn on cocaine recording Roger Stone giving it to some page boy or peg boy, not that there was anything so wrong with that, per se, but it had to be hidden because the party was pandering to the religious right, marketing themselves to the so-called faithful masses, so they could serve Wall Street and ship jobs to China while blowing coke smuggled in by the CIA. Yeah, maybe that was fun but it had never been a moral nation since the day he was born. And it pretended to be—wasn't lying wrong?

At least his parents had been trying to be moral, once, in a cult, although that got complicated by sexual escapades, weapons, issues with child abuse and other diddling blithering nonsense that happens when people stop thinking for themselves. So what? As above, so below.

Whatever his parents learned back at their cult, it hadn't helped. Mom was a hypochondriac and Dad a hysterical, violent drunk. Home was a world of furious chaos muffled to the outside by the soundproofing qualities of stacked cash. He was told that if he caught a cold, he just needed to pray and believe rightly and he would be immediately healed. True Christianity was about manifestation too, right?

Life was whatever you determined, so it was also kind of all your fault. Everybody in the house, tucked in the Ohio woods—before the family moved to Oregon—was under the spell that life was a wet, wild dream ride through God's Kingdom, as First Lady Nancy Reagan held the famous sign that read *Just Say No* from the back of her Anglo-Arabian horse, No Strings, on the Reagan ranch in Santa Ynez, just outside of

Santa Barbara. She probably had a fantastic pussy—First Lady Nancy Reagan, not the horse, but No Strings was indeed a fine mare. Peter and his brother said "no" at first, and then "maybe," and then "yes" after they realized their parents were hypocritical rich assholes. Her pussy probably tasted like Diet Coke. They were told someone at the top knew something, but the people they saw running things didn't know anything at all. God didn't seem to be in charge. The country was fucking insane, even then. Urban decay, rampant violence, corruption, drugs, MTV, AIDS. Crack. The oil companies hiding the coming climate catastrophe. None of it was a threat to the greatest empire on Earth. Societies crash for three reasons: war, famine, and revolution. Marlboro men rode across giant billboards and mounted the signs of corner stores. Women wore their hair as high as their aspirations. *Life* was going on swimmingly and the country was thriving! Who would ever say no to Coke?

In that famous *Just Say No* photo, Nancy sat beside Ronny, who was saddled on his own white Arabian stallion, El Alamein, a gift from Mexico's president. The CIA had worked with Mexico's Federal Ministerial Police collecting billions in American dollars as bribes to assure the unfettered free flow of cocaine across the border. The CIA was running the Iran-Contra Affair, backing guerilla terrorists, and picking sides over who to support among Latin kingpins like Pablo Escobar and Miguel Angel Felix Gallardo, while providing for the common defense, promoting the common good, and also slinging crack. Peter remembered watching the little Zenith television from his parents' bed and seeing President Reagan (MCA's brainchild and Wasserman's dutiful servant) with his foundation, polish, blush, and lip gloss, plus that statesmanlike, dark-slicked-back-wavy hair. He wasn't a human, more like an animated corpse speaking with uncanny half-there charisma. He was Mr. Rogers mixed with Hitler, but of course that wasn't true. He looked like his first wife, Jane Wyman, mixed with a Labrador who could read off a teleprompter. There was something so beautiful about Ronald, like Richard Prince's wet dream. Everything the country hoped to be. The Republicans could always play the tricks of illusion, manifesting one reality by displacing another. The old slick moneyed handjob. In other words, they knew how to practice politics. Out front, it was liberty for all, in backrooms it was libertinism, freak parties, swinging dicks; Republicans on acid, the CIA in leather headbands with the kings of industry—cracking skulls for the head banana at United Fruit or whatever altar they were paid to pray to then.

Is that what "the killings" were? Politics? Who had cut the throat of Shirley Iko across town? Was it just a sicko for the Orange Candidate, someone who hated the poor and the addicted? Or was it something else, something far more conspiratorial, more corporate, and more focused? The hair had been cut from her head with a knife, leaving it longer in patches, and in other sections revealing chunks of scalp, and removing bleeding patches that dried to look like a dog's hide with mange.

The question about the chronology of "the killings" remains, as there had been a first "killing" possibly linked to the murders that fall, which occurred before Ash was even found at the Cecil Hotel. Roger Lyne had been stabbed with a knife through the back of his skull at the Bevenoshire Lodge on Beverly Boulevard. The knife had pushed through the hypothalamus and thalamus, as the curved blade speared into the parietal and occipital lobes, blood and spinal fluid cascading down his back. His long hair hadn't been cut, but several chunks had been pulled out, with bits of scalp attached, and these sections of hair tossed on the floor. Lyne's toxicology report showed he'd used Oxy in the hours before his murder. It was never officially connected to "the killings." Maybe it was just random vice.

Peter was glad the latest victim wasn't his brother, but other than that, he probably didn't feel much about Shirley Iko's body being discovered at the Full Moon Inn. Was that evil? To be so callous? Even if he cared, it wasn't like he'd done it. Was he levitating everything, floating all earthly objects into their orbits? The Church said this was the case; that the fundamental truth of all existence was he was responsible for all reality, *semper in perpetuum*. Although there was a ring of truth to that stump, it was but one of the innumerable rings of the ancient tree of knowledge. Or else it wasn't really a tree at all but an illusion of the tree. Wasn't God still in charge? Just because he'd stolen God's wig and beard didn't mean he was Lord Supreme himself, right? *God?*

"Pe-ter! Pe-ter!"

His devotees were chanting his name.

In two days, the papers would report the discovery of another dead unhoused addict, Fred Harkin, at the Snooty Fox Motor Inn. Fred's killing would look different, as the authorities stated and the papers reported: more private, more "blood motivated," more occult. His nipples had been snipped off with a pair of tailor's shears. Either a killer was getting bolder or it was the work of someone else. Someone who wanted to change peoples' minds about how society looked at, or didn't look at, people who were addicted to opiates, living on the streets in tents to survive, just barely, at the fraying edge of so-called "society." Or maybe it was some guy who got off on cutting off hair and fingers, reprograming the physical world in some kind of bloody occultist apocalypse of his own making.

In his suite at the Villa, Peter untied his monogrammed Ralph Lauren red silk twill robe and let it drop to the ground as he put a smoldering cigarette in the ashtray. He was wearing white Turnbull and Asser silk boxers. Down below, the Surlies and guests were romping and sending up alarms, shouting for theater and their afternoon drugs and calling Peter's name. Peter sweated. It was not from nervousness, but from the two tablets of Adderall he'd swallowed earlier. He stood, looking through his wardrobe, which Royal-Lee had meticulously color coded. He wanted to look perfect for his performance.

First, he threw on a white poplin Brunello Cucinelli chalk stripe shirt. Over his boxers, Oxford blue-and-white-striped pajama pants, into which he tucked the crisp dress shirt, thinking he looked casual and enlightened, jittering and fumbling with the buttons. A blue Moncler windbreaker half zipped over the dress shirt, with twin front pockets and a tri-colored ribbed collar—after all, the afternoon heat was nothing to him. Finally, large-frame Ray-Ban Wayfarers to shield his eyes from the glare of the lights for his lecture. He would take them off each time he made a profound point. It was the trick Jim Jones used in the Peoples Temple in Guyana. His long wig, the thick wig beard, silk socks, and embroidered Crocket and Jones slippers finished his costume. He admired himself in the full-length mirror. He thought of his brother. He would tell him he looked idiotic in this outfit, he figured. He would tell him what a phony he looked like. So would Susie. He hated himself. He loved himself so much. He didn't even feel like he existed to himself, especially not on this much Adderall and Valium.

Maybe Peter was destined for *phoniness.* He'd been destined to come to LA, after all, the epicenter of illusion in the United States. His name wasn't real. His hair wasn't real. The Church he went to wasn't a real church. No more than the Villa was a *real* rehab. In their towels in the spa or naked in the gym's locker room—the smell of talcum and cologne—there was something refreshingly male about The Church, earnestly grounded in communal faith and the ambition to seize and hold power. They were real men. Men who didn't complain about their identities or their feelings. They took action. Dried their balls with the hand dryer in front of everyone. Maybe it was all an act. Maybe all identity was a play. But The Church was like a grand theater, cast with the elite—playing out their fantasies in the real world—the ruling class of LA.

To that point, so far, he and this year's other recruits had performed plays including *War in Heaven*, from which he'd stolen the wig and beard, *The Salem Witch Trials*, *Genghis Khan's Wedding*, and *The Beheading of Marie Antoinette.* The Church must see something special in him, Peter thought; how good he was at pretending to be someone else. The success in his bloodline. They greeted him warmly when he arrived in his convertible in his Ray-Bans. They parked the vintage Lincoln Continental. It gleamed jet black under the golden sun.

"*Pe-ter*!" The summons from the Villa's auditorium grew louder. He knew exactly how long to make them wait.

Royal-Lee was still returning from Dr. Delray. Peter was beginning to worry, but then fear was a big part of the high of his new lifestyle, and the Adderall was making him jumpy, but the Valium helped. He'd always been so high strung. He still felt the way he had in high school, sweating through his shirts on the bus thinking about how he should carry himself as he walked down the hall from calculus to history and whether people would see something flawed in his bearing, see there was no center to him, know that he was funny, fussy, angry at the world. He'd always wanted his brother to comfort him back then, as he wanted now, if only he could find him. He always wanted his brother to be his best friend.

Maybe a phony could do things a non-phony couldn't. Wasn't that what all the theater was about, all the performances in this capitalist system—wasn't he just hiding who he really was, the loneliness, the self-hatred, lameness and the fact that he wasn't a *real* man? He *was* a real man, he was the realest man. He was the only man.

It was the whole point of joining the Church of White Illumination. You could become whoever you wanted—he could *be* someone else. He could pretend his way into his new identity as the new emperor of the moon. He was getting closer to the elite who ran the world, who sold more opiates than the Ayatollah, and he was learning the secrets of their "secret" society, without losing his soul down the rabbit hole. He had yet to contact Susie, reaching out with the news of his infiltration of her inner social circle. *In time, in time.* First, he had to work his way down the nest and properly position himself among the lavish fluffle.

To be the activist he might become, he knew he might need to destroy them all. He wanted to smash Dick in fulfilment of his lifelong desire to do something good, taking action against a man who had helped kill hundreds of thousands of people with opioids under his corporate greed and manipulation of the proceedings of law and at the FDA. His brother could be next. Dead.

He wanted to do something to help change the world. Was that because he just wanted to be in charge himself? He was desperately trying to run his own house, this Villa with its unruly villagers. He took another five-milligram Valium. Hadn't the Sicklers been connected to Valium? Hadn't Mortimer Sickler marketed Valium as a miracle drug to replace Haldol? Think of all those crazy people. All those people locked up in institutions. All those people in pain who just needed a fix to get through life at home. Thank God there was help for people with real mental illness. Maybe the world was becoming a better place. He chewed the Valium, which tasted like sugar on his numbed tongue. Some people needed a way to manage their pain, but Oxy had been used against everyone with physical and mental discomfort who turned to Dick for relief. It was a killer. The *real* "Pain Killer." You couldn't put a drug on trial for murder. You couldn't lock up a compound. It didn't end that clean.

Would working his way up The Church make him into the very people he hated? Would he become a dick like all of them? He was invited to a private meeting with a woman called "The Conduit" every week as part of his apprenticeship. All new recruits had a "conduit"—it was how inside information was passed from the organization to "pledges" like himself.

His conduit worked out of her satellite office on the top floor of a nine-story medical spa building just off Sunset, where people came for cosmetic procedures—teeth implants and veneers, lipo and lapband, breast augmentation or reduction, rhinoplasty, tummy tuck, the Mona Lisa touch, Brazilian Butt Lifts, Botox, Dermal Fills, CoolSculpting, Fraxel, and every injectable and chemical peel under the sun. Praise science! No one with cash in hand had to remain ugly, The Conduit said she had received many procedures herself, and she flaunted it. Society was curing homeliness if not homelessness. Physical alteration wasn't about sex, she said, but a way to feel real in an increasingly post-body world. The pain hurt so good.

He and The Conduit always convened in the same room. Last session, she wore white Wolford nylons, a high-waisted, multicolored Miu Miu wool-blend miniskirt with grosgrain trim, side-zip closure, patch pockets, and pearl buttons. On top, a Courrèges short-sleeve knit top with embroidered lace trim neckline offered peekaboo views to her augmented freckled bust.

She didn't give him her real name, just her title: *The Conduit*. She looked like the advertisements he'd seen on windows of MedSpas up Sunset Boulevard and assumed she was paid to act severe in her countenance, clearly *acting*, not knowing the Fraternal Secrets, but Peter was acting, too—pretending like he had no qualms with the organization when he probably knew better than to trust the ultra-rich—acting like a schoolboy, so many years too late—still trying to ingratiate himself with the cool kids he claimed to despise, or the hot teachers everyone wanted to suck off, or everyone's rich parents.

Peter and The Conduit sat upon a rattan loveseat and matching armchair across from one another at a beveled McGuire glass table as the sun shone through floor-to-ceiling gold-tinted windows onto a platinum, brown, and tan tropical rug. It felt to Peter like the décor of a country club, or a suite at the Four Seasons Maui—it was perfectly Beverly Hills, from what he'd seen. He felt poor on this side of town, where everything was still styled tacky as at the height of empire even in this New Age of Oligarchs.

A vintage Christian Dior lucite and rattan magazine rack displayed issues of *OK!*, *Time*, *People*, and *The New Yorker*. It reminded him of a magazine bin his mother had kept in their kitchen, where he and his brother once hung onto one another, eating sliced apples with peanut butter and watching *Shaka Zulu* and then later *90210*, studying the world through the Sony screen while Matsushita bought MCA and its prize, Universal. He'd always wanted to be Luke Perry.

He'd hated himself then for not feeling as cool as Dylan, who was sixteen, played by the twenty-four-year-old actor who did things to his ten-year-old body when he stared at those softly chiseled, subtly pouty, eternally smoldering lips. A little stubble, his hair perfectly gelled, an earring in his left ear. After each weekly episode, he would stand outside his parents' door debating going in and confessing to homoerotic urges that created a tug of war between his religious upbringing and the desires that existed deep inside. Was it because he'd experienced the violent, physical passion of his father? So now no love could feel real without a man involved? Lacan and Gore Vidal and Jean Laplanche. His father's violence "invaded" his childhood and created confusion between affection, sexuality, and rage. Everyone wrote about it from Judith Butler to Jessica Benjamin. It wasn't like Dad fucked him, but he certainly fucked him up. Dad was, at times, so easy to throw under the therapeutic bus—to classify as simply another guy who drank too much and lost his temper, going to a fancy job in dress clothes and flying in corporate jets before his wife inherited millions and they moved to Portland, where Dad bought into the liquor industry. But he was more complicated than that—more confusing, and more confounded by his own unique path that had led him from rags to riches—or at least from bandanas and T-shirts to Hickey Freeman blazers, 24K gold-pinned ties, fine wine, cash-thick thin calfskin billfolds, and soft packs of cigarettes stashed in silk-lined pockets—back in the '80s, feeling good, coming from shit and landing in a gold mine he got to oversee for a time, having made something of himself in a way Peter never had. Dad's realm had become the boardroom. Peter's room to grow was The Conduit's office and the rituals of The Church—and his rehab scam. He didn't hate his father, he loved him, which was confusing, and he'd become adept, as so many abused people are, at "reading the room" and could usually gauge exactly how far he could go. It just never felt far enough. You became a psychic slave to the abuser, addicted to the abuse. Or maybe he was just a people-pleaser and wanted to be loved, because his mother ignored him. It made him strong.

Was he afraid of his mother and all women? Was Luke Perry not just *too* hot? The feelings bubbled and danced inside him, tickling his shoulders, rippling through his abdomen and twitching inside his boy cock.

Some evenings, their father fell asleep beside him, on a rattan couch, while he watched Luke Perry. Dad drunk on single malt, comfortable in his heteronormative body, while his son squirmed with desire. He prayed for guidance and deliverance from evil, wanting to be delivered to the Peach Pit, served à la mode, by a hot young waitress in gingham, and he felt hot for her, too. He wanted to be so hot, maybe even popular.

He'd always wanted something, some connection to male coolness, some way to get closer to someone who had the right looks, the right soul, their finger on God's abs. He was just, in truth, into empire, and Peter had begun to have feelings about The Conduit, although *truth* was something she said didn't exist. He imagined her forcing him to do things with Royal-Lee, and then joining in. It felt sort of like when he'd watch *90210*. This really *was* Beverly Hills. Was any of this or the past even real? Especially now that the past was gone and he was aging, older than his father was then?

At Peter's level of things as a low-ranking "pledge," the concept of *reality* was pretty slippery. According to The Conduit and The Church, reality was solipsistic: everyone created everything in his own personal holographic orbit.

"It's *all* projection," The Conduit laughed during their first office meeting. "There is, was, and never could be any history before your singular consciousness came into being. How could there have been, if you're perceiving it all through your totally unique self? Don't you believe you're special? Reality isn't *real* without *you*, is it? There's no 'we' in reality. Just an 'I.' The 'I' at the top of the pyramid. That's a lot of responsibility. There's no room in 'I.' You're all alone at the top, just a dot on a pillar."

Peter nodded, pretending to understand.

"Okay. How do I know this is safe? Could I lose my soul if I join? Is this like *Mulholland Drive*?"

"You won't lose your soul. Your soul belongs to God. You and God are one. No one loses anything, Peter. Religion has fucked with you. You are not beholden to your past programming. Get real. This is Plastictown. Be moldable. The people you're trying to save, they're just the failed versions of yourself, help them quickly and toss them aside. Don't make a fetish out of it. Find your brother. We talked about this."

"So, I need to determine my own etiology? Then free myself from it? Project my destiny from a new identity? But what about my essence? I'm still worried about my soul."

The Conduit laughed. "You're not a bug, Peter. You're *too* brilliant. Like Bugs Bunny. You need to stop asking me for all *your* answers. I am giving you a template, but you ultimately decide. You are the true temple, the ultimate lodge. Anyhow, we are just you in multiple form. Are you trying to play stupid? Say something."

"'The killer' . . ." Peter froze.

"'The killer' what?"

"They want me to help distract everyone from 'the killer.' But I don't know if I want to."

"Who is *they*, Peter? Is it really *you*? What do you not want to distract them from?"

"The Emmys I guess."

"The Emmys? What are you talking about? Are you 'The Pain Killer'? I could see the idealist in you being motivated to use dead addicts to raise awareness. Are you a bleeding heart? Are you trying to make a stand?"

"Don't you know I want to be like Dick Sickler, not fight with him?"

"Is this about your inadequacies? Your blurry creation? You want to be an actor? A director? You ought to start forming the edges of your kingdom. Look at it this way," she faked a smile, "People want their illusions. But they want them to be simple. Do you like Kubrick? Make it simple, stupid. Wake up, Peter. It's a metaphor. A dream. The sooner you embrace the mystery, the sooner we can move on. You're making it up. All of it. You're everyone. You're God. Nothing can stop you."

"Okay," Peter said. "But why? What if I like God as God?"

"*Why*? You're opening a doorway to the most powerful secrets of ruling society, dating back to prerecorded history, carried by ritual and word of mouth, mystical magic, practiced by Jews, many whites, Asians, etc. Too fucking bad. Let's work on your 'reality map' again."

Peter hated this part. He had to explain everything he thought had ever happened. Starting at the beginning of time. *What was there*? He pondered. *The Earth covered in water? Little amoebas turning into fish lizards? Lizards becoming dinosaurs. Then an ice age? Dinosaurs becoming lizards again? Whales had lived on land, walking around on legs. A bear and a seal had the same skull. He had taught—what had he taught? Writing? That wasn't a subject, it was a process of bullshitting. Saussure assured us language was arbitrary outside of syntagmatic relations. We could never produce the essential truth of a natural signifier. It was all manipulation. So make some decisions,* she was urging him, *execute some big moves.*

"Your *Oedipus Complex* shit is too much," she'd exclaimed later, once he'd gotten to modernity (which surprisingly took very little time, as he knew almost no ancient history). "Wait until the other men hear about this: sex with his own *mother*! Over and over and over. Is that what you really want? Old UnclePus works away inside his mother, creampies her, sires his progeny as sister daughters, and the founder of psychology 2,300 years later—on cocaine—licks it up and says *this* is what every man wants? Incest with mommy? You're setting yourself up with that one. This is the world you're writing? You perv."

"Well . . . according to history. And academia."

"History!" she gasped. "School! You're hilarious dipshit." She dabbed the corner of her eye with her pinky. "With all due respect." She held up the palm of a manicured hand. "You believe humans have been around for over a million years and you've badly penned five thousand of those years, with a seven-hundred-year gap between the fall of Western Rome and the establishment of England? Do you know that Eastern Rome fell thirty-nine years before Columbus discovered the Americas? Wooly mammoths roamed the Earth while the Great Pyramids were built? Abraham Lincoln and the samurais were concurrent. The Otto-manEmpire was intact when Disney made his first cartoons. There are Greenland sharks alive today that lived when Henry VIII became king. The T-Rex existed closer in time to us than it did to the stegosaurus. Only 1.5 percent of human history has been recorded, so I get it, but you've written about mostly white people, really only white men. You run a life off this? This world concept is shit. You're a narcissist."

"Jews," Peter interjected.

"What?"

"Not just white people. Many were Jews. And Egyptians."

"Do you realize how much you admit to not knowing? What gives you the right to hold any opinions? No one will believe this."

"No. I don't know. That's why I'm here."

"Exactly! Do you even *know* any Chinese people?"

"Of course I do."

"Name one."

"Mao Zedong."

"Dubious. What if Black people ruled the world? What would be your sense of history then?"

"That would be great. I *love* Black people."

"Right. Then why aren't you one, Peter?"

"Because that's appropriation."

"You're an idiot. How do you know they don't rule the world? What about Khazaria?"

"What about it? What is that?" He furrowed his brow.

"You tell me—you're making this all up. Sixth century, somewhere around modern-day Turkey. You know these red-state neo-Nazis under the Orange Candidate are blue in the face with talk about secret sorcerer Jews, Revelations, fake Jews, fake news, fake everything. Phantom time conspiracy. CERN portals. Time travel. Your fear of us is part of the conspiracy thinking that started the Holocaust. Tell me, Peter, are you antisemitic?"

"Don't be ridiculous. I'm a quarter Jewish."

"You don't *look* Jewish."

"That's antisemitic."

"No it isn't. My husband is Jewish. Shalom, shithead. We're on the same team. You can't be a quarter Jewish, idiot. What do you understand about the current election?"

"It's all about sexism?"

"Peter . . . *please.* Try harder. I hope you're not voting. I think you're confused. You probably should do whatever you need to do to get somewhere in this organization faster. You're a rube. You lack creativity. You have no meaningful place in your own so-called history. Try again."

After attempting to explain himself and his understandings, she gave him a three-ring binder. It held a blank 100-page timeline of world history starting at 1,000,000 BC and she handed him a mechanical pencil.

"Fill this out, please," she directed him calmly. "No gaps this time. Include some diversity. Aliens. Antigravity. Nephilim. Anything."

After he penciled in the timeline, using his phone, she paced and smoked, gazing over his work in the binder.

"Why do you still call it the Dark Ages?" she asked, squinting.

"I didn't *name* it. The Catholic Church ruled and tribes of people lived together without nation states after the fall of Rome . . . so history kind of went dark. Progress ground to a halt. At least for a couple centuries. 500–1,000? I believe Petrarch named it."

"Wrong. There was a volcano. A big one. You think *history* can go *dark*? Just because some people were in turmoil the rest of life took a giant commercial break? The sun didn't shine for five hundred years across the Byzantine Empire, or on the native peoples of what we now call the Americas, or Eastern Rome, or sub-Saharan Africa? You have written here: *Aquinas meets with Pope to get ancient texts back from Muslims.* Peter, do you hear how fucking stupid that actually sounds? You're covering something up. Maybe it's a period you don't want to shed light on because of your religious indoctrination and childhood trauma. Or is it because you understand our teaching: 'With no true history, the future can be anything imagined'? Are you playing hardball? That would be good."

"Me?"

"The world's story is falling apart, and you don't seem to have anything to hold it together with; *think,* you idiot. What is the meaning of this *all*?" Peter wanted to interrupt and say something smarter than what she thought he was capable of saying, but made himself wait. Maybe The Church could help him? Maybe everything was Spinozian and he should abandon all previous morality and select his own reality? He needed a minute to think.

"Haven't you ever noticed everything in your life just works out? Horrible things happen to the good people all around the world while you sit in perfect safety and bliss, able to survive and thrive in spite of impossible odds?"

"Well, I've had a lot of opportunities."

"Peter, if you try that privilege shit with me again, we will end the session right now. You're one of our most principal souls. You're on the top floor. I can't even join the club." She suddenly eyed him suspiciously. "Do you even want to see who's behind the curtain?"

"I'm sorry. Wasn't that wizard in *The Wizard of Oz* a fake?"

"I think you totally misunderstood the movie. Nan Goldin says, 'You are who you pretend to be.' Do you know who she is? She's an enemy of The Church. She's not wrong."

"So why is she an enemy of The Church?"

"We do believe that there are absolutes of power. One has to be a little emotionally fascistic to tap into internal strength. This world isn't run on pity parties and sharing feelings and free fucking ice cream. You have to lift yourself. Do you know the ortolans?"

"No."

She clucked her tongue. "Pity. Delicious. The aristocracy still has them boiled in cauldrons of Armagnac, and then they are eaten whole, bones and all."

"Birds?"

"Yes. The birds, *Hitchcock*. Not the aristocrats. They keep their faces hidden under a cloth while they eat them. The people I mean, not the birds. That would be ridiculous. Do you know why we eat them? It's not only their delectable flavor. It's a symbol. And a French tradition."

"Interesting," he said.

"And they're illegal."

"Okay."

"A killing of innocence . . . Look, some of the elder counselors have taken an interest in you, Mr. Holiday, especially one of our most esteemed members, the pharmaceutical mogul: Master Richard Sickler. *Drugs* are very powerful, Peter. They are one of the essential means of rule and control. Have you ever seen *Eyes Wide Shut?* Let me tell you a secret. The elders approved your application because Dick Sickler wants to conduct studies on addiction. He's glad you let your addicts keep using. He thinks your rehab might be an interesting resource. *You see?* You're doing it . . . manifesting! People are looking to depend on you a little. Did you know the FDA lets drug companies conduct their own research? You can have whatever you imagine and let yourself acquire. And I mean *whatever* . . . Any kink. Any pleasure. Children. A wife even. Or husband. A palace in the hills."

Peter squirmed a bit on the sofa. "I don't have any real kinks."

"That's not what I heard," she gasped, laughing. "I've listened to the recording of your initial call to The Church. *Feminization. Gender shifting.* How do you feel about life and death, Peter?"

"All life and death?"

"Do you believe in an afterlife?"

"Not sure."

"Do you think it's better to be alive or dead?"

"Alive. Definitely."

"Hmmmm. Would you consider testing a new drug? One to keep your patients *alive*? To help advance science and help others, and get paid?"

Peter thought about it. He knew he ought to not say anything and wait to see what kind of deal The Church was offering him, but he was too impatient.

"What kind of deal are you offering?"

The Conduit laughed. "You've been invited to the Sickler's big soiree this year on Election Day. Dick throws a lot of masked balls. He hosts them all the time—to draw forth opportunities better suited to satisfy his tastes. But this one is going to be truly exceptionally over the top. You should feel honored. Let me ask you, what do you know about the Temple of Dendur?"

She sounded scripted all of a sudden, testing him like he'd tested students, trying to find out what their abilities were, and how much they might each let him influence their young minds, before bringing out the planned teaching material. *Lesson plans. Pedagogy. Program-Wide Grading Standards. Term Papers.* Like a student, Peter needed to respond. She stared at him, then parted her lips and blinked once. Twice. Three times. Her eyes were wide, vacant, and staring.

"It was a fake," Peter began. "Erected by Emperor Augustus of Ancient Rome in occupied Egypt."

He'd seen it at the Met plenty of times back in New York. He had read the introduction before the squatty stone structure, while thinking of his brother. Seen it in photos of the Met Gala every year. The Sicklers had donated the temple, paying to have it moved from Egypt to the Upper East Side and housed in a new wing they'd built for it, even constructing a dry moat. The moat said: "We are here, you are there."

"The Temple of Dendur's hieroglyphs portray Emperor Augustus as an Egyptian pharaoh. He's making sacrifices to Egyptian gods, though he was a Roman Emperor," Peter said.

She interrupted him. "To do what? *Why* did Emperor Augustus of Rome have a temple built in an occupied land showing him as an Egyptian Pharaoh wearing an Egyptian war helmet instead of as a Roman Emperor?"

"I don't know. A power move?"

"*To change history.* Why did Sickler move it? *To appropriate the power of a human God.* To transmogrify his soul. Like the obelisks in Rome. The statues upon St. Peter's in the Vatican. Geffen buying Lew Wasserman's house. Do you understand the difference between art and entertainment yet? Do you understand anything?"

Knowing whatever answers he gave would be scorned, he remained silent. He knew from teaching he was in the being-broken-down phase of the process. She would refuse any answers he gave, no matter how good they were, so that he'd be eager to accept her teachings. It was basic brainwashing, the root of all educational practice.

"Art is divinity. Entertainment is religion. Personally, I say moving that temple was genius. Still, the Sicklers need a new strategy. That was a long time ago. They thought they could control the art world and be gods forever. You have to control entertainment. Art is not for the masses. TV is—by which I mean the Internet, by which I mean phones, by which I now mean 'reality,' by which I mean everyone. Life is being eaten by the eye of media, for good or bad, in every area of culture, even in the museums and collector circles. Everything is streamed online now. As such, everyone is watched and policed. Voluntary self-imprisonment. Self-imposed mental slavery. *Brilliant.* The Sicklers should be getting their children into the Senate, their daughter married to the next president's son, or taking over a media company to control the world. Entertainment is religion. Now it is. Maybe always was." She clutched her cigarette purse. "That's what I'd do, anyhow," she said and pulled out a Superking from her pack of 100s.

"Okay."

"You're so stiff, Peter," she said, brightening. "Lighten up." She ignited her long cigarette. "They want you there. You're the only initiate who got invited to the party on Election Day."

"How much is that going to cost?" he said, "Sometimes I feel like this is a scam. I didn't create all this. Trust me, if I was in charge I would make the world better."

"That's what everybody says at first. Maybe it's not all your fault," she said while passing the ashtray to Peter, humoring him. "You *can* manifest a whole new reality. You *can* have anything you believe in. You're just not very good at believing things yet. You've been surrounding yourself with *losers*. So, manifest some winners."

"What about my brother?"

"You tell me. What's *his* offer?"

* * *

Sometimes Peter dreamed of his twin, seeing him return home to the family in repentant attempts to prove himself worthy and recovered. Eating buttered green beans at the family table with the good silver from their mother's side. In other dreams, his brother died of a heroin overdose in one scene, but then came back and Peter had to cement in his dream mind that his brother hadn't actually died, or that he'd come back to life somehow. Right as he'd assimilate his brother's return to life, dissembled the sense his brother had ever died, he'd wake up remembering he hadn't died at all, not as far as he knew, not in real life, not yet. Maybe it was a psychic sign that he *had* died and they hadn't found him yet. Was he dead? It was all very confusing. It was all very . . . sad.

It was easy to love his brother when he wasn't there. To want to call out to him from the balcony: *Peter, Peter, Peter!* The very name he'd stolen. To send his Surlies out searching, and to learn The Church's secrets for manifesting his return. Although, sometimes he felt all the love he had was just a story he told himself, when really, it was better to be without the people you loved, who could only make you sad. Or piss you off. Let you down. The past was a dream. Like in *The Wizard of Oz*. You could never really go home, not by hot air balloon, by bus, by storm, or by witchcraft. Even if you had bright red shoes. It was all really in your heart, and it could break. Actually it was in your head and if you hit it just the right way you could change the channel and see all the colors.

A beautiful songbird sat on the balustrade of the balcony outside his suite at the Villa. Beyond the open French doors, it was puffing itself with air and cleaning its feathers. For a moment, Peter thought it looked unrealistic.

Yellow finches came and chased it away. Had he done that by not believing in it? Summoned the finches with his mind to chase the vision away? He wasn't aware of doing it. He tried to summon them back. He closed his eyes and pressed "rewind," imagined the birds in reverse, flying back to the balustrade, the finches retreating, the songbird preening. But no, a tiny lizard poked its head out of a crack in the stucco and ducked away like a joke.

His musings were interrupted by a knock on the door. It was Royal-Lee, Peter intuited. More and more they could read one another's minds, know what the other was doing and feeling, probably because Peter had willed it. Or Royal-Lee had. Or it was something deeper at work.

"Can I come in? I need to tell you something."

Peter took a short drag off his cigarette and smashed the cherry out into the ashtray.

"Come in." Royal-Lee entered, looking stricken.

"What is it?"

"It's about Dr. Delray."

"What about him?"

"He quit."

* * *

Had I been in the audience for the lecture Peter delivered to the Surlies and house guests just after Royal-Lee delivered that news, I'd know if I'm right about what I believe happened. What I will now have to perform for you in writing, as best as I can imagine it, is based on the events that I am certain unfolded later.

In the construction of the scene, I'd like to imagine Peter playing "Requiem" by Mozart over the loudspeakers of the house for the visitors that afternoon. I see the next victim, Mr. Harkin, forties and ultra-thin, with sad jaundiced eyes buried deep in the gray sockets beneath an ashy bald head—Mr. Harkin, whose corpse was delivered to, then removed from, its brief star turn at the Emmy Awards the next day only to be later found cut up in the Snooty Fox Motor Inn—I see Fred shooting up in the corner to the sound of the brave music—a song Mozart was unwittingly writing for himself. His final reunion with

God, the divine pursuit of human beauty facing the mystery of its own end. When life gets deeper and has a whisper to it. Cigarettes and the acrid blue smoke of speed and opiates lifted as the haze blurred the lights and a rattle of whispers rustled through the crowd.

Peter rocked back and forth on his wooden-heeled slippers and smiled through his beard, clutching the microphone. Clicking the remote, he dimmed the lights and turned down the music.

The house goes dark and falls to a relative hush.

Peter begins. "Welcome, everybody."

The crowd groans and some cheer like maniacs.

"You want to listen to the rest of the music, don't you?"

The crowd grumbles. "Give us drugs."

"How beautiful! Mozart at his finest, beseeching the Lord for salvation. A mad genius trampled under the foot of elite swine. They began using him when he was six years old. They tried to control him all of his adult life. His father tried to make him a slave to the rich."

"Fuck Mozart. He's a bitch," a woman with jeggings and hair the texture of glue yelled. "*He* raped children. Everyone knows it. He came down on a UFO with the ice queen of France and they were fucking Mr. Rogers's head with a knife penis."

"Go ahead and begin handing out the medication, Royal-Lee, and gather up a few of the house members and have them help you. As my guests, make sure the house members don't pocket all the pills for themselves. *No, no!* Make sure they are distributing to you visitors first. You live on streets of trash. You don't live in a beautiful home like this. You deserve comfort. There are no trees where you live. No shade. No Earthly bosom to pluck fruit forth to eat or beautiful game to hunt. You could only hunt each other if you wanted to hunt for meat. Or rats. You only pick through trash. That's how they keep you and use you. The flowers that give you comfort, the poppies are controlled and watered by the hoarders of resources. You're born into slavery in a system that poisons everything, has ruined food, has made Earth the playground for their Satanic destruction, greed, and perversion. So we all delight in the evil of their systems of Babylon, and that's what's killing you. They're killing you in motels for sport. They want to eat you. They want to profit off your bodies and souls while they murder you. As you sleepwalk through their cities on dope. These people are the Sicklers!"

The pills have been handed out. People are smoking them and shooting them. They aren't listening anymore. Peter feels alone.

"They are killing you and will continue to kill you." He needs to get to the subject of his brother.

"You can create a new world. You can rise up against them. You have to wake up. They've taught us to hate one another. They've set the forest on fire." Peter lowers his sunglasses and gives his most open-hearted glare. "I want to speak with you tonight about one of the most corrupt cultural institutions of our times. It's called the Emmy Awards. And it's happening right here, in this city, tomorrow."

"We need more drugs," someone complains. The others agree.

"My dearly beloved," he sighs. "You've seen the future. There are two options: drain the swamp or fight for visibility in a world controlled by billionaires. The secret that no one has told you is that you are free to imagine a new world. There is no going to Mars. The billionaires are lying to you. You have to wake up."

"This guy is dead," someone calls out. "He's dead!" the man shouts at Peter, who freezes for a moment, removing his glasses. Guests and house addicts startle a little, moving groggily. Some begin to stumble out of the house. Others gather around the fallen man's body. Peter catches a glimpse of his brother, he thinks, leaving the living room and he calls out through the microphone.

"Peter! Hey, Peter! Stop." The man is gone. He turns to Royal-Lee. "Did you see that man? That's my brother. That's Peter. Follow him, Royal-Lee; quickly. Get him to come back."

Royal-Lee runs for the door and into the light.

"Out," he calls into the mic. "Everyone needs to leave now. I'll take care of this guy. He's not dead. Everyone go, back to your rooms, back to the street. The lecture is over."

The Surlies and visitors aren't listening. They are talking to each other, indecisive.

"I am serious. Get out!" Peter screams into the microphone, which rings with feedback. "Get out!" People begin to leave. Surlies push the street people out and follow suit. Soon the place is empty, except for Peter and the dead man in the corner, whose skull gleams softly in the smoke-diffused light.

8

In the Villa's Basement . . .

We found my father's dog dead. Dad really was a gangster. He never seemed to find it necessary to search his conscience, even in the face of over half a million deaths from opioids in the United States since he came to serve Dick Sickler. He didn't care—they were all useless drug addicts to him, losers who would have merely found something else to kill them. I hated him for not feeling any remorse. From his perspective, everything he did was for the family. I was the recipient of his protection, his care, the produce of his hard work—but the yield I ate from his trees was fruit born of trauma. I used to have nightmares involving my father killing people, and then disposing of them in our backyard, under the fruit trees, like he did my giant Flemish rabbit after he snapped her thick neck. I saw him do it but he denies it to this day.

During the time of "the killings," I more than once asked myself: Could he have been "the killer?" Dad was the one who tracked me, knew my whereabouts, and had the most to protect. I wondered if he was perpetrating the more gruesome deaths to distract the public from its increasing ire at his client's refusal to claim any responsibility for the opioid crisis. Or to set into motion that which would essentially save him. I could never really trust my father.

Since the discovery of Shirley Iko at the Full Moon Inn, there had been three more motel "killings." Fred Harkin was found first, at the Snooty Fox. After that, two more bodies were discovered—one at the Hollywood Stars Inn, on Sunset and Western, the other at the Hollywood Premiere Motel, between Hollywood Boulevard and Loma Linda. These all looked different, and the papers reported as much:

the killer was getting bolder—or it was the work of someone else. A copycat "Pain Killer." For one thing, there were no pills in these rooms.

Fred Harkin was found in bed at the Snooty Fox, his nipples glued to his eyelids, blood down his chest and stomach like milk from a wet nurse. His blood was smeared across the sheets, like he'd been moved after the operation. The radio was left on in the room. Playing Classical California KUSC at 91.5 FM. The second body was discovered at the Hollywood Stars Inn, lying on the floor in front of the TV, throat slashed, blood pooled beneath the head, but the rest of the room was untouched. The third was at the Hollywood Premiere Motel, face down on the bed, blood soaked into the mattress, no visible wounds except for the absence of a head.

Experts know serial murderers are a lot like drug addicts. The escalation of spectacle demonstrates their growing confidence, desensitization to violence, and desire for deeper psychological or physical stimulation in the act of the kill or in the post-mortem defiling of the body. It mimics our society's lust for more, and growing confidence in letting go of all former mores, embracing the emptiness and incivility of modern life.

I'm pretty sure there were multiple killers that fall. I understand why several killers had to distract from the other. I thought of my dad. I had seen the series that was going to win the Emmys. The population was learning too much about the opioid epidemic in the US. It was bad for business and business was making a killing.

Imagine 500,000 people in one place, the narrator of the series, nominated for the Emmy that fall, says early on, over the coming footage of what is invoked. *Twenty times the number of refugees at the Superdome during Katrina. Eight times the number of US soldiers who died in Vietnam. Fifty times the number of people who died from Chernobyl. Twice the participants in the March on Washington. Most of the prisoners killed at Belzec. Each person stolen from their family and friends by Oxy is a silent murder, committed by systems of bureaucracy, corporate greed, and governmental corruption—at least in part with the Sicklers as accomplices. As a return, their family has netted over eight billion dollars.*

My father slapped me around and terrorized me like a mobster. This had an effect on the canvas of my nervous system, where the colors of my emotions are painted as Rorschach. I suffer from physical ailments related to stress and trauma. I tremble, I have overactive bladder and stress incontinence, tinnitus, and ocular migraines. Maybe everything has made me tougher than a lot of women. Perhaps it got me in touch with my anger, which plenty of females still are told not to embrace, as the world now pretends we are being treated as equals—today we are told that really, it's young men who are being raised to be submissive to the boiling rage of the female uprising and that we are causing the suffering of incels—which is complete nonsense—as Neanderthalic men walk around shooting people with assault rifles, and elite males continue to dominate, control, and manipulate from above, watching YouTube videos about ice baths and how to sculpt their abs, while women have to continue to fashion ourselves as sex rabbits or dogs, painting our faces in ever more complicated ways, augmenting every major aspect of our physiques to appear more like swollen sex organs, and as I work overtime to conceive and fabricate my art to be sold at blue chip galleries capable of enhancing my provenance, while I get treated like a moron on the streets because of how I look.

Ever notice successful women still wearing high heels? Who dress carefully? Ever notice how successful creative men walk around like washed up salty dogs just waking up from a bender, who throw on a crocheted sweater and a misshapen hat with some breezy low-tied pants, a few strands of beads, and look like their dick will slop out of their pants at any moment and their shoes will bounce off and they won't even realize it because they are too brilliant to care what they look like, thinking their Big D thoughts, imagining the great worlds inside them. Hipsters are worse. Fake Versace-print T-shirts tucked into a tracksuit with a trucker hat, ironic wannabe edgelords or like my lame sponsor, really, living off her parents, everyone tending to their social media gardens, pretending they're little demons while going to Ralphs for cat food.

I suppose my anger informs my art. Dad treating me like some dog to be kicked around is what helped me to become the artist I am. His actual dog was killed the morning after the poisoning at the Emmys.

He prized her like the love of his life, sexualizing Fifi, his fluffy teacup white Yorkie, kissing her neck and ears and letting her lick his face like ice cream. Their romance was beyond anything I ever witnessed between him and my mother, thank God. My parents never fucked. I was made in a laboratory. No fornication necessary.

He would hold a cracker in his mouth and feed the little teacup the croccantini from his lips. We found Fifi slit open like a martyr from a Caravaggio painting. Pale sun streaming from the east on her white coat, her little departed form in chiaroscuro. The dramatic realism of the bloody scene was heightened by a stick caught between her tongue and the roof of her mouth, exposing her little white fangs. A horrible spectacle of death, one of many that fall. Who could it have been that murdered her? I still wonder.

It made me afraid "the killer" was coming nearer, wanting to tell me something—I was sure they had a message for my family, or Dick's clan—but not knowing who he was, or what he wanted, made my blood run cold, giving me a chill that hot fall. Or maybe "the killer" worked for Dick—or one of "the killers" did? There was something called *heat rage* that had begun happening that summer before the fall in question; people snapped. They killed each other on the freeways, downtown, and in cars from LA to New York City. Maybe Fifi wasn't murdered. In all likelihood, she was probably attacked by a coyote or a raccoon or a big cat. Finding her made me feel connected to my parents in some terrible way, like we shared a common animal instinct, crouched in fear, waiting for "The Pain Killer's" hand to come close enough to bite, to strike back, unleashing the animal of self-protection that clawed in our hearts. I remember once again my father's warning to me that my mother couldn't protect herself.

Only my heart was left awake to the killer instinct. My mother barely flinched and left me alone with Dad standing in the grass. *Who could have done this? Someone we knew?*

"Who did this? Is it 'The Pain Killer'?"

"What do you know about that? Susie, did you do this? Are you involved? Why was your roommate's hair cut off from her head?"

"Remember, I am an animal lover. A vegan, Dad. I would never hurt a living creature."

"Why don't you get this into your head? It's not my problem. Don't make it my problem. Just shut it, Susie. Bury the dog."

Then he went inside through the slider and left the door open. I wanted to ask questions but he just went in the house. It was like he understood who had sent the message and I was sure someone was watching us, someone who had just moments before slit Fifi with a knife. Was this the same person who killed the unhoused and addicted in motels? I had to bury Fifi myself with a spade the landscaper left leaning against an olive tree. I fantasized about bashing my parents' skulls in with it.

At the Emmys, Fred Harkin's body was served up on a rolling service cart, dressed in stinking clothes, real "streetwear," surrounded by decoratively cut lemons whose ridges held small briny green capers, scattered pleasingly to provide contrast against the jeweled cells of the pale-yellow fruit. In a thickened balsamic reduction was written "SICKLERS" across the only clean item Fred Harkin wore, a white Balmain T-shirt, as he was laid out like food for the Governors Ball Emmys after-party. The balsamic of course looked like blood across his chest. Then he was stolen . . .

I remember the terrible incision of the dog's belly, the tiny parts hanging out like little links in a string of sausages, the torn intestines leaking waste . . . it really could have been another animal that had gotten her, which I interrupted when I opened the slider; perhaps it wasn't the work of a killer at all. Except she was lying dead just under the patio that was shaded by the bump-out of my father's upstairs study, below the exact spot where he had been sitting at the time she would have been killed, Dad taking in the news that had shocked Hollywood and the nation. My hands were trembling and covered in hair and blood as I lifted her, looking her in the face, her eyes blank. I was used to this death look. I felt the wound in her side, from a bite or a blade. How the stick had become jammed between her pink tongue and the roof of her mouth remains a mystery. I wanted Oxy; I wanted my parents to comfort me. But Dad had followed Mom inside, seemingly unfazed—or in shock?—to sit at his desk in the company of his Montblanc Atelier Prive Meisterstück Solitaire pen (a gift from Dick) and a Berluti Venezia Scritto desk blotter and his false respectability, the morning sunlight mantling his shoulders.

Is it because of my father that I understand men who feel they have no other choice but to act like brutes or psychopaths? He was terrifying. Men like my father fight against the force of life in order to be seen, heard, and to make their rise known against the immense gravity of failure they feel pulling them down. I can see it every time my father walks in a room. How he bites and picks at his fingers, and his other obsessive habits, stooped posture, and the way he struggles in his countenance to appear strong when really he's a weakling. The way he lets his mouth hang open just the slightest bit to seem vigorous, as if he's been chasing a gazelle through the Serengeti, when really he's just got high cholesterol from the pasta sauce at Spago and the Bistecca at Toscana.

And as for Peter . . . I would come to see what happened later that fall, and how he handled things as the man of the Villa. I imagine he waited in the basement for Royal-Lee to come downstairs after the speech—to join him so they could talk. Was Fred Harkin dead? Was he down in the basement, hidden away? Or had Fred left, and someone else followed him? I have my thoughts. Either way, I imagine Royal-Lee hearing about the political action against the Emmys being considered for the following night. It was to be his lordship's foray into putting on a real-life "performance."

He'd been told on his first encounter with The Church that they worked at the higher levels of the organization to influence "consensual reality" by staging "plays" enacted out of real-life events. These enactments appeared to happen by chance, but they were purposefully planned to shift public consciousness, he was told, and they were immensely powerful. It was rather irresponsible for The Church to use him for this kind of an assignment, which would otherwise be enacted by members ascending into their final and highest degree of membership.

Maybe it wasn't The Church. Maybe it was Dick. Or maybe it was a rogue member of the Sickler family who put him up to it. Maybe anything, because we can't know, and I know that gets tiring, but you wouldn't want me to lie to you, would you? I can lie to you, but it would break the sacred bond of storytelling. The truth is that Peter later told me he had been assigned to stage this "play" as a less-than-first-degree "pledge," by Dick Sickler's brother-in-law, Ed, in the steam room, at The Church's luxury campus in Bel Air. Was Ed acting as Dick's official emissary or on behalf of The Church, or both? I don't know.

He was eager to take direct action for a good cause in a time when real protest needed a rebirth—now more than ever—something outside of the free speech abattoirs and the federal red tape of anti-terror laws that had brought the protest world of direct political activism in America to its knees, with a bag over its head, heading to Guantanamo. There was so much that needed protesting in America. There was so much, in fact, that people had gone numb, and posting online was about as effective as talking to yourself in the shower. It felt like we were already in the camps. Here was an opportunity for my old teacher to make up for his past failures as an activist. No longer would he be too chicken to break into an animal laboratory or too cool to burn down a ski lodge or too stuck to chain himself to a giant tree. All he had to do was poison some champagne and the revolution would be televised. He was in the basement at the Villa, and likely thinking of a way to drag me into his revolution—a Patty Hearst for the new American millennium—although he knew there was no way to change the world, surely.

If low-level members were to take part in false flag actions, he was once instructed at The Church, it could jeopardize the secrecy of the organization and its operations and do real harm to the reality map of any newer member. It's hard enough to accept the idea that reality may not be real, but then to imagine that the major stories of the world may all be fabricated as episodes of social engineering could quickly lead to major depression and other forms of mental collapse. So why did they ask him to do it? Because he was controlling everything. And was he afraid? Was he excited? His thoughts were interrupted by the familiar sound of youth's descent, creaking down the stairs.

Royal-Lee's small frame was coming down—sporting an oversized pale-blue Celine Paris homme cotton jersey T-shirt over faux-leather wet-look leggings—with bangs in their eyes from a wig, which, Peter had to admit, made them look pretty *banging.*

I do believe Royal-Lee tested the ipecac that night in some bathroom where projectile vomit would have roared against the back of the raised seat and bowl and maybe speckled the wall in reddish browns, like fecal waste. It would make sounds. Maybe it wouldn't feel right, pleasurable like it should. It would come too fast, thick lumps rushing hard through their throat, fluid spurting from their nose. Their intestines feeling like they were coming up through their throat and out their nostrils. They would have to work the movements of their mouth and neck and throat to allow the passage of that much vomit. Perhaps it would be like fucking or sucking or praying. Maybe it would feel like hard won liberation.

9

Back in Brentwood Circle . . .

First Susie was sitting on the black marble toilet in the downstairs half-bath, staring at the faded hand-painted wallpaper—chinoiserie of pink and yellow roses on a bloodred background with spider monkeys poking out of teapots, holding sunbrellas, and fishing, and others pruriently hugging banana leaves with jocular elan; the paper was from the early aughts.

The walls were like a Looney Tunes symphony, full of bending hilarity, swinging mischief, and floating opiate dreamsong. There was a continental gold stripe around the rim of the toilet seat. Her mother's interior designer had always had a sense of humor. Last night's attack at the Emmys had a sense of humor—at first, if you weren't hopped up on ultra-sensitivity—but then it darkened. The politics creeped in and made a worse show of it all. Everyone was upset. Reality bled through the illusion.

Her father would be traveling to Las Vegas after traffic died down to the airport. He'd been invited by Dick on a trip to celebrate the recent inadvertent media victory. Private jet, private car, private chef, private elevator to the Marcus Aurelius suite, blah, blah. In an attempt to recover some self-esteem through bettering herself, Susie had been reading a book about creativity. She was on page two. The book wasn't very creative. What was? She flushed the toilet.

Whoosh.

Maybe *everything* was creative.

Next, she was sitting on the floral cushion of the rattan chair at the kitchen table watching her dad iron her mother's dress, which made her feel like she was a child, again, caught in a dreamworld. Her father had woken her up at 8 a.m. Why? The dog, Fifi, now came running into the kitchen and her father gave it a pat. Was his dog alive? What the fuck had happened earlier—when she had found Fifi with her belly slit, a wound in her side, the stinky sausages of intestines hanging out? What was wrong with Susie? Was she losing her fucking mind? She had just buried that dog.

She'd found him watching the Emmys coverage and reading the papers when she'd gone up to see her father in his office, the sun stippled through the half-open blinds, looking out over the pool. Who had wheeled Fred Harkin's body out on a tablecloth draped over a produce cart, with the Sickler's name written across his chest? Was *that* real? She worried for her sanity but didn't dare ask for a reality check, because the last thing she wanted to do, if she were cracking up, would be to let Dad in on the secret so he could shock her with 450V, and have her locked up at Resnick, or Mission Harbor, or Summit Malibu, or worse.

Lately, Oxy was either too much, all at once, or not enough. She should try heroin; she'd actually thought about it It could help her dig deeper into her artistic daring, summon the forces of some dark mystical shit inside, finally help her let go of her inhibition and mortality. Maybe it would help her relax—drift the way LA is meant to drift, in the early sunshine, slow and easy beneath the palms and the tinted blue sky, now filled with smoke, but the thing about LA was that even when it burned, it didn't burn *that* much. It wasn't like Mendocino, or Oregon, or wherever. Boston burned, San Francisco burned, and Chicago had its great fire. Nothing could burn down LA because nothing could burn up a dream. Dreams just evaporated into the mirages of other dreams. Maybe she could learn something from heroin. She could learn to let go.

She'd been too stoned, or too tired, or too lazy to spend the long time she would need to poop to completion. She'd seen a brochure at that shrink Dr. Delray's office—the *twit* who wanted to be a *twunk* but was a *twaint*—for drugs to treat opioid-induced constipation. The unpooped poop lodged in the chute taunted her butthole. That woman on the brochure had been fifty years old wearing a neon orange bicycle helmet and was cycling down a hill past a wheat field. That's what pooping again would feel like. She should get some of those. She thought of a kid going down a brown water slide as another possible brochure image option. She knew McKinsey & Company was behind all the worst pharmaceutical campaigns, including Oxy.

Her father had hollered at her from the kitchen, the giant sweaty brute, now bent over the ironing board in his undershirt and boxers, gold Star of David nesting in his damp chest hair which, to Susie, looked especially pubic this morning. Her head was still in the toilet. She'd thought Fifi was dead. She'd thought Dad was in shock. The bathroom had smelled of oil diffusers: gardenias or lavender or lilac. Lily of the valley? He was always sabotaging her. She couldn't even take a fucking shit. She picked up the Diptyque Figuier room spray and slipped it from its box, which still had the price tag: *Eighty bucks.* Susie read the box.

> *The woody scent of fig trees stretching endlessly across a Mediterranean landscape . . . the sun at its peak . . .*

"Are you conscious? Are you even alive in there?" her father had pounded. She'd stood and peered down at the toilet bowl imagining ribbon-flat poops like serpents in a pale lagoon, a nest of snakes in a porcelain swamp. And the darker pellets at the bottom like black Flemish bunny rabbit shits. The ones on top would have been lighter tan and squished like pappardelle at Osteria Mozza, coiled together and alive, writhing like a hydra. The top poop pastas leaking brown oils into the water, and for some reason (she could probably do a hundred sessions with a psychoanalyst about this and never get to the bottom of it) she thought of Faia and imagined her in the world of the clear upper strata of the water, swimming in a sparkling pool and emerging, wrapped in a fluffy white towel, climbing up the cement steps and out onto a perfect green lawn. As she picked an orange, a dense glowing sphere, a killer stabbed through the orange into Faia's hand, blood coating the skin, mixing with the thin juice, as he pulled the blade out and slashed her across the face. Blood splattered the orange leaves. Then the vision was gone, and the cinematic quality of the scene made Susie feel happy and uncomfortable all at once.

It showed how deeply ingrained violence against women was in her own mind. Psychopathic killers were media fun, especially when their victims were female, although she didn't want to get preachy. She was upset with Faia still. Susie would later come to memorize that 70 percent of violent acts against women went unpunished. She'd learn women made up 75 percent of serial killers' victims, and 85 percent of murderers were male. The scene dissipated as she flushed clear water into the bowl.

Why did Faia still bother her so much? Was she in love with Faia? Was Faia the only person who had ever really loved Susie? Was Susie still trying to think of some way to get her attention? The Emmys must have gotten her attention and certainly had captured her dad's mind that morning but what had happened with Fifi? Had it been the neighbor's dog? Did her dad now have two dogs?

"I'm fine," she'd called through the door back to her father. Then washed her hands with Woods of Windsor soap, scrubbing hard for no reason—no shit or pee, no wipe—feeling her insides still twisted. There was nothing worth much in this world, and she suddenly felt it, a new level of darkness reaching her that reflected in her eyes in the mirror, alluring in a perverse way. Shit. She still had blood under her fingernails. She tried to think of something she liked, to bring some light back into them. Flowers, she thought. It didn't work. The stereo was playing a song from the '80s. "Cruel Summer." Not as good as "Pictures of You." The '80s felt so perverse, so violent and excessive and greedy, and she liked it. The design was spectacular, the return of art deco, mixed with futurism. It was so sexy, so masculine, the rockers with their long hair, bangs in their eyes, top hats, cigarettes dangling from pursed lips, wearing silver skulls and crosses and black makeup and dripping in leather and sleeping on waterbeds. Annie Lennox and Grace Jones, the bold shoulder pads on coifed men and women with slicked back hair, confused silhouettes that went either way, and real gender experimentation mixed with bold new design. Hope and capitalism as one. The Bennington baddies. The Sheen/Esteves empire and River Jude and Joaquin Rafael Phoenix and Corey Feldman and Miramax and the Menendez brothers, who ended the decade and their parents' lives in a Beverly Hills mansion worth fifteen million that nobody wants to buy on Elm Drive off Lomitas about ten blocks from the Beverly Hills Hotel, where Susie's own story could have once easily ended in the flick of a wrist.

It was Joni Mitchell, actually, on the family-room stereo. Susie had misheard or time had sped forward. She was singing about cumulus clouds, or was it *The Creation of Adam* on the Sistine Chapel? Adam's cock looked like a used bandage—wet and sticky—but still, he had been pushing the limits, Michelangelo, painting God in a pink slip dress. Everything ornate was hilarious, yet there was a pure earnestness in her singing about sunshine and gold in that voice, aching with a bygone dream of California loveliness. What was he playing? Stupid sentimentalist fascist. She suddenly wanted to die. Time ached inside her bones, and she thought of the Emmys again. Fred Harkin had been wheeled out on the cart while everyone's focus had been on the celebrities who were throwing up, made sick by the tainted champagne. It had all looked like a gag, a prank—except it wasn't. The press photographed the moment, leaving the question of whether they were witnessing art or activism to posterity. That Fred had died of an overdose would be discovered later.

In the bathroom mirror it could have been a shorter, much-less-perfect Kate Moss for CK, Claudia Schiffer for Guess, or Christy Turlington for Maybelline. Girls spiritually dead from the exhaustion of partying and playing beautiful. Susie was spiritually dead, too. Who could survive in a time when every woman was supposed to be twerking in everyone's face, and recording it on Instagram or YouTube, while being a feminist girl-boss and making a billion dollars off showing her tits? Honestly, most women today on advertisements, in magazines, on the street, looked more imprisoned by implausible beauty standards and sexist expectations than ever before, more oppressed by the systems of capitalism that made them into designer objects. It pissed Susie off. Women now were expected to fulfill all sides of impossible dualities more than ever—leaning into the erotic inhumanity of the uncanny valley, face first, ending up doggy style. The hope was we were supposed to be offered more respect, more opportunity, more power. We could do *anything.* No one was giving Susie a break or a step up. Her father was a knucklehead. Her mother was probably sleeping with the enemy.

Today was Monday. Weekdays were a real thing now that she was living back at home, regulated by her father's work schedule. In college, any day could have been a weekend, be it crisp and sunny in autumn, with the leaves changing on the maples and ash, or snowing in the West Village around Thanksgiving or Christmas.

Back then Susie was getting drunk and high. She so admired old New Yorkers but she didn't really ever feel like she could become one. Either you were a smartly dressed person with the East Coast in your bloodline, flowing seamlessly down the street, behaving as a collective member of the city, or you were something feral that could not be calmed, and couldn't be fed, and wanted blood. Her Oxy habit had many times multiplied since then. She was feeling more feral. She saw him that winter of her first year—a dead man hunched over a heap of black trash bags, blood and vomit pooled beneath his cheek like a ruined halo—two fingers, bitten off, stuck in the sick shine of it. Who had bitten them off? Maybe it hadn't really happened. Maybe she'd dreamed him near Gramercy Park that night, high on her pills, buzzing on her new way of life—drugged and dazzled, thinking about what it would feel like to hold a key to those locked gardens. What else could success look like? To fit a key in a private gate. But then she saw him—this man, this heap of death—and the dream went sour in her mouth.

Her father was talking to her.

"I want you to start thinking seriously about going back to school. UCLA. I don't care. USC. Pepperdine. Spring semester. Money is no issue, lucky for you. But you're going to study something useful this time. Something practical and profitable. Nothing creative. Creativity just means it's for losers! In college, anything that has the word 'creative' in the name, just stay away from it. It's for rich-kid fuckups. You can be creative once you're successful and grown. Until then, creativity is for the mentally ill! Why be Jasper Johns when you can be Ovitz marveling at *White Flag* from your stairwell while it increases in value and you go up and down the levels of your house? Are you listening? I love you."

"Yes."

"Stop looking at your phone while I talk to you. I didn't raise a loser. You're not too old to get a spanking."

Susie woke out of a half-nod, her phone in her lap and head down. She opened her eyes. Birds were chirping outside. She heard them over the hum of the AC, singing the prettiest songs. Birds in the flowering dogwood, in the tea roses, in the pachysandras and plum tree. She listened: the birds were singing a song she knew from somewhere. She knew this one. It was The Zombies' "She's Not There."

"Do you hear that?"

"Oh, good, you're listening," her father said.

"Also, do you feel that? The tide that runs from your forehead down to your toes and up your back?" She slowed her voice as she said it. This was time-release Oxy. It must have kicked in again. "Like, *whoosh*," she whispered. A boa up the sequined back of a showgirl. Bob Dylan was playing.

"Honey, do you even *hear* yourself? You sound like an *idiot*. You sound like a stupid voodoo hippy selling incense to fools smoking marijuana on Venice Beach. Do you hear me?"

Bob Dylan was playing "Idiot Wind" through the tube stereo. How had she heard another melody in the birdsong? The organ and guitar had a haunting stillness, a slow, uneasy pulse that felt like weather rolling in. The sun shone outside, and the song rasped through two Altec speakers her father had salvaged from a movie theater that went under decades ago—huge wooden boxes built on Christmas Eve, 1942, in the height of the war effort. Their tone was crystalline and sharp, like the edge of memory, and Dylan's mouth, tight and underbitten, spat a jeremiad of spit and grief across a ghostly microphone in a room echoing lonely anger and intelligence—an understanding of misunderstanding itself—filled with grief that pleaded to be drugged into peace of mind.

The wind whooshed across the world's unrelenting stupidity. The same horrors that haunted that Christmas Eve—the assembly lines of death and industry—had only evolved. The trickery of man remained: violently hopeful, stupidly ingenious, callously smashing in the skulls of the old and the newborn, greedy for obscene wealth. The tide had not turned; it had merely pulled back and come again, multiplied in force since the day those speakers were glued together by chapped working hands. Susie's mind was getting out from under her again. *Whoosh.* Sweet lady, she thought.

"What's that smell?" Susie wrinkled her nose.

"Goddamnit!"

Her father had burnt the buttery fabric of her mother's Diane Von Furstenberg diamond stripe silk dress. Why was he always ironing? Had he heard of a steamer? Where was the housekeeper? Had *she* died?

Susie wanted to be rich.

He turned off the iron, shoved the burnt garment in the trash compactor and poured a cup of steaming coffee. While she studied the cheesy outdated bunched window valance, like she had a million times, her father sat down beside her and smacked his lips. He studied her arms, like you would a junkie's.

"Forget college. You're not ready."

"Dad, can you stop talking to me so much?"

He exhaled heavily through his nose and sifted again through his stack of daily newspapers on the kitchen table, looking for something more to say, knowing he wanted to talk to her about drugs. It was obvious. *Or was she paranoid?* There was a tension between them like razor wire barbed with little plushy heart emojis; he wanted to connect. What did she do all day, he wondered? He didn't really want to know. He wanted it not to be true. He held up the *Financial Times.*

"Do you know why this is printed on orange paper? Orange is the color of champions! I went to University of Virginia Law, you know, top three; it used to be the color of champs, anyhow. Now *this* paper," he picked up the *L.A. Times*, "is for star-fucking idiots! What did I tell you? Look at this story! You think this is *real* news? The celebrities regurgitating at the Emmys after-party?"

"Regurgitating? Who says that?"

"It's all over the internet. Photos of Peter Dinklage puking on the skirt of Halle Berry's dress. Will Ferrell puking on Padma Lakshmi. How crazy can things get? Don't tell me you haven't seen these!"

Of course she had. Did he really think she was an idiot? The entire cast of a Black comedy show was in a photograph in the paper, all vomiting: Tracee Ellis Ross, Anthony Anderson, Yara Shahidi, and Marsai Martin.

"Listen to this," he began reading aloud, Dadsplaining the news. "Forensic testing of champagne bottles served at this year's Emmys after-party, The Governors Ball, have come back positive for ipecac and Oxycodone after testing at LAPD labs and the FBI at Quantico.

"Investigations into the case began after press captured images and posted them to social media. Victims include: Maggie Smith, Jon Hamm, Jeffrey Tambor, Julia Louis-Dreyfus, Aziz Ansari, RuPaul, Tina Fey, the Kardashians, Amy Poehler, Rami Malek, and nearly a hundred other stars.

"Several guests became incapacitated and some sought medical care for Oxycontin poisoning. This resulted in attendees waiting for their vehicles for hours as they attempted to leave the awards show after-party amidst arriving first responders.

"Newly embroiled Hollywood A-list executive, Rupert Wasserfield, accused yesterday of sexual assault by over a dozen female actors in an open letter published at the *New York Times*, was transferred from Cedars-Sinai to a private medical facility in Bel Air. He was the only celebrity to be hospitalized overnight. At the time of this story's publication, neither he nor his agency has responded for comment.

"The FBI has issued this statement: 'We are taking this act of domestic terrorism very seriously and looking into the possibility of this being a hate crime.'"

Her father looked over the top of the newspaper.

"I hate Faia Sickler and all of them," Susie murmured.

"I'll never forget how she's hurt you. Faia Sickler is a spoiled brat. Whether it's 9/11 or puking at the Emmys, someone with money is always out to make more."

Susie was almost asleep.

"Bunch of fucking Nazis. It's free advertising. It's smart."

"Not Nazis, Dad."

"All these drugs started out in German labs a hundred years ago. The Nazis invented speed and heroin; look it up. IG Farben. Operation Paperclip. Operation Bluebird. Operation Artichoke. MK Ultra. It has nothing to do with us Jews. The Germans invented the pharmaceutical industry."

"Dad."

"He is not a saint, Dick. I'll tell you that much."

"So why do you still work for him?"

"For the money! I wish I could get out of this industry. If I could I would. You don't understand."

"People have been using opium for thousands of years."

"Oh, so that's it, huh? You do care about something?"

"So what if I care? It's medicine. It makes people feel better. I'm defending you."

"You think I'm that naïve? So that is it, isn't it? You're on their shit, aren't you? Do you really think I'm that fucking stupid? You didn't think I'd know?"

"You don't even know what you're talking about."

"No, I do know. I've been watching that show *Intervention*. I'm not an idiot."

Susie put her hands on the table and tested to see if she could stand up. She could.

"Welp, I'm out of here."

"Where do you think you're going? You know what? Fuck college. You're going to *rehab* this fall. I'm going to get those morons at Passages to blood test you. Don't say you're drunk, I know what drunk looks like and you're not it. You're stoned on Oxy."

She took a pitcher of OJ and flung the juice at him. As she walked away, her father knocked his chair backwards leaping to grab her arm.

"I know now. The jig is up. You're going to rehab. Game over." The juice dripped down his face like egg yolk.

He held her arm in his fist and it hurt her. Susie could smell her father's cologne through the juice, as she tried to ride the smell back into her high, snuggling with the memory of the smell of yachts and sunshine and the scent of the sea, but it was all gone, and he was just yelling at her. This was how Natalie Wood died. And Nicole Simpson. She should kill him first.

"Or you can forget about your inheritance!"

There was a sound upstairs—heels clicking across the floor.

"Come down then, Mom! For once! Bitch!" Susie shouted, nearly exhausting herself, fake crying. She tried to break free of her father's grip but he took her by both shoulders. "Let go," she whined. He shook her.

"Your mother thinks I give you a hard time," he yelled toward the box beams of the coffered ceiling. "Meanwhile, you're on hard drugs. I've got you now and you're going to do exactly what I say."

She felt too high again, and the birdsongs came back, or was it just her father's heavy nostril breathing?

"Let me go. I had some Chardonnay. That's it."

"It's 10 a.m.! We don't have Chardonnay in the house since your mother quit drinking, you fucking dork. When I get back from Vegas, we are going to have a serious talk," he said. "Until then, I'm locking you in the bunker." He gripped her shoulders tighter. "You can eat canned soup and drink water and use the gym. I'll be back to let you out on Thursday morning. Watch TV. Work out."

"No!"

"If you aren't on anything, what's two fucking days in the bunker? It's not like you have a job! It's not like you work! If there's a time for me to be wrong, let it be now. Susie! Prove to me that you're not on their junk."

"Fuck you, Dad. It's your junk. And I'm not on it!"

"You *are* on junk!"

"No! I'm not. No one says junk. You fucking idiot."

She tried to break free, but he had his hands on her, and he was not letting go. He released one hand to slap her hard across the mouth, then grabbed her with both hands again.

"Fuck you, Dad."

He slapped her again. Her ears rang. It felt like victory.

10

Susie's House, Underground . . .

The bunker was a prison for one. It looked like the love child of *Better Homes and Gardens* and *Ballistic* magazine. Like Martha Stewart holding an AK-47. It was no joke. Her father had it built out of radiation-proof concrete—whatever that was—after the city passed its "anti-mansionization" ordinance in 2009. Legislature limited the square feet you could add to your house, relative to lot size, but basements didn't count, so building the subpar bunker at the time made perfect sense.

It had a dining room, kitchen, two bedrooms, office, gym, media room, plus various supply pantries filled with everything from gluten-free matzo to submachine guns. A room to monitor air, water, radiation, satellite news, and communication. He had been well ahead of the silo curve but had fallen behind—it didn't even have a well.

His idiot boy-box failed to include newer bunker essentials like a hydroponic garden, decontamination chamber, and garage filled with bug-out vehicles to withstand EMP attacks. This was before companies like Vivos or Oppidum made museum-quality bunkers for the ultra-rich, island fortresses with cutting-edge tactical systems, Mars-inspired space-aesthetic underground layers designed by Al Corbi, on par with NSA headquarters, employing biometric recognition software, steel-reinforced caissons, ballistic-proof panic suites, and Naisome gas billows to disable intruders.

It was for the race war. The American holocaust. The rise of the white nationalists. A civil war that would erupt, baldheaded brigands murdering and burning down the entire West Side. As a Jew, Susie's father saw everyone as a possible threat. The city burned twenty-four years ago, during the Rodney King riots, before she was born. Then riots erupted again in 2000. Of course, there were also the brushfires. The earthquakes. The threat of nuclear war. Plagues. Cannibals eating the rich. The Illuminati. What a joke. In fifteen years, global warming would cause extreme climate destruction, intense heat waves, storms, rising sea levels, accelerate biodiversity loss, strain food and water resources, and deepen economic and social inequities around the world. Hundreds of millions were going to die while right now everyone navel-gazed at their precious identities, bleating like distracted sheep, completely immobilized, blaming each other, or some shadow-world government, or even worse, *the Jews.* The oligarchs were preparing for the day they would be hunted by the hungry masses. *Bunkers.* It was bonkers.

Maybe the bunker *would* come in handy. Especially if the election went the wrong way—whichever way that might be—which was the great obsession of her father's miniscule mind: what outcome could be worse. Which ruler would end the show. The show wouldn't end. It would just be fascism back in fashion. Right now, the bunker was Susie's prison.

Dad liked acting like he was Floyd Abrams, but he was on the wrong side of the needle. Having notorious clients, like the Sicklers, meant power as an attorney—just look at the Kardashians. O.J. cut off his ex-wife's head and Bobby's kid got famous off her sex tape. Now she's a billionaire. Still tacky though. Neighbors looked at Dad when he walked into Amandine Patisserie Café in a python Gucci by Tom Ford tracksuit and neon-yellow Balenciaga Bouncers. Over two hundred pounds in a town of waifish joggers and millennial dweebs, people whispered when he tactically entered La Scala, Juice Crafters, or Chaumont for an egg bun. Living his survivalist fantasy, bitching about both the Orange Candidate and the cost of bullets under Obama, sometimes he carried, but secretly, of course.

"Call Dad," she told her phone. *Straight to voicemail.* "Dad, this isn't funny, I'm not a drug addict. Come back and let me out of here. This is inhumane."

In order to get in or out of the bunker, one needed a code, a series of seventeen digits—her father's social security number and mother's full birthdate—which at this point in her drug career, she absolutely could not recall.

Next voicemail: "Dad, text me the code. Or else I'm calling 911 and reporting you for child abuse, and kidnapping . . . I'm an adult! Let me out you fuck-suck dick-jerk. Don't you believe in the fourth amendment? The American Bar Association sure as hell does. I have their number right here. I'm calling them."

Following voicemail: "(Fake crying) Dad, I can't believe you don't love me more than this. I'm your only child and your only friend. I thought I could count on you. I am so sad now. (Sob. Sob. Sniffle. Sniffle.) Okay, bye."

She rifled through the drawers, looking for a pill. Her mother must have one somewhere. Everyone had pills for when the going got tough. Things were pretty tough. She found a travel-sized bottle of mouthwash, chugged it, riding the minty buzz, but it was bullshit. It made perfect sense why she'd failed as an artist. She found a glock in the back of the drawer. He didn't need all of these guns. Or did he? He was probably being cucked by his wife and boss. He still thought he was Tony Soprano ordering extra meatballs.

He had no class or creative intelligence. She hated both of her parents. He had tricked her in such a basic way. At the end of the fight about the Emmys, he grabbed her phone. Susie chased him down the stairs. She was afraid he'd see her texts to Royal-Lee. He threw the phone on the carpeted landing and she went for it, like a dummy.

He slammed the door. It was such a witless trick. He was such a *fucking moron*. He had none of her creative talents. She should call the police. She hated the police. She hated everyone. She loved humanity, she just hated most of what it did and all its individual people.

"Hi, Asshole. I will fucking end you. Mom is going to hear about this and I think she's having an affair. Because you're fat! Right here in your own house. I'm here every day watching her fuck Richard Sickler like he's the pool boy."

Whose dog was it she had found in the yard? A white van had driven by when she'd found the white dog. How was she going to survive without pills in this preppy-prison designed by her dumb daddy?

She flipped on the TV. It was a shock to see mainstream news. So fake, so preposterously basic. Fred Harkin's body had just been autopsied. His eyelids severed. His nipples had in fact been removed with the pair of steel scissors found on the bedside table. The nipples had been superglued over his eyes. The eyelids placed over his missing nipples. What did this have to do with his appearance and disappearance at the Emmys? The news was asking this question over and over.

According to the Snooty Fox Motor Inn's records, the room, rented by Fred, was paid in cash. The networks didn't show the room, its mirrored ceiling, the blood, or the body. A female newscaster said LAPD was reviewing security footage for the motel, but so far, no further details were being released. When asked if it was the work of "The Pain Killer," police said, "No comment." Although the room had only been rented that morning, Fred Harkin's time of death was being placed days before. There was the usual news footage: police tape, cop cars, appropriate distancing between footage captured by the news and the "work" of the police. It looked like a television procedural. She watched the national, then the local, then turned it off.

Who was killing people? What was this world? Did life matter to anyone? Hers or someone else's? Her father had ruined hers. Did he even know that? Did he care?

Maybe he read the *Financial Times* because it was so completely devoid of any proof that there was beauty, or such things as subtlety, or shades of gray. He lived in a black and white universe, an old photocopy, completely blind to his daughter who had—miraculously—developed into a human with actual depth. What did he know about art and creativity?

He could dismiss her as a loser, but that's because he didn't know who Linda Nochlin or Cindy Sherman, Diane Arbus or Nan Goldin were. Or how hard it was to become a thriving, self-sustaining artist. He couldn't even recall the difference between Charles Ray and Ray Charles. Couldn't pick out the difference between chiaroscuro or impasto, a Van Gogh or a Vermeer, a shape or a plane—identify chartreuse from cerulean. He was an idiot, a dolt, a buffoon. He was the biggest loser. He was her problem, not drugs. *What was her problem?* She didn't have a problem.

She was just taking a year or two off from NYU, trying to relax, and he'd trapped her in a sub-basement for it? Like she was an extension of his kingdom? If she *were* on drugs . . . she really *was* . . . how could he know she wouldn't die from unmedically-supervised detox? At least this was all a good setup for her origin story as artist. She absentmindedly moisturized her face with iCare Private Label cream before the mirror and then realized it contained snail peptides. She wiped her face. *Vegan.*

She thought of Fred and "the killings" and how it was all connected to her, the opioid overdoses, the dead NYU roommate, her old classmate Asher, the Emmys, the documentary, her dad and the cults of Los Angeles he had warned her about so long ago, when he was teaching her to protect his kingdom while he was off at work, sucking Dick, and helping him peddle opium to the masses.

She thought of how many motels there were in Los Angeles. She would learn the names of so many in the weeks to come. The Alvarado Palms Motel. The Hollywood Stars Inn. The Roxy. The Banana Bungalow. The Welcome Inn. The Randolph. The Lincoln. The Ramona. The Oak Tree, The Paradise Motel, The Tropicana Inn. Jay. The Notel Motel. Her father's favorite author once wrote: "There is a motel in the heart of every man." In the heart of these motels was the desperation of humankind being exhibited in "the killings." Maybe behind every shooter, serial killer, and terrorist was simply this crying out of angst against dehumanizing systems and technology. Look, this is what we made of life. This is what we did to everyone. The news showed the outside of the Snooty Fox Motor Inn. Who had done this to Fred Harkin? Who had done this to the world?

11

Royal-Lee Takes Over at the Villa . . .

By the time Royal-Lee tried talking to Peter's brother—PETER KROLIK—the man was standing on stage, shirtless and sweaty, a trickle sluicing down the V of his strong lower abdominals. He was impressively thin and Royal-Lee surveyed his physique, more intensely after he climbed up on the stage and dropped his sweatpants, freed the strap from his gunnysack, and went searching for usable veins in his lower extremities. Royal-Lee stared at his gray briefs. Their stretched-out waistband caused them to slip down, flashing glossy black pubic hair.

This casual encounter would happen later on that day.

First, Royal-Lee had to host group therapy.

He had to let the addicted plebes know they were out of Oxy and were going to have to stay sober until pills arrived that afternoon. He had to enact group therapy in place of the boss in order to distract the residents from their collective withdrawals. Meanwhile, upstairs, in fine sheets and silk pajamas, the leader of the Villa rested like a fat cat in the sun.

"Hey," Royal-Lee managed. No one listened to him. "You all know me." The eyes of the house members scanned the room and fell on their face.

"So, as you know, I'm Royal-Lee. Normally I don't run group therapy, but . . ."

"What do you think you're doing?" It was Tom, green-eyed, half Puerto Rican, half Black, with tattoos up his neck. One read *Marthar* in cursive, a tribute to Martha, who had OD'd while he was with her. The tail of the *a* had accidentally been inked too high, making it an unintended lower-case *r*. It was a mistake but looked tougher that way, anyhow. He had a crown on his chin. Tears on one cheek. A dagger on the other. Despite the blue and black ink, Tom's face was as expressionless as Royal-Lee wanted to be; he had a sophisticated style and a pacifistic demeanor. He might not be rich or intellectual but he was confident, chill even without drugs, casting a slow eye that captured everything in the periphery.

"We know all about your bitch ass," Gloria scoffed. Gloria was an apple-faced woman with crazy eyes that beamed through crooked glasses.

"Go ahead and get fucked up bitch. If you don't give us some Oxy, we will destroy you. We will eat your ass." This was Clay.

Royal-Lee twitched. They were pretty sure Clay didn't mean it the way it sounded.

"Give us our shit." He was about twice their age, with spiky hair and nipple rings, and a red square cover-up on his bicep. Royal-Lee could guess what was under the tattoo. Clay came from Yucaipa and had another tattoo that said W.A.R., which stood for White Aryan Resistance. There were lots of Nazis out east in the desert towns. Peckerwoods, house members called racist whites. They said these peckerwoods would come to LA to fight in a second if commanded by the rising Orange Dick.

Royal-Lee understood why the Surlies weren't happy. Still, shouldn't every addict want to get clean for a moment or two before going back to dope? Like smokers quitting for a day before going back to the corner store for another pack? Even when Peter was in the group-therapy circle, there was resistance and rivalry. Fights broke out with each addict trying to outdo others by comparing privilege—race, gender, sexual victimization, immigration, sexual identity, military experience, trauma, class, ability—nearly all of which Royal-Lee could hold their own in comparison to the rest, but they never said so because therapy could be so ruthless.

The circle would rise in support of one opponent over another. It felt like a bad reality TV show reunion, except there was no reason to care about any of them. None of the characters had done anything worth a shit all season—they *were* entertaining to watch, sometimes, especially when one really opened up, and there was so much pain that it was unimaginable to think they could get better, and that made it real because the stakes were so high, and Royal-Lee cared—and *wanted to listen*, as they said today, *and to learn*, and it was almost true. No one spoke up.

"Guys, I've been fucked with, too," Royal-Lee leaned in.

"*Fuck you.* We want dope," someone grumbled. "We did the Emmys."

"Okay. Right. Okay, okay." Royal-Lee had to get through to them. "I've been hurt and manipulated, just like you. I've been abused sexually, physically, emotionally, and spiritually. Maybe there's no point in comparing stories, like we always do, because does it really matter how low your bottom is when you were programmed to fail? If you come from the streets or land here all on your own, it's all the same. We're trying to find what made us lose our way. What made us losers. To find the path that can lead our lives back towards success. We can still win."

"You're definitely a bottom, you bitch-ass trick."

"When I was a kid and things happened to me . . . I wasn't allowed to complain or talk about it. Look, I was raped . . . Then I had to go home and be told I was selfish and greedy to not be satisfied with the pittance of love my mother bestowed. I didn't know how to respect myself. I couldn't tell her. I've never told anyone. Not until now." Royal-Lee shook their head at the profundity. They were finally telling the truth and it terrified them. It felt Christian. It felt real. This was getting therapy. This was shining a new light. Everyone could sense the problems in the world, the systems Peter knew how to explain that made everyone feel like they couldn't take it anymore, but Royal-Lee was bringing the solution, bridging the pain with the bright light of the human heart and soul, that almost desperately delicate twinkling of hope and love—they stepped boldly into healing by showing these hurt people they could get better.

"We will rape you," Clay said.

"I want to hear your stories." Royal-Lee asked, "Who wants to go next?"

"Where is Peter?" Melissa with impetigo snapped, shivering. "Goddammit." She looked like an overgrown child with a flesh-eating rash;

her lower lip stuck out and her upper lip collapsed from having no teeth—a tiny skin wave crashing at the bottom of a jagged cliff. Her pale blue eyes were red with burst veins in the whites from meth. She could be in turns quiet and brooding or angry and nasty. Melissa's eyelids were granulated and her gray face covered in welts where she dug into herself with a razor blade.

"Where are our meds? Do I look like I'm fucking well?" she threw up a little diaphanous foam on stage, which probably amounted to spit she'd been saving in her mouth. "I'm going to call the police. I'm gonna turn us all in and kill myself. I have a gun. I have a fucking Glock 9. No stamp!"

"Melissa," Royal-Lee said slowly, as if poise could spread; they could be fairly certain she didn't have a gun. But she might. "He said you can't use this morning, so . . ."

"Fuck you," Melissa said. "We will *hurt* you."

There was talk about where to get Oxy and heroin.

"If you all just participate . . ."

"Alright, I'll go," Brenda said, scraping her chair across the floor.

"Thank you, Brenda," some patients muttered.

"I got taken into the Villa off Skid Row at seventeen." Brenda was the youngest junkie in the house. It was a classic runaway story. Abused by her stepfather, kicked out of her boyfriend's house, found the streets, got sex trafficked by a pimp who broke her jaw. Ended up living with another woman named Kym in a tent on Gladys Street, working with her, trading off tricks in a pay-by-the-hour motel room, while the other shot up in the alley. Kym was in the circle, too, nodding. Her partner in what probably shouldn't be a crime, not on their side, anyhow, especially at seventeen. These women had it way worse than Royal-Lee. Every single time group therapy was successfully enacted they were reminded how bad these people had been off. She'd been off Skid Row for four months now.

Royal-Lee looked around the circle. It was a horrible mess of victimization.

"And what happened to set you off your course, Brenda?"

"In ninth grade, I had this older boyfriend who introduced me to dope, and I fell for it. You know, it was like, so much better high than going back to my mom's house, where her boyfriend hated me and made me eat shit every night for not making straight A's. Not real shit, not actually eat shit. I mean, my mom just let him rail, like she was ashamed of me. He drank and he fucked with me. Cuz she was so desperate, I guess, for a guy with a decent job and an old Camaro. But everything was okay when I was high, because none of it mattered; I could laugh about it. But then some really fucked up shit happened. That's it."

"Thanks, Brenda," Royal-Lee said.

"Thanks, Brenda," everyone said.

"Can I ask you a question?" Royal-Lee asked.

"Not what fucked up shit happened. I don't wanna go there."

"No. Did you have any brothers or sisters growing up?"

"I had a half-sister. I don't know where she is. Why?"

"Well, if you had one wish for your sister, what would it be?"

"I don't know, that she has enough money. That she doesn't have to sell her ass like I did."

"You're not selling your ass anymore, are you?"

"Not since I moved in here. Nope. Hopefully never again . . . unless there's no dope today. And I mean soon."

"Would you want to fall in love one day?"

"Who are *you* to ask *me* that? Not with you. If that's what you mean."

The circle oohed.

"I need a real man, like Peter." She stared at Royal. "Not a bitch."

"I want you to start imagining a new life. A new life where you're not ruled by addiction."

"Wait," Kym called from her place in the circle. "Are you saying you're not going to give us any more Oxy, like, ever?"

Kym had been a tweaker before becoming a junkie in the Villa. She had dyed purple hair, a lip ring with a green plastic bead, and she used the word "voluptuous" whenever she talked about herself.

"No, that's not what I'm saying, Kym."

"Because when we came here," Kym interrupted, bobbing her knee. "Peter said we could stay here for free as long as we came to these meetings, and we'd get all the pills we needed. So, if that's not the deal anymore and you're asking my girl if she wants to fall in love and get married, then what the fuck are we talking about here? Why are we here? I thought we were going to change the world."

"There's no deal, Kym. We are in talk therapy. I'm not trying to trick you. It's just to get the feelings out. We're all dying because someone hurt us. With that we hurt ourselves. We hurt others. Things aren't happening to us, they're happening for us. So we can learn."

"So you're still going to give us pills?"

"You'll get them," Royal-Lee said. "As soon as they're delivered."

"Okay," Kym nodded her head over and over. "Okay, okay, fine, you wanna know my story?" She rubbed her nose. "I was born in 1991. I'm from Hemet, California. We got a lake out there but I never learnt how to swim. Played volleyball in junior high and the girls made fun of me because my tits were so big. I was always voluptuous. My town was full of pick-up trucks, hicks; everybody liked drinking, but I couldn't give a shit—I hit the meth when I was twelve. That's when I got born, twelve. *Mystical.* I took a bus later on to Los Angeles. You know the drill, I was living in a tent with the Sixth Street crew. *Whooot-whoot!* Fifteen years and I still make a living. Wake up and just reach for the pipe. When you smoke meth it gives you these big ass hits, but you have to smoke it all the time. So, I got onto heroin, instead, and now I reach for the needle. Of course, in here, we mostly get Oxy, which kinda sucks, but it's free."

The residents looked bored. It was the same story everybody else had. The same thing every day.

"Can you imagine waking up in a beautiful room filled with soft morning light, and reaching for something else?" Royal-Lee asked. "Like a kitten, or a silk robe?"

"Okay, that's a-fucking-nough out of you." Melissa stood and looked at the circle. "Kick his ass. Right? Fuck him up."

Jomari stood, Filipino and quiet—he had strange using habits—one of the Surlies who worried Royal-Lee most. Royal-Lee had needed to use Narcan with Jomari several times already, but Narcan wouldn't work for most drugs, and that's what scared them. He'd use LSD, heroin, PCP, meth and stay up for days, acting nuts.

"It's dope time," Jomari grinned.

Tom interrupted, "Everybody chill. We partied last night. Let's sleep it off and wait. It sucks out there, guys, remember? Were you listening?"

Josiah, a lank Black guy with lipomas under his muscle tissue, stood up. He'd been a baseball player in high school and had that all-American thing about him, like he would wear Aeropostale and smell like Polo Blue, sign your yearbook *GOOD LUCK BRO,* before going on scholarship to state school. Except he'd smashed his skull and collarbone in a crash on the 10 and it left him with an ugly knot on his shoulder. Screwed up his pitching arm. He had a speech impediment and brain damage and was addicted to Oxy. He was aimless. To Royal-Lee, he seemed destined to die young, like he'd just get hit by a bus or be murdered or fall off a bridge. A scar ran across his forehead over his eyebrows and down the bridge of his nose, the glabella, in skincare, it was called.

"Fuck you," Josiah agreed. "Drugs or death."

Clay stood up.

The Surlies all stood.

"That's it," Royal-Lee said, suddenly brave. "You're not going to *hurt* me. You're not going to *do* anything. You know why? Because we are manifesting everything. You're manifesting *shit* lives. Total shit. Sit down. Or you'll get nothing. He'll give you nothing if I say you didn't listen to me. You'll go back and live on the street where you belong. Go to your rooms and wait quietly. He put *me* in charge. And you'll do what I say."

"Either punch the kid, or let's take five," Tom said. "Don't hit him. He's right."

Royal-Lee nodded. "Yeah. Thanks."

"You're still a bitch," Melissa said.

"I'm sure. Okay. Go envision yourself in your caves. Go upstairs."

Everyone got up and walked away toward their rooms. Many soon congregated outside Peter's door, banging on the oak. Royal-Lee felt stressed. He didn't want Peter to think they were irresponsible. That's when the relentless banging shook the front door.

12

Moments Later, Same Place . . .

Royal-Lee opened the front door and let the real Peter Krolik inside. He looked war-torn and slapped his legs like he was putting out a fire, which was still in the hills and mountains and nearing the beaches, far from West Adams. His teeth were brown. His eyes were weary but clever, winking with light. He made his way up onto the stage and dropped his sweatpants. He let his gunnysack fall to the stage with a thud.

"Um, hi?" Royal-Lee said.

The brother's eyes scanned the room and fell briefly on Royal-Lee's heavily contoured face. He pulled the cord from the bag that held his possessions and found his dopp kit. Royal-Lee gawked at the man's sharp, boney shins and ropey thighs, legs covered with dark scabby bruises and lightning-shaped thromboses, lined with seeping red sores. The brother went searching for a good vein. All of them were collapsed or lined with stormy, infected tracks. His scruffy upper lip jutted around a syringe, which he bit between his teeth, before filling the rig. Without tying off, he plunged the needle into the brachial artery of his left shoulder like an expert tailor, heaving with a sartorial grunt, then slammed the trigger.

He exhaled, arm forgetting itself and its tension, and his hand dropped the shot. Blood trickled down his arm in a sloppy line, weaving into the warp and weft of the oriental rug and Royal-Lee knew to go get Peter, but didn't. Why was this sexy? Watching the brother's expressions alternating between the joy of opiated relief and sudden inner agonies, dreaming with eyes open like a sleeping dog. It was impossible to know if it was a dream about running in pursuit or being chased away.

He glistened with sweat, arms covered in gooseflesh. Royal-Lee impulsively thought to reach their hand down the waistband of this guy's sweats, as disgusting as he was, and check if he and his brother were a match in the crucial way. Why would he want to do that? Fucking bums were disgusting. No, no. They would all be better off dead. No, no. A wave of shame washed over Royal-Lee. It couldn't rinse the guilt off that they felt for thinking these words for no reason whatsoever, except there was always a reason for every thought, every prayer.

A Surly named Vic walked towards the stage. He looked like the kind of guy who would sell crank on a BMX at night on Venice Beach. Vic had really pretty, long wavy hair and wore a black cap with a red bill, looked surfer-ish and street druggie, and had a tattoo of Santa Muerte.

"How did *he* get high?" Vic shot Royal-Lee a betrayed look, then noticed the dopp kit.

"You can't use today," Royal-Lee reminded him.

"*He* did. Looks like he's too far out too, bro."

Royal-Lee squatted down to peer at the brother.

"I wouldn't get any closer," Vic said. "This guy looks like he'd punch you in the face if you woke him up."

"He's breathing too slowly."

"*Fentanyl*," Vic said, finding it in the dopp kit.

Royal-Lee could barely see his chest shifting up and down. He held a finger under his nose.

"Barely breathing. Wait here and watch."

Royal-Lee ran upstairs. They grabbed the Narcan from the pack, seeing his lordship slumbering in the bed, half of his naked ass exposed, one cheek pale and smooth, the other under the tan silk sheet. He was beautiful, sleeping, and Royal-Lee hated to wake him. They'd like to turn him over, suck his cock, make him squirm, before telling him how his brother was found, more than found, was downstairs, right now, but there was no time for Royal-Lee to learn to give a man oral pleasure, and they blurted out, "Peter, wake up, your brother is home."

"Huh?" He shot up from bed. "What did you say?"

"He's here. He's high. Do you want to come down and see him? I'm bringing the Narcan."

Peter's balls were swinging as he threw on a white Burberry tee and Calvin Klein sweats, and rushed down the stairs, with Royal-Lee trailing behind, Narcan in hand.

Peter touched his twin brother's face. The twin didn't move.

"Peter?" Peter said.

"Why do you both have the same name?" Vic was smart.

"My real name is Phil," Peter said. "I named myself after him until I could find him. Because I love him so much."

So, the three of them conveyed the brother into the basement, shuffling like a group of bad movers. They laid him on a cot. His pants were still at his ankles. Royal-Lee stared into the brother's eyes, which fluttered. He was out of the danger zone.

"You wanna get high?" the brother mumbled. He gave his twin a knowing look.

The doorbell rang and Royal-Lee jumped and went upstairs.

They peeked through the peephole, expecting FBI agents swinging a battering ram, hot TV-star-looking agents, pomade in their hair, glocks drawn at Royal-Lee's head, played by Jon Hamm and Christopher Meloni. Instead, they opened the door to a man wearing a limp dress shirt, wrinkle-resistant tan slacks, and nondescript Cole Haan shoes. He looked like a guy who would vote for the Orange Candidate and laugh about it at the hotel bar.

"He represents the common man," he'd say, guzzling a lager.

Royal-Lee wobbled his head a little. The guy looked at him like he was searching for a piece to a jigsaw puzzle. Royal-Lee realized what they were wearing themself. A vest designed by Gary Baseman for Coach with a cartoon baby leopard bat monkey on it. A Gucci cotton-jersey tank top midriff, black Guess women's jean cutoffs, and his favorite white belt sporting chunky pink gems with matching Gucci flashtrek sneakers whose removable crystals glinted in the light coming through the opened door.

The man handed a card to them. It was from The Conduit. Royal-Lee pulled the stiff card from the envelope. *The Church of White*

Illumination was embossed on heavyweight cardstock, along with The Church's raised insignia. Below were the date and time for Peter to be at the office. It was today, in half an hour. *Don't be late, Sir. It's v urgent*, was scrawled in red on the back. *xx, The Conduit. P.S. you're in MAJOR trouble.*

Royal-Lee muttered "Thanks" and shut the door in the guy's face.

Would it be too gauche to borrow one of Peter's black silk ties to deliver this card? He felt like dressing like a mortician, suited up, clean and precise, in order to mask the dread they felt about the situation. Fashion always alleviated stress. Royal-Lee felt stressed and didn't want Peter to think them irresponsible, in Guess cut-offs, highlighting gender fey, given the gravity of the present situation. After so many months of being a tag-along, Royal-Lee had the opportunity to show up as someone with initiative, managing the house all morning, and wanted to look like some kind of high fashion executive, or a gangster from a Tarantino movie when delivering this card.

What if things went wrong and they went to prison? Getting out with a record and having to work selling pills on the street in bold and bright colors, rocking Tommy Hilfiger velour tracksuits? If they transitioned, would Royal-Lee go to a women's prison? Was that better? Making cup-o-noodles with a stinger, hanging around rough women acting like undignified bitches, Royal-Lee playing at appearing undignified, too. It sounded terrible.

Was "*Phil*" in trouble with the cops? What did the card mean? There was no time for dressing up. Downstairs, Royal-Lee found all three men high. Phil blinked, seemed to be falling asleep, but then opened his eyelids like the rising of two dim blue suns that looked at Royal-Lee but failed to even notice. Heroin eyes were always sort of clear. The drug pulled the curtain of troubles away from the windows of the soul. He blinked and closed his blue eyes. His boss couldn't go see The Conduit like this. His lordship was high. They held out the card for him but he closed his eyes. The real Peter Krolik snatched it away, read it, considered it for a moment, and then, with a scoff, said, "I'll fuckin' go."

13

Back in the Bunker . . .

Susie knew the greatest artists were always lured into inner sanctums of wealth by assholes. Just like being rich made you attracted to your own family. When she escaped, she'd dig the gold bars up from under the flowering plum, if her father wasn't watching her. Could she wait three days to get out on good terms with all that gold? Or would he come down tomorrow to find her sick and detoxing, having canceled his Vegas trip? Would he fuck her in a fever dream? That was her father. Yanked between the poles of love and hate. A villain and a validator. He was her twisted husband, her nasty brother, and her benefactor. The mystique of wealth clung to him, but he was basic . . . not billionaire class. He reified the divine right to rule for powerful families—like the Sicklers—that kept the "people" looking up worshipfully. He was a marquis, nothing more. He kept the interlopers from the borders, serving the crown. That was what museums and the world of galleries and auction houses did today. She grew up in the Sicklers' palace half-time. If only she'd been born there, the artistic protests she eventually created would have hit harder, but then she would probably never have succeeded on her own and would have hooked up with her sister.

"Do you know what a eunuch is?" Susie wished she could ask her dad.

Eunuchs were kept in the palace because they were so loyal and good at keeping secrets. The key to remaining seen as king, as god, was to have strict secrecy all around. Eunuchs had nowhere else to turn, no church or society-approved sexual desires to fulfill, and no place in the social hierarchies outside of the palace. That was what her father was trying to do with her, make her a eunuch, ashamed and trapped in his kingdom. But she was no eunuch! *He* was *Dick's eunuch.* And fuck Faia, too. Susie didn't need her, or any of them.

Artists today, fashion houses, musicians, actors, influencers, and celebrities were still part of the same mystification of wealth. Art was ruled by godlike men pretending to be sovereign in games of illusion that objectified "outsiders" into works of art for their private collections, diversified via diversity, and perpetuated imperialism, all while running tax and investment scams. Gary Indiana said, "I was aware at an early age that this country is rotten to the core, but it took years to begin to understand why it was rotten." Susie knew from the start. It was her dad and her friend's dad. She was never going to attach herself to one of those little dick jerks, just to feel in touch with the art world. She would make her own way. She would not be taxidermied while alive, stuffed with their shit, botulism, silicone, dick, and stupidity. She would make her own installations.

* * *

I know how perverse it is up at the top. I knew it then. I'd watched the Sicklers play the art world. My father explained long ago how tax breaks worked, and how top collectors went about influencing the value of the artists they collected, augmented their provenance, and how they pressured museums. He had a collection of his own, following Richard's advice, collecting ancient Chinese art and a few pieces of Qi Baishi's fruit, and Jasper Johns's flags. Buy two, donate one, write it off, and get the one you collected for yourself for way less.

Someday they would all be mine, maybe. I just wanted to get high. I had to. Did he know how hard it was growing up in this house, in his world, and suddenly it was like poof, all of the trauma was supposedly gone, just because some rich old cunt was running for president. Fuck her. My dad wanted to rub it in my face, how I had so much privilege and opportunity now that the world was turning in my favor, after he yelled at me and put me down, kept hitting me with an open hand, and as a kid even killed my rabbit, on purpose, supposedly because she scratched me but really because he was always complaining about the way she smelled.

I went back into my parents' bunker bedroom and blasted through my mother's drawers again, pulling them open and searching. I tore through a Hartman duffel. Her roller board. Tote. Attaché. I wanted to cut all the buttons off my father's clothes, do something to show how much I hated him. Swallow the buttons and take a shit in his shoe. In this metaphor, were buttons pills? Was I his dog? *I would not be his dog!*

I should paint him as *my* dog, next to a pile of shit, with a micro-penis in chastity, eating the shit while on a leash, with Hitler's mustache. Or have it sculpted by Carlson Baker Arts. Sell it to my mom or Sickler or anyone after I left my dad—make a million dollars. It's what rich families were about, power games that meant life and death. Especially in Los Angeles. It was Grecian. It was eternal. This was how rich kids died.

I found an Advil. Took it. My head was pounding. I felt strangely turned on.

My phone rang. *Dad? Royal-Lee?* I had texted them, where were they? It was my mother, the woman who had locked whatever was real inside her away behind a wall of jewelry and skin rejuvenation and charades. What the fuck did she want?

"Hello?"

"Susie," she said cloyingly.

"Yes. What?" My heart was skipping beats.

"What are you doing?"

"Alone time. Have you talked to Dad?"

"There's someone I want you to see."

I was stunned, staring in the mirror. I squeezed a blackhead. "I'm sort of stuck . . ."

"You're in the bunker. Yes. I see you on my tablet. My drawers are all over the floor. I'll send someone. They'll let you out with the code. Susie . . . get cleaned up."

"I *am* clean. What the fuck, Mom? Who do you want me to meet?"

"*WTF?* You speak three languages, young lady. Susie, if you prefer to continue living as a loser-victim, cosplaying poverty, waiting for your daddy to help you destroy yourself, stay down there. *Après moi, le déluge*, right? What do *you* want?"

"What do *I* want?"

"Yes. Why are you doing all of this? You think I don't know what you're up to?"

"A red."

"A red what?"

"You know, Mom. A red Oxy."

"Someone will come let you out. Your pills are upstairs in your father's underwear drawer. He's already left town."

"He found them? Then why are we doing this?"

"Hildegard the Nun was from a noble household, Susie. She saw God for five seconds. She authored books on botany, invented a language, and wrote orchestral music in melisma and monophony, wrote plays, poems, medical texts, and natural histories with illuminations she designed. Why are any of us doing anything? Love and worship. Think about that while you wait."

I thought about it. It made me angry.

Was my mother paying me a compliment for the first time? Or did she just want to lock me in a different kind of bunker for the rest of my life; one of emotional bondage, playing mommy mind games? Supping together at Bestia, or Shutters, or Felix Trattoria. Actually liking each other, just before she died.

"Hello?"

Mom hung up.

My mother had wanted to be an artist and had failed. Was that why she liked Dick? His connection to art? I'd seen a few of her childhood sketches and paintings. They weren't great but they weren't total shit. She was just too rich to force herself to pursue her outlandish dreams and juvenile desires to the degree necessary to become a famous artist, or a dancer, or any of the creative impulses she'd once felt that ultimately left her feeling a failure for not making them her reality. No one cared about white women anyway. I worried I was the same kind of person. I had the same genes.

What did I have in common with Hildegard von Bingen, a Catholic saint? Was she calling me the family mystic? I was also a child of lower nobility from a family in service to the Sicklers. Like Hildegard's family had long been in service to some count. The count was probably a pervert, like Dick, like everyone rich. Hildegard had been handed over to a convent.

If only I had been given up as a child to something wiser than the west side of Los Angeles. *Moloch.* Raised outside of the idiocy and vulgarity of my parents' home and the Sickler palace. I thought about it and waited for the hero my mother had promised, ready for a vision, even if it came in pill form again.

On my phone I studied one of Hildegard's illuminations: a red angel holding a lamb that looked like the Lion of Judah. The angel was stomping on a green demon, who was being kissed by a serpent, and the head of Jesus appeared above the angel's head. There was a bird coming off one of the angel's wings. Above the other wing was the red face of a soul who seemed particularly devout. I felt it all. I was the whole cast of characters.

Von Bingen held the entire world in her soul just like maybe everyone did. But fuck everyone. I didn't have open-eyed visions in the shades of pure living light better than Rothko's *Chapel* or Turrell's *Twilight Epiphany*, but I understood it all when I looked at it, and felt the burning faces pressing inside mine. My need to express, to capture, to be a master. To master myself. I had my own light, my own fire, and visions that were beautiful, even if they required Oxy. Even if I was just a pill-hungry junkie in LA, trying to get fucked up to find a little peace on Earth.

I would need to devote myself entirely to my purpose, something Mom never accomplished, but maybe she was proud of me that I was digging into my addiction so deeply at such a young age, so I could get it out of the way, and become who I was meant to be as mystic, as the family's only hope, as a pure artist, as Apollo. Or was she just fucking with me?

It didn't matter in the long run. It was my world to determine entirely for myself, just like everyone else in town. My own etiology. That was the only game worth playing.

14

The Medical Spa, Doheny Road . . .

The real Peter was sunblind. He came in from the brightness of Sunset Boulevard, stepping into the black marble foyer. He wanted to smoke but he couldn't see. He didn't want to ash willy-nilly on the building floor, plus he was pretty sure there were guards in the lobby. Most lobbies had them. They were always throwing him out. He had taken the last bump of some crank from his speed bag. Now it was wearing off.

Was that Genesis on the speakers? "Invisible Touch"? He couldn't be completely sure. It ended and now it was something else. Why did he always feel so alone in the dark? What was it like to be Phil Collins, someone who knew how to create pop music about successful life? Love and shit. Once music held the hope for not being completely alone. That was pop. Pop was about not being alone in life. Peter wasn't popular anymore. How could he be? With how blind and lonely he felt, how dark, even in the sunlight? How dirty he always looked. He was in his brother's clothes. These felt nice. He had been a bum too long. It was good to be wearing decent clothes, coming to a nice place, where a woman named The Conduit was waiting for him and supposedly would give him whatever he wanted to drink and chocolate or cookies or whatever. She was mad at his brother for something. He had to act like he was his brother, Phil, drink coffee, eat a cookie, say sorry or some stupid shit. She'd better not be a real bitch. He still couldn't see.

Blindness and darkness everywhere. Wasn't that how everyone felt lately? Strange blinking days. Dim groping hours. Heading toward the worst election in the history of the nation. Fuck the nation. *No . . .* he *was* an American. Perched precariously above the cliffs of disaster, ready for the smashing of the democratic pillars that kept the whole system from tumbling down; a lot of losers were rooting for it, total destruction. They leaned into it, the vertigo, desperate for the plunge. He wasn't so stupid. He wasn't wearing a Guy Fawkes mask, jerking off in his parents' basement.

Fucking losers couldn't get laid—even worse, they were fake activists, fake carers, liberal bullshit fucks, while the whole world baked to a sun crisp. Africa would have no food. They could always get food. They could always get help. They just had to call home. But now they didn't have to call home. Now he had his brother. His brother always hoped the Western world would fall. His brother fancied himself an anarchist, but how much of an anarchist could you be when he grew up drinking Orange Julius at the mall? He remembered The Sharper Image. Walking around with a hard-on for all the girls in Abercrombie. Waiting to get rich as soon as everyone with money in his family died and give it all to him. In high school, getting drunk on wine and stoned in Washington Park under the massive trees, he would gaze into the purple sky and blow smoke from a Camel wide or a joint and feel connected to the roots of the ancient forest. He didn't want them to die before sharing their fortune with him, he wanted them to share it while they were all still alive, so they could enjoy it together. Idiots. They wanted to make him wait.

He and his brother would eat those beautiful dried purple and white mushrooms and occasionally snort cocaine and take Ritalin. But his brother didn't really like to party. His brother would always take his magazines from the top shelf of his closet where he kept a photo of the first girl he ever kissed, at summer camp. He wondered what happened to her. He never liked the way his dad treated his brother, but Phil was so annoying, he kind of asked for it, and he never learned. Their dad was difficult, it was true, but he never broke a bone or anything. It wasn't like they'd lived through the Civil War. Dad left him alone, and really only focused on Phil, who kept provoking everyone because he couldn't sit still with the difficulties of life and the concepts of death, God, reality, and just watch TV. Phil could never survive on the streets, he was soft. Still, it had been painful to watch and to have to distance himself from his twin, growing up in a house with so much anger and violence.

Who was this woman he was coming to see? This Conduit? Would she be angry? What would she know about why he was wearing this wig? Was the wig a strength or a weakness? It was good to disappear. So people couldn't see you. His brother said she would eventually compliment him and give him the pills she owed. If he didn't act stupidly. It had been a long time since anyone had complimented him. He wanted to smell good again and be with people who smelled good, who were glowing and looked beautiful, like his grandfather had looked, who bought expensive things for his nice home and drove luxury cars and was hilarious. He'd once dreamed as a kid that he might be like the people he watched on TV. He had dreams like this when he was young. To be funny and charming and to not worry about a thing.

He was still sunblinded, having come in from the brightness of glimmering cars on Sunset, below movie-theater-screen-sized billboards advertising shows whose actors and producers were poisoned last night. Why had his brother said he would get in trouble and then get praise? That made sense, it was how women generally operated. Or was it the opposite? Was this a trap? Was his brother against him? Setting him up for something? Intervention? The card said he was in trouble. If they were setting him up, the card would have said he had won a prize or something. He was his brother now. What was she going to say to him?

"Oh, Peter, great job, Peter! We are all so impressed with how you look," she'd tell him soon. "You really clean up, don't you? Do you want a massage?" Why did she think his brother's name was Peter? That was his own name.

Praise would feel good. He hadn't felt proud of himself in a long time. He didn't remember what it was like. He'd felt he'd ruined himself in that respect long ago.

He knew exactly when it had happened.

In 2001, his brother had flown to Fort Benning, Georgia, to see him, when he had broken his back during basic training. The trip was supposed to be a celebratory one to toast that he wouldn't be off to Kabul to get blown up. Flowers in vases from the family filled the room, but each bouquet carried its own ledger of debts and accusations. He lay in traction with pins in his vertebra; stargazers and daisies and roses opened all around the room. Where were his family members? Daisies were cheap. He hated the name Daisy. Only Phil had shown up. It was both of their ideas to smoke the Oxys like a party drug. Phil had brought a few bottles from his hotel's mini-bar.

They'd toweled the door as they'd done in college, used the straw from the iced water and the aluminum foil off a half-eaten baked potato. They smoked one pill giggling and joshing one another, the smoke burning their throats. Then they smoked the other. The high came on fast, blood-dilating, slowing down the rush of life. The wondrousness of breathing became apparent. His eyes glistened like a doll's. There was always something uncanny and slightly terrifying about having a twin, like if something happened to him, it would happen to you, too, and there was this shared knowledge between them. And if you did something, the other one would sense it. If you died, half of them died. In that first drugged moment, it was all part of the magic as every cell that had been starved for air and water finally let in the light and they took a deep fucking breath. He could kiss his brother on the lips. Was that too far? The world was too far. The world wasn't far enough. Newsstands full of stupid magazines, no one gives you matches anymore, everything comes in plastic, no hot girls who want to pay you attention or suck your dick. Or kiss you or anything nice.

Once the high was over his pain became unbearable.

"I need something," he'd shouted, desperation flashing in his eyes. He'd been trying to get back there ever since. Brotherly love, youth, the first great sparkling high, like when you see something beautiful glistening as the darkness recedes through the windows of a Mercedes.

His brother had become a university professor. He guessed he'd dropped out though. If he himself had become a professor, too, what would he have to teach? He knew the answer: the soil, dirt under the lawns and in the lots of apartment buildings around town. The dog shit in the little patches of soil between the sidewalks and trees. The sandy soil detached from the business of the day. LA soil was great. It grew flowers and fruit and all that was lovely and sunbaked and timeless. This town should be free. He liked movies. He'd always felt like he was in a movie. Wasn't life like a movie theater? You were either on screen or sitting in the reclining chairs, stuffing your mouth with popcorn. What about love, friends, and weddings? Actually living life? His old life. All he felt was panic now and dope and no one understood how much he was doing to try to find his way in the world. Why couldn't he be like Phil Collins? Or Peter Gabriel?

He'd known Fred Harkin. Fred was dead. Bye, Fred.

What the hell was going on? These motels. "These killings." He knew what was happening. He knew what happened last night. The news was talking about the award show's focus on race and how the attack was racist. The liberals were racist; all they cared about was race. He knew the rules of the street game. Things were fucked up. Everyone was going crazy. They didn't even know it. He knew it. They might have all been played, but that didn't mean they were all played out. Did people know that sometimes you went blind when you came in out of the sun? And then you could see again. He couldn't see the people, but he felt them. Heard their slip, scuff, and grip of shoes across the stone floor. Their breathing. The ache of public, the groaning of mass anxiety. He listened for where the footsteps ended. That was where the elevators would be in any place. He heard one open. Ding.

He waited until his sight was returning to step into the elevator car. Was he alone? He still couldn't focus on anything clearly. His brother could be just before his nose, right now. Ready to flick him between the eyes. That was the sort of joke his brother always made. To be there a few moments sooner, ready to flick him right between the eyeballs. Annoying. His brother was high now. Why had he done that? So he would be less annoying and on his side.

He hadn't waited. He felt the elevator going up. He remembered a sweet hot summer day in August when the students trudged up the stairs toward their grade-school classroom, and the smell of cut Ohio grass and humid cornfields beyond the town, summer sweetness of crops in the air all lingered. Their village was neat and pedestrian and the students traipsed squarely into the hall in Bengals shirts and backpacks—sunblindness. He and his brother were the children of industrialists, empire builders. The other kids' families worked for them. Then the formless world took shape as he floated and wondered if it was just *his* eyes, some ancient vision, some secret power, no one else sharing in the wonderment of how the miracle of sight had been suspended, not even his brother, and it returned in oranges and yellows. Purples, grays, blobs and bulbs of green. Who cared about the past? The past was gone. He had gone from something to nothing. He was a waste. No, he wasn't. He wanted his Fentanyl.

At the top floor, he stared at his reflection in the long black glass walls. He inspected his fake hair, eyeglasses, distressed T-shirt under a long white trench coat with three-quarter-length sleeves, gold Fendi hi-top sneakers, and 24K-gold chain. That weird kid had helped him get dressed after a shower. He looked like a drug dealer now—or worse, an out-of-touch record producer. He knew that what remained just below the surface, in his face and eyes, if he peeled the years back—and removed the wig and these silly clothes—if he got a shave—would look exactly like a founding father of the United States of America. Or at least, he had—once upon a time—looked that way. It had been a long time since he'd had a haircut and a shave. The wig over his hair itched. He hadn't needed a fake beard, he had the real one his brother only wished he could grow. Maybe his brother was right. This country really needed their help. They were the great men of America. They'd always been and they were true brothers. He knew what was happening, more or less, having seen Fred go, back at his brother's joint, yesterday, and then the news. He figured something funny was up. Phil was making moves. He would find out more, but what are you gonna do with a dead junkie?

Earl-eye in the morning!
Shave his belly with a rusty razor
Shave his belly with a rusty razor
Shave his belly with a rusty razor
Earl-eye in the morning!
Way hay and up she rises
Way hay and up she rises

Way hay up she rises
Earl-eye in the morning
Throw him in the lock-up 'til he's sober
Throw him in the lock-up 'til he's sober
Throw him in the lock-up 'til he's sober
Earl-eye in the morning!

One of Chopin's preludes gently pounded, watery through invisible speakers, as he studied the double doors. His mom liked Chopin. Or she just had the CD in her Bentley. The doors were locked. He didn't like Chopin. He didn't like Mozart either. He liked Bach. Bach was the best composer. His brother should know that. Everyone should. Inlaid symbols wound around marble pillars. He didn't know what any of these were: arrows, swastikas, a snake with a tail in its mouth, the Egyptian cross. What the fuck had his brother gotten into?

He stroked his beard and pushed on the doors. He pressed the buzzer. These doors were shiny like a movie set. Even the dust on the marble doorjamb looked fancy. It was fancy dust. That was this part of LA. The mix of reality and delusion. Out of it came TV. He looked up and saw a security camera tracking him. He was on TV. He smiled. He waved. A buzzing, then a clanking sound indicated the doors were opening.

He slipped into the marble hallway and stared at a long tiger-maple buffet covered in Fabergé eggs emblazoned with iron crosses and double eagles, the Madonna, animals and bees, royal figures, images of czars and czarinas. It'd all be pretty punk rock if it wasn't so earnest, and there were scepters and paintings of Catherine the Great, and solid gold eggs set with diamonds and precious stones, and Chopin kept diddling, blither-blathering on. He pocketed an egg. It'd been a long time since he'd seen shit like this. He could go for a steak. His hands were dry. He spit in his palms and rubbed them together hard and bent down and wiped his hands on his brother's nice socks. There were two jade dragon statues with planet Earths in their mouths. A 3D yarn icon of the flaming heart sat in a spiked birdcage on an ionic columnar pedestal by the gas fireplace burning a hot spot in the AC. He lit a cigarette. What was this place? Had his brother become a billionaire?

A woman appeared to meet him. Her hair was in a bob. She wore no shirt underneath a suit jacket with pink high heels. She had a huge diamond ring that flashed a rainbow on the walls.

"Look at you with all your swagger, the Holiday that poisoned Hollywood," she whispered. Was she talking to him? His eyes bulged. Was this The Conduit? She was hot. He wanted to lick her teeth. Women didn't really talk to him anymore.

They walked into her office together. A man was sitting in a chair wearing unbelted tan slacks, his large gut stuffed inside a blazer with gold buttons. Flat-screen TVs played news on different channels. The anchor talked about dog whistles and the Orange Candidate. Fred Harkin dead at the Emmys, his body stolen, found dismembered in a motel. Somehow this was related to the election. A lady said the candidate's father had been arrested at a KKK rally. She seemed so happy to be saying it. *KKK.* She frowned on TV, but you could tell she was smiling underneath. A scientist said "misuse of ipecac can be fatal." He said it over and over. There was a hotline to call if anyone knew anything. Whoopi Goldberg asked some woman who looked like Drew Carey how to explain this to children. He needed to get high. This was getting boring. Then Whoopi said, "Hold up, hold up," and read something coming through from somewhere. "This is BREAKING: 'The Pain Killer' confession letter has been exposed as a hoax—the real killer is still unknown. Authorities now confirm the letter previously attributed to the alleged Pain Killer was a fabrication. What is known about the real killer is nothing at all. *What!*" Whoopi exclaimed. "Is the killer a far-right extremist, a lone psychopath, a teenage troll, or a cult of predators targeting the vulnerable? What *is* happening *here*? A fake! So it was all a fake?"

"How are you today, Peter?" The Conduit lady tilted her head. She was like the world's sexiest social worker. He remembered his disguise. How did she know his real name? *Peter Peter Pumpkin Eater.* Right, Phil had said this would happen.

"This is Lieutenant Polachek of the central division." Peter saluted but remained sitting. The lieutenant cleared his throat. He stopped saluting. "He just wants to ask you a few questions." Had his brother set him up? In the military, a lieutenant was a senior officer. He remembered John Cusack's speech from *Say Anything* about kickboxing. He hummed a few bars of "The Killing Moon."

La
La, la, la, la
La, la, la, la
La, la, la, la
La, la, la, la, la, la

In 1998, or so, McDonalds offered a Thanksgiving breakfast meal. The Thanksgiving breakfast was designed to cater to early morning holiday travelers who didn't want to cook first thing on Thanksgiving Day. It was also a nod to the changing behaviors of the nation when more and more people appreciated the flexibility of grabbing a meal on the go. It was his senior year in high school. He got one with his dad and told his dad he was joining the military, and his dad cried in his coffee. He had waited two more years to join.

"Can I get either of you a coffee? Espresso, lieutenant?" That was nice. She was doing a good job. He could use a *shot* of dope.

"No. Thank you," Polachek smiled. Peter waved and tried to read The Conduit. It was impossible. His heart was trying to blow up inside his chest.

"I'll have some water." He licked his lips. Dry.

The Conduit got up and poured him a glass and brought it back to him. She smiled really big like she was on that TV with Whoopi Goldberg. He smiled back. People were so stupid, or were they smart? He'd better be careful. He was always surprised by how dumb people were and the things they liked, but then right when you underestimated them, they bit you in the ass. This lady was rich, and rich people were always smarter than poor people, even if they didn't seem like it at first.

"So . . ." The Conduit said, then stopped talking like she wanted to make a big deal of this meeting. It was a stupid rich person trick, the kind of thing people with too much time on their hands did to people with real shit to do. He wanted to get high. He should leave.

"This is about my daughter," she said.

"Of course," he said. He didn't know why he'd said it. She said she had a daughter. And he was in a hurry. So of course he said *of course*, like, let's go. Let's get going. Now, he had to act like he knew what he and she were even talking about. This was so boring. He remembered Johnny from *Naked*, talking about how stupid it was that people were bored. He'd always liked that guy.

"Susie is my daughter."

He sat stunned. So this was Susie's mother. Whoever *that* was. Hmmmm. His brother would know what this was all about? He needed to get out of here and back to him. He wasn't really getting anywhere.

"Wasn't she your student?" Lieutenant Polachek looked at him.

"Of course. Of course." There it was again. *Of course*. Why was he so agreeable? He should be the one demonstrating that he wasn't someone to fuck with, at all, because he wasn't. "Back in college." He spitballed, nodding his head. "Yes. Before I fucked that all up."

"The reason I'm here today is that she was on the security footage at the Cecil Hotel where her former classmate Ashley Sinclair was found dead of an overdose with severe head wounds. Susie entered the hotel with Ashley the day that she died."

"That's too bad. Too bad. Dead is bad. Sad story."

"We would like to talk to Susie. Have you seen her?"

"No. Nope. No. Definitely not. I haven't seen *anyone*."

"What do you mean, you haven't seen anyone?"

"I mean I see people, but not her. I really don't like to go out."

"I had been led to believe otherwise," Polachek looked at Peter, then The Conduit, furrowing his brow. It had the leathery texture of a B-film star. Sometimes everything in LA looked just right. Even when things went wrong. He wished that happened more often.

"I heard you're a rising star here in a society of powerful men. That must require some significant socializing."

"I came here. That's it. I'm very busy. I haven't seen Susie at all."

Lieutenant Polachek nodded.

"So that's it?" The Conduit said.

"Yeah, I haven't seen her. I barely knew her. She was not that great in class, if I'm honest."

"I thought she won a prize for writing an essay in your class," Polachek said. He'd done his homework. Someone had.

"Just by chance."

"Chance?" Polachek raised an eyebrow.

"Yeah, she won by luck. She picked the right number out of a hat."

"Well, if you do see her." Polachek stood up and handed him a business card. "Tell her we'd like to talk to her. She's not in any trouble. I just want to speak to her." He made a big deal of saying *I* like he was so important that he got to be the first person more than anyone else. *I. I. I. I. I.* He'd like to punch him in the eye. Militaristic capitalistic colonialistic imperialistic fuckery. He hated the military. They hated him, too. That's where he'd started shooting dope. They'd kicked him out.

"Me, too."

The lieutenant made a confused face. It was like he was considering saying something else but then he just walked away, losing the fight. *Idiot.*

"What the hell was that about?" The Conduit said.

"You tell me. What's any of this about?"

"Peter, I need you to know that she's addicted to Oxy . . . so I don't want her talking to detectives right now. I don't understand how she could be connected to an Oxy OD and the mutilation of a friend she went to school with; she never leaves the pool. You know her father is Dick Sickler's principal attorney? My husband, of course . . . at least for now. You poisoned the Emmys? What the hell happened with Fred Harkin? Tsk tsk. Did you really have to go and do all that?"

"No, of course not. Are you kidding? I didn't do it."

"Oh, come on. Still, I need her to enter your rehab." She stared at him. Her eyes were bright green. You didn't see a lot of bright green eyes anymore. Usually it's only when the sun hits them.

"So, that's a rehab?" he said distractedly, rubbing his tooth with his finger, and then licking his tooth to taste the salt. Where was his cigarette? Did he eat it? Where did it go?

"You've got your affairs in order, I'm sure. You better get them in order if not. He might come looking for her. Still, I want her there with you. It's a risk. I'm sending you to pick her up at my place. She's locked in the basement. I'll give you the code, okay? And make sure before you let her out, you get the pills that are upstairs in her father's underwear drawer. I'll give you all the details. Without the pills, she won't do what she's told. She is a true brat."

"So, you know I *could* use a *real* drink."

"Listen, Phil. Yes, I know plenty. I know your real name. I've been helping you since you called me, before you moved from New York."

"Of course."

"I helped you become a member. This organization takes its membership very seriously. We keep our members *safe*. Every member is accountable to each other. This is the real true lodge. The keepers of wisdom and time's eternal knowledge." She brushed her lapel. "You have committed an act of domestic terrorism. It isn't what it used to be. Once upon a time, this would have been a practical joke, and they would have made it all look like bad clams," she smiled. "Bravo, you're nuts."

"Well you're nuts."

"Hardly. Your plans were never discussed with me, and I can prove that. We have the tapes. And don't worry. If anyone asks for them, we'll say we taped *Seinfeld* over them."

"I love *Seinfeld*."

She turned on the TV with a remote, pressed a button that activated a VHS. His brother was on the TV, in a room full of fine furniture. On the wall hung a reproduction of *The Treachery of Images*, CECI N'EST PAS UNE PIPE.

"When you want to suppress a story or a movement," some man said, sitting in a silk-upholstered chair in an oatmeal linen suit, opposite his brother. "What do you think you ought to do?"

"Release a story that says the opposite," Phil answered, wearing a towel.

"Don't be stupid," the man said. "So much ancient wisdom. Too many bouncing balls. No one can watch them all. You're not supposed to. That's not what a brain is for, a mind, I mean. You know. The wise mind. The knowing mind."

"So I'll poison the Emmys?" Phil looked stupid.

She turned off the tape. "We are imposing a fine of a quarter million dollars. Bring it in cash to the election party at Richard's."

"Don't be ridiculous. We're not paying the fine. *No fine*. We can't do it, so we're not doing it, because I say so."

"That's not how manifestation works. I'm a Conduit. Do you know what a Conduit is? I pass information. It's in the handbook you were given."

"I'll read it again, but you're not doing a very good job."

"I beg your pardon."

"You heard me."

"There's something else. I didn't want to tell you until you had calmed down. But you obviously aren't going to. Wasserfield is dead."

"Well, that's too bad."

"Wasserfield recently suffered a life-threatening attack and, sadly, died from complications." She smiled conspiratorially. "We've handled his remains at our crematorium. No coroner needed, no nonsense, no big deal. Do you get what I'm saying? He left his money to The Church, tax free. Now he's gone. Poof." She made a motion like a magician.

Peter stayed seated with his shoulder forward. A pigeon on the ledge outside the window was lying on its belly.

"You seem unfazed," she said.

"Everybody dies. I don't even know what I'm doing here."

"You're here because Richard Sickler wants to meet with you. I'm in full support of this plan, this time. You'll be rewarded and you can use the reward to pay the fine. You're going to be a very rich man, Peter. All of your dreams will come true."

"So, it's a circle jerk. What about my brother?"

"We'll find him. Maybe Susie can help you look. You'll take good care of her. She can paint or take photos. Bums make good subjects. Like Diane Arbus. Walking around with her paper bag purse."

"Diane Arbus."

"Whatever," The Conduit waved. "You know Susie."

"I know where my brother is."

"Come on, let's go talk to Dick. He's great."

She led him down the corridor and one floor below to Dick's office, where they waited. He wanted to get high. It was all he could think about. High. High. High. This was taking too long. These people were ridiculous. A thin man in a tall suit came and lead them into a library, where he saw an ugly old man with a settlement of moles colonizing his pale face, who looked extremely rich. He was in a high-backed chair tapping on an iPad. He didn't even look up. *Dick.* Or maybe he was having a stroke, tap, tap. In the corner there were flags, like the ones at the White House on TV. He remembered being in the Boy Scouts. He remembered the building from across the grocery store where the Scout meetings were held. The Quonset huts that were used for grain or warehouse storage for some business he never understood that had closed long ago.

"Mr. Holiday," the man said. Who the fuck was he talking to? "I understand you're an Oxy enthusiast of sorts." The man kept poking at his iPad as he spoke.

"Do you have any?"

"Yes, yes. We will take care of you. Although we shouldn't, what the hell were you thinking? Trying to make a complete mess of the night? Sort of smart, though—sort of good. A lot of filth, a lot of mixed messages. But my pills are in the punchline. That's not good. Pretty stupid, bottom line." He squinted. Peter's eyes bulged again.

"And Fred Harkin, not funny. Are you stupid or something?"

"I agree."

"Nipples for eyelids. His dick split open like a hot dog. Trying to show us all you have teeth for more than smiling? Exploiting this killer business? She tells me you've started a little church of your own." The spit in his throat crackled. Old men were gross. "Good for you. Good for you. Good for you. Good to have people who depend on you. Isn't it? Practice manifestation. But we know Susie was at the first hotel, Cecil, no shit. It's demented."

"Of course."

"It's good when you get to make the rules. I'm sending you home with some new pills that really work miracles. Miracle drug. Amazing stuff. My driver, Federico, will meet you out front and give them to you. We've found the cure to addiction and we're starting a test trial at your rehab."

Peter blinked. "Ummmm." He muttered, "I'm gonna need some pills before I get home."

"For Susie?" The Conduit said, scraping a little lipstick off the corner of her mouth. "I already told you they're upstairs, in her father's desk drawer. They'll tide her over."

"No, no. He's thinking big picture. He's a manifestor! I want to keep him up and running. Freddie will take care of him downstairs. As much as I don't like it, you saw the footage from the smoking lounge. My idiot brother-in-law put him up to it and promised him pills. What were you two thinking? Are you trying to fuck me? You wouldn't do that. No. Of course not. Think this has been easy? You think I don't deal with hatred? You don't think everything that's happened to addiction would have happened anyhow? You don't think fentanyl would be coming from overseas? You think this isn't all planned, all rigged? It will blow over. What doesn't, right? So will these lame killings. Someone can't stand their own mind. Nothing new. Killers come and go. It's all a dream, it's all your dream, never let anyone outdream you. You're the one who is awake. Dreaming while awake. That's it. Total autonomy, you know the drill. Anyhow, just give them both kinds of pills and I'll be in touch again soon. You're doing fine. You're one of us now. You're the best. Enemies only make us stronger."

"Can Freddie take Peter to pick up Susie, Dick? We're having some trouble with her. You don't mind, do you?"

"No," he tsked. "Anything for my old friend. Too bad she's having a rough time. For the time being. She'll turn around. Artists are kind of pathetic when they're not famous yet. We'll work on her."

Peter stood there blinking.

"Let's go, Peter." The Conduit grabbed him by the arm. He stuttered a few steps forward. "Come on, people have work to do. Pick up Susie and go back to your drug addicts and patients. It's time to get to work."

"Yes. Federico will meet you out front. He goes by Freddie. But it's Federico, don't let him fool you. The name means Peaceful Ruler. While the world is held together by invisible knots, and while we are each our own peaceful ruler, he's just a chauffeur. A damn good driver. Good day, Phillip. Phillip Krolik. Yep, we have all the knowledge and we have the wisdom. Bye-bye."

15

Peter and Susie Ride in a Rolls Royce . . .

Life drifted hourlessly along the Westside in cars with mahogany folding tray tables and quilted leather seats, rich men and women with puffed-up lips gliding by in G-Wagons sipping Moon Juice collagen smoothies through paper straws, and somewhere in that slow, glimmering drift, with the partition up and the world held at bay, Federico drove Susie and Peter—both high, eyes half-lidded, floating—in the back of Dick Sickler's Rolls Royce.

Okay, so Susie'd hole up in some shithole, where—so her old teacher had said—she could keep using, get the gorilla that was her father off her back for a few days, and maybe bust loose after crashing in some dump Phil Krolik ran. *Fine.*

But why was he even here? She blinked and her head drooped and it took real determination to raise her chin back up, and then she felt proud of herself for winning her fight against gravity. Wasn't that what life was all about, the sheer determination to rise in the face of so much difficulty?

The entire cabin of the Phantom was white. White leather seats. White carpets. White ceiling. It was like a white leather coffin, except with AC blasting. They probably would have coffins with AC at Forest Lawn now. Or maybe not *yet.* Everything took forever. You could die waiting for change. Or you could kill for it. The car's engine was silent. Partition up, there was no sound at all, and Susie's ears rang. The ear-ringing had been happening since she'd been Narcaned at the shrink's office. Next to her, her old friendly professor from NYU was fiddling with his buckle and, she thought, avoiding eye contact. *Was that really her old teacher?* Something seemed off, or was she just high, in a Rolls Royce, in the typical weirdness of Westside life?

Susie had demanded to see her mother, but by the time they reached the Medical Spa building at Doheny she was too high and changed her mind. Past the Chateau, cars dragged along in the sun. She imagined the pool glittering just below the giant billboard, people in swimwear. For some reason, that made her think of her old roommate, worm-food at eighteen. Supermodels starved themselves for money in New York. Everyone in LA wanted that fat ass. Was there anything central to the integrity of life, or was it all just passing fancy, infinitudes of luxury, gauchely driven toward silent nothingness? Maybe her roommate had gotten cut right in time—once you turned eighteen, life was no fun.

Would she have a counselor at this new place who wore turquoise jewelry and Eileen Fisher? Being dead didn't sound too bad. *Whoosh.* Would they have WiFi? Room service? Would she have a roommate? She didn't think she could handle any comingling of personal space at present, aside from perhaps the shared air of the communal residence, collective trash, and clay sewage pipes full of all their mixed together shit. We were all one, right? Is that what they'd try to tell her?

Why didn't she just go to Betty Ford? Because she wanted pills! Her old teacher already had her pills by the time he opened the door to the bunker using the code. He gave her two and he took two. She guessed he had kept using Oxy after The Carlyle. Was it somehow her fault? So how could he be running a rehab? What kind of brilliant scam was this? She smiled. *Good.*

She'd probably be the hottest person in rehab, anyhow. She guessed that was like being the youngest person in a nursing home. Or would it be run by The Church and filled with beautiful men and women drinking cucumber water with their sunglasses on, mourning their lost drugs, like Demi Lovato, Winona Ryder, or Ben Affleck. Whatever perdants du jour were in the pot. And Susie would be the only one without luggage. What would she wear? Was Phil in The Church?

Would her old teacher loan her some pajamas? Or Church-issued tracksuits? That might be cool, she kind of appreciated how Scientologists dressed around their complex in East Hollywood. Skinny ties, shawl-collar suits, classic blue and white (or black and white), she couldn't remember. They carried radios, clipboards, seemed official.

In dress clothes, they played casual with the secrets of the universe. Like if you knew those secrets of course you'd build a pyramid scheme and start conducting personality tests on the street. Trap Tom Cruise. Make him fuck your uncle. *You can't handle the truth!*

They looked official in a time when nothing was official, not cops or politicians or priests or musicians or ambulance drivers or anything, except firemen. Everyone loved firemen, because they were so young and hot. Blah blah blah blah. Firefighters was the term with no gender. The Scientologists had a draw, like they really believed that the mysteries of life had been solved by their higher ups.

She looked at Phil. Was he pathetic? His outfit, yes, but his sea-blue eyes behind the lenses of his gray glasses were interesting. He looked like he belonged at Madame Tussaud's—a nonhuman—which is what everybody wanted to be now, to not exist but to still be on Earth. A wax idiot. She didn't know what to say now. The old professor looked nervous and, actually, quite nuts, wringing his hands and staring at the TV screen set into the partition in front of them. Drugs fucked him up?

"Are you gonna vote?" she asked.

"Legally, nah," he replied.

"Me neither, I never . . . pointless."

"Uh huh."

In the past, back at NYU, he would have prepared a long soliloquy on the illusion of power given to the masses through the electoral college. She ventured another provocation.

"I mean you're only given two options? And you're not in a swing state?" But he said nothing, just stared at the screen.

Fine.

She didn't want to hear any bullshit anyway. She hoped the Female Candidate won, she guessed. Or did she? She was in the back of a Rolls against the white leather, high in an orbit of failure, hoping her mom would relapse and OD and burn to death from smoking in bed so Susie could just light a cigarette at the funeral, blow her an air kiss, blanket her father in silent comfort, patting his dumb fat head and kissing it, and taking control of his finances, ordering the groceries and buying party poodles; she didn't give a fuck who won.

She had to fart but held it in. The dash glowed in rich red. She farted. The partition wall was white leather accented with dark mahogany. In the partition frame there was another clock set into leather that glowed blue. What was this car, a time machine? A rolling watch? A Rolls Royce . . . a Rolex . . . why did the fat cats always want to roll? So lazy. Couldn't they walk? Her fart didn't even smell above the leather stink. *That* was true luxury. A platinum timepiece was set into the passenger's dash panel of gold, laser-cut art deco.

Why was her old teacher stoned and running a rehab? What was real? Would she get high and talk in group therapy all day? That sounded kind of *nice*. Maybe she'd have something important to say, like on television shows about the addicted where they solved the mystery for each addict about why they were so fucked up, and then some subjects got clean and others died.

Her old teacher looked perturbed. He was chewing his nails and spitting bits onto the carpet with wet puffs of air, which was like what some artists called an intervention, which was different from the other, boring kind; smarter, more creative. It *was* kind of brilliant, this *intervention*: spitting in a car that probably cost 700,000 dollars, the same Kim Kardashian and the Queen of England rode in. Why was he so quiet? He looked at Susie but quickly broke eye contact. Maybe he wasn't too happy to see her? Or maybe he was too happy and was trying to hide it. *The absence of proof is not the proof of absence* was one of her father's famous lawyerisms. Something like that. She should kill her father. Or get someone to do it. Maybe this guy. Was it even him? Something still didn't feel right. Maybe they needed to go back to The Carlyle, she thought, as he lit a cigarette, a different brand than in New York, a white and green pack of menthol Basics, and powered down his window.

"Sir, you can't smoke in here," the driver said, over the intercom. "Sorry."

"Dick said I control all reality. He told me everything." He looked around for a response. "I'm just smoking." He took a drag.

Warm wind coming in through the open window felt good on her face and on the cold skin of her arms, overly refrigerated by the car. It felt like wind through wet hair. The cigarette smoke—mixed with the leathery, fartless air—smelled good.

"Can I have one, pleeease?" she moaned.

Why wouldn't he look at her? He had always been self-conscious around her. She'd had that effect on him in and out of class. Whenever he looked at her playing cool in her chair-desk combo, he'd fumble to catch his thoughts mid-speech. Did he still like her or something? Why was he wearing that wig, and outfit, and glasses? She missed school. She sighed. Art and narrative were endless cycles of degradation and fetishization of success. If you wanted to succeed, you had to show people what they already recognized, but make it twisted, like you weren't asking for permission and were simply way smarter and more jaded than everyone else. You had to be able to talk in NPR voice, voice rising and falling, saying almost nothing, but sounding like you were profound and fresh in a way that accepted the whole world while criticizing it, or didn't criticize it at all, just understood it from the highest apex. Or did criticize the world but didn't seem like it.

"Hello?" he said. "Hello? Do you *hear* me?" She turned to look at him.

He was looking for some way to speak to the driver, a button or a microphone or a telephone. Was he stupid? Was this her old teacher? He spoke differently; was he putting on an act? Was that a new mole? From the sunshine?

Susie began glaring out the window. The sun baked the tall green palm trees. Susie saw dirty fishtail stucco on Spanish architecture. Gray and white under the high blue sky, not as smoky today. This part of town was ugly. The driver pulled over beside a building and parked the Rolls. A partition came down and the driver handed a briefcase through the opening, which Peter ignored. Susie grabbed for the case but the man refused to let go.

"Peter," the man said.

Peter? Phil, he meant?

Prying her hand off the handle and opening it, Krolik pulled out bags of pills of so many colors, shapes, and sizes.

"Holy shit," she said and tried to think how she could get her hands inside the case as he greedily snapped it shut.

"So, how do you know my mom?"

"I don't."

"Yeah, right."

"I don't know her."

"Are you part of The Church? You idiot."

"I don't know."

"It's not like we fucked," she said and felt young and gauche and wanted to be truly free. Rob the gold bars from her dad's garden, kidnap herself for a large ransom. Was he devoted to The Church now, too, like her mom? Protective of their secrets? Hiding some made-up spirit math?

"You're riding in Sickler's limo, acting like *you* can help *me*? I think *you* need help."

"This isn't a limo."

"Remember this?" She twisted herself in her seat to show him the stripe of scar across her throat.

He looked and nodded. "What about it?"

She laughed and scrunched her nose. "You're so LA now."

"I'm not interested. Let's go in." He put out his hand for her to shake. His palm was hot and dry against hers. Had they ever touched each other so earnestly before? She pulled her hand away, a little unnerved. Why was she nervous?

"Is it nice in there? No, right? Is there WiFi?"

"It's great."

"It's a shithole, huh."

"A shithole is a hole you shit in."

16

Royal-Lee's Locked in the Basement . . .

Royal-Lee crawled around the basement, feeling pitiful, awed by visions in the dark. Their eye burned and throbbed, hot with blood, with an outer ring of numb flesh, like flame burning through ice. In blackness, specters of colors bloomed electric pink and teal, with gold dotting the periphery. Purples floated through the inky dark. It had been a completely unnecessary attack; surely motivated from a place of nationalistic hatred.

Or why the punch?

They'd been cooperating. After Peter left, and after making sure Phil was okay, Royal-Lee went to change upstairs and before they could return to Phil, chilling stoned in the basement, they had been robbed by Surlies. Shoved through the basement door, they'd fallen down the stairs, catching the handrail, trying to turn back and rush up through the door, but then an asshole named Simon hit them hard in the eye. The door was slammed shut and the power went out. There was no light, no fan, no humming of the horizontal cooler in the basement where Royal-Lee fell and crawled along the floor in a Tom Ford Dylan Wool-Silk Twill suit.

God always seemed like the director of a horror flick, full of slashings and possessions, heads spinning around, walls moving and spirits growling from hell. But that wasn't real, Peter—no, *PHIL*—had said. The film projector was run down here. There was science. There was reason . . . but Royal-Lee didn't know what reason actually meant. Did anyone? This basement was real . . . or was it? Was anything? Was this pain they felt? What we thought about colored our reality, like the lights playing through their head from the impact to their eye, or from falling down the stairs, which was a result of the day's misfortunes, which was a result of Delray quitting, and the result of Phil at The Church, which Royal-Lee had always felt was a sketchy organization with diabolic ideas and occultist practices that no one should be messing around with, but it was all about how you processed it, right? What you felt and believed created reality . . . and they believed it might be time to leave the Villa for good. Melissa had orchestrated the robbery; she had the gun, like she'd said.

Their left eye throbbed and red bands of light floated like silk scarves through the dark theatre of their mind. Royal-Lee did some CBT and looked for Phil, who was high, somewhere down here, where Royal-Lee was now trapped.

"Phil?" It sounded weird to call out this new name.

Everything felt wrong today. Maybe it had always felt wrong. It had taken a lot of justification to make it seem right. They brought their hand over their eye, as if holding an icepack, and felt it throb and swell and went looking for their lordship and knocked their shin into something.

In the grainy blackness, trying to find the cot where Phil was chilling gave them the impression of being in two different worlds, both in the basement and in the space of some theater of their consciousness. Was there someone with a knife down here? Would they feel the hot blade pierce through their organs at any moment? Royal-Lee couldn't tell if they were being childish, and felt with both hands, bending low, searching for the cot.

"Hello?" they called. "Hello? Phil?"

Royal-Lee swung an arm out and ducked still lower, searching for their lordship, and bashed their head into the long horizontal freezer. Finally, they found the flat, muscled stomach and sunken abdomen of a man lying on his back. There was a large bulge where the man's hands were gathered across his groin and Royal's hands skimmed up the torso and chest and neck, and then found his face.

"Phil?"

Royal-Lee felt for air coming out of the man's nostrils, but there was nothing. Just a lot of moisture at his mouth—sticky wetness and loose flesh. *This can't be right*, Royal-Lee thought, tapping at the wet cheeks with one hand. Was his heart beating? *No heartbeat*. The wrist. *No pulse*. At the man's nose, no air. Was he really dead? *Phil?*

"Vic," they whispered hoarsely into the black. "Vic—where are you?" Where was Vic with his stupid tattoo of death and his bullshit? For some reason, Royal-Lee kissed the lips of the body of Phil. It didn't work, he wasn't moving or breathing.

He's still breathing, they tried to convince themself, thinking they felt something moving in his torso. They knelt down and put an ear against his heart and heard it beating, but it was just their own pulse throbbing in their own head. Royal-Lee almost smiled for a moment, leaning into the darkness, and then pulled their trembling hands away from the man's face. Was that a breath? They needed help.

Suddenly, as though Royal-Lee had manifested it in their mind, Peter was hollering upstairs.

"Hello? Hello, anyone?" Then murmurs. A nervous laugh, familiarly selfish, a voice recognizable from somewhere but not yet placeable.

"Hello? Anybody?" Peter was calling from upstairs.

"Help us!" Royal-Lee cried in a false voice, as if setting a trap. "Help, we're down here."

We, Royal-Lee thought, but didn't know what else to say. *Your brother is dead*, they almost yelled but stopped. They put their hand on his lordship's throat, hoping for a pulse; to do something drastic enough that it would bring their loved one back, they squeezed a little harder. Royal-Lee's eyes roved the darkness, big globs of hallucinatory lights in every corner. The lights had gone red and silvery now. *The Devil is down here. No. I'm just seeing stars*. They gagged and gasped and sobbed.

"Relax," the familiar voice said from the darkness.

Royal-Lee was shaking. They threw up on the dirt floor and although it was too dark to see the mess, they smelled its acrid stink, felt its warm miasma rising. In their mind, blue windows sat to either side of the darkness, off to the periphery of their inner vision. "I hear my twin upstairs. We don't wanna scare him off. Help me grab

Vic. Let's place him in the freezer." *It was Vic he'd kissed?* A first kiss with death?

"We have to tell someone."

"We definitely don't."

"What?"

"What do you mean, *what*? I'll deal with the body. For now, we just need to put him in to chill. Help me."

They couldn't believe any of this was real. What was wrong with them? What had they done? The wire bins were in the way and they put him down to pull those out and then lifted him again, lid held open by their heads.

"Higher, babe." Royal-Lee's heart soared.

They struggled to lift Vic over the freezer ledge. They thought words that were directed to God. *Please help me, free me, destroy me or save me or kill me, just put me where I belong.* Royal-Lee gulped. *Don't judge me. I didn't know . . . how could I know . . .*

They felt the lid slam down and knew they could never tell anyone.

"Hey, hey! We're down in the basement!" It wasn't Royal-Lee speaking, but for a moment they thought it was their own voice.

"Hello?"

"Peter," Phil called. *Phil*, Royal-Lee thought the name in their mind, turning it around: *Phil. Phil. Phil.* The man he loved, his name was Phil. Peter was a miserable bum. Phil was a beautiful man, and he was alive. Vic was dead in the ice box.

17

The First Time at the Villa . . .

Upstairs, I waited at the foot of the stage. The patients came down until there were over a dozen, all banded together, a mob of penniless, addicted foot soldiers. They demanded pills. A druggie mutiny against Royal-Lee, who had crawled up through the stage, their Tom Ford suit torn and bloodied and filthy. I wanted pills, too. I almost joined the shouting. Then Phil emerged out of the basement looking haggard and exhausted. If I had been closer to the front door, maybe I would have bailed, escaping the Villa forever. *Whoosh.* A thousand unanswered questions. Why had he just shaved his beard in the basement? He looked suddenly bigger.

At least Daddy wouldn't bother me now. Mom would tell him I was here to get better. Would he miss his soulmate, try to bust me out? Amy Winehouse syndrome? Turns out he didn't even give a shit. I didn't make him money. Although I would. I climbed onto the stage to extricate myself even a tiny bit from the all-too-human stink of piss and shit, bacteria and mildew, methane masked by incense as the patients grew nearer. I wanted to denude myself from a wreath of disgust at the Villa, deranged patients encroaching at the edge of the stage and my sanity. Soon enough it would be Xmas. Xanax. Chanukah. Manischewitz. But first Halloween. Ketamine. Then the election. Heroin. It was always funny how closely Halloween fell every four years to the horrors of election night. Thanksgiving. *Fuck my life.*

Was this to be my new life? I'd always been aroused socio-sexually by the popular girls in high school. Gilles Deleuze said: "A person's real charm is the side that shows them as somewhat unhinged, the side where even they don't really know their whereabouts . . . if you can't grasp the root or seed of madness in someone, you can't truly like them. You can't love them." But the people he said that about were the ones who didn't fall apart. The popular bitches with secret problems. I still wanted a future in the world of the elite. I didn't want to be like those bitches at Marlborough, their hair in ponytails, straight A's, driving Land Rovers in Umbro shorts that showed their symmetrically perfect young legs. Who smelled like perfume and lip gloss and gum. But even as a closet weirdo, I still had been sort of a popular girl, and now I was a dope fiend. These people had fallen through the cracks. An attractive dope fiend, which was dangerous in this house, this *Villa*. Anywhere. A rat scurried across the floor and I froze. The rat froze. Then it descended into the basement through a hole in the stage. Peter emerged from the basement with short hair.

I looked at Peter and then I looked at Phil, oh, dumb me, they were twins. I knew he had a fucking twin. How did I not get it? In Dick's phantom? Idiot! Well, one face was almost exactly the other. Only one had worn itself out. Like a poster on an old wall that had lost its color, protecting the wall behind it while everything else faded, ruining both. Like a room you returned to after so many years and peeled back the image to reveal the ravaged time you suddenly knew you could never get back. One brother had taken all the sun's damage while the other remained protected. One hadn't actually lived, while the other had experienced too much, was way too damaged. They ruined one another.

Peter was scruffy, wearing glasses, and holding the briefcase. Phil whispered in the ear of his brother, who begrudgingly crouched to open the case and pulled out two bags, one full of red Oxy and another that looked like birth control.

I'm sure Phil had no idea what the trial pills would do. How could he?

He later would be informed that the test drug was formulated to increase HU receptor availability in order to counteract the way Oxy trailed off in efficacy later in its delayed-release lifespan. But you had to take it in its prescribed form. To shoot the drug or smoke it or snort it would simply mean the increased receptivity afforded later in the drug's life would be made irrelevant by short-circuiting the delayed release quality of the medication, so the new drug would then augment nothing. The Villa's residents weren't interested in the details, just the big-picture news that the new drug would boost the Oxy.

The result, however, was that many of the "rehab" patients would refuse to follow protocols, would leave the Villa permanently, would overdose out on the streets, and those who did stay simply tongued the Oxy and trial pill, spit them out in a bathroom, flushed the trial pill, and shot the Oxy, claiming it was working *so good*.

Over the next month, Peter was the only addicted person in the house to successfully complete the drug trial. His situation improved, while Phil hit the skids. The rehab lost money, Dick Sickler got pissed, my dad left me alone, my mom went AWOL, and "the killer" stopped killing. I think those last motel scenes were already a copycat, as I've said, and I don't know how culpable Phil or Peter or even I may have been in inspiring more copycats to disfigure the poorest of the poor in our great town by the sea. If you do anything radical in this world, you risk incurring unwanted consequences—but as a younger artist, if you are not radical, you are a silent sellout. Silence does equal death. So does expression, sometimes.

For whatever reason, no new unhoused victims were discovered dismembered or dismantled or dissembled or disemboweled or disfigured for several weeks in any of the shitbag motels that stay filled with occupants from the ranks of lower nobility across Hollywood and Downtown and West Adams and Compton and the Valley and Canyon Country and Long Beach and Santa Ana and Anaheim and where-the-fuck-ever. More and more people can't afford housing, and permanently live in motels.

I watched the horde of addicts from the stage and debated making a run for it. I was semi-relieved that this was a place where addicts could get high. I was intimidated but intrigued and wondered whether there was any inspiration to be gained from spending a little time in a place like this with losers like these. Maybe there was some pleasure to be found being in a place that nobody took care of, like you didn't have to worry about period-staining the sheets or knocking over an antique vase. You could relax. Would it be a relief to be free from the uptight confines of my prior life? Could I learn anything from these shit people? Could I get my share of those large bags of red Oxy? Whose dick did I have to suck to get a constant supply? JK. I'd suck my own dick, get all the pills I wanted, and figure out how to manifest a better situation. Done, Dick, done.

18

Dick Sickler's, Holmby Hills . . .

My dad had been called over for an "emergency meeting" with his client, and Dick's corgis, Diana and Fergie, were out on the terrace, like two huge hamsters—shrunken pet versions of the Orange Candidate—scampering on all fours for treats. The house was a newly constructed six-story cube of black glass on stilts, paid for by an insurance settlement.

The new structure increased the value of the land it sat on, which had been purchased primarily with profits made, of course, off OxyContin. The irony of all this was not lost on my dad today, now that his daughter, moi, had been in rehab for several weeks.

He dreaded the meeting and maybe even missed me as he lifted and banged the front door's huge knocker, waiting with an edge of resentment on the ground-level patio and glancing up at the rest of the house. Potted palms and hibiscus, queen of the night, some other plants were reflected in the black mirrored glass of the tall facade. It was like a reversed California ranch had been bred with a Beverly Hills office building. It was a mini-Mecca with gold-railed wraparound patios on the fourth and fifth levels.

What was he even doing here? There was a big party happening on the property tonight and catering trucks and florists and decorators and service professionals of all kinds were parked on the huge paved drive and under the porte-cochere. Yet no one could open the fucking door? Where was Mitchel?

Dad stood in braided blue Ferragamo drivers, sockless, under a shiny Valentino sweatsuit with his salt-and-pepper hair gelled back. The suit was making him sweat like a jerk. He knew how to pick up his feet and walk, in spite of the hatred he felt for himself, which was rooted somewhere in boyhood abandonment and internalized antisemitism. He'd watched his brother get beat up as a kid for being Jewish, back in Chicago, and had been too powerless or chicken to interrupt the fight and save his own blood.

Today, maybe he felt hatred for Dick and this estate, but he could stand by and let things happen still, just as long as someone would open the fucking door so he could walk up and out onto the terrace. He knocked again and smashed the bell.

Should he drop Dick as his sole client, he'd often wondered? Be done with the Sickos? But how did you do that? You drop someone like Richard and who do you go work for next? Some tech-startup-idiots? What did a man do without his work? Take the boat out? Look at a swirly blue-breasted Picasso painting? He hated art. He didn't know anything about the arts except the LACMA A+F Gala each year where he drank too much. He didn't know that Jeffrey Deitch in his goggle glasses had been pushed out of MOCA for being too pop. What did he know about LA? He liked movies by Baz Luhrmann but couldn't remember his name. If he retired, he would do what: eat lobster and gamble more of his money?

They'd come back early from that trip to Vegas, which was inane; one stupid night and Dick got tired of his own lousy indiscretions, and canceled the rest of their stay, saying he had to throw together a last-minute party ahead of the big masked ball on election night. Call it a sneak peek. A preview. A rehearsal for *Big Dick November*. Dick hoped that tonight's masquerade would earn his redemption among his fellow Church elders. He needed forgiveness, or at least forgetfulness, for the bad press that "the killings" and the Emmys had brought. It was one thing to help kill over 500,000 people, but now Dick had something worse on his hands than the blood and genocide of the poor and the addicted; he had a PR crisis.

Dad had blood on his hands, too, even if he wasn't allowed to wash them clean at the party. He couldn't attend—he wasn't a member. Forget washing his hands in Dick's politicking; my father didn't like to look at himself in the mirror anymore. He was a loser facing the last third of his pathetic life, trapped, working for a madman. Of course, that was the world today.

The culture around money had changed rapidly. Dick and his family had recently lived at Hotel Bel-Air during their rebuild after the original house burned. It was set ablaze by his own birthday cake, which he had thrown off the balcony after being unwilling to blow out the seventy-some candles that his assistant Mitchel had lit, he thought, too slowly.

He could see Dick and the corgis out on the patio. Why wasn't anyone opening the door?

He pounded harder. He shouted up at Dick.

"Dick, it's me. Come down and open it yourself, maybe?"

The man couldn't hear him. He tried calling on his cell.

The estate felt like a redo of a tropical Eastern monastery: shaded and removed from the world. The fire had spared its original infrastructure of large bricked patios, with an outdoor fireplace and brick walls beyond modular couches on the lawn below. The lawn and hillsides were lush with mature landscaping: palmetto palms, blue butterfly bushes, forget-me-nots, fishtail palms, and golden wreath, plus the native oaks. Beyond this property, in the distance at Dick's brother-in-law's, with the horse barns and the tack house, was the arena where Faia and I had ridden as girls.

I had helped Mom teach my father the names of plants and flowers. He probably felt I had a wonderful fascination with botany and he couldn't help learning from me, before the drugs. Was I out fucking for pills now, he'd worry; being abused by some skinny little Hollywood pimp? Or worse yet, someone *his* own age and size? I was far tougher than that. Maybe I'd been just chipping Oxy, he'd hope. Maybe it wasn't so bad.

He remembered me painting, perhaps, and drawing, looking up at him through my long hair that grew soft and wispy near my bangs. Along the edge of the brick were pachysandra, hibiscus in bloom, wild pansies, cactus and ornamental agave, and he didn't know the names of the rest. I would know. *I would know.*

It wasn't a life he would have chosen for me, for his only child, and how did I get so fucked up, by people like his client, who wouldn't open the door? He'd tried to protect me behind a guard shack with that butch girl-guard and the other guards, their life stories we all knew, were kept informed of, sent flowers for the guards' losses. We had all been, me and my neighborhood friends, either very attractive or at least moderately well-formed, smartly dressed, emblem-adorned, and well-raised, even when we went through cuntish phases or shit ourselves from too many laxatives. He'd never expected I would turn into a dope fiend. Maybe I would have sooner, if I'd thought of it back in my cotillion days, if I knew it would get his attention.

Sure, we had our first underage tastes of semen and pussy in one another's homes. Our fathers were *not* captains of industry, but they *were* producers, lawyers, intelligent helpers of the upper echelon. Our mothers were lookers, engaged, involved in extracurricular or, well—what was the word? *Involved* in things. Some worked. But at college, at NYU, students had ambition and drive and some even came from crazy poor upbringings. James Franco was there. Not in LA where he *belonged*. Everyone was exceptional or trying be, and some got their work hung places, shitty places, but hung, while the only place I'd ever had my art plastered was all over the walls of my parents' house.

Anyhow, LA had been a lot of parties growing up, throughout high school, and we had been close, closer than I could explain, as if in some way me and Faia were united in the expanse of that blue sea off the coast of Malibu and our private beach clubs, our identities coterminous with Beverly Hills, Bel-Air, the Hollywood Hills, movies and music, a world of dreams only as expansive as our city and the streets named famous names, and all that sky and sun of the west, the music on our car speakers cruising the canyons. Our bodies. Our last names. Our identities. It had faded so fucking fast like a winter sunset, reminding me the dream of California had died before I was born.

In high school we had partied in the old house on this property that had since been reduced to ash. When our parents were out of town, on vacations, or business, we would sit in the cushioned marble conversation pit and spill imported beers, liquor, champagne, and orange juice on the fine, handwoven rugs and crank Dick's tube stereo and play with our iPhones and text and Facebook and fuck with boys and girls, and always there were Bentleys and Aston Martins, Alfa Romeos, and a '69 Porsche 917 all in the many garages to joyride—every industry had its problems, every elite circle, every fucking predatory practice . . . you didn't need to prove there were problems in the world, and make the case. *Grow up.* This was real life. Back then . . . fuck it. The fireplaces turned on by remote. We blew coke on Christmas, us Jews.

My dad continued to beat the brass door knocker against the giant doors. It was sculpted in the image of a spread eagle nude man with huge thighs and massive pecs, a pair of oversized solid testicles swinging from a ring where the figure's penis would otherwise be. Dad gripped the balls between his fingers and banged the knocker's load against the sunburst doors.

Sure, there was the pill epidemic, but there were low-orbit space condos to be built, environmental devastation to overcome . . . missions to Mars to save humanity. The human predicament at present was reaching critical mass and that would shield them, hopefully, by deflecting attention away from the drug crisis while increasing the urgent demand for their product. The world was losing itself. People were hopeless, and that was good for business. It was all about survival. There would be assassins, vigilantes, comic book incels, vainglorious shooters. Protect your neck and your own family, that was the name of the game.

Everyone would come for Dick, for Jews, for white people, for Dad, and the ultrarich. Dick always said it was time to stockpile wealth, to build silos, and connect with other people who had silos of their own, and that's why Dad had built his bunker. Dick said he should join his special society, but Dad just didn't have it in him. He didn't like other people that much, and he wasn't that rich. He knew it.

Plus, those societies were often linked to antisemitic theories. Dick said these theories could be used for good. Mom said he was OCD about being prepared for the end of the world. She was working for The Church now, since she'd gotten sober, some third act, and he knew her diagnosis of him was bullshit. He knew how to organize, prepare, but also how to relax.

Sometimes he could smoke a joint and watch a drop of water seep into the rug, the liquid spreading like the borders of an invading army, while watering his plants in his upstairs office. He smoked a cigar every now and then, the nicotine regrooving old routes of pleasure in his brain as he felt the blood pulsing in his thick fingers around the smoking leaf.

He liked handling his business, running in the mornings, reading the paper, knowing he was prepared for any disaster. But not this. Not his daughter on drugs. He loved me.

Without knowing, little things gave him pleasure but now everywhere he looked, the capitalist system he loved so much felt like it was under attack. The nation seemed second-rate, cheap, and meaningless. The people were turning on the empire. Things were heading for World War III. His daughter was a lost soul. How would he protect her as the world turned on them?

For the first time in many years, he wanted a cigarette. Even that would probably feel empty and cheap but what else was there to do? Life went on, as they say. He took a deep breath. I had no money. I would come home when I got desperate, like a cat, he thought. Or sober. I was too lazy to work—the thought made him anxious. There was always money to lure me back. That's right. He could assure himself that everyone was a brat, and as a man with wealth he was still the gold standard of power—Daddy Warbucks obsessed with revolution and gold bricks under the plum tree.

Dick Sickler was totally insane. He was convinced that Ingersoll Lockwood had written books about the Orange Nightmare being a time traveler and becoming president, and that dimensions were not fixed, but constantly being rearranged by our thoughts, or rather *his* thoughts, and that we were all living in a very different dimension than we had been in any period of human history before. I guess that may be true because we are living in a world full of conspiracies, ancient occult mystery schools, and it is the coming of the next age of tyrants and fascists and the new world war ahead, but this time it will be set in climate catastrophe and tech dystopia. They were getting prepared.

Dick was very high up in the secret society and my mother was attending the party here at his house tonight. Dad wasn't invited or allowed on site. Mom had gone missing

"Hello, Dick," he shouted toward the house from the brick walkway again, before pounding on the door and getting his phone out to call some more. Dick didn't seem to hear. Dad left a voicemail, his voice sounding falsely baritone, covering up the pain of my absence.

Dick had joined the fraternal order early in their business relationship and often insinuated he was privy to the secrets of the ordering of the free world. Many of LA's elite had been closely imbedded in secret societies since the dawn of Hollywood. Freemasons, Scottish Rite, The League, Ordo Templi Orientis, Knights Templar, Order of the Golden Dawn, The Knights of the Golden Circle, JPL, Disney's Club 33, and hell, even the Bohemian Grove up north, and the Bilderberg Group. Dick could and did go on and on about it, often. He liked to act like a soothsayer in Bel-Air, constantly rubbing his nose in knowing ways. He loved raising his eyebrows, blowing out his cheeks, and drinking, acting like he was aware that he was revealing too much and putting himself in grave danger with every empty aphorism. Maybe he really was in danger. Either way, he was annoying. He had graduated from a conspiracist into a paranoic with the money to afford all of his delusions.

His paranoia and money manifested in the car in his driveway: an armored bulletproof Mercedes S680. It was a BR6-level package with reinforced door hinges, total perimeter protection of passenger compartment, layered bullet-resistant glass, reinforced suspension, run-flat devices, and a weapons package.

When working to convince Dad to put a bunker in the Brentwood home, Dick said he already knew what was coming. He and his friends were extremely well prepared—had been for centuries. "Have you ever seen *Eyes Wide Shut?*" Dick had asked him. "Kubrick was a genius and and an occultist. He didn't really expose anything. It's all real, except it's far better than you could ever imagine. Of course, they would have killed both of them: Bill and Mandy, maybe Alice, too. Their kid. Just kidding. You really should join us, I mean, if you want, if you ever want, you can ask me anything."

Dad's IBS was flaring up, and he felt panicked. He hadn't taken a solid shit in years. Maybe it was stress, maybe it was Zoloft. Mitchel, a nearly seven-foot-tall Swede with thinning red hair, finally opened the door.

"Mr. Sickler has been waiting for you out on the balcony."

He moved down the pink runner, across the black-and-white checkered floor. Nothing held his attention anymore. Just thirst traps, memes, and the Internet, and wherever a bathroom lay waiting ahead of him. The news each day, however insane it got, was wearing him out. He went into the marble powder room and quickly played his deuce. Sitting at home in Brentwood and staring at the gold brocaded curtains in his office hadn't been helping so he'd answered this call. Came over. It would be a total waste of time, he was sure. He wiped and washed, hating to be without his bidet. Hemorrhoids. He climbed the stairs, as the elevator was out of service. Put first your common humanity, he told himself.

Out on the terrace, he said, "Dick," and stood clearing his throat, unsure if it was from acid reflux or to announce himself. Stoicism and service were the masks of the day. That was a good title: *The Masks of the Day.* Perhaps he could write a book. Fat chance; he might sooner paper the master bedroom of this home with all the NDAs he'd signed.

Dick was looking through a Nikon bino-telescope at the canyon's brim.

"Shhh, shhhh," Dick whispered.

"Oh, please," Dad said. Dick always pretended he was miffed at being interrupted, like he was the main character in a story of the world splitting apart. Dad had no patience for it. In the world of Dick, it was still sort of the age of Victorian romances, engagements, lords, and luxury, but totally perverted to the max.

Tonight there would be secret scenes, dances, and meetings Dad would never know; mingling in the society he had always wanted to be a part of back when he read domestic novels at boarding school back at Exeter, written mostly by women. It was all the same; who's who, rumors and secrets and mutually assured silence. Things were always twisted and what was his wife doing? He saw a bee, buzzing hard into the ceiling above them, so singularly occupied, headed for escape toward other bees with whom to nest. He felt like quitting. Hive collapse. Cuckoldry.

What was a blue sky for?

He was getting rather philosophical. LA asked for philosophy and intrigue, then fabricated a quick gesture. Lately, nothing seemed real. Not these last few years. Things kept changing around, like dimensions were shifting. Were we all antennas? What had his wife been doing with Dick so much of the time? Before she disappeared? He'd asked before and Dick always scoffed. *We're just friends.*

"What are you doing, Dick?"

"Watching the birds," he said and then lowered the glass and his eyes were flat slices of wet stone. Dick loved to waste his time like this, having him on retainer.

"There are no accidents," he said, setting the bino-scope down. He rubbed his nose with a silk pocket square like he was sending a secret semaphore to the bushes. "None. Not at the upper levels of society anyhow. Of course, the rest of society is just a mess. Who could live in it? In Claremont, shopping for mystical experiences at the yoga and crystal shops? Meanwhile we have the secrets. You know . . . if you *really* want to protect your family . . . just ask. Then you could come to the parties."

Diana, one of Dick's corgis, kept bottle-nosing his privates. He wanted to pick her up and throw her off the deck. He hated himself for being here today.

"Diana, stop that!" Dick said. "Forgive Diana; she's just a nosy little bitch, that's what got her namesake killed, am I right? Am I right?" He laughed with a big wet cough. "Just kidding. Just kidding. The place is probably bugged. Just kidding."

"Dick," he sighed, "What can I do for you?"

"Mr. V.," he began. He smiled to show a perfect row of caps, shaped like a tidy little village by the sea in gleaming white. He wore a colorful woven charm bracelet like a sex tourist in Thailand would wear. "How is Susie?"

"To be honest, not great," he could feel his face tightening into a grimace as his eyes watered.

"I'm sure she'll be fine! Young girls. We know what they like. Nothing so wrong about it. She will grow out of her party-girl years. We are being led by superior beings. Those of us on the inside are incredibly optimistic. I think she's in good hands. Good, good hands. Nice boy, sporty dresser."

Dick was wearing skin-tight, tan-through workout wear with UV protection, dotted with red wine drips down the shirtfront, under a zippered oatmeal Luca Faloni silk-cashmere top, and a visor Velcro-ed around silver hair under the bright orange Styrene brim. He looked pallidly vampiric and old. Was he a vampire? Was he not?

"I see you're checking out my workout clothes. They're fire retardant, most everything you see on me, and I like how slippery it feels on my skin. Diana and Fergie love it, too, because their paws don't catch on my fabric."

"You called me here, and you said it was an emergency. What is it? Forgive my saying so, but I need to get on with my personal day and I'm hungry, Dick."

"Oh, I could have Mitchel get you some soup."

"I hate soup. It's so weak, just lying there."

"Do you want a cookie?"

"No. I'm back on the diet."

"Right, well. I want to show you something very upsetting. I'm very upset about it, and I think you will be, too. Now, as they say on the news, what I'm about to show you is extremely graphic. Mitchel! Bring the document!"

Mitchel strolled onto the patio with a piece of paper in a three-hole-punch plastic sheet protector. "Sir."

"Thank you, Mitchel. Give it straight to Master Vogelman. I don't want to see it. My eyes can't take it again." He was playing his game.

It was a crayon drawing of a swirl of pink under a swirl of yellow.

"What am I looking at, Dick?"

"It's elder abuse. My four-year old granddaughter thinks it's funny to draw pictures of her grandfather either using symbology she learned from her predator family members who are molesting her mind as part of the family legacy of control, or merely as an obese swirl . . . she thinks I look *fat*, or she's referencing the minotaur and child sacrifice. Of course, her mother, my own child, is menacing me or she wouldn't have let me see it. I catch them only on holidays. She brought it to me as an act of violence. She wants to separate me from the family. I've tried to be very close to this little girl. After this I want her taken out of my will, which means her mother must be cut as well. I don't want one drop of my riches going to those people. Not that it will affect her much. The entire family is so rich her mother has started using the term 'Social Entrepreneur.' Trust me . . . it's not meaningless language. She's inventing new ways to profit off of what was once our realm of pure philanthropy. Like those stupid videos my cousin's daughter made. It's a new world, David: you can profit off philanthropy, especially in art. You know how it works. Give a little, get nothing. Give a lot, get on the board, influence what enters museums, have a private collection in your wings that sky-rockets, plus you write off the gift. The good old days are now. That and surveillance capitalism—making money off seeing the most from the highest point. It works. We know it works. Know what's coming before it comes. Why aren't you doing that? Legally speaking? Before everyone sues us over our drugs. You know your signature is on that document. You need a Trust Protector who will enforce the proper distribution of your estate if anything happens to you. What, it's like painkillers could ever come without a price? Nothing can be created or destroyed. That's what Einstein said. Or Epstein. Pain can only be transferred. That's what you're for. You transfer my pain. So it's not my problem. It's yours. You're on the line."

"I know all of this. Actually, that was Antoine Lavoisier."

"Never heard of him. Do you know Kate Middleton, sweetheart of a woman, back when she saw our courtyard at the consecration of some museum in London, she mouthed to me, 'Wow.' Do you understand what I'm saying? Dad would be so pleased to see we have Sickler staircases in museums, escalators, crossings and roses, asteroids and everything named after us. Trust me. True they blackballed us from some boards, and rented our temple to that goddamn designer.

They stopped letting us store our private collection in a few museum basements. Fuck 'em. The will needs to be amended immediately. Given my fragile state, I could go in a moment. I could go tonight. That's why I have Mitchel here. He's trained in CPR. Cut her from my will! My daughter the ingrate! I never hear from her and now this."

"Are you sure you want to do that? Your granddaughter is only a child. She doesn't have the motor skills to draw a person accurately."

"Oh, don't give me that motor skills nonsense. Grow a pair! You dickless simp. My own granddaughter drawing me as a blob. In a circle of hell! You have to understand, the new generation of American children are being raised to be completely inept. Startling that this child can even hold a crayon. I won't fund a loser like that. Kids now have no ideas. They're manufactured to live in liberal groupthink. The Millennials are nothing but mild-mannered servants, collectivist thinkers doing group projects for a living, unable to form a personality aside from their monstrous online outrage against the patriarchy. And the generation after, god help us all. That's what they say now: *patriarchy. Leftist.* Led by graduate school think, they gesture at large fuzzy concepts with complaints they got from someone else, hoping the empire that protects them will fall. They'll try to come for us. I've done the research. I have a *Facebook*. They post pictures of their oiled-up asses."

Dad was getting sweaty again.

He didn't want to hear Dick talking about his daughter's generation like this. This was all for what? Dick was a disgusting, visor-wearing, flame-retardant billionaire whack job. US doctors wrote 300 million prescriptions yearly for opioid painkillers. The US consumed 39 tons of the "pain medicine," which is 99 percent of the world's supply. We had 70,000 overdoses per year in this country. The chances of recovering were pretty slim. This childish crayon swirl. It brought back memories. The Sicklers were killing his daughter. Dick and Dad were killing me.

"So, I want to give all *her* money to elderly corgis and soup kitchens. I want you to amend my will, tonight," he cupped his hand around his visor like a halfhearted salute. "Mitchel has already taken her and her family off of the invite lists to all my holiday parties and fundraisers and removed photos of them from the virtual albums. Or I'll give all of her money to her sister, Faia. Yes, do that. Fuck Soup kitchens. You're right, it all just lays there, anyway, like the lazy people waiting to receive it. Fuck Oliver Twist. *The idiots always want more.* I've been doing Pilates and working with a trainer for forty years. Do you know what kind of sacrifice that takes? Skipped cocktails? Skipped carbs? Fat-free everything? She makes me a fucking swirl." He let go of the visor and bobbled his head like he was stunned.

"Dick . . . it makes me nervous to see you becoming so reliant on this young Mitchel . . . but as you like." He got up to leave and Dick grabbed his sleeve.

"Wait. Wait. Mr. V., what's your rush? Have a drink? Loosen that tie?" He reached over and pulled on his tie playfully. "Mitchel, come out here. Mitchel!" he cried.

"Mitch. Put these stereo speakers on out here. That's what we paid so much to that lousy subcontractor for. *So* . . . Let's have some music. And bring a bottle of Dom. And charcuterie. That duck cognac pâté."

Dad was stuck. He'd sit out on the patio and drink wine and eat duck with Dick until the sun went down beyond the canyon and then he'd drive home and we'd arrive hours later at around 10:15 p.m. for the party, fashionably late, reasonably attired, although clearly sporting cheap costumes among people who took their masks and cloaks seriously. We were obvious interlopers among the masters of the universe, who wore faces and robes handed down for decades and centuries, or else had them custom-made in recent years by the likes of Sergio Boldrin, or other even more secretive and selective makers of the finest Venetian masquerade masks in the world. We would show up like Manson and his girls, unannounced, infiltrating the crowd, but at this time, we were merely scouting.

19

The Party, Holmby Hills . . .

LA has its own force field of reality absence—it doesn't matter who the president is so much as who's currently running MGM, Universal, or Sony; who are the chief executive officers at A24 or Netflix; who's directing LACMA or MOCA. As long as you're in Los Angeles, you're inside the dream. And if you're famous, you've *found* the dream. You just hope you can hold onto it—keep to yourself and to others who are crucial—everyone caught in the push-pull of being seen and unseen while staying relevant.

Then you're *in*. And if you're on top, you're already disappointed—disillusioned and wanting more. Because the dream, once achieved, becomes nothing. Unless you're a true creative.

I'd seen it so many times: fuckboys, fuckheads, actors, rich dicks. If you aren't *of it*, you stick out. The cool thing to be in LA is incognito. No one cared who came to the party, as long as they had the password.

Which is why, when Peter, Phil, Royal-Lee, and I pulled up to Dick's house in the Continental—drop-top up—in robes and masks, no one even blinked an eye.

You can still trust this novelization. It's all true, mostly, although Dick was right, you can't actually say what happens at the parties, so take this chapter for what it is, an homage to cinema, a play within a play, a dream within a dream, which is the genius of Kubrick's *second* greatest film, next only to the 1975 seven-category Oscar-nominated and four-time Oscar winner *Barry Lyndon*—adapted of course from William Makepeace Thackeray's *The Luck of Barry Lyndon: A Romance of the Last Century*. The luck, indeed.

Peter pulled up to the valet and gave the keys to an oldish Filipino gentleman and this white guy, who both seemed like surfers in their pink khakis, dressed like valets at the Parker hotel in Palm Springs. They were the sort of men who would listen to *The Beach Boys*, smoke a joint, put their feet up, and smile all the time, like they were back in the days when it was cool to be cool, and then drive down to Huntington Beach for an early morning surf session.

These guys didn't care about secret society perverts who carried out the ancient occultism of Egyptian or Roman pagan mystery schools through the magic of new dark arts, employing traditions that work—for power, for faith, for cover—while executing the time-tested tactics of infiltrating and stealing the last of the world from the poor and selling it to one another, while trapping one another. I have to be honest. I can't *really* tell you what happened at this party. I can tell you I am afraid if I actually write and publish it, even as autofiction, or whatever, it could get me and my family . . . well, *fucked* . . . look, it is too attractive to create a story to explain why everything seems awful and ludicrous, and I need you to understand these people do not rule the world, per se, but also, I need you to know they are powerful, and it all fits so perfectly together with what Kant named the *a priori* categories of humankind, how rumor and fear and religion and myth are all forms of something inside of us that actually form the universe—a vastly expanding, limitless universe of infinitudes . . . and these people tap into that by existing outside of the brainwash of conformity and the limitation of law. *The Killers*. The lobbyists, the lawmakers, the money movers.

The solipsists say one constructs one's own universe . . . and there is a level of truth to this which Phil told me The Church taught him, while acknowledging the predicament of Immanuel Kant and the moral imperative that assumes the presence of others to be valid.

They, too, wrestled with Kierkegaard's maxim that we must assume the presence of God, and yet they suggested that God could be anything one chooses . . . the entire joy and terror of life was in not knowing if anything was real, and that was the true existential hell and heavenly wonder of living. It opens the door to Spinoza and from Spinoza you can spin yourself dizzy with anything you wish to create, to do, to experience, and to control. The only true maxim: you must fully experience all that life offers or you are cheating yourself out of your opportunity to thrive on this psychic plane, the only true given: *experience*.

Phil remembered riding his bike past the Masonic hall in their town when he was a kid, and the weird spooky stuff on the dollar bills, and his friend's parents saying that the Devil lived in Hollywood, and could snatch him and his brother right through the VCR.

His parents and their friends sometimes met in Quaker halls and held prayer circles and read from the Bible. He had never been inside a Masonic lodge. How was that possible? Were they more or less powerful than The Church? Something was always lurking under the surface of America and he'd felt it as a child in the classes he took, learning to write with pencil on paper; he'd always felt it, something *bigger*. Something was training the population to be docile, scared, disempowered . . . he lost his train of thought. This always happened to him right at the most crucial moment. The valet guys had the doors open and we'd all gotten out of the car and Peter, who was sober enough to drive, was hiking up his robe to search his pants for cash.

"Sir, we do not accept tips."

* * *

Lights reflected from the surface of the pool floating in the dark of the grass beyond the path of potted fishtail palms. At the large brutalist sunburst doors, a guard with a thin, wiry frame and oyster eyes stood stiffly in a black Securitas uniform, with a .44 strapped to one thigh, doing his job inside the entrance of the marble foyer and hall, watching Peter as he entered. The guard caught his glance through the mask and nodded almost imperceptibly.

LA didn't often do guards with guns at parties but this guy looked like he was packing a few. Sometimes Phil felt like he was part of the problem with his white skin and his penis, but in this mask and cape no one knew your face or race. He had taken a red pill and a few pinks and floated into the foyer in the company of three others: me, his brother, and Royal-Lee. Wasn't it better to be without an identity? When everyone hated everyone, and people meant death for the planet—when the whole notion of an identity rested on the idea that an individual life was either worth living only if it reflected in a huge bank account, or else it was just a burden for legal purposes—anonymity was liberating. To be high and to be masked and cloaked was liberating. Thank God for drugs, he thought, and then the irony of the full circle of events came crashing down on him like the wave of calm the pills gave him. Phil was high. Fuck it. It felt good. Bring on the coke. Bring on the dope. Bring on the hors d'oeuvres. Bring on the hardcore fucking.

Peter wasn't *high*. He and I were both on a low dose of Oxy and the trial pills. I felt okay, just okay, on a little more Oxy than he was, and curious about the party inside. I guess I was nervous. I took a deep breath but it didn't work. It never worked. Breathing was fucking stupid. I felt like a criminal, like they could all see me under the robe and mask, and look through my scalp down into my brain, see *my double identity as the Susie who had grown up playing around this estate, and the one now sleepwalking through it like a stranger.* An infiltrator, a traitor, or just an emptiness, like the absence that Nietzsche wrote was at the heart of every great artwork. Johnny Depp's eye winked at me in the vestibule from behind a mask of the three faces of the *Commedia dell'arte*, and the dimmed glow of sconces reflected off the mask's glazing. There was no way it was him, right?

There *were* boys modeling women's panties in the lower library, others in women's high fashion. There were naked trans girls with budding breasts dancing with large silk scarves through the ballroom, women in men's underwear—stuffing, or not stuffing—women in men's suits, outfits made of what looked like dried human skin, but they couldn't be, could they? An old man with a giant bulbous phallus followed, in a mask, weaving between people in cloaks, all wearing masks. A tall copper alloy statue of a cat-headed god lurked against a stone wall.

Royal-Lee stood trembling and took a step and tripped and got back up with Peter's help. He absent-mindedly patted Royal-Lee's groin through the silk cape, tapping little circles with the palm of his hand over the material and then stopped. I could almost feel the sensation inside of my own body, sending an electric line to the center of me that was hungry, spasming, unfucked, while all these people touched one another, kissed mask to mask, lead another person or persons to private rooms. Peter held Royal-Lee's hand.

Where was Mom? I wanted to ask her: in sum total, was the world really owned and run by occult hermeticism, holding perverted orgies like this, like people suspected, in top-secret conspiring societies, who'd taken, a thousand or more years ago, false knowledge to the extreme? Was it all really just sex rituals, entrapment, liberation through perversity and shared excess?

I was feeling a little funny. I said it over again to myself. *I feel sort of funny,* like I was practicing for what I'd say to anyone if I ever explained my being at this party. I was dressed poorly. We had gone to Ursula's Costumes to get the carnival masks and capes. Phil was wearing a Prince mask from *Purple Rain* and Royal-Lee wore a black Uma wig from *Pulp Fiction* above a gold Venetian Madonna mask made from recycled paper, decorated in gold and silver leaf with a red ribbon tie. Peter wore a Maschera Tragica Bianca. I donned a traditional baroque Venetian sun mask, which would normally be made of paper mache, but was cheap acrylic, with macramé and passementerie; glitter and plastic crystals inside the mouth, along the brow, and in each of the sun's triangular rays. I wore a white macramé cape over a silver robe. I hoped we weren't fucking this up. My hair was cleaned up but it didn't matter. The cloaks and masks made us all holographic. I forced myself back into a fine carved wooden chair and watched. I took off the macramé; it had been a bad choice.

What was tonight's message? Whether you were going to save it or love it, this last of it, as the world rushed toward robots and totalitarian states, toward extinction and collapse—even if it could redefine itself and its systems in a best-case scenario, Earth as we knew it wasn't going to remain the same, and you had to worship it, feel it on your skin, in your very being, all you ever knew, tonight, and then turn yourself upon it to devour it, either through destruction or total engagement and enjoyment, guiltlessly, wordlessly. The sounds of opera, classical music, the clarinet, violin, human voice, the beauty of the music from that golden era of classical renaissance, emanated gently from the study; was it live? Of course it was.

In the music was the sound of us all, the majesty and thrill and the hunger and boredom, and you could ride it over and out with your mind but even more than that I could feel it in each episode of being in my body—my organs, my clitoris, my cells, my mitochondria, my Golgi apparatus, my atoms, my subatoms, my nucleus, my subnucleus, the space and dots that made up the subnucleus—and then the space itself, and the pure being of eternity. There was no bottom. There was no top. The floor was black and white, a symbol, like everything in this party at the micro-palace on this micro-plane of existence.

Phil examined his hair in the mirror on the wall.

Peter went and stood beside him. Their masks reflected back in the glass. It was like they were speaking to one another without language, without sound: Who is the one who does nothing, changes nothing, who affords nothing to be done in the face of brute injustice, irreligious piety, and social sickness? *Hi*, they were talking to the dying era. Damn the ego and damn the self that doesn't make the world change, but do not *damn* the self. These people be damned! Phil Krolik, before he was Peter Holiday, had passed through this world an outrageous slave, a plebeian, a choiceless user of worlds designed by others, unaware of the enormity of his complicity. Peter Krolik had been its junkie. Not raging, not swollen with righteous anger, not feeling the passion for his time being alive; they'd surrendered their deepest feelings as children under parental abuse to the fleets of power and control. Who were they? If they had a collision in mind, and effectuated it, choosing grave crimes, they could awaken each other to every moment of sun and dark, every stone in and above the city of LA. They could find real life. Look where they were now! Look what they had found! The inner sanctum of power. Not wardens or past masters. The flowers of privilege. This garden of night.

It was a time in America. Post-America. Where the dream was a pantomime as it always has been. Now it was all clear. In any liberal city, any wealthy city, you could see it so clearly. How meaningless it all was. All art had become marketing. Branding. The beautiful people weren't beautiful, although these bodies around them on display were attractive, and they were getting sexually excited, but people were turning into emojis, as the world was shifting rapidly and the shift was away from humans, away from the value of any life, and always toward hatred and systemization. Systems were trumping humanity—and everyone was lining up like families at Disneyland, or people boarding the trains to the camps that would surely come again from the wing.

We all wandered into the cigar room, on the third floor, where there was an art hoard of South Asian sculpture, paintings by Manet and Monet, Pissarro and Picasso (who I'd someday see that Larry Gagosian also hung both in his home), Chagall and Courbet, as well as various hunks of jade, jewelry and pottery, and other shit that meant nothing to the world today. A man in an ancient large leather horsehead mask with a movable tongue was speaking to a group of men in tuxedos with assorted masks ranging in shapes from animals playing cards to Greek gods and former presidents of the United States of America. They had young hands and the shiny new shoes of youth. These were not the grand elders, but a captive audience of underlings, bobbing their heads and holding drinks and sipping through straws to avoid lifting their masks.

"It's going to be a *grand* election. Disinformation's better than ever. The media? Useless. Can't keep their eye on the ball, crying about 'American reality.' The Democrats? They couldn't elect themselves out of a blood-soaked paper bag. They're betting on a woman now? Against a golden god from New York? What do they think—crying'll save them? Organizing? Collective pouting? We've got theurgy, they've got pity parties."

"Ha. Ha. Ha," the underlings laughed.

"Yes, indeed, ours is the last generation that'll know the planet before it grows inhospitable. This is it. Last breaths of the old world. After this? It's strip-mining the moon and surveillance forever. The riff-raff'll die off. That's not on me. Don't look at me. The Emmys. A goldmine. A grand performance. Wasn't mine. Doesn't hurt. Yes, some losers carved up in motels. So what? Fred who? Won't stick. It never does. We've got the next story already written. We've got people in the rooms where it gets shaped. Transmutation begins with acceptance, and then alchemy, making it all One. Some people want off the train, some people want on the train. It's cosmic transportation.

"It's no tragedy. This is nature. Evolution. Don't we owe the race *something*? Our souls? Our cunning? We're not people anymore. People is a word of the past. Think bigger. Think outside the body. You're not human—you're alien now. Interdimensional. Independent. Yes, I recall my hermetic axioms: one is to become god not by becoming less human, but by realizing what is truly human. Well, this *is* what being truly human looks like. Renouncing the old and embracing the new. I renounce my old country. I renounce the cowardice of this whole pathetic species. *Humanity. Is. Over.* Let 'em dig for cobalt. Let 'em choke on deep sea gas. He's going to free us—*through* nationalism. That's the joke. That's the magic trick. You already know. You've already joined. You gave up your past the moment you chose power."

"Hear, hear," the young men agreed.

"So grab a partner. Grab anyone you want. The rules are gone. You're not a citizen anymore. You're not a person. You're *one of us.*

"And me? I'll be fine. This'll blow over. The ones dying? They're losers. They were always gonna die. I'm never going to die. Why would I? And lose all this money?"

It was Dick Sickler talking.

He came over and touched my hand, lifted it, and studied it like he recognized the lines of my knuckles. He put his hands over my breasts through the silky material of the cloak. He tried to lead me by my hand upstairs, but Phil took my other hand and waved a finger. People in cloaks circled us, terrifying masks coming near as if to smell us out.

"I don't feel well," I muttered. "I feel sort of funny," I said, as I'd practiced before in my head, and pulled myself away from everyone, rushing up the stairs and finding the Tuscan bathroom off the master bedroom on the fifth floor.

It held a large tub in the center of the room beneath a recessed ceiling. There were people in the shower, fucking, and people in both of the toilet areas, and people snorting ketamine, or coke, or heroin off silver plates at the various vanities. And there were two figures in Venetian cat masks—sleek and ivory, sculpted like the faces of indifferent gods, their mouths left open to expose the lips, working loosely beneath—lying on top of each other in a lazy sixty-nine. Around them, bodies performed other acts, sex acts, but all of it felt disinterested, mechanical, like a looped demonstration, everyone just going through what they were supposed to do, in the ways that each thing could be done, spread across the tile floors and quartz counters. The warm fall air drifted through the open windows, mixing with the manufactured coolness from the ductwork, the chemical perfume of commercial air fresheners pumping in scent to chase away the stink of sex. And outside, the richest neighborhood in LA exhaled—cars, noise, sirens, all a million miles away and also so close you could feel the city pressing its nose to the glass. The pure being of eternity shimmering on the edge of the city's shore.

"It is the time of preparations," a voice echoed from outside the door as I went to leave the bathroom. It was Dick again.

"We are free, free of it all. Let's fuck. Let's have sex with that small young person. Let's love each other through them."

"Fine, Dick." I think I heard my mom's voice. She was talking to Dick, in his horse mask. She was wearing a buckram green hummingbird mask made from silk velvet wire lace and felt, decorated with a jeweled baroque wire beak, which was the half-stick by which her mask was held to her face.

I went and sat on the patio furniture and smoked a cigarette that Phil had given me. I'd dug the jewel out of the hole where the mouth opening was in the mask. People were talking about swimming. They were going to take a dip. I didn't have a suit. Someone asked me to skinny dip and I said no. Sure, I wanted to feel free. Freer than in years of reading Jacques Lacan or about Desdemona when I was Phil's student, filling in scantrons for art history exams and writing my student ID number on tests in lecture halls, but I couldn't let anyone see me at this party. I was afraid Dick already knew who I was, and that I was here, and he would tell my mom, but also, who cared? I *cared*, suddenly, less high than usual, afraid of this party. It was scary to me, I admit, being there, uninvited, among these people. I suddenly realized

I lived in a world of very serious men and women and they were all around me. I was sad about Mom and Dad. I was sad.

The city shone out there just waiting to be loved, to be given the gift of my art that could be used to save the world, somehow—the animals, the people, the entire planet, the strange phenomenon of being—rescued from total ruin. I wanted to help. I wanted to love the world. I wanted to be able to look into the eyes of all, homeless, rich, average. I wanted connection. Maybe it was from watching the skin of nudity, the fucking, the shadow and reveal of genitals, animal poses, force and movement, approaching, reapproaching, the smell, that made me think of the eyes of the people in the world and how they seemed trapped: wanting, waiting, hopeful, desperate, but also locked inside from all the years of hatred and hurt, from toxic messages, and programming from the pervasive endless information era about how wrong everything was, the systems of oppression, each macroaggression and microaggression, each bomb, each murder, the sad trap of our minds and bodies, and the indomitable persistence of *hope*. What was *hope*? I wanted to experience some of the kind of release I'd seen happening inside those rooms where people were letting go and fucking, moving their bodies, feeling connection. Then my thoughts were interrupted, and I was watching both Phil and Peter talking to Dick, who was giving them some sort of stern lecture from his horse-head mask, probably because they hadn't paid the fine and weren't going to, as they had no money.

Royal-Lee came and sat next to me and I put my arm around their shoulders and we watched, wondering what was being said. Would the brothers let him penetrate me or Royal-Lee as tribute? In place of the fine they couldn't afford? How was the drug trial going? Later I'd learn they'd explained they'd lost a lot of patients, because no one liked the new drug—Phil was thinking of leaving The Church—and Peter was asking for advice.

"Impossible," Sickler had said. "Give them more. More Oxy. More trial pills. Fake the data. I just need reports to turn over to the FDA. This guy, he's on our side, they're all on our side. They're here. See that monkey? Big time. Just give me something I can work with." His hands shook. A man in a Plague Doctor mask was entering another man's asshole, who was bent over the balustrade, with his fist.

Royal-Lee's eyes met mine so easily and were innocent but also shocked in a sort of silent shame, their programming triggered, the expression of "What am I doing here?"—a glance of childlike embarrassment, turning to outrage mixed with desire. I smiled with my eyes. I was ready to go home to the Villa, or somewhere. Dick wasn't letting the two brothers go yet. He was shaking his finger at them. He was making a gesture that was threatening, and I waited, and held Royal-Lee's hand, and knew that things were never going to be the same after this party. The wind tousled my hair and lifted the smoke from my cigarette. The Uma Thurman wig didn't move.

"Don't let your junkies lie around. Get them online spreading information. Involve them in politics. It works. Haven't you been learning anything? Are you some kind of buffoon? Are you an idiot?"

Whatever was happening with Dick and Peter and Phil, it didn't look good, and I would later learn what Dick was pushing them to do—rig the drug trial, help get the right guy elected, and that it was all part of the plan, this party, this meeting on the balcony, this election, and the empire; it was all part of the plans of the most powerful men in town. I didn't know it then, but there were Saudis and Russians and Israelis, Koreans and Chinese and American politicians, and tech giants, and artists, all celebrating at the party, living their dream, pumping the world for whatever could come next, all in the Los Angeles night in a world of flesh and human puppet theater—brought from the culture where the masquerade ball had emanated five thousand years ago in the land of Greece, that, ecologically and geographically speaking, looked a lot like LA.

20

Epiphany Strikes Susie on Skid Row . . .

A week after the party, my mother—who had been involved in a cuckold orchestrated by Dick Sickler and employing a younger man at that godawful party—still hadn't come home to my father, and he'd been rapid-fire texting me.

HELL is going on, Susie? Your mother is GONE and no one will tell me a goddamn thing.

I'm not playing detective in a porno. This is your MOTHER. Where is she???

You think this is a joke? You think it's some bohemian game?

She's your mother. Doesn't she tell you anything? Doesn't she text you?

Every woman in this family is a stupid cunt? Are you SOBER?

I'm sorry . . . I'm just upset.

Susie?

Phil didn't want me to respond, and neither did Peter, until they had more residents at the rehab for the drug trial. It all seemed stupid to me, but Dick had made a deal with the two brothers and he was going to pay them a lot of money as long as they played ball. I was unsure how politics fit into my life, or what the drug trial had to do with the Orange Candidate, and really, I was having a hard time telling Peter and Phil apart, as they were switching off wearing the beard or wig or combo. Or maybe I was making that up, as I couldn't stay sober, not really, and every time I got too high, I saw Faia's face—judging me like I was some pill-popping clown from a family of monsters. At the last minute, the brothers bailed on taking to the streets to find new comrade addicts in need; I don't know why.

They designated Tom, the guy with the neck and face tats—who'd been so usefully chill when Royal-Lee had conducted the bumpy group therapy session at the Villa on the day of my arrival and who had lived on Skid Row before coming to the Villa—along with Gretchen, another former Skidder, to go in their place. I volunteered to go along as a third because I was curious, and Royal-Lee was assigned to accompany us and watch over me.

With all the anticapitalistic educational blither-blather Phil espoused, you would think he would be willing to sally out into the dregs of poverty and lend a helping hand, but he didn't. He taught, inspired, handed out pills, and Phil used and Peter occassionaly slipped, and they talked about *Thus Spoke Zarathustra*. They got high and asked: Is the Orange Candidate an Ubermensch? What did recurrence look like in the face of global climate change? Then they'd discuss Luddites and technocracy and how the state made smashing machines a capital offense. They talked about *Das Kapital, Mein Kampf,* and 4Chan. They were bro-ing out.

* * *

"Skid Row used to be one street only," Gretchen lectured to me, sweating like a teenage boy on a tennis court and gesturing past tents on the sidewalks. "Now it's six full blocks," she said.

The sculpture students at NYU were a hundred years behind these street vagrants who had assembled their camps out of found objects. There were tents tagged with words like "hope" and "soul," and one of them, scraps of American flags had been sewn onto a wall to create the effect of stained glass. It looked like a medical tent in some insane street war, but for now there was peace—and peacetime was flying as high as police helicopters. Everyone was a loaded street soldier. And it was kind of beautiful. There were canopies of fleece blankets and shimmering tarps strung from posts, angled out from pallets of weathered wood, and tent poles festooned with sparkling ribbon that hung gamely in the sun. I felt limp, not high enough, still taking the trial drug, trying to get my life sorted, and to not snort too much Oxy with my silver spoon up my nose.

It all looked a little like the Tracey Emin installation *Everyone I Have Ever Slept With 1963–1995* in the dissolution of boundaries between public and private life. Except these encampments out on the street weren't made up of clean cozy tents like you'd find in a kid's room on a rainy day. No one was cutting out letters to spell the names of people they'd slept with. They were sleeping with people to pay the Street Boss to keep their tents on the sidewalk—not sell them to Charles Saatchi. They wouldn't carry the £2,546,500 auction house price tag that *The Tent,* as the Emin piece was commonly known, had fetched.

Walls of private possessions were held in stacked milkcrates fashioned into curio shelves. Overturned bicycles stood on torn seats in front of tent doors, their frames draped with clothes. I almost liked it here, but I didn't want to stay too long. Although I had to admire the abject aesthetic, Skid Row was like a shitty Coachella for junkies and tweakers, a festival that never ended with no musical acts, no selfieing brats, no twenty-dollar avocado toast. But it felt like real art. Real creativity. A world uncorrupted by the Internet. No corporate greed. Just humanity, plain and simple. No waste. No vanity.

This was the first time I felt I had stepped into anything remotely resembling a "community," in spite of having heard the word all my life in private schools. Tapestries and prayer flags hung from white fencing along the old real estate, put there, Gretchen told me, to keep people from living too close to the buildings. I wanted to kill Dick Sickler all of a sudden. Sure, but did I really want to kill him? Gretchen had been talking nonstop, so high she seemed to shiver with every bit of information she oozed, chewing her words like Starbursts. The fencing looked like those wire grid racks you see in mall kiosks hawking sunglasses and cheap jewelry.

"Greeeeeeetchennn, do you have any more Oxy?" I thought it was worth a shot. She looked at me, considering. "Here. Have a bump,"

Gretchen said, holding out an open envelope and passing me a straw from McDonald's. I snorted the powder and rubbed my nose, letting it burn. The taste in the back of my throat was a fucking orgasm. I don't know what it was she gave me; some kind of snowy LA miracle.

There hadn't been actual snow in LA for a thousand years. But something about this place reminded me of wintertime in New York, where kids decorated snowmen out of whatever was lying around, the snow rolled into big cold stucco balls poked with sticks or carrots or pieces of broken blacktop. A stray scarf. Some hat with a silly pom-pom. I missed the New York subway. I looked down at the Skid Row gutters. What could I use here to decorate a snowman? Spent needles, pill bottle caps, beer cans in paper sacks, crushed orange plastic, and corners torn off baggies. Every day there was snow on Sunset Boulevard. We scored it in high school and snorted it at school, or home, or in public toilets. Faia even snorted it after getting a nose job, while her nose was still healing. Of course she did. She was reading *The Secret History.*

From old brick buildings, half-naked people leaned through their windows, watching me like aliens, or like I was the alien. Was I? Had I been so deprived of my humanity that I had none left? These people were instinct-driven, immediate. They were free. Birds silently flapped their wings on the ground among people gambling, hustling, selling EBT food cards. A woman lying against the crook of a building looked dead. Nobody drove down the side streets—it was all foot traffic. It felt kind of like a Jill Mulleady painting, hellish but fun. Or it had snowed in the '60s, I remembered someone saying once, maybe my dad.

The thought of him made everything less pure than it felt in the moments before. That's what family did, stole your buzz, itched your asshole, and ruined the power of your authentic vision. Maybe I should have said pussy. Where was my mom, that bitch? Probably getting off on being important, or was she in trouble? Black magic? More and more, I, too, blamed Dick. Always Dick. Dick. Dick. Dick. It was popular to blame Dick at the Villa. In fact, everyone I knew hated Dick. It was down with Dick every day.

"This is Broadway, and from Fifth to Sixth, you get your pills,"

Gretchen told me, scratching her nose. "Corder is heroin only. Every street's got its own Street Boss. You need to have their permission to twist or grind. You gotta get their permission to set up camp. You need permission to fucking breathe.

"It's always a big Black guy, too. It just always is, sorry, they keep the hustle going. *Don't look at me like that.*"

"All these buildings around here are SRO. Means single resident occupancy, but people say it's 'shit right out.' It's where you live when you're just out of prison, so you'll definitely go straight back to prison. Who could stay sober here, right? Everybody's keeping industry alive."

"Right," I said, noting Gretchen, too, had been educated on anti-capitalist theory.

"Who could live a straight life even if they wanted to? Work a fry line at Carl's Junior? Save up for a regular apartment someday, right on the 10, not even subsidized, filthy-ass carpet, living alone and watching TV, filling a bong or glass cock? Like our culture is so full of healthy people? Peter's right, this is the best alternative, until there's a better world. At least drugs work."

"At least they don't have bitchy parents breathing down their necks," I nodded.

"Uh huh." Gretchen yawned.

Cecil Hotel was just a few blocks away, and I shuddered at the memory of my classmate Ashley's murder there—Ash, who might still be alive if she hadn't played a part in Sickler's circus of addicts. And of the security footage that co-starred me, entering the Cecil with her. What was I doing here? What was the long game? How was I going to make this story mine—make it work, bend fate to my will, manifest a Campbellian hero's journey, or a bright Hermetic dawn?

A car backfired in the distance. I didn't even flinch. This felt like fate. The shit people talked about on social media or in college was a joke when a place like this existed. Did Dad think I'd never figure out the truth—that freedom wasn't something you bought with prestige or power and money you earned playing their game, but something you found within yourself as soon as you quit playing?

"I should quit," I thought, and then realized I already had. That's why my parents were so pissed. They were jealous. Slaves to the system, and I was completely outside of it, free to make anything I wanted out of myself.

I'd quit a long time ago.

The sun was hot, but cumulous clouds were overhead, darker ones coming from the northeast. It hadn't rained in a year by my memory, although my sense of time over the last year or so was mostly cloudy. I was holding a Diet Coke. Where did that come from? Holy shit. It was still cold.

"It doesn't even make any sense," Gretchen was saying.

"I know," I said.

"It costs five times more to live in the shitty SRO's over there with no bathrooms." She pointed to a building with a neon sign of a palm tree. "Five times more than the nicer SRO's on San Juan and they have private bathrooms, but you have to be in the system to get those, come from inside, be out on parole, or fully mental, plus you gotta piss clean. Lots of people can't get the expensive ones or the cheapies and they stay at the Mission. You can sleep in their courtyard until 5 a.m. if you can't get a bed."

"Four people died last week," Tom chimed in. "OD's. This heat, fentanyl, fake Oxy, street methadone; it's nothing like living at the Villa. The Villa is cush."

"What's street methadone?" I asked Tom as we turned this corner and could see smoke hovering over the mountains.

"Get it prescribed to take at home. Cut it, sell it, and buy real dope. Good hustle if you're in the system, but the strength's always different. People die. Everyone dies. We all die."

"There was this girl from Ranchos Palos Verdes last year," Gretchen said. "Died. Got to Skid Row, maxed her ATM out, five hundred a day, took everyone partying at the bars: The High Tide, Nexus, King Eddy. She smoked it up, came out here in a green Jaguar, looking young and fresh as a flower. In two weeks, she was barefoot, covered in sores, used up and fucked up by everyone from the top to the bottom. Whored out, strung out, dead at the Loraine, which is a Blue-run crack spot, you know? Dead in someone else's room, worse off than any of these whores out here today. Thought she could fuck with it, but she couldn't."

"She sounds like a privileged idiot," I said. "I wouldn't drive a Jag down here. That's just tacky."

Gretchen stared at me. "Bitch, that's you. If you don't have us. If you end up street. You don't know? *That* is *you*."

I did not know. "Blue-run? You mean the Crips?" I asked like I was on a field trip. I felt insulted. I wanted to fight but was too high. What had I snorted? We were supposed to be involved in a drug trial.

"The cops. They run the Loraine. The cops love to run crack, shoot people, rape women. And men. What do you think they do all day? Eat donuts? They'll put a dick in your fucking donut." She made a face like duh. "Then blame you for the hole you got in you. Cream filled."

In the dim, musty room at the Cecil Hotel, I had leaned against the faded wallpaper and looked at Ash, her dark eyes a mixture of exhaustion and resilience. There was a rare kindness to her gaze. She reminisced in subdued tones about high school days and about Faia's smile.

"More than anything, really, I wish she would've looked at me the way she looked at you. She loved you in a way no one ever loved me. I just wanted someone to look at me like that," she said in a voice tethered to addiction and regret. "Just one time, you know?"

I had no idea what she was talking about at the time, but when I thought of Faia while on Skid Row it elicited a longing inside of me for the girls we'd once been on the Westside, cushioned in our little protective bubbles while our fathers wreaked havoc on the losers of the world. On these streets, I wanted to free myself from my father, which seems so simple when you're out on a field trip for the day in the drag of poverty, but was never so easily accomplished, and I wanted to free Faia from her father, and from his legacy, and from the reputation she would never escape as the daughter of one of the deadliest men in history. I wanted her back. I wanted her to see past last names, past the pills, past the shame. But that wasn't gonna happen.

The detritus lining the gutters was like some post-flood reckoning, a storm that had come and gone, leaving all the poor unharmed. If the meek would really inherit the Earth, like Jesus supposedly said, these freaks were going to need to figure out what to do with their country, because it was all going to be theirs. It was over ninety degrees a month before Halloween and there was no shade and everyone was half-clothed, except the tweakers who wore puffy full-length coats and somehow didn't ever break a sweat.

I stole side-glances into the tents and lean-tos. Inside, people lay in their underwear or naked in the heat, smoking crack, completely at ease. A bony-faced Black woman made her face up from a little white plastic case of cheap cosmetics that looked like a toy for a kid at Christmas. The woman was probably in her twenties but looked ancient.

"That was the front line over there where Green Apple was on Winston. That's where people go when they say, 'I'm going to the front line,'" Gretchen was saying. I guessed that's where I got the Diet Coke. "This is Stanford. It's usually going off, but maybe the cops came. It's dead now. Must have busted it up. At night, people turn their music up on boom boxes and dance. I miss that . . . but things are so much better at the Villa."

An old white man with a beard sat in stretched-out white underwear in his open lean-to and picked at an infected wound on his leg with a folding knife that had a turtle shell handle. I thought I saw green puss oozing out but didn't look again.

"That's Sniper," Gretchen said. "He was in Vietnam. Came back and has been homeless ever since. Swore off violence and weapons and the society that uses them. He's seen these streets change and they haven't gotten any better. Like that building, that brick one, guess what it was."

"A mortuary?"

"Good guess. Close though. A church. Guess what it's now?"

"SRO?"

"Nope. Hardcore porn studio. Corder is heroin and porn. Stay off Corder. Imagine what kind of porn that looks like. Or don't bother."

"SBH" was spray painted on the wall of the porno church. Tom said it meant sad bitches hour. "Eight years of Obama and this's all still here," he said. "He didn't do shit. I already had Medicare. Lyndon-fucking-Johnson started that shit."

"Remember, Stanford has a big palm tree on it. Seafood companies start there. They're over on Gladys, too. In the summer, they'll stink like shit to low hell."

Everyone was staring at me like I was from another dimension. Like I was a juicy cut of prime rib in a cartoon where the starving characters start to see the other character as meat, a big brown turkey basted in a roasting pan. I was a little baby turkey for sure. I could feel their glares and sense the stronger characters on the street considering me as an investment opportunity. Were it not for Tom and Royal-Lee and Gretchen, I figured the whole block would come swarming me, but Tom was keeping watch, making eye contact with the right people, and every now and then he said "what's up" to some large man on the street. He must know the bosses, I thought.

Skid Row was the counterbalance to the rest of LA, I thought. Or the one I had grown up inside, anyhow, with golden-brown bodies on the beach and miles of tan sand and lifeguard towers. Golden Globes parties and cheesy red carpets with logo backdrops. Rich people in Malibu smelling like coconut and Scotch and synthetic musk. Kids in high school who drove Porsche 911 Targas and got into college from family donations. Elites with villas above the PCH and behind the gates of the Malibu Colony. Huge estates in the canyons, where entry was as given as oxygen—and pools and tennis courts sat behind tall black iron fences, lined with bougainvillea and holly shrubs, ficus trees and face lifts, fake boobs and butts, pusillanimous mommies and daddies with organic spray tans, deep-clean dentistry, and catered dinner parties for birthday girls who left the smell of perfume and vomit in the bathroom when they left.

Whoosh.

Skid Row was the most honest place I'd ever seen: the balance of life resting just on its surface. Nothing was hidden. It made me want to embrace it all, to fall down high in the street and worship failure as a permanent excuse to bang dope. To become it, like one succumbs to the indigo visions of dreams in the last moment before falling back to sleep. This made America great again. Could I capture its apocalyptic surrealism, somehow? Pay homage to its human resourcefulness in the wake of corporate tyranny? I felt I was walking among the better angels here, souls far purer than anyone I'd ever known. Nothing was hidden. The ghost of humanity showed its true, primitive grin and was jarringly awake and honest. Part of me kept picturing these people cut up in motels.

Phil had taught that capitalism perpetuates the exploitation of the poor in so much as financial institutions and wealthier elites profit from exorbitant interest rates on loans, entrenching poverty and inequality. Marxism explains how this system of usurious lending traps the working class into perpetual debt, siphoning their labor value and reinforcing a cycle of economic dependence. Rich parasites get richer at the direct expense of the impoverished. Then sells them booze, drugs, and cigarettes.

Shouldn't my artistic practice be about reaching into this world of exploitation and representing it, as an act of war against the forces that would use me?

"Can you believe this place, Royal-Lee?" I said, overwhelmed and hot. "Isn't it . . ." I paused. I didn't know what else to say.

"Disgusting. Yes. It's terrible."

I was going to say amazing.

"It's the only place rich people don't own, yet," I brightened, emboldened. "It's so honest, it's so real," my eyes sparkled.

"Yeah, if you want your honesty brutal and your reality grim, with no choices, you privileged idiot. Look at all this food from handouts," they said, pointing at slices of bread smashed into the sidewalk, hard cooked eggs smooshed on the blacktop in chevron patterns of car tires. "These people don't need food. They need help. I thought that's what I was doing here, once upon a time, looking for people to give sandwiches. Trying to save people with Narcan."

I looked. And in the back of my mind came a nagging itch. Was it guilt? Or shame? Or pride? My parents' wealth had all come from the Sicklers. It paid for everything, from the shoes on my feet to my overpriced tee, to the Oxy I'd bought from Royal-Lee so many times. There was no answer to the streets. You could decorate a thousand motel rooms with their dead skins. They'd keep coming and dying and coating the walls in blood and gore. Shouldn't *I* do something?

"Okay, but what about these tents?" I said.

"What about the people dying in these tents, you mean?"

"If the right name were placed on these tents, they'd be masterpieces. What's this street we're on, again?"

"Gladys," Gretchen sneered like some fellow art major back at NYU who thought I was a fool for not remembering the details of the docent's tour.

I walked over to where Tom was talking to a boss of the street, another tall man with dark skin. I made myself hold my head up high and tried to nose myself into their conversation, but with respect. I wobbled and the Street Boss caught me. "I just need to sit down. I don't feel good." I felt embarrassed. Everything glittered in sweat, and the hot sun was rainbow colored on my eyelashes and across the street.

"Don't sit here. People shit here." He held me up by my arm and guided me to a small piece of aquamarine sheeting someone had left on the sidewalk. I sat down and looked around in a daze. Gretchen stared at me like something in a pet shop window, curious, but unsure about my white ass dripping in sweat, like a wet puppy she didn't want.

"Look, here's the deal: we need people to come live with us, and we can pay," Tom was saying. "We've got medicine for them, you know? How much you want for all these people on your street?"

"Sell my people? What the fuck do you think I am? What are you saying?"

"How much for them to come live with us? Indoors. You can find new ones."

"Their tents, too," I said, butting in from my seat on the sidewalk. "And this whole street for the two days through Halloween," I said.

"Who is this?" the boss flirted and smiled.

"I'm Susie," I said, standing and woozily reaching my arm out towards him.

He laughed and said, "I'm Rodney. Call me Rod."

We shook hands.

"How much would that cost, Rod?" I asked. I felt like my dad.

"I'm sorry. I'm talking business with my man here. You need to wait while we work something out."

"Bitch, get the fuck out of here," Tom warned.

"Who are you calling a bitch? Don't fuck with me." I couldn't believe I'd just said that to Tom. Hot and high, I trembled when I said it, but I'd seen shows and read books about jail and the street and you had to show you weren't weak. Tom and the boss both stared at me like I was some drugged-out whore. I walked off back to Royal-Lee and stood fuming. I needed a bottle of water, maybe a line, maybe just a new life. I needed Faia to believe I wasn't trash. But she already knew I was. Where did people get water?

Then Rod laughed and coughed and Tom mumbled something about more dead addicts in rental rooms. The whole street was suddenly quiet. I looked around feeling embarrassed. Like I'd farted in a place that didn't let me deny the stink. Like I was responsible for the silence. I'd ruined everybody's fun, the whole street. Poor people held you accountable when you shit in their mouths.

"Uhuh," I heard Rod say. "Whatever. I hear they feel like they stepped in shit and slid into Christmas. Till they dead. Fred Harkin. Y'all are fucked up?"

"Naw," Tom gave him a look. "It's all good. Motherfuckers overdose."

I walked back toward the two men. "Look, I really need to use the tents and this street for two days."

"Here's two," Tom passed bills.

They all waited while the Street Boss rounded people up out of their tents. Calling people on his cellphone, Rod also whistled at women and guys on the corner. "Yo, Green Eyes, come here. Nancy."

"Okay, but seriously, what about these tents?" I said again.

Yeah, call me whatever names you want. I did my time on the stand, I stood trial, I was in jail. I'm going to dip out again for a bit, let you twist and grind in your high holy seat. Like you do anything but read.

* * *

When Susie came back from Skid Row, she went down to the basement to pitch her art project to Peter or Phil, whoever was down there. The first floor of the house was dark and quiet, with everyone upstairs.

Royal-Lee, Gretchen, and Tom showed the thirteen new homeless people to their bedrooms, introduced them to the original house members. Royal-Lee gave them red Oxys and white trial pills and asked each newbie questions off of the pink intake forms.

Susie had to do hers, because she'd never filled one out, and the twins needed her as another number for the drug trial; they used her mother's maiden name on her paperwork to avoid any conflicts of interest; she circled "no" on every line and rushed down to the basement.

Do you prefer to think for yourself wrongly rather than follow someone else's thinking that is more correct?	N	Y
Do you believe that all reality is your invention and dream?	N	Y
Are you willing to do anything it takes to save yourself?	N	Y
Would you kill your best friend if it would dramatically change the world for the better?	N	Y
Do you have any family that you are still in contact with?	N	Y
Are you susceptible to the power of suggestion?	N	Y

Susie had found Phil—or was it Peter—squatting next to the freezer. There was blood on its dimpled wall. Lit only by a candle in a glass bottle, he licked his split knuckles. Susie couldn't say for sure, but it seemed like he'd been crying. After a silence, he asked what she wanted. His presence was eerie, like they were strangers. Were they? Had she painted him, or had he taught her at NYU? Or was it the other one?

"I've got an idea for an art piece that will have real social impact," she began.

"Go ahead."

She explained her concept—of appropriating the homeless tents on Skid Row and signing them as if they were art. They *were* art.

"It could be like an art walk. And we could advertise it like the Sicklers are our corporate sponsors. That will piss off my dad—and maybe crack the whole Sickler façade. We could hang banners."

"I don't think so," he said listlessly. "It would also piss off the Sicklers, and we can't do that. We need them. You need them. There's a detective sniffing around. Something about you at the Cecil Hotel."

Of course. That was always coming, she'd figured.

"I don't care. They're genocidal maniacs!" she countered. "And they're huge art snobs. They'll be so embarrassed if people think they're behind a show featuring their name on Skid Row. They won't get it at all. You know, maybe they don't deserve the free press."

She sounded stupider than she was. It was the drugs. In her mind, she understood that the show would expose Dick Sickler's hypocrisy and call out everyone who pretended to care so much about minorities and underprivileged people, but really just fetishized them and weaponized and collected them, and when it came to the real truth of the most obviously traumatized people, society couldn't give a shit. They would only look if it was called "art," and if it was art endorsed by a corporate sponsor. But she couldn't articulate all of this to him, if he was even listening.

"How far are you willing to go?" He stared at her.

"How far are you willing to go?" She stared back at him.

21

The Day of the Art Walk . . .

The heroin was kicking in, her first shot, as quick as the liquid hit her blood. Susie felt like one of the birds that darted into the glass sliders at her parents' house: temporarily paralyzed and confused. She'd pick the birds up and hold them in her hands and bring them in the house until they sobered up. They looked at her like she was a giant angel, incredulous that she wasn't hurting them. As if everything birds had heard about humans was wrong, and people weren't destructive, shitty monsters, if that wasn't too much personification for the minds of birds in her brain on dope. *Ceci n'est pas un oiseau.* White light was entering her mind. Heroin was innocence, absolution, and guilt all at once.

Phil had cleaned the injection site with an antiseptic wipe, gently swabbing the skin of her pale forearm. Then he held the syringe at the appropriate angle, forty degrees, and slid the needle smoothly into her arm and up the vein, and pulled gently back on the plunger to mix blood, ensuring he was in. He'd slowly injected the drug, removing the needle quickly and pressing a wad of toilet paper to the tiny hole in her vein.

There was no pool at the Villa, no huge sliding glass doors. No housekeeper down in the kitchen filling the glass pitcher with iced tea and sliced lemons from the tree in the front yard. Susie felt everything everywhere fall limp and runny. HEROIN. It was the best feeling she'd ever felt in her life.

Woods of Windsor?

Woodland Peony?

Whoosh.

"Isolation" by Iggy Pop played on the bedroom stereo.

Needed you, you were only using
Needing you just tore me down
Here I stand in isolation
Feeling emptiness and doubt . . .

Neither her eyes nor her thoughts would focus. The obvious truth was she'd gotten her first intravenous hit of heroin. Her veins were new leaves. It felt nauseating and ticklish. She'd also made her first art in so long . . . or, really, the illusion of art, which was the best kind of art, she supposed, second only to masterpieces. Better to make an art illusion that worked than a real piece of art that was mediocre. Better a Tim Hawkinson than an Anselm Kiefer, because simple sincerity in art was not a lasting strength. Plenty of art acquired by museums was made by fabricators: UAP or Ted Lawson or Carlson Baker Arts. Having her tents fabricated would cost a quarter mil, plus they'd look too clean, too new for this protest. She should do that in five years, though, as an homage to her first show: *The Sickler Halloween Art Walk*. She'd tell everyone about how she'd been homeless at the time.

The only problem with the show on Skid Row was that Susie was missing it. Somehow she'd ended up sprawled on this floor, head against the toilet, free as fuck. But that was pretty punk rock. Like not going to your own birthday party. It's probably for the best, she thought. It was tacky to be front and center at your own debut. Better to be smoking cigarettes in the alley. Better to be right here, sucking sugar, beneath the bowl.

Walking down the broken highway
Sucking sugar plain and sweet
Did your mother ever tell you
That the joyful are the free?

"Hey," Phil said, propped up against the wall tiles.

She closed her eyes. Was she going to pray now? *To what?* What could she see? She was smiling and smelled the shit smell of the toilet or she was imagining it. It didn't matter. Phil could take a dookie right above her and she'd keep smiling, head right between his feet, looking up at the pair of his swinging balls as he stood. Phil wasn't taking a dump, he was talking. *Talking, talking, talking.* She saw him, but didn't understand what he was saying. Did she love him? What was love? *Please don't hurt me. No more.*

"We are the sole architects of our lives. Or are they lying to me over at that fancy church? '*Where I found the living, there I found the will to power; and even in the will of those who serve, I found the will to be master,*' thus spake Zarathustra. This was how God crafted us, different from the angels. Free to act, and act wrongly. Divine prurience is the free will that is our power."

"Fuck spake Zarathustra," she muttered.

"Sure. We aren't in control of everything. Or are we? I was taught I was not meant to be responsible for my life, you know, I was beaten and raised in a cult of submission . . . now they say my thoughts equal my words equal my actions equal my habits equal my destiny. If I think I just manifest my desires then what do I owe my life's design? All things have amounted to this need to seek revenge on Dick, or am I a fool? Or is it not about trying to force the world to bend to our will? Have I been fucking it all up? '*To have and to want to have more—growth, in one word—that is life itself,*' thus spake Zarathustra."

"Shut up, Phil." Susie had never believed in any of The Church's manifestation and bullshit that Phil was talking about. It was just a way to manipulate people into working harder to make more money so they could pay more dues. Nobody ever said, "Manifest a sandwich," or "Manifest some dog shit to step in." It was always about power or money or a connection that would result in more power or more money. All of these thoughts were just clouds in a sky.

She saw a warm red chalice in her mind; even as a Jew, she was having her Catholic vision. Did her mom really believe she could manifest reality? If so, why hadn't she used her will to care for Susie as a child? Use the power she'd actually had? Susie knew her mom didn't care. The one time she spilled paints on the living room's velvet pile carpet, her father had lost it. He hit her, pushed her, then grabbed her up by the hair and slapped her face and her ears rang. Mom had come in wearing a white eyelet summer dress, drunk, screaming "*I hate you, David.*" For a moment Susie felt she would be saved, protected, but then Mom recoiled into her own selfishness and ran upstairs in her mules, leaving her in his domain. Susie didn't forgive her, but she didn't care anymore. Her mother was still missing. A warm rope of ink sank through Susie's veins. Her mouth was warm and the perfect moisture. She lost herself, disappearing so far away it made her stomach drop.

Whoosh.

Mom later sobbed in her bedroom as Susie crept up the stairs for comfort, but her mother just asked her to rub her feet with rose cream.

So, did she believe she'd manifested a drug addict daughter?

Both her parents were so sad. She forgave them now completely in this perfect, twinkling moment. She was in a heroin bubble.

She smiled inwardly to herself and the curling of her lips felt so sweet.

Everyone was downstairs on their meds, hooked to the Internet, reading and posting conspiracy theories. It was what Dick had demanded. *Distract, employ, drug.* The Church and Dick looked to be winning again. *The will to power.*

Phil was talking. "You know what happened to Fred Harkin? He overdosed in this house. We killed him, it was you and me, whether you were here yet or not. I put his body on that serving cart. What else was I going to do with him? Well, I had them do it. My lovelies, who don't even listen to me anymore. They only listen to my brother."

"He's staying sober, Phil. Mostly sober," she muttered. She couldn't open her eyes. She wanted to get fucked. Someday. The red ring of the light bulb on the ceiling burned in her brain but she'd never opened her eyes to see it.

Had her mom come back home to her dad yet? She sort of hoped so. She sort of hoped not. *Did* Mom believe she'd manifested a drug addict daughter?

Maybe she was at the art walk now, showing some fucking support.

Maybe she was blaming herself for the shit her daughter had pulled, and that she'd just stepped in. Dick would be mad. Faia would burn with rage. Susie smiled.

Was any part of her mother or father going to be proud that their daughter had signed each tent with gold paint in perfect cursive: *Susie Vogelman*? Maybe she should have signed them *Susie Sickler*. But now it was too late to change it—was it raining? Maybe the event on Skid Row wouldn't work; the sun better come out. What was a name, anyway? How did you make it a brand, a destiny, a work of art and fate? What about all the people on the street? The hundreds of thousands more who would die? Why couldn't they all crawl into her heart right now, like a big dry tent? Did she want to be famous or did she want to see God, herself, her world? Wasn't this the job of the artist? To try to talk to God? To be with God? Which meant to not be with people but alone, working. Where was God? She loved God so much right now. She hoped she could always have this feeling, with God, with everyone in her heart, with her art show, hopefully making a great big hole in the heart of the evil that Phil was still talking about.

"Dick Sickler is a dick. He's such a dick. I hate him," Phil said. "I am so proud of my brother. My brother is the good one. I'm not good. I've never been any good. I'm so glad I found him. At least I've done that right. At least I found him and he's doing great on the new drug, right?"

"Hey," Peter came in. She could barely keep her eyes open as she watched Peter fail to stay sober on the new pills, reaching for the spoon and the powder and the little container of water, and begin cooking his dope, the good brother, tossing the cotton from a cigarette filter into the pool of silver in the spoon, and go reaching for the needle, and she saw Phil smile.

Got a lot to do, got a lot to say
Got a life to live, got a lot to do
Got a lot to say, got a life to live
Got a lot to do . . .

* * *

Driving felt liberating. The sound of the water through the old tire radials was a new sensation and there was some slippage Royal-Lee hadn't experienced before while driving the flimsy cabriolet. He listened to the rude voice on the map-app telling them what to do and then the rain stopped.

They liked feeling the car zipping with its little engine, the smell of spent gasoline, the funny shape of the car, the torn upholstery, and the windows in the chrome frames. Royal-Lee looked at her nails and then remembered to drive. They were passing Popeye's Chicken across from the St. Vincent de Paul Roman Catholic Church; Royal-Lee wanted to get a box of chicken and a biscuit, and a spicy chicken sandwich and cajun fries, and then go into the beautiful cathedral and digest and pray and talk to God and explain things about Vic and being so sorry. Royal-Lee was so sorry and didn't know what Phil was going to do with his body in the freezer. Dreams about Vic's body haunted them nearly every sleepless night, as did "the killings" around town, Fred Harkin, the fires on the Westside, up in the hills, burning private homes behind their tall iron gates, palm trees exploding in flames.

West Adams Boulevard became East Adams Boulevard just past Figueroa, near Main Street. They took a left up South Central Avenue. They were looking for the banners but they didn't see any. Why were they even out here doing this for Susie? It's not like they were sisters. Or even friends, really. What would God think? Did God even care if you stayed one gender? She'd asked Peter and Phil. They said God didn't care as long as you loved Him. Sometimes Royal-Lee couldn't remember who God was, what they'd learned all those Sundays at the Worship Hall, all the stories in the Bible. What did they all mean? Was God a *Him*? They knew something in their heart, and prayed they were forgiven. That love was enough, but who were they loving? Who were they really, truly loving? Themself.

Not Susie. She came from a world they'd never know, the part of Los Angeles connected to Ivy League educations and old-world schools out East, Hollywood agents, lawyers, doctors, manicured lawns and trees filled with flowers, figs, lawn statues and Bentleys in garages, paying colossal property taxes to feel they owned the world. Susie didn't need her love. Their mother did . . .

There were alleyways between old brick buildings with roll-up metal door covers and graffiti everywhere. Royal-Lee passed *Baba's Electronics*, *Rush Exotic Wheels*, and felt free in the car, drifting, not married to anywhere, passing a Coca-Cola bottling plant with a big sculpture of a Coca-Cola bottle next to a red marque on the roof with *Coca-Cola* in white script.

Phil said Southern California wouldn't survive global warming. Not the homeless, or the trees, or the birds, or the golden city. They couldn't imagine that the empty heart of Los Angeles would ever stop beating, its agents and actors and singers all gone, and those beautiful homes they'd never been inside of, out in Malibu, the equestrian stables Susie described, the tilting palms of Wilshire Boulevard, the corridors of Laurel Canyon, the fetishized homes up Benedict or Coldwater, and huge mansions with libraries full of books beyond their wildest dreams. All could be reduced to a beggar's banquet, piles of ash and rubble, according to Phil. The Coca-Cola building was shaped like a giant boat, Royal-Lee realized, and it went on for*ever.* It had big riveted windows and round porthole windows and railings all around the second floor like a modern-day Ark. Could Coca-Cola save us? Could LA flood instead of burn?

They cruised past old brown wooden electric poles and abandoned-looking buildings and warehouses and a cement building covered in metal bars with the name Karlido Hotel painted in black, a liquor store on the ground level. It looked like one of the hotels where "the killer" would gut out one of their next victims. Royal-Lee ached with the gnawing guilt they couldn't shake since finding Vic dead in the basement. The feeling was mortal, heart-wrenching, like a sledgehammer to the brain—and it had taken Royal-Lee a few days to accept the truth of what had happened.

They didn't feel at home in their body now that they'd held the body of Victor's dead remains and helped put him in the freezer. It made them think of God all the time. God. God. God. Who was He? If you could burn up a body in a furnace, turning it to bone and ash, why couldn't you freeze it? What difference did it make? Why were some people allowed to get rid of a body and others couldn't? Was it law or morality? It's not like they had killed him . . . still they felt terrible.

Death was terrible. Secrets. Crimes. Victor was young. They sort of wished someone would cut him up in a motel, make use of him, make people know his name. Was "the killer" hot? Like *The Dating Game* Killer? Was it *Phil*? Was it *Peter*? *Susie*? They weren't ready to deal with the dead body, so freezing him actually seemed sort of like the right thing to do. People freeze until they know what to do. It's just a trauma response. Fight. Flight. Freeze. Fawn. Fuck. Phil had explained it all.

A woman with a rolling walker wheeled out into the road, and Royal-Lee swiveled and stared, thinking it was their mother, but didn't see her face and that was ridiculous, it wasn't her. Royal-Lee kept driving, knew she needed to be careful what not to manifest, and zoomed into the Piñata District. Should they move home and live with a sticky mother again? She was like a depressing piñata, full of snack cakes and candies and diabetes and sorrow. But a child loved their mother. A few blocks later, Royal-Lee turned left on Sixth Street, past Triangle Plaza and Bank of America, heading toward taller buildings downtown.

They saw the seafood company on the corner of Sixth and Gladys with people breathing through their shirt sleeves. There was a little park that had been overtaken by people in blank hats, preppy clothes, rounded eyewear with glossy frames, and good shoes. Their cars were parked along the curbs, edging out the local beaters who'd been forced to find spots elsewhere. Two cop cars were parked by a brown brick building with AC units in the windows with words dented into the coils. Overgrown bushes crowded a fenced area near a mural of parrots on the side of the Regal Hotel, which wasn't regal, across from the basketball courts where homeless people in sleeping bags talked to each other. Royal-Lee circled the block.

There was a sawhorse roadblock across Gladys. *STREET CLOSED FOR ART WALK* was hand painted in red. The wet concrete from the brief rain steamed in the sunshine like a movie set. The tents and tarps were bedazzled with the last drops of moisture, and it all felt like a small town somewhere, or a storybook. The place was packed with normies.

Dozens of people were turning the corner at the B&P Seafood Corp on Gladys, heading to Sixth Street. Royal-Lee hoped to fit in with the visitors on Skid Row, having used concealer to even out her skin tone and texture, contouring to add depth and structure by creating shadows under the cheekbones, along the jawline, and on the sides of her nose, enhancing the bone structure and creating a sculpted appearance. She wore highlighter, blush, lip liner, lipstick, eyeliner, and a little eyeshadow. BALENCIAGA was printed in gray on the cotton jersey sweatshirt they wore, but it seemed ridiculous now, just like Susie had said it was. *As if Cristobal Balenciaga would ever be caught dead in a sweatsuit.* She'd said that. Royal-Lee at least felt skinny in the sweats as the clothes hung off her frame in an elegant way.

There were dozens of art tourists already looking at the first tent on Sixth Street. Amidst the spectators, Royal-Lee recognized ArtFag21, a gay boy influencer she followed on their socials. Royal-Lee thought ArtFag21 was hot, and he wore bright neon color blocking and was live streaming for his followers in a hushed, awed voice. There were little signs on all the electric poles saying, "No Photos! No Videos!" Susie predicted no one would obey the signs anyway, and she was right; everyone was posing in front of the tents, taking selfies and pics of one another pretending to duck inside. Some were holding their noses. Others rolled their eyes at those being disrespectful of the art walk. "No photos!" a middle-aged guy with a dad-bod called. He was taking notes on his cellphone.

The Surlies had pasted the signs up overnight after hanging art banners around town. Royal-Lee had been part of that mission, to hang banners for the art walk. Susie had talked to Phil and told him about this idea for her art show. Royal-Lee had heard about it later in the suite while all sharing a bed together.

"Just make it look like the Sicklers are corporate sponsors," Phil had said.

"I already said that. That's my idea," Susie said.

"Yeah. Make them look like the assholes they are. Hang signs," Peter said, smoking.

"Like, put their names on banners?" Susie said.

"You'll figure it out," Peter had said.

"Why don't you take down those ones for museums and hang yours. The ones up in Miracle Mile." Royal-Lee had said it without thinking.

Why was she even helping her? They just wanted to act smart in front of the twin brothers.

"Smart," Susie said. "We can stick them up over the banners for real museum shows. That's genius."

"Okay, how do you get the banners hung?" Phil asked.

"We wear orange vests. Rent a bucket truck from Home Depot under your fake credit card and ID," Peter nudged him.

Later, they had all watched *Project Runway* together in bed—an old episode—trying to pretend time was infinite and Vic wasn't frozen. Everyone but Royal-Lee was high.

The episode's challenge was to do a makeover while designing an outfit to be modeled by one of the show's crewmembers, but for the tacky, horrible *JustFab* accessory line and clothing company. The winner of the challenge would have their work up for sale on the *JustFab* website. Tim Gunn hated *JustFab*, it was obvious, and who wouldn't? Royal-Lee loved Tim Gunn. *JustFab* was just trashy.

A contestant named Swapnil—a beautiful blue-eyed Indian designer—had been paired with a woman who seemed like she was high on Oxy or heroin, and who of course didn't want her arms to show, either because she *was* a junkie or because she had nasty, flabby arms. She didn't appreciate anything Swapnil did and was impossible to work with. All the familiar judges, Heidi, Zac, Nina, were harsh with Swapnil in critique, because they had all decided in the previous episode that Swapnil was wasting his gifts and slacking, taking smoke breaks, and worst of all, Swapnil just took it. He accepted their criticism as his own truth, even though he'd made three different outfits just to try and please his model in the time all the other contestants had made just one outfit. Their critique killed something inside of Swapnil. He was so sensitive, and the TV show was destroying his joy, and then, *Auf Wiedersehen—you're out!* You weren't really out until you were dead. Once you died, what was the best thing to do with your body? If you overdosed? If you were another victim of the epidemic? Royal-Lee learned a lot from that episode: don't let anyone steal your joy. Don't internalize criticism. Oh . . . and even Tim Gunn yelled at Swapnil and swore at him, which was totally out of character. Phil hadn't even yelled when he saw Vic was dead. What was going on? Was the episode fake? Scripted? What was happening?

The banners were obviously still hanging today, even if Royal-Lee hadn't found any; just look at all these fools out here on Skid Row, like it was a living museum of the deranged and addicted. People were posing in front of the tents. Some girls were smoking around a green tent with a hot-pink rainfly giving peace signs to each other's phones. There were stacks of Rock View Family Farm milk crates stacked in front. Inside a crate was a soaking wet stuffie of a valentine frog with sleepy, close-set eyes holding a pink sateen heart stitched: *I LOVE YOU.* In another crate was a porcelain statuette of Jesus with the Sacred Heart. Royal-Lee didn't like idols, it made it seem like Jesus was just another fame junkie.

Another tent was orange and gray in tiger-stripe camouflage, covered with a brown tarp with silver grommets. Tent poles came through the grommets with wands of sparkly streamers and a large pink dipper from a bubble-blowing kit. A bulky desert-camo sleeping bag was bungeed around a hunk of furniture that looked like a piano bench or a large footstool, and an American flag hung to one side from a chain link fence by zip ties. Zip ties had been used in several killings. Royal-Lee watched a homeless man—someone from down the block, they supposed—studying them. Had this man been a visitor at the Villa last week? He looked vaguely familiar.

At the next tent, the crowd kept its distance, a few people bending at the waist to try and peek inside: a man was sleeping and snoring loudly. "Be quiet!" someone said in a sharp whisper. "No, it's fine. He's not really sleeping. He's part of the installation." "Oh." What was going to happen when these homeless people and the art crowd started to mix? Royal-Lee wondered.

ArtFag21 filmed inside another tent. Vic was lying on the floor, thawed, his body flattened against the plastic tent floor, hair cut off, the long beautiful brown sections of hair laid out in the shape of a star, still shiny and lit carob-brown, in the light of ArtFag21's flash that was recording a live stream on his iPhone.

"Oh my God. Oh, fuck. I don't think this is part of the show," ArtFag21 reeled out of the tent, gagging and regurgitating what looked like green energy drink on the tent corner. Royal-Lee rushed over and ducked into the tent and saw Vic, blue-gray with black lips, dead as fuck, lying there like he'd melted into the tent floor. The man had oozed out of himself.

Was this Susie's idea?

Peter's?

Not Phil's, right? Or was Phil connected to "the killings" all along, she wondered. The shock hit and the smell of Vic got into her nose and Royal-Lee also threw up in the tent. Their DNA was now in the tent. *Fuck.* She took off her sweatshirt and used it to wipe up the vomit, shaking, trying not to look at Vic. The T-shirt wasn't enough to stay warm. Or the shivering was from fear. As she came out of the tent with a puke-coated BALENCIAGA jumper held out in her arms, they saw a familiar-looking woman who appeared like she'd been wandering the desert and who came strutting down the center of the road in sweatpants and a tank top, wearing a blue backpack across her chest like a suicide bomber. She was accompanied by a skinny guy with no shirt and black tattoos.

Some man in light-washed designer jeans and a crisp white shirt nodded to her. She scowled and yelled at him and at the rest of the normies. "What the fuck are you all doing here?" As she walked on, she shouted, "What the hell is this? Invasion of the body snatchers? Hey," she hollered at three guys standing together all wearing the same glasses. "Get the fuck out of here before you get beat down!"

The three guys looked around for someone in charge. Then one of them said, "We're here for the art event." They all nodded. "This could really turn your neighborhood around."

"We don't want it turned around, asshole! You turn around, bitch." She walked over to three Black people on the corner. Royal-Lee could see them huddled together, the angry woman gesticulating violently at the crowds. Tourists started taking videos on their cell phones. Royal-Lee felt a little sorry for the art tourists. They looked scared, not sure if the combative street people were part of the art or not. It felt like something was about to pop off. Everyone had stilled and was looking around, waiting for an eruption or a show. ArtFag21 was talking to his phone crying on video. Royal-Lee felt the moment of no return arriving. And then, as if manifested—breaking the silence—someone threw a bottle over the crowd. It sailed and smashed against a wall. Everyone ducked. More flew through the air. A bottle hit a man in the head and he fell to the ground and bled. Another man in a blue hat ducked down to help the man who was bleeding from the gash in his skull, now curled in a ball, going into shock.

Up ahead, a tent with a bright rain cover had the words DON'T SAVE ME spelled out in silver duct tape. Susie's gold signature sparkled.

"Who threw that?" some art tourist asked.

"Those Black people," a white tourist said.

"No," some Black tourist said. "That woman."

People began running awkwardly. Some were giggling as if they were on a ride at Six Flags. Homeless locals rushed up on the imposters, pulling punches and making them flinch. More bottles broke. Someone fell down. Then a man started screaming. Royal-Lee began jogging.

There was a block to go before Royal-Lee reached the end of Gladys, where Catch 21 stood, the restaurant that served seafood from all the warehouses on the street. She could see the big shade tarps and blue-tarp-covered tents together under an American flag along the big white hotel on Fifth Street. Royal-Lee's mom appeared, ten feet away, with a rolling cart-rack of brochures from the Jehovah's and another Jehovah lady Royal-Lee didn't recognize, in an all-purple outfit. Had they manifested Mom by thinking of her earlier? Whoa. Phil was right about everything. It was real. Royal-Lee felt like a lost little girl and then, there she was: *Mom*.

Quickly, they hid behind a utility pole. They couldn't let her see him like this. She had lost weight. Royal-Lee couldn't believe it was her . . . and how good she looked. Part of Royal-Lee felt she must have stopped existing the moment they left her. They felt jealous; but she was doing better without them. How was she so mobile? A prosthetic leg! It had a brown sock and orthopedic shoe, like the other leg, but it was plastic. It looked cheap, at least. So, she did still need someone.

She was standing, watching the street break into chaos, and she prayed with her hands together. How was she doing so much better since they left her for Phil? There was a streak of shame, as though they were the reason all along that she had been so sick and miserable. She had gotten her hair colored.

Packs of homeless people were flooding onto the street from nearby avenues, and the art attendees were fleeing in both directions. Mother clutched a Bible and lifted it into the air. "You don't have to live this way!" she cried. "God loves you and wants your love for Him. Come, save yourselves! Turn your lives over to Jesus." It sounded like a hostage negotiator: TURN YOURSELF IN. SURRENDER TO THE POLICE.

"You need to go, lady," that woman with the Steel Reserve can said. "Get the *fuck* out of here. You're a good lady. Don't get hurt. Get off this street." Drunk, she tugged hard on the hem of Mom's shorts to demonstrate urgency. Mom's above-the-knee prosthetic fell off and the lady with the beer was there to help her up after she fell to the concrete. She helped her get her leg back on.

Royal-Lee slunk out from behind the pole. But then froze. She saw. "Royal-Lee?" They turned away. "Wait! Son. Don't run. I want to help you. We can help, but you have to come back. I've been looking for you everywhere. That's why I'm here."

Royal-Lee turned to her. She was in tears.

"Mom," Royal-Lee began. "I'm sorry."

Royal-Lee would go back to her. At the Villa, there was no true goodness, only Phil, who would never love Royal-Lee the way Royal-Lee wanted him to.

"Are you wearing makeup?" she asked, horrified, as though it was the worst thing on Earth. "Makeup! In front of all these people?" She laughed bitterly.

Royal-Lee turned away in shame and then ran. There were things to tell her someday, but not today. She was better off without her, and she could never help her. God would never love Royal-Lee because if God had ever loved them, God would have given Royal-Lee a better mother. Royal-Lee ran back to the Beetle, not caring anymore that the mud in the puddles was splashing up onto their brand-new white Air Force 1s. Already, there were helicopters overhead. Running, she felt like a criminal, complicit in the death and decay of Victor, stashed back in that signed tent made into a self-serving artwork for a stoned idiot princess. She was running and knew she had nothing to run toward and everything to run away from, but that everything was their God, their story, their trauma, and as the blades whooped and whooshed overhead, she ran until she reached her shitty car.

22

Susie Reads the News . . .

It was the day after Halloween and Susie was dressed like a sober person, back on the trial pills, plus a low dose of Oxy, which after H, felt like children's Tylenol. Pain throbbed in her chest and temples. For a moment, she felt nostalgia for her Georgian four-poster canopy bed at home, carved with laurels and roses and cherubs, its Frette linen sheets scented by silk Santa Maria Novella potpourri bags, suffused with the distant memory of childhood's easy sleep.

She held the *L.A. Times*, arms propped on the table where she sat. She thought of her father's obsession with the paper; he might be reading the article about her show by now. Although he always said that if you wanted to disappear in plain sight, get featured in the *L.A. Times*; no one would ever see it. He also said if she ever made the *L.A. Times*, he would frame it and hang it by the rat poison. Fuck him. Holding the physical newspaper felt reassuring, a tangible connection to history. It made her feel sane and sober. She chewed a bagel with cream cheese and dripped schmear on the paper, which smelled of shit and sawdust. "The paper." What movie was it where the lady sculpted bagels with cream cheese out of plaster of Paris? *After Hours*, with Linda Fiorentino . . . "Surrender Dorothy!" If she were higher, she would smile.

The idea of "the paper" as a means of communication was a relatively recent one. At its most charming, it felt like the days of steamer ships when women wore poplin slacks and skirts, even poor men wore suits, and everyone read the news. She lit a cigarette and heard a foghorn in her mind. *Boooooooring.* Of course, nothing could be further from the truth now. No one read. No one had class. Class was war. She chewed and smoked. War was media. Since their inception, newspapers were entirely tools of propaganda. Ted Turner and Rupert Murdoch sailed racing yachts against one another and divided the nation politically for profit. Hearst was insane and the only correct karma for a man like that was his daughter becoming a radicalized killer. Hint, hint, *Daddy*.

She turned to other pages: Protests at the Dakota Pipeline. Police killed Black men in New Jersey, in Tulsa, in Columbus and San Diego. Obama made a $38 billion deal with Netanyahu. Angelina Jolie filed for divorce. ISIS responsible for stabbing at a Minnesota mall. Samsung Galaxies exploded. Another school shooting. Bombs in New York and New Jersey. Zika swarmed Miami. LAPD still searching for the perpetrator of the "motel killings." The Orange Candidate polling up.

The important news in today's paper was really about her. The front-page article outed the Art Walk as forgery, sponsored not by the Sicklers, as erroneously advertised, but devised by an ambitious young deviant artist, which was fine by Susie, who always admired the enfants terribles and shit instigators of the art world and was pleased to be included in their ranks. The article was titled, "An 'Art' Walk on the Wild Side," and Susie read it over and over again. *Artforum* had an article online about the walk that included videos of the riot she'd supposedly caused. Her social media accounts she had resuscitated were soaring by the tens of thousands.

There was definitely a buzz. She was a rising star. The riot had gone viral. Someone had songified footage into a "Bed Intruder" version.

A video of The Sickler Art Walk played on her phone.

"Ugh. Can you turn your volume off?" Royal-Lee asked. "You've watched that five times already."

"Be quiet, both of you," Phil murmured in the corner, from which he had not moved in hours.

"Congratulations," Peter said, studying videos on Snapchat. "You're a bona fide brat. Where did you find the dead guy?"

Did he not know?

It had to have been one of them who put him in her tent. The body had been frozen, the article said, and was thawing in the installation, oozing out after the degradation of cell walls damaged from the freeze. He was a puddle of what used to be street-cool. Who could carry that weight?

They'd had to work together, she'd figured. She remembered the bloody split knuckles of one of the twins, and the blood on the freezer wall, the night she came back from touring Skid Row.

"Don't make a big deal out of it," Phil said. "You don't need to know." Was he pissed off, thinking that he was the true visionary, and she was just a dumb social media addict, a young attention whore? People hated what had happened at the Emmys.

Although, people were also trolling her social media. Some called her a killer. There were plenty of people calling her a whore and they were growing more vicious: "stupid rich slut," "privileged white bitch," "ugly and too skinny," and "you exploit homeless addicts and appropriate the cultures of others," plus "get a real job." This *was* a real job. The show had made the papers. She was an artist! Only a barbarian would think that wasn't a real job. Trolls and haters demanded pussy pics and information about her tits, asked for deets about her sex life, while other people wanted words of wisdom on how to get famous. Then she saw the latest article mentioning her, on her feed, from *The New York Times* about "the killings" in LA and about the most recent victim being found in a Long Beach motel. There'd been another one.

The news ran a photo of the Sandpiper Motel in Long Beach, its pink stucco exterior bloated and peeling like waterlogged flesh, sand flowering in the seams of the walls like rot beneath a scab. A rusted beach cruiser lay collapsed against the building, half-swallowed by weeds, its frame warped like something dragged from the ocean floor. The latest victim had been a man—mid-twenties, unhoused, his body discovered in Room 7 with his eyelids stitched shut, his mouth stuffed with marigolds and chamomile, a crown of wildflowers pressed into his scalp like a wreath on a drowned king. Blood had soaked the mattress, then dried in hard, black waves. Susie scrolled without breathing, nausea rising up her throat like tidewater thick with gasoline. Then came the quote, halfway down the article, like a splinter in the middle of a bruise: "'*We can't let performance art like Susie Vogelman's recent Skid Row debacle or politics distract us from real lives,' said Faia Sickler, daughter of pharmaceutical mogul Richard Sickler, and founder of CHRYSALIS LA, a new nonprofit dedicated to transforming the city's approach to addiction and recovery. 'Some people still know things. People close to all this. Susie—if you see this, please talk to someone. People are still dying.'"* Susie stared at the screen. The name—*CHRYSALIS*—landed like a threat wrapped in silk. Faia always believed in transformation, so did Susie, who believed in breaking life down until it begged to be made into something else. But this? This wasn't transformation. This was a setup with her name written underneath it. This was personal.

Her phone dinged. Peter jumped.

"Oh, PLEASE, Susie, turn your notifications off," Royal-Lee sighed.

"That's not me," Susie said.

"It's me," Phil said. "Who's texting me?" He looked at his phone. "It's your dad."

"Let's kill him," Peter said.

"What did he say? I've been ignoring him."

"*You stepped in it deep. Dick is pissed. Tell Susie lunch. Pa Ord on Sunset, 1PM. Don't let her post anything until we meet. Stand down,*" Phil read.

* * *

Downstairs, the Skidders and Surlies were on the new drugs, their usual doses of Oxy, and the Internet. They scrolled the posts with patterns of integers for GETS that got thousands of comments. Online, incels were singing praises to their KEK god, predicting the election of the Orange Candidate. Memes and GIFs flashed across their screens, stealing their minds down the rabbit hole.

"There was no Egyptian God named KEK, right?" Gloria said, chewing on a hummus sandwich. "It's a racist hate symbol."

Tom wasn't listening. "The stuff I'm finding out about ancient Egypt is insane. Do you know about the guy from Blink 182?"

"What about him?" Gretchen asked. "I listened to them as a kid."

"Ancient Egyptian," Tom answered.

"You know where the word 'pizza' comes from?" This was Brenda, the seventeen-year-old at an attached cubicle.

"Where?" Kym asked, slumped against the wall before the kitchen, slurping a La Croix.

"It's Greek for kiddie porn."

"The Queen of England, the Female Candidate, the Rothchilds, and most other globalist billionaires are lizard people. They eat humans. The meetings of the true elite rulers of the world are held in tunnels, deep inside the hollow earth. They eat people, especially sex-trafficked victims. The bodies have to be alive for the lizard people to munch on them. Opioids keep the victims alive while they're munched on; it's how the power of poppies first came to be discovered. Human sacrifice. I can't believe Sickler wants us to know all this. It's the whole open secret shit. It's their law, to tell everyone what they are doing. Or is he actually good?"

Susie leaned back and put the paper down. Outside, hummingbirds floated in the air, their wings as invisible as time. Finches stood and chirped before the tall cyclone fence on the balustrades and porches.

Susie imagined the world beyond LA: deserts stretching across the San Gabriels. The Los Angeles forest, the prison complex in Victorville that she hoped she wouldn't go to; shaggy palms and brittlebush and goldfinger, boulders, mountains, live oak and buckeye, soft dust powdering the leaves of holly shrubs. Twin Peaks and Lake Arrowhead. Palmetto palms, blue butterfly bushes, forget-me-nots, fishtail palms, golden wreaths, and the native oaks. And then sand. The great divide. The Rubicon. And the empty nation. New York and the Old World. She was an artist. Most of it would burn. Fuck her dad.

She remembered Aubrey, the male figure model from her painting studio at NYU, their dorm-room trysts and the shape of his engorged penis, his uncircumcised hood her tongue would slide up in when he was not fully erect, and how she'd dressed him in her crotchless underwear once, in a black silk teddy, his shapely bulbous penis hanging below the hem. Why would she think of him now? His asshole used to taste like coffee and cinnamon. Who cared? Why was she thinking of him? Was it because of what happened to Asher? They were similarly named. Aubrey. Ashley. Laura Ashley. Ashley Olsen. Ashley Furniture. *Fuck it.*

Peter was acting strangely today, drawn inward, mumbling about being hungry and having no appetite, nearly comatose on his back. Every now and then, he wiped his eyes as if he were crying and then talked about Crayola crayons and how there are infinite colors, and who used crayons anymore anyway? They always just broke. As soon as one broke, you wanted to buy a brand-new set. They designed the boxes to make you feel that way. He wanted to go back in time with his brother. He wasn't going to shoot any more dope. Phil shouldn't either—Peter was worried about him. Remember when they played with crayons?

"Shut up, man," Phil muttered. "I never should have found you."

Maybe she'd do an installation of a palm tree fabricated out of polyethylene, with a huge beard or bush or whatever the shaggy brown part of those palm trees on Palm Canyon in Palm Springs was called. She'd known, once. Her brain was toast. How could she not recall? On each wall of the room would be a painting of the sky in LA in each season. Summer, fall, winter, spring, so that when you looked at the palm tree from different places in the room, you'd see the sky with the name of the season in black letters. They'd all look the same, the skies in different seasons. LA barely changed. Or maybe it would be a penis coming up out of the skirted palm with more fronds erupting from the urethra. *Trunk fibers.* That's what the hairy part of palms were called. *No.* She was getting ahead of herself.

Her phone dinged. Royal-Lee had texted a link. Hannity had done a story on her and launched a tirade about spoiled brats in Hollywood. The Orange Candidate tweeted that it was very interesting how someone had attacked the Sicklers:

"Nobody's done more on opioids than I have—believe me. It's a TOTAL DISASTER, a horrible crisis, and I care deeply about the people suffering. The addicts, the families—we're going to take care of it." Then: "We're going to FIX IT, and we're going to fix it fast. No one's going to do it like me. Everyone knows that." And then another: "Look, the opioid thing? It's a disaster—total mess. But I care, I really do. I've seen it, I've talked to people—it's heartbreaking." And finally: "Let me tell you, nobody is going to FIX IT like I will. We're gonna clean it up, FAST. The other guys? They talk. I DO. We're gonna take care of our people—the addicts, the families—we're not leaving them behind. Not on my watch."

The phone dinged again. Another link. On the sidewalk on Gladys, three severed fingers had been found, but just the top halves, taken off at the second knuckle.

"I better meet my dad for lunch, don't you think?"

"Do whatever you want," Phil sighed.

"Okay," Susie, said, turning slowly, disbelieving Phil's blessing was so easily earned. But why should she need his blessing? It was her town, and her life. Whose fucking fingers were those anyhow?

"Just know you wouldn't even be in the news if it weren't for me. You made the papers and the nightly news, and you didn't have to do anything but sign your name? This isn't just about you getting famous."

"Are you okay?" Susie had asked. Phil was acting like he was being operated by remote control.

"I'm fine. I just need some time alone, in the dark."

"This isn't over," Peter said. "We should kill your dad."

Susie said, "What?"

She envisioned getting dressed for her next opening. She'd have a balcony of her own and the light of the afternoon sun on a tall eucalyptus, the sky's color darkening at sundown. The blast of a car's horn or a fire engine's siren would scream as she'd go inside to put on an oversized Reebok sweatshirt over a dress from Rodarte, and weird sandals. A show at LACMA—tents in plaster of Paris, gold-coated and bejeweled. She'd show up late, air-kiss a few old friends, and duck out early for dinner at Musso & Frank with Alex Israel, Carmen Argote, Young Joon Kwak, and maybe Erwin Wurm would be in town. Or China Chow. "Tell us about your first show, the Skid Row one," China would ask.

"Susie, are you aware that my brother is a junkie who's been living in one of those tents on the streets for years?" Phil said. She dropped the paper. He was staring at her.

"Yeah, I knew that, Phil. He's right there."

Peter spoke up. "You guys don't need to worry about me. Worry about Dick. Worry about the rest of the world. We ship our trash to third-world countries but how come my mom never came to my school plays? What was she doing that was so much more important all those evenings?" He looked off into the distance, rapt in memory, then came to, remembering where he was. "We've all been fucked with, we've all been hurt. It's not about us anymore. It's about this next generation. I mean they tell them that they don't deserve to feel hurt, to keep their heads up. Stiff upper lip. Whenever we complained, our parents would just tell us it was our fault, that we were useless. Meanwhile, they were the most spoiled people on the planet. They used us for comfort, and when we couldn't make them feel better with hugs and kisses, they turned on us. Remember, Phil? We were the lucky ones. Think of all those people out on the streets. No one gives a fuck. All the addicts. These trial pills aren't going to work. These people downstairs are doomed. They're getting sucked into the opiate of the masses, conspiracy theories, antisemitism, and they're still hooked on dope. The Church never took you seriously as a member. They fucked us all. Everyone gets erased and the world burns. It's all luck. Unless you take action—and then everyone thinks you did it to get famous, rather than to save your own heart from the guilt of being a fuck."

Royal-Lee sighed. "Come on, man. Enough. We aren't a real army of resistance. We don't save actual lives."

She seemed tired of everyone. She'd contoured her oval face to look a bit more heart-shaped, like Susie's, but nobody even cared. They tightened their long Bonsoir silk wrap, smoothed it over their long tan legs, and tried to breathe deeply. They had more important things on their mind; they positioned their head to convey it. She couldn't go home, couldn't stay here, and she was definitely going to make a run for it. Meanwhile, the brothers were making speeches and griping at each other without any real communication, just their separate thoughts bouncing around their lonely, drug-addicted minds.

"The Earth is a prison state run by billionaires," Phil said. "To quote Juvenal, 'Everything now restrains itself and anxiously hopes for just two things: bread and circus.' There's more to life than bread and circus, guys. But if you're gonna live at the circus, you'd better at least get on stage. We could die waiting for someone to come around tickling us with free sandwiches made with ciabatta bread and caviar."

"You don't eat caviar with ciabatta," Susie interrupted. "Idiot."

"Whatever! You're not Cinderella and you don't need new shoes. You can just take a fucking car to lunch with Daddy. And you can watch yourself on your little screen playing out America's schizophrenia with you in one of its little shows, your TV riding around in the palm of your hand, the snow-globe world that's going to melt before it ever learns to love itself. I just want to get high. You made a name for yourself off the backs of the poor and the addicted. Go see your dad. Get lunch. I already gave you an A plus, what else do you want from me? But first, Suz, come get high with me. Peter, please don't come with us."

23

The Fires . . .

What does it mean to be a serious person? The things that happened—that will happen—in this chapter require some differentiation between Susie the character and me, now, in my day to day. I'm not the young foolish girl I was back then, at the Villa, blind to the world, grasping for some means to strike back against the little society of my humbler beginnings. Not that they were all that humble. Humility is something that I still struggle with in my program and life. You see . . . I'm not *like* you. I don't mean that in some flagrantly entitled sense. I'm not playing a social trump card. It's simply true.

You are probably someone who is completely in society, in the mainstream, whether you want to admit that to yourself or not, and I am part of a different order. I want to be humble and gracious. I want to appear magnanimous and gentle. I know this is the time of the "suave and considerate" creative. The truth is, however, that you know too much about me, and the world knows too much about me, for me to pass myself off under the cloak and mask of clandestine calm. I take direct action

I'm a killer.

You're a killer.

We are all killers.

That's the baseline, the rest is what good you can do to make up for it and save someone else.

I am sure by now you've figured something out about me and this whole story. I do have to let you know that Faia is coming by in a little while, and I have my studio manager stopping by later this afternoon, so I have to keep this brief. I don't much like talking about what happened next anyhow, and I want to preserve the option of letting you think for yourself after this book has ended, and question it all, count the killings on the severed fingers of the dead, which of course you're going to; how much of what I'm writing here is the stark truth, naked as the eyes of a clown, as someone once put it so brilliantly, and how much is the business of compromise, living with others, existing in a society, having a name and a bank account. All that good business of life. I have already told you that my father taught me to have cash on hand, jewels, gold, a boat, protection, resources at the ready.

My father never joined The Church, or *The Society*, as it has come to be renamed and rebranded after the events that unfolded that fall, and they have begun accepting women into their fold, as actual members, but I will let you in on a little secret: Faia, myself, my mother for a time, we were all invited to join. We refused. I want you to know that some things are very serious with real consequences, but *The Society* is not one of them. It's a joke, and it always was. It is more serious perhaps than the truly unserious people walking their dogs in Los Angeles, their blank, pathetic faces, ready to be good little boys and girls, hoping they'll be rewarded with a nice life if they just behave like they were taught in school, but neither they nor those who roam scowling, mad on the streets, know—really know—the truth of where this world is going next. I know more than they do and that keeps me from false humility. My father taught me more than survival skills; he taught me how to thrive. I know not to trust this world and not to keep everything I have in one place. The shit is going to hit the fan again.

I will sit under the canvas awnings this afternoon with Faia and drink my iced tea with lemon, and admire the feel of the wet crease of the cut crystal glass and the slide of my fingertip up and down the groove, the sunlight split through the prisms of the palm fronds, and feel something like the meek of the earth must feel, a little breeze on my face, something of God, which my sponsor continues to preach to me, and who the losers in the meetings I go to talk about alongside their gratitude lists and their groveling before one another to be the most humble, the most healed, offering petitions to the Lord of the Twelve Steps, but I know the truth. It's awfully hard to respect anyone who isn't in a position to know how the world works, who isn't privy to the secret workings of the powerful and doesn't understand how powerbrokers keep the world radiating like the NIST cesium fountain clock, as billionaires promise to take us to Mars . . . right? You think you know how things are going to go but it takes three days for a society to fall apart when the banks stop working. Don't be a liberal idiot. Or a conservative fascist. *Think, think, think,* as they say in meetings.

After all I've done, and all I have seen, and still see, I know how things *really* work; what the big picture looks like. I try to find God and humility. I really do. Back then, at the Villa, reading the paper, it was a simpler time. I was still on the outside of the power game, more or less, and thrilled to see my name in print, the papers that never stop being printed with new names, the movies that no one believes in anymore—the bygone times of make-believe dreamers of a better world made up on the old 20th Century Fox lot are over—and I'm almost glad we don't believe in that toxic dreamworld anymore—and that I don't live back then, a prisoner in a man's world of racists and sexists and semi-secret Jews and Jew haters—even though that world is still with us. We dare not blink before the truth, which is that my father is right: antisemitism is rising, racism is a puppet master that never stops pulling the strings, and the world is run by serious people who use hate to make money.

I am not one of those people.

Who am I?

I am a player.

* * *

How things played out at the Villa that day, and at lunch with my father a week later, when I agreed to meet with him—on Election Day—and what prompted me to accept his lunch invitation are painful memories to recount. Why had Phil sacrificed his sobriety to be close to his brother? All to watch Peter then achieve a new relative-sobriety without him—intermittent and chemically dependent on a maintenance dose of opioids and opioid enhancers as it was—and then it was Peter who was to go to loggerheads with Phil's enemy, Dick Sickler?

I guess Phil didn't have the force of will to manifest his vendetta against the Sicklers. I guess he was always too weak, too privileged, too damaged, too demure, too squeamish to go all the way. He should have had a smarter army. His brother, Peter, would prove the stronger of the twins. He'd already seized control of the Villa, was leading group therapy, sermonizing from the stage in wig and beard at night, and guiding the addicted house members to try and try again at opioid-supported recovery.

In his talks, Peter's increasing anger at the world inflamed his preaching about our duty to strike back against the Orange Candidate's rhetoric, the opioid industry, the cops, society, and, not neglecting our distinctively local ills, against whoever had been dissecting even more addicts in hotels in Los Angeles, in increasingly heinous ways. Whoever it was, they were leaving messages now at the crime scenes about the useless leeches on society they were murdering, "junkies who suck tax-payer dollars," "the immigrants," "the lazy poor," "the weak," and "the impure."

The Vagabond Inn in San Pedro was a scene from a coastal John Carpenter flick, blood splattered on the vinyl blackout curtains, walls brown with dried gore, flesh cut from bone, the terrible low linoleum counter with the brown faux-leather ice bucket, and amber ashtray, the toilet full of blood, towels stuffed inside the slashed abdomen of the victim, a robust woman in her fifties named Linda Valentine, her name like a joke, like a book, or a De Palma movie, but the messages written on the walls were not from a fiction.

At the Roxy Hotel on Western Avenue between Hollywood and Sunset, a young male body was suspended in a closet, hanging by a steel double-sided shark hook. Connor Fredrickson's skull was impaled on one end of a twin hook that straddled the adjustable chrome closet rod. The Roxy Hotel's royal blue, star-studded sign was displayed against the faded green stucco when photographed in the papers. The victim's impaled head was not shown, but photos had been leaked online to

Facebook and to various sites that traded in the unsavory and ghoulish predilections of the perverse.

Then there were the fires. Someone was setting homes on fire in the canyons and to the west, all owned by prominent people—but only the homes of people of color and Jews. Something very sick was happening in America. Or it had always been part of the nation, but it was now rising to the surface in bright boils, and Peter was angry. It was on Election Day, before I went to lunch, that Phil slumped into the bathroom with a needle and a spoon from the dopp kit that had been his brother's, having invited me, but I'd stalled, and prepared to die.

I still don't know if he meant to go, or if his soul was just finished, or if God wanted him, or if anything like that is ever true. I just know he slipped into the bathroom, and slipped away from this world. Maybe it's fitting that he died before the election was called that night at midnight LA time, Phil not even making it to noon that day, November 8, 2016. By the time I realized he'd been gone too long, was not in the room, and went to find him, going to get high myself, he was collapsed against the wall, a cone of foam down his shirtfront, his eyes rolled back; another number adding up to zero.

I came out and told Peter, who went crazy, and I slipped downstairs, myself unable or unwilling to bear witness to one brother screaming at his dead twin. Royal-Lee stayed in the room. I called a car on my father's rideshare app, and slamming on my Gentle Monster shades against the brilliance of midday, went to lunch.

24

Susie Meets Dad in Thai Town . . .

Pa Ord was a cheap, fluorescently lit restaurant on the north side of Sunset at the border of Hollywood. It wasn't like her father to meet her in a place like this for lunch. He preferred contemporary spaces with gleaming open kitchens or classic old Hollywood haunts, or the occasional grand sweeping patio with good-looking waiters, crisply dressed, serving overpriced California cuisine. He'd obviously chosen this place as an act of psychological warfare: the dark yellow walls, the drop ceiling, and black faux-marble countertops, everything about it seemed to be telling her she was exiled from his circle of privilege. She was in trouble. She was a *bad girl. He* was a *bad dad*—he hadn't even visited her in rehab. It had been over a month.

Her father watched her waltz to the table, his gaze tracking her like a cop: Susie was his criminal. He had on his weekend T-shirt and slacks combo, as though he were trying to blend in with the commoners. His shoes gave him away. Chalmers—crocodile, purple label, with penny slots at the vamp—super cheese. It wasn't Spago, or La Scala, or The Tower Bar, or Maude. She didn't care. She'd rather die than go back to any of those places and sit like a petulant child captured in the miserable scenic details of their old familiars—she wasn't her father's subject anymore. She was the main character, and he couldn't stand it. The world knew her name. Of course she was still wanted for questioning by the police. She'd rather go to prison for being free than be free and live like she were in a cage. Phil was dead. Peter was going crazy. Her phone dinged. She ignored the message.

She was embarrassed for him—his heft, his sloppiness despite the fastidiousness of his self-grooming, how truly subservient he was, how lonely and clueless and scared—a drug dealer's hired bully with self-esteem issues.

What really bothered her: she might be a lot like *him*. Except he hadn't done anything for social good. Quite the opposite. It showed. Now Dad had been living alone for weeks. Men were so pathetic. It was pathetic to hide behind wealth all your life, Susie thought, especially someone else's money. She was better than all of that. She wasn't at this restaurant ironically. She was going to *eat* the food and actually savor it. The restaurant smelled like bone broth and spices, roasted duck, and chili oil. She'd get vegan spring rolls. People chatted and chewed. Her eyes stung. She was a fugitive artist. Would anyone recognize her? Not here. Maybe that was why her father had chosen Pa Ord. Maybe he was looking out for her.

She wore a new uniform to lunch, one that advertised her status as a subversive proletariat artist: a greased-up mechanic's onesie that one of the Surlies had left behind when they'd evacuated, failing the drug trial.

She'd worn it every day now without deodorant, so her smell permeated the stiff poly-cotton and became an extension of her body and aura. The group at the Villa had grown on her over the past month and a half. She'd been part of a movement, she felt now; Phil, its once leader, was dead. The house had turned into a den of trolls, medicated incels, and Illuminati-obsessed neo-cons. But her first show had been written up everywhere. She would have to leave the rehab soon, she felt. Actually, she could never return. Someday perhaps she'd write a memoir about it. "We had a Dadaist drug cult, with my old professor acting as opiate shaman, or LA Jesus. I wasn't involved in any adoration of him, not even close—actually he was kind of an idiot—but at the Villa, I felt powerful, in a real-life, post-abstract kind of way." It was that simple, to turn her back on the truth. To deny she'd believed in his radicalism since she'd laid on eyes on him. To say he hadn't given her so much impetus.

It was good copy.

She was in the zone. She had some Oxy zinging in her pocket and more in her bloodstream. Her followers were skyrocketing. She was sad about Phil.

The sun through the tinted storefront glass barely lit the dingy brown table, hiding her tears. The dream wasn't success in the here and now; the dream was to start something that would go on after your death. She didn't want that something to be revolution. Revolution was boring. She didn't want other people using bodies for art. She had decided her next project would be to sculpt victims out of non-human materials, a dream she would later accomplish. She'd grabbed pills off the dresser on her way out of the suite at the Villa, and used in the car ride over to Pa Ord.

"Hi, Dad," she said, as he sipped his Diet Coke through a non-compostable straw.

"Hi, love," he said like a desperate schmuck.

"Hey. I have to go to the bathroom real quick. Actually, I have to *shit*. It might take a bit." She ran a hand through her dirty hair. She looked down at him. "It's just hard to go at the Villa." She nodded her head and kept talking. "Because there's always a line. So I save up my shit for when it's convenient, you know?" She'd just smashed his power game. *Take that, motherfucker.* He was her mother's fucker, once upon a time, although apparently not anymore.

She turned and walked toward the back, where a sign said "Toilet." When she glanced across the room, Dad was fuming, violently flapping a laminated menu at a fly. Did he really think that he was too good for this place? She tried to remember seeing a fly at Peppone or La Dolce Vita. She'd seen one at Musso & Frank, several at Dan Tana's. And they flew into the Polo Lounge from the patio, but that was different. Those flies were on vacation, like tourists.

All Dad cared about was work. He'd gotten several Sicklers off of felony charges in his famous plea deal of 2006. Did they give him a billion dollars for it? Surely not. They were fined and given misdemeanors after he'd argued in court they didn't know Oxy was addictive until after 2000. Another lie. *Mom* was hooked on Oxy back then already. When they were fined, Dick Sickler tore my father a new asshole. He berated him in his office, "Are you a fucking idiot? Are you so fucking stupid? Are you worthless? Maybe I should fire you, you rotten little coward." She was going to blow this place up.

Dick dressed him down from the other side of a mahogany desk the size of a truck. As a kid, Susie would overhear her father talking to management consultants on speakerphone, pushing for shaping the company toward an "end-to-end pain management approach." Using code words, "Fidelio" and "Fellatio." Whatever it all meant, she knew the picture. Once you got on, you never got off. It was so *dick*. It was . . . inhumane. It was just capitalism on the new drugs as always.

Susie looked at herself in the mirror. She was glad she had grabbed a bottle of reds back at the suite after she saw Phil OD; her old trick, grabbing the pills off a dead victim, flinching at the prospect of taking heroin now that Phil had OD'd on it; she wasn't that tough. She wanted to live. She *was* strong. Her father didn't see that, or appreciate it, or give a shit, obviously, or else he'd have booked them a table at Delilah and apologized for busting in on her territory. "I'm so sorry, Susie. You're obviously more in tune with the world than I am, as evidenced by your radical genius art project. Daring. Searingly sardonic. The only thing I can't figure out is if you put the body in the tent. If so, your art show is even more of something to be proud of. However, no matter what, you have ruined me with your brilliance and I would like to buy you a *Bugatti*." Those were so tacky. Her father was tacky. And maybe it was cool to be tacky but not when you were rich, but most rich people were totally tacky. Even the word *rich* was tacky. The correct word was *influential*.

Her father's influence wasn't real influence. He was a tool. He drew up exit plans and nondisclosure agreements—lobbied politicians, made donations, and pushed to have government documents sealed—practicing good lawyering. If it were up to her dad, she'd be married within five years to some Jewish guy with a crooked penis who looked like Ben Platt from *Pitch Perfect*. Fat chance now. Fat cock. She didn't need a cock.

She double-checked the door. It smelled like chemicals and Thai iced tea in the can. She used a black permanent marker she'd pocketed from the Villa that morning—always planning ahead!—to crush a red pill. Susie railed the red powder on the buttery plastic counter of the Pa Ord bathroom. She checked her skin in the mirror, then studied the walls of greasy fake wood. She popped a pimple. There was an orange sign that said *don't put paper in the toilet.* Did it mean *don't flush toilet paper*? Were people really supposed to take their shit-streaked TP and put it in the trash? Was this El Salvador?

She rolled a dollar bill into a wide straw and jammed it up her nose. She snorted the powder greedily. The Oxy tasted bitter and medicinal. She licked her lips and cleared her throat, gulping back nasal drip, feeling it hit her system. She took the dollar bill, crumpled it up, and threw it in the toilet and flushed. She checked her nose in the mirror. She rolled up her sleeves. She had no tattoos, several scars, bruises, and three track marks. She rolled down her sleeve. This looked like a bathroom you could cut someone up in.

"How was your poop?" Dad asked when she returned from the bathroom, high as fuck. "I ordered us duck soup."

"Great. I'm vegan. So, I'm totally sober now." Her head lolled a little.

"You don't look sober. You can expect riots to start any day if the Orange Guy wins. Can you believe this Comey fellow? I wonder what side *he's* really working for, and what they got on him. Sickler says he's fey as a rabbit." The waitress put down another fizzy Diet Coke and two more non-compostable straws. "Completely crazy."

Susie thought of her rabbit. She'd loved her. Her name was June. Who cared? The world was still spinning. Everyone would be buried in it.

"What?" She'd completely forgotten what he'd said.

"James Comey, don't you read? Head of the FBI. Stupid. What's wrong with you? Your face looks . . . bad."

"I look like this, because . . . I'm on the new drug."

"Your hair is a mess. You can't brush your hair?"

"What do you care?"

"You're my only child, Susie. I care about you." This other waitress with bad acne brought two big bowls of steaming duck soup. He coughed into his napkin and placed it still folded on one wide thigh.

"Yeah, sure. Dad of the Year. You didn't even visit me."

"Well that's gonna change. I need to talk to Phil. I need to talk to him today."

"That won't be possible." She flinched.

Her father slurped some soup, coughed, patted his mouth with the paper napkin, and cocked his head in a way she'd never seen before.

"Have you heard from your mother in the last few weeks?" he asked.

"No, Dad. Last I heard from her, she was telling me to take it a day at a time, or some bullshit."

"Have you tried calling her?" His eye twitched. She noticed a mole on his eyelid she'd never seen. He had a rather broad Midwestern face. He was aging.

"Why?"

"She hasn't come home in a month," her father said, swirling his noodles around with his chopsticks. "It's probably nothing, but her phone is off."

"She ran away?"

"Oh, no, I'm sure she's just out of range, out of service."

"For a month?"

"Did she tell you where she was going?" he asked.

"She never tells me anything."

"This . . . affair she's having. Do you know if it's real?"

"I don't know, Dad. Your marriage is none of my business."

"I'm concerned, Susie, that your mother has been kidnapped."

"By who?"

Her father was silent. Susie pictured her mother tied up in the back of a '68 Plymouth convertible, lipstick smearing against the nylon rope bound around her jaw, like the rich white lady in that Rihanna video. "Bitch Better Have My Money."

"Excuse me?"

Had she just said that out loud?

"No, nothing."

"What money does she owe you? What's going on? Has your friend at the rehab been in touch with her?" he said, slurping and then setting the chopsticks across the bowl. "Dick thinks he might be 'the killer.' I don't know. Something your mother told me he said before they disappeared together. I don't know where she's been. Dick's been hiding out until his election party tonight. Phil's been uninvited. Dick thinks he's gonna kill him. These Oxy deaths have gotten too close for comfort, they really are fucked up." He looked around to make sure no one was within earshot. "To be honest, if Dick were dead, our lives could get a whole lot easier. That son of a bitch could really turn on us. If he says I knew everything and hid it from the Feds, I could spend time in prison. If Sickler's dead, our money's safe. Mom comes home. I won't get dragged through congressional hearings for the second half of my life. I could finally chill."

"What the fuck are you talking about?"

"Look, I know you had your little art show and got some attention, but Victor Hernandez was found dead in one of your tents. This dectective has been looking for you and ringing my phone off the hook. Cecil Hotel, Susie? Ring a bell? Your old roommate at NYU. This all connects you to these 'killings,' whether you like it or not. You can never go back to that rehab. It's obviously not working anyhow. You should come home and live with your daddy."

"Daddy . . .? What did you mean about the Feds? Are you in trouble with the law?"

"Dick and I have had a little friction over the last few weeks, about this drug trial." He was whispering now. "It's completely outside FDA regulations. I told him not to tell me about it, but once *you* got involved—"

"I'm not involved!"

"Please, Susie. These are dangerous people."

"The bums? They're not dangerous. They're mellow as shit now that they're on your new drugs. All they do is fuck around on computers."

"No, not them. The Sicklers. The Church."

"Well, shit." She was feeling woozy again, like she was melting in the steam from the soup.

"I'm going to resign," her father said. "The Nazis are coming. Do you have any idea what kind of shit riot it's going to be if this clown gets elected? Someday soon these will seem like simpler old times."

"What about Mom?"

"I'm hoping that if the drug trial finishes, no problems, nothing happens, Sickler gets what he wants, we can sweep it under the rug. Forgotten. And your mother will come back with a new nose or something. But if something goes wrong . . ." Her father leaned over his soup, the steam fogging his transition lenses.

"Are you saying you *want* us to kill Dick?"

"Now, hold on, back up." Her father was serious. He pushed his soup away. "Susie, there's something called the 'Prosecution Memo.' You need to know about this now. If that memo comes out, if things go in that direction, you'd be a poor woman for the rest of your life. The Feds have proof that we misled Congress, but the document is sealed. I had it sealed. If and when that gets released, all our money-on-paper is gone . . . anything they can trace to me can be taken in civil courts for victims' families. But not if it's been transferred to your trust. If Sickler dies, this will all disappear. Trust me."

"Kill him, huh?"

"I never said that."

"Yeah, we should just kill Dick." Susie didn't mean it. She was high and testing his limits, daring to find out what kind of man her father really was and what his limitations would always be.

"Kill Dick. You said it, not me," her father said.

So this was the kind of person she came from.

He really was a fuck. Had this been his plan all along? First she was a good-for-nothing junkie, and now she was his go-to murderer for hire? Was her mother in on it? Was anyone else? Was she misunderstanding?

"What do I get out of it?" she asked.

"I'll give you the house. It's worth fifteen million, but safe harbored and distributed to your trust at the original purchase price," he whispered. "It's always been my plan for you. I want you to have the house. I'll do all the paperwork, put money aside for the taxes, and you can have it."

"I could make it look like a sex thing," Susie said. Her wheels were turning. Was she so high? Susie closed her eyes. Was her father fucking with her? Or was her mom working for her dad as a mole inside The Church? Was she missing or not? Who had been committing "the killings"?

"Whatever you want," he was saying.

She opened her eyes and looked down at her soup. There was a black hair in it, not hers. She pulled it out, uncoiling it off the oily surface of the broth. It just kept uncoiling, longer and longer. It was at least three feet long. She held it up and looked at it, almost invisible in the bad lighting. It wasn't human. It was horse. Maybe it was one of Phil's? From his wig? Too long. She was so disappointed in her father.

"Susie?"

Was it Faia's hair? Impossible. She closed her eyes again and imagined going back to New York. She could go to the Guggenheim, some galleries. Maybe she'd get recognized. Meet the Bells, or the Blacks, or the Boros. Fake hotdogs. Mustard and ketchup. Relish. Coffee and pills . . . her eyes were closed. She opened them to her father clearing his throat.

"You lie for a living, Dad. Why should I trust you now?"

"You never know who you can trust. But I am your father. If you can't trust me, who will you?"

She watched him slurp some soup and nodded at him. She looked at her phone. Faia had texted.

My dad got a call from the Beverly Hills Hotel . . . Do you know about this?

"Faia's staying at the Beverly Hills Hotel," Susie said blankly.

"Oh, that's a great idea. I'll get you a room. Spend time with her."

"What would Mom say if I killed Sickler?"

"Susie. Stop it. Your mother has a vested interest in whatever is good for this family. And you should too. So, are you going to the election party tonight?"

"Okay. Mom sucks."

"She sucks, but she's the only mom you have. Now, listen to me, Susie. The code for Sickler's gate is 1984 . . . And the password is Gutenberg."

25

Body in the Bungalow . . .

Farther on the Westside after lunch with Dad at the Thai restaurant, I barely knew how I'd gotten there, but found myself strolling like a zombie into the Beverly Hills Hotel. I floated through the preppy pink pillars of the porte-cochère, with its green-and-white striped ceiling, and over the bold, bloodred carpeted walkway and across the inlaid palm-patterned floors and rising columns of the lobby, past the Polo Lounge, and out onto the paths toward the bungalows.

I wound my way toward the Presidential Bungalow through the wind. By the time I caught up with my vampire-self, I was nearly stoned outside of consciousness, fighting the gusts and the grit in my eyes, almost having forgotten why I'd been summoned at all. I had to find out why Faia had been told to come to this place, and if she would be there after I'd told her I was coming . . . something was happening and I couldn't go back to the Villa and I had no real place to be. I looked back at her texts.

My dad got a call from the Beverly Hills Hotel . . . Do you know about this?
They say there's flowers all over the Pres suite.

I texted back.

Hello, Faia. How would I know?
Can I meet you there?

She texted back.

Don't. I'll call the cops if you come near me.

I'd forgotten if I'd come by rideshare. Maybe my dad had gotten me a black car from his personal service, since he was trying to persuade me to do what he wanted, or so I thought? I flipped through my phone for receipts.

Should I be hurt?

I was conflicted. He'd offered me our house! There was always a catch; he probably meant when he was dead. He should be more worried about me getting sober. Where was the human element, the patriarchal heart? I had been in *rehab* . . . did either of my parents think to *visit?* Those mechanical mothers covered in spikes that blew air on baby monkeys—that Phil taught about in class, furious about animal experimentation, and Skinner boxes, deranged torture, Satanic mistreatment of living things, why I had become a vegan—were an apt metaphor for my parents. Except now those monkeys would give me fifteen million dollars? I wouldn't take it. Maybe I'd take it. The world was in shambles, and I was walking along the winding paths of the rich. Dad only cared about generational planning, wealth, control. He hadn't ever given a moment's thought to me as a real person, an addict who could die, his only child in the midst of so many deaths. He should be worried about me. Maybe I should grow up, stop blaming him, and be responsible. I texted my mom; she said she was fine but couldn't talk or text.

Locked inside his miserable ways, Dad concocted only the most heinous scenarios because his mind had become addicted to fear and violence, and he was as chemically dependent on paranoia as I was on dope. He was only looking for the big crash and couldn't be helped. There was something profoundly human about his helplessness that I could almost respect—I couldn't be helped either. He helped kill a half million people.

I felt hopeless, drifting through the sun with the winds that were whipping the palms like plastic pompoms. *Rah-rah-rah*. They had inspired everyone from Homer to Hockney, Baldessari to Ruscha, Israel to Versace. Fuck fucking everyone. They would burn. No one had really sculpted palm trees perfectly yet. I would, I told myself—

but I never have and don't want to. If I'd done it then, there would be bloodred Oxy pills descending the cables like fruit, and on that day, as it would turn out, a head atop the highest fronds.

I'd had one show. People hadn't all loved it, on account of Vic's body being left in one of the tents, but it had made a splash and that's what counts. Was I in trouble? Would the art world shun me? Peter and Phil had told me six weeks ago of the detective asking about me, but my dad hadn't ratted me out to Lieutenant Polachek and neither had Mom. Whatever was floating on the turbulent air, fate was awaiting me and maybe I would find it in the bungalow. I felt fear rippling up my back as the drug receded but I pushed on into the rough wind. I found myself ringing the bungalow's bell and knocking.

It's all sort of a blur.

Royal-Lee opened the door with a puffy face and big cheeks streaked with tears. What was she doing here?

"What's wrong?" I said, as if I'd forgotten Phil was dead.

She just shook their head without giving me any answer.

"I'm so sorry," I held Royal. She crumpled in my arms and I stood there as long as I could and then shook her off.

I was high enough not to give a fuck. Tears felt like a performance—some sensitive baby having a too-long moment. But part of me saw it. Felt it. Filed it away. Because what if I needed it later? Did Royal-Lee know Peter was coming with the body? Did Royal-Lee know anything at all or had she just been sent there to check on me? I will never know what they knew.

Whoosh.

The winds were whipping wildly outside around the hotel compound. I looked around the place and yawned and rubbed my eyes. I wasn't sure where Royal-Lee had gone and realized I'd been staring out of the sliding doors onto the wind-driven waves of the private pool. Next to me, there was a big flower arrangement with a card that said, *Welcome Faia, With Our Compliments.* I winced. Compliments for what—being rich?

This place was nice. But I wasn't satisfied. I didn't want to be here *or* in squalor at the Villa. The luxury aesthetic was a mere substitute for our time's version of real art or music or social events. People fetishized *spaces*. Nothing was fun. You didn't go to a hotel to *visit* somewhere, or *do* something, you went to look at the hotel and post it, have drinks by the pool, and if you were lucky, or maybe unlucky, fuck in the same bed where so many other people had fucked before you.

It was fancy jail for fancy prisoners, caged by their own minds. I'd spent plenty of my time at The Carlyle and my parents never blinked an eye at the credit card receipts because they knew it was all a prison anyhow. Would I go to real jail? Was I really on the run, hiding out from some detective with a last name I couldn't remember, and would I end up incarcerated? How had Royal-Lee checked in before Faia? My ID, listed on the reservation, in a wig as disguise? The place was too quiet, no music, the weird hum, and the too-cold air.

The bungalow's pool, secluded behind tall pink stucco walls, had one living wall of succulents in a color scale of oranges, teals, light blues, dense greens, limes, and yellows. It looked like a part of an inner courtyard at one of the finer hotels in Marrakesh, or some shit off Pinterest. Plants grew from built-in planters near a table and chairs for six, poolside lounge chairs and sunbrellas, with oversized slider doors spanning the living room. Royal purple bougainvillea grew from other planters as did a citrus tree from a large brutalist box planter. There were three extremely long white steps into the pool with a railing, and gleaming white coping around the ledge of the pool.

Velvet chairs and ottomans, glass, wood, white rugs, orchids, mirrors, long white linen drapes, leather overstuffed dining chairs, and a mirrored-glass dining room table were arranged inside, and beyond, the long open foyer of windows and mirrors.

I found myself in the bathroom. It was a nice place. It was fine. I wished I could pass a single shit. When I was younger, I would have dreamed of having a luxurious bath in this soaking tub, sipping a glass of champagne, wiggling my toes in the dissolving bubbles. It's just that I had been on drugs long enough that being unable to go was constant discomfort, and I could care less about taking a fucking bath.

You can forget weighing art and culture against an idealized past, the trappings of nostalgia, a romance of narcissism. I would have just loved to *go*. To eliminate, to expel, to banish. It was like Judith Butler wrote about that I'd learned at NYU from Phil, reading *Bodies That Matter.* I heard a thump, outside the room, and blamed it on the wind. The body must have permeable boundaries; if you didn't allow things to come out, you became so full of shit you died. What did I want to come out of me? What did I want to let go of? There was so much of me that I didn't want to hold onto anymore. I didn't want any part of me, maybe, and that's why I stayed so doped up. Society wasn't letting go of its bullshit. Boundaries weren't permeable. We were way too walled off. That's what the Orange Candidate was about. Walls. I was guilty, too.

Identity, like all else that is legally enforced, is fraudulent, and yet the dream awakens to reality for the mind that has dreamed it, right? If I could shed my mortal coil and become something else, it was time to try. I'd been going somewhere I knew I shouldn't be going for a long time, as if pulled by a net dragged behind people who were more sober and in control than me—Dad, Mom, Dick—and, for a time, Phil. I was ready to become the originator of my own existence. I was about to come into contact with my subject; my muse, once again. I didn't know it, but looking back, I had some kind of feeling, that premonition of a puzzle piece about to click into place. It was the most intricately made piece on the planet. A simulation would mean nothing. Damien Hirst had figured that out, with his taxidermized animal sculptures. Looking back now, I shudder to think how I'd comported myself so coolly around death at that time. I didn't kill anyone. I didn't seek anything out. Art did it to me! I saw the vanishing point of the circumstances of my life converging into this very center, around a single subject, and I considered it and ultimately did not use it to speak for myself, but speak it would. Or its brother would speak for it. Having a brother must be the most important thing in the world, more important than a religion or a country, or anything else I could imagine.

A wheelchair is how they moved him. While I was at lunch with Dad, a wheelchair had been purchased, a bucket hat loaned by Royal-Lee; the Montclair windbreaker and a pair of Gucci glasses donned, and the reservation made for the Presidential Bungalow—it had been the only bungalow available but it had been unreserved. A stroke of luck?

Or just the result of the hefty price? Manifestation? I don't remember how I learned of it all.

Dignity has no price but it has a pedigree. I would go on to be welcomed back into the fold. My time with Phil and Peter and Royal-Lee was brief. My parents would become unwelcome scoundrels after my trial. I can't help that. A body, alive or dead, should be useful to a good cause. That's something I believe. It's the punk version of Churchill's "Never let a good crisis go to waste."

I didn't place Vic in that tent.

I didn't even know about it, if you take my word for it on the stand and in this book. Even if I'm a black widow woman and I'm lying—those cliché ideas of womanhood—let's say they're true in my case; what did I actually do? Say I put a dead body in a tent knowingly, which I didn't. Say I planned this demonstration at the Beverly Hills Hotel, which I didn't and didn't even execute. If I planned everything that came before and was about to follow, which there's no way I could have, as you know, and will further read about, the big juicy ending, wouldn't I have merely been a drugged follower living under the indoctrination of a charismatic cult leader? I could be guilty of—what? Being an accomplice? Repurposing dead bodies as protest? We know there was the Orange Candidate Killer. That's not what they called him. The nationalistic psycho who was caught and confessed and killed himself in his cell. Another copycat. That's what he was. The follower of the Orange Monster who mimicked "the killings" to attack the poor and addicted and actually murdered them, trying to make it look like they, too, had OD'd. Fuck him. Patty Hearst went to prison for seven years. Most of the Manson girls were convicted. I was out on bail by the afternoon. Never served a day, innocent and free as the birds.

Evil is just a name we give to the unwanted hand that forces the world to bend to its will. I've found *ideas* aren't the true cause of most evil. Ideas aren't events or objects, like Phil taught me Descartes argued. Movements of thought convince people to do terrible things. But it's systems that prompt these movements of thoughts. It's all cumulative. Ideas are symptoms of systems. Systems are the result of habituated actions. Habituated actions are the result of social arrangements. It comes down to the essential flip of the cartesian model. Descartes was solipsistic and secluded, but we are not disembodied thinkers alone in our holographic isolation. It's all how we treat each other. I was subject to becoming an idea, like anyone who made conceptual art, but I didn't hold any evil notions. I didn't even know why I was at the bungalow. I had gotten a message. I missed Faia. I wanted to see her. Is that so bad? Things happened. A volcano is not evil. It's just pressure that builds up. A snake is not evil, it's just that my skin crawls to think of that pink play palace on Election Day, as the fate of the nation was decided by voters—or, really, by the electoral college, which very well may be evil itself. It was maybe two o'clock. I was about to meet God, as I've come to understand God. God is the antithesis of ideas.

The bathroom had a glass wall with a shower door, and a tiled shower wall held another glass door, which opened to the outdoor shower for the pool. Along the adjacent wall was a long marble counter, holding two sinks, and plush rolled towels on a lower shelf. There certainly must have been green fronds and foliage in white vases on the countertop. It was the era of monstera leaves. The freestanding white porcelain tub was large enough for two. On the wall adjacent to the tub, directly across from the shower, was a tiger maple and mahogany vanity with a creamy, coffee-colored leather chair. Nearby, the front legs of two cross-back chairs stuck boldly out in downward dog. Much of this would become covered in blood. I imagined kids fucking or being fucked in the tub, or on the chairs, teens, golden bodies in the Golden Age of Hollywood. How much young talent had this town destroyed? Wasserfeld. Another pervert dead. Even still, I loved LA.

I was sitting in the leather chair, watching my hands shake, wondering if my life would take a curtsy or a flail. Upon the vanity was a glass tray with slender bottles of toiletries. The bathroom was the nicest part of the bungalow. I twisted my torso to look in the long horizontal mirror to see how high I was, but I didn't feel it. I felt . . . only calm. This had been Howard Hughes's private place, once upon a time. Everyone knows, he had owned it.

"Royal-Lee," I yelled. I didn't know what I was going to ask.

It didn't matter; no one came to the door with a tissue in hand, raised to a puffy eye; there was no sign of life. Where were the signs of life? Was this the height of ambition, to be alone in this bungalow? At least I had Oxy. I needed something. Should I order a steak from room service with a beurre blanc, duck fat or truffle fries or whatever they would have, give up on veganism, and any and all of my moral principals? I was considering it. Was anyone here? I wanted a cigarette.

"Why am I here?" I yelled. "How did you get us into Faia's suite?"

"Who?" Had someone said that? Or was I hearing things? My ears rang.

"Faia. Faia Sickler. My best friend."

I put my hand on a door lever and pushed. The door opened. I immediately understood this game. I saw Phil's body on the bed, the bedding elevating his corpse, his open mouth, the way the sunlight fell on the floor but *not* his face, the back of his head on high-thread-count six-star Presidential Bungalow goose-down pillows. Even in death he looked outraged at the material. His penis was small, retracted in rigor mortis. I gasped, amazed at the physicality of his body laid out in the Presidential Bungalow bedroom, a memory of The Carlyle and our short time together. Pressure in the abdomen pushed out a small amount of waste onto the comforter with a fart.

Inside the bungalow, modern and classic design met with Mediterranean influence, built-in floor-to-ceiling white shelves and an entertainment area, oak floors, twelve-foot ceilings, the signature pink and green colors of the hotel, but very little green. Lots of white, from carpet to bedding—even recessed white leather wall panels that held nooked headboards and night tables and lamps to the master bed area all tucked back into its receded cove. It was classical and contemporary elegance, in white. Whiteness. Silver mirrors and fine handmade lampshades and fixture accents stood by like discreet servants. The walls were painted crème, the oriental rugs were thin, antique, Persian, the modern furniture robin's-egg blue or crème leather. It was beyond boringly underwhelming. It said *I paid too much*. I hated it. Maybe it was seeing Phil laid out on the bed that definitely twisted my stomach against it all.

The one good feature was the fireplace in the bedroom: a very classic 1920s Spanish stucco plaster, from a time when the moguls were doing everything in Louis XIV furniture, but this was the real classic everyman style of LA. With its lack of pretense and the evidence of the workers' hands who had fashioned it, the fireplace was the highlight of the bungalow.

"The killer" had a new body in a hotel. A nice room this time. But *which* killer? Me. Everything was a perfect setup so that if this body was left in the room under Faia's name, we would be bound together by everything that happened that fall, she and I. So far, the story of my life had been written about me but not *by* me. Not until this moment at the bungalow. It felt sort of tacky, grotesque, and advantageous, the thought I was having. But there was an angle, as an insider, almost dying myself, and living among the addicts who died . . . all great actions were disruptive, dangerous. I could either go along with the flow of the world, or I could make something of myself that was even more daring.

Otherwise, I was basically a part of the decorations at the Beverly Hills Hotel. A piece of the capitalist machine. Like Phil had taught. It wasn't a bad idea. I grasped it. Faia probably wasn't coming. It would be a human spectacle. I would shave his head. Why not? All the suffering in the world, all the pain, all those bodies I saw, like you see, everywhere I go in this country, the tents, the people with their pants down and shit in their undies, the fentanyl stupors, the women who look dead in doorways on doormats and by tents, so stoned they can't breathe. I came from this family, these families, that were trying to kill me, too. I had something I owed the world. That was what Phil had taught me, that death meant nothing without transformation. That if I didn't use it, I'd become just another ghost in this place, another decorative corpse in white sheets. And maybe I was already. *But if I did it I'd take the fall.*

I tried to hold it all in my mind. The thought of my once best friend, Faia. She would never accept me now. Not after the Art Walk. Not when I was linked to "the killings" in any way. I was looking at his body and I was getting emotional. She had turned away long ago.

Maybe I would die of an OD soon. I could take credit for this one, let them think I'd used Phil, let my father know he could fuck off, and let the police sort the dead from the dead. Let society figure it out. I wouldn't do Daddy's bidding.

I did have a knack for turning scenes into sculptures. I didn't ask for this body in the bungalow but one doesn't always ask for their art to come to them, it just comes, and it had and I could already feel him asking me to make him bear witness, a testament in death. This beautiful man. And then what? I'd clean myself up, I'd change my life, and the evidence would prove me innocent. I'd admit I did just this one *intervention.*

I can see him now in ways that are different from the photos that were posted and shared on the news and all over, which would not be taken in this hotel room. On the bed, there was a spiritual sense of what life was that I still only understand from those deaths that fall. I knew what it was by then. I can't explain it in a million years, but I'd known it from the moment I'd found my roommate on the floor in my dorm room, her skin in the sunlight like warm butter in the late fall glow, almost translucent—it was around this same time of year—and then a shadow fell across her freckled nose. I remember her crinkly eyelids crusted by mascara as if painted in heavy oil on an a completely relaxed face. Death was the absolute authority on life. The death face is uncanny and unmistakable. Something remains inside each dead body. A seeming mistake of perception. A light trapped inside waiting to be let out. *Is that love?*

This need for death to be a mistake; is that what love is? *The mistake.* It's truer than the faces that get photographed to annihilation in selfies and candids every minute of our lives; we're practiced at being perceived, made up in make-believe, totally against the question of life. This was a still life. It wasn't still alive. If that's not too cheesy. This was the frozen beauty of not wanting to let go. As Butler said, "People need to be grieved; loss needs to be acknowledged." Right? There are no words for certain things, the heart of the moon, the way it feels to be alive.

All these dead bodies sent me tunneling into my own corporality. I needed more Oxy. Death may be absolutely silent, but life bangs on whether you're ready to look it in the face or not. I chewed my fingernail. I got closer to him. The Santa Ana winds whipped outside the bungalow, breathing, loud enough to be felt, through the palms. The world was shaking alive, coming for me like a storm, like the story of my own creation.

I remembered The Carlyle. He'd worn Calvin Klein white bikini-briefs and I'd worn royal blue Wolford underwear with a see-through underwire bra, like I was trying to feel some sense of titillation; my life was still collegiate and kempt back then. It wasn't really for me. It wasn't my reality. I'd had him step out of his underwear to paint him as a white blur, my professor, seeing his big dick, his balls, like Rilke's Apollo. The smile that ran to his dark center. I thought about the Sicklers, who they were, and how I felt about them, and my father, and my mother, and the wake of tyranny and death they pulled behind them in their net, and I was thinking of the idea of signing his body as art, and then I was doing it with that black marker I'd been carrying around in my jumpsuit.

I guess it remains an interesting question in terms of praxis. Was his dead body a work of political art? Was I being manipulated? Or was I manifesting it all? Would my mother be proud? What would Faia think? Was it totally unfair to put this on her permanent online record, socially, publicly? Didn't she owe something for all her family had done to help kill so many people? She was never going to speak out. Not against her father, who had done so much to hurt her. Not against their billions. I wasn't the only one with daddy issues. I realized that I had been touching his body, holding his hand, squeezing it. Was this the most profound artistic statement of my lifetime? Was I insane?

I heard a movement at the door.

"Hello!" I yelled.

"Shut up," Faia said.

I turned and saw her in the doorway, wielding a knife. I'd been expecting Peter—but it was Faia. My best friend. Her forehead looked larger than I remembered, like her brain had swelled with suspicion. Her blonde eyebrows, stupid as ever, carried no hint of kindness. She looked like a parody of herself: a tall blonde in an early-2000s CK logo sweatshirt, mom jeans, Gucci backless loafers, and that JW Anderson "Pierce" bag slung over the shoulder of the arm not wielding the knife. A Japanese Kotetsu, probably from the kitchen block. For a second, I felt caught—like I'd been caught *doing something*. Like I was in trouble. But what had I done? Was I the bad guy? Was Faia here for justice, or revenge? Was she the real killer? Did she think *I* was the killer? Maybe I was. It would make sense if she thought so. She had the knife. There are so many knives in the world, and this one was in *her* hand—gleaming like a threat or a test. And I didn't have one. So how could she think I was "the killer"? And how could I not, for a moment, feel my heart drop and wonder—had she been following me? Was she involved in all this?

"He's dead," I offered.

"What?"

"He died of an overdose."

The silence hovered.

"You killed Ash? Are you the fucking killer?" Faia held the knife out.

"You're the one with the knife. Do I look like I'm hurting him? He's dead. And you can't stab with a knife like that, only chop."

I looked back at Phil and all I could see was a man who should have tried harder. Was I like that? All he knew how to do was argue. What was his point? Who cared? We watched TV on laptops now. The revolution was live-streamed by people who would never revolt. We lived on our phones and got our kicks from prescription bottles. Phil would want to be used as direct action. His body could become a legendary statement. Photos would be taken by the press and the police and I could tell the world we made art out of death and fucked with billionaires. Anyone could do it. Anytime. Or maybe just me. You could kill them. You could get away with it. Or I was special. I was privileged. Had Faia known Phil? Were they all using me? My head spun. Would I be blamed for all "the killings"? I was tired of the questions.

I stood and watched the light on Faia's face. Her lips had a cupid's bow, and her nose had a slightly deviated septum I could see from feet away. I felt something for her that I still can't explain, the fear of being rejected I'd felt all of my life, the need I had for her to love me, and the power imbalance between our families. I charged at her and picked up a lamp and bashed her in the head, but it didn't break. Her head started bleeding a little. The purse strap fell into the crook of her elbow.

She swung the knife and it sliced across my cheek and it felt like a hilarious kiss. Hot tears ran down my wet face, it was a river of blood. I pushed her into the side jamb and knocked the knife out of her hand, skirting by, the hot blood rushing down my face and down my neck into the collar of my jumpsuit. She crouched to pick up the knife and I tossed a vase I'd grabbed off the credenza. It was full of idiotic dried pampas grass that looked like roaring feathers. When I chucked it at her it shattered near her head, and she covered one eye with her hand, but had the knife and was racing at me.

Was Faia "the killer"?

Was her dad using her like my dad was trying to use me? I picked up a large square cushion from the couch. It was thick and covered in velvet. The knife came through the cover and the batting and stopped just before my face, which was still bleeding heavily. I reached around the cushion and grabbed her hand. I dug my nails in and somehow managed to shake the pillow and blade from between us. Faia leapt over the couch and her big basic athletic body landed on top of mine, where I fell on my back into the glass coffee table. She spit in my face. I don't know what her fucking problem was. I spit in her face. We glared at each other and she spit in my face again and I licked the spit off my lips and cheek and laughed as I saw Peter coming into the room. He grabbed her by the throat from behind and dragged her into the bathroom, slamming the door and wedging a chair under the door handle.

"My hero," I said, laughing and coughing.

He didn't laugh. I felt nothing for Faia. The spell of our love was broken, for the moment. Royal-Lee came in with the wheelchair and they went into the bedroom, returning moments later with Phil's body, wearing the bucket hat and the windbreaker. Faia was banging on the door, screaming that she was going to kill me. She obviously was obsessed. I hadn't done anything to her. It was really irrational. I pressed a small throw pillow against my face to stop the bleeding and left the Beverly Hills Hotel campus with Royal-Lee and Peter, who had each driven their own cars. Royal-Lee parked with the valet and I went with them to wait for the Beetle. Peter had parked the Continental on the street, on the North Crescent Drive side of the hotel, under the palm trees, which were whipping like hell in the wind. I swallowed my last pill as they told me we were still going to the masked election party. The masks and cloaks were in the Beetle's trunk from Dick's costume party, a happy accident. I knew just how to do it. I knew where to place the body. I had the code and the password. I knew every inch of the property.

We decided we would take two cars to avoid looking suspicious—all piled together, which no one did in LA—although the Beetle was a bit Manson. A bit suspicious in its own right. I didn't have to drive it. I would drive the Lincoln since I didn't drive a stick. It was a masked ball. No one would know who we were. If you stacked half a million bodies on top of one another and placed them on the Sickler estate, you'd have the opposite of an idea. We had only one. Peter instructed Royal-Lee that after the party, they were to fairly distribute the small stacks of cash and pills from the safe to the addicts of the Villa. Royal-Lee should take whatever personal compensation she wanted.

"Why don't you just leave?" I asked Royal-Lee as we got into the Continental, after switching cars outside of the hotel, after we found Peter leaning against the side of the Lincoln like a boss, smoking. I still don't know why Royal-Lee rode with me. Probably to make sure I would go to the party with them both, although I had no intention of missing it.

"Peter says he loves me. At least Phil's body will get noticed and respected. Everyone will see him. I don't know. Maybe it's what he'd want." She started crying.

"You think Peter's your boyfriend now? But if he likes you, I guess, and you like him. I get it. Sometimes you gotta get what you can. No one will ever know about you and all of this. I won't tell anyone, I swear. I think Phil was in love with you. I really do. He just couldn't let himself have what he wanted. You know, right? But, Royal-Lee, listen to me—Peter's not Phil. Phil was a sweetheart."

"Peter says he's going to disappear after this. I will, too. Forget you knew me."

"I didn't know you. We were ghosts together is all. Everyone is a ghost now. It's the media overload. We live our entire lives in ideas, separate from each other and everything we are meant to love. It's business. It's the basis of our entire society. That's what Phil understood, art isn't real, ideas aren't real. People aren't real. The world isn't real."

"What are you saying?"

"Don't worry about it."

26

Heading West into the Sunset . . .

I wiped my blood on the arm of my jumpsuit as I started the Lincoln. I was sweating and trembling and starting to itch, but I wasn't sure if it was from jonesing or nervousness, and I tried to put things out of my head. The little pillow was soaked in blood, staunching the wound on my face. Peter stopped the Beetle and came out and told me we had to go back to the Villa. He would need to destroy all the records first, gather all the money from the safes, and get rid of the pills. We could leave no trace.

I pocketed a handful of Royal-Lee's ten-milligram cannabis sour watermelon gummies from their stash in the suite as we cleaned out the apartment building on West Adams. I ate one as we fled and I drove the Continental west. I don't know why we couldn't have any more Oxy, but Peter was a fucker about it, and had flushed them all. There were tons. The toilet water was bloodred. He said no more drugs.

There would be photos of Phil's body with my signature on his foot. "Renegade Artist Strikes Again." The photos would hang in a museum. Was I crazy? What was I doing? Would I release a statement? His body was in the trunk. Maybe I should black out my signature. Maybe I should back down.

After Oxy, weed felt like needing to pay attention to all the little intricacies of how I felt at each moment, every aesthetic element of my environment, and whatever creative bullshit my imagination was feeding me. It was maddening. The opposite of being drugged out, because I could hear myself thinking, amplified. I could feel my thoughts imposed on the world. I'd have to learn how to love my mind. This was also a maddening thought. I was finally coming out of my long dalliance with opioids. Could I crawl out of this? Could I survive? It felt like a fever dream—like in a storybook I'd read as a child about a traveler I couldn't remember anything about who fell ill with malaria. At some point someone from housekeeping would let Faia out of that bathroom but she'd have to wait because she didn't have her phone; I'd seen it on the floor as we left the bungalow and I'd taken the sim card and smashed it.

Whoosh.

I told Royal-Lee that after we got to the party, and once we'd unloaded, she should just keep the car, keep going; this would be our goodbye.

"Hey, Royal," I said. I studied her face for a moment before looking back at the road. "I'm sure you're going to be fine. Cheer up."

Peter followed us in the Beetle. I watched him in the rearview. On the way to the freeway, we passed graffitied buildings, a painting of the Lady of Guadalupe, auto parts stores, income tax service signs flapping in the breeze, an abandoned gas station, RVs. We drove past boarded-up buildings, a coin-op laundry, fading murals, a woman giving out parking tickets.

"Take West Adams to the 10 to the 405," Royal-Lee said from the passenger seat.

"I know where I'm going," I said. "This is my town."

"You don't know West Adams," Royal-Lee countered. "You don't know downtown. Or the east side. This is *my* town."

"Fine. But the freeways belong to everybody."

Royal-Lee was quiet in agreement. "Peter's sober," she said. "I'm proud of him."

I nodded. Most of the buildings were dilapidated, boarded over, encased with iron bars over entrances and windows, but occasionally there was an Iglesia Cristiana or a beauty salon with bare windows, glass doors. Risky businesses. There were people riding bicycles and carrying basketballs, standing on the side of the road, talking in couples. Happy Faces Party Supply next to the Royal Liberty Mart sold *cold beer, grocery, liquor.* It was getting darker earlier but there was still plenty of sunlight. Pink and terracotta and brown stucco everywhere, signs in Spanish, and the thud of car stereos; I heard the world. Two identical homeless people were living under a giant electrical tower on the corner of Fairfax and West Adams. Their camp stood across from the Jiffy Lube, on the median of grass between Fairfax and Genesee Avenue, heading toward Electric Drive. I got in the right turning lane by mistake and Peter beeped the Beetle. He was following closely behind me. I'd take a left in two blocks onto the Santa Monica Freeway. I corrected and got into the left lane.

Tent camps lined the on-ramp. I pressed the gas and heard and felt the engine as I merged onto the 10, looking out over a fleet of electric company bucket-lift boom trucks for working on power lines, more encampments farther off into the bamboo and eucalyptus. People liked to live near traffic; it was less lonely, someone had said.

Heading west, traffic was opening up and I could see the mountains out toward Santa Monica and up to Will Rogers State Beach, where the waves never stopped lapping the shore. Peter's Beetle weaved in and out of the lanes behind me. Was he having second thoughts? Maybe we should just take Phil's body to the beach. Leave him by a lifeguard stand. No, that wasn't going to happen. I'd seen too much to stop now.

To the right and out was Beverly Hills. The fading dream of empire. The sky was a theater of gray and silver with patches of blue and edges of white against the darker clouds. The blue sky and the sun were alive. I crinkled my eyes against the orange ball dropping west and slipped on some cheap scratched-up sunglasses I was happy to find hanging from the rearview mirror. Ahead, the mountains were lush green, lit up almost monochromatically by the sun.

The 405 was glossy, light on cars, the familiar feeling of somewhere to go. Air through the windows. There were wine lockers and cannabis dispensaries off the freeway. *Somewhere* there would be *something*, the freeway promised me, some great beautiful thing that would be all mine—a home of my own. A dream. We passed terracotta condominiums with banners that read *LIVE LA YOUR WAY* on green and white vinyl. There was a sign for Wilshire. More condos along the freeway. We'd get there sort of early, perfect timing. Where on the property would we put him? I was having second and third thoughts.

I wanted to take exit 57A for Sunset Boulevard, cruise past the Bel-Air Country Club, Marymount, wind around UCLA, and turn down Comstock. I didn't want to take Wilshire through Westwood and be reminded of college. I saw the Beetle in my mirrors. Sickler's house awaited in Holmby Hills. I suddenly felt very weird. It was getting darker. I remembered the election. There were cranes in the distance, four red, one blue, one white. I heard a sharp rapid popping sound like my tire had gone out, but it was driving fine. The Jetta in front of us had a handicap plate, and die-cast palm trees and a silver wave for its frame. I heard fireworks, and suddenly the cars started to veer. A Rolls Royce hit a Tesla, knocking its gray bumper off. I saw Peter swerve past me in the Beetle, cruising on ahead. I drove, glad I had avoided this collision. Then another car veered and crashed into the wall of the off-ramp. Then the snapping sounds were growing louder. I saw two figures that looked like hitchhikers over by the retaining wall of the freeway.

"Stop!" Royal-Lee yelled. Cars were hitting one another, then the snapping sounds popped louder. "No!" Royal-Lee cried. "Stop. They're shooting at us."

I saw the two figures more clearly. They wore jeans and tight white T-shirts. They were shooting assault rifles into traffic. Something clicked in my mind. Déjà vu like something I had practiced in a dream. I drove onto the shoulder and yelled for Royal-Lee to get down. Royal-Lee was screaming, but things fell silent for me, and I drove, swerving around a BMW on the shoulder. The driver inside was bleeding and in shock, studying the blood on her hands. I ducked and drove, glancing up occasionally as I felt I could, while flooring it. The engine lagged and caught up. Cars swerved. They knocked into each other and broke apart into plastic. People were bleeding.

I realized the radio was on as I saw the first gunman approaching fast in my vision, firing at cars like anyone practiced shooting an AR-15 would. I'd done the same so many times. I ducked and slammed the gas as I hit the shooter hard with the chrome bumper and grill of the Continental. His body was flung up and flew over the hood and long roof like in a movie. I sat up, my foot easing a little off the gas, and I braked as I hit the second gunman and smashed him into the retaining wall of the freeway embankment. I heard Royal-Lee and me catch in our seatbelts and the metal crunch as we flung forward after we hit. The second shooter was between the crumpled front of the Lincoln and the cement wall. I kept pushing the gas, the car pressing harder against the wall, the engine growling. I let out a loud war cry. With each press of the pedal, the crushed body jumped a little less, bowing like some broken mechanized doll. Blood ran out of the shooter's mouth and ears and spilled on the hood of the car. Vehicles were stopped across the freeway. I put the car in park and got out. This was my moment.

The teenager I'd just crushed into the wall wasn't moving. He was pinned tightly. The bald-headed teen was dead, a faint mustache on his upper lip, cheeks pubescent and acned. He looked like he should be in high school. The rifle lay a few feet away. I grabbed it. I walked over to the boy and checked his breathing. I could smell his sweat. And Ivory soap. Was there anything as strange as a dead teen boy? All the masculine posturing was gone, the spark and hope and angst and passion departed; just the body remained. Just like my roommate at NYU. I had caught a whiff of her shampoo when I'd knelt down to check her pulse. The girl's watch was still ticking. The beginning of the end. *Whoosh.*

The other shooter was still on the ground. I ran over to him with the rifle up. He was dead, blood pooling out of his head. His bloody ears were glowing in the sun like red poppies against pink tulips.

I went back to the Continental and killed the engine. Royal-Lee was trembling in the passenger seat. I opened the door.

"Let's get Phil out there," I said. "Get out and help!" I yelled over the blare of car horns and screaming.

We placed his body on the shoulder of the road by the first dead shooter. Sirens were getting louder, whooshing like the wind down the 405. This was the point that was discussed many times at the trial. Why did I leave the signed body? Why would I have brought the body out of the trunk of the Lincoln and placed it beside the dead shooters? Why had Phil Krolik been transported in the trunk of the car registered to his brother? What was my connection to the unsolved killings of the most vulnerable members of society? All I can say is this: I was trying to speak in univocal support of the poor and addicted, and to speak against the Sicklers. My old teacher helped me share in his agenda of direct action and protest. But I think Phil lost his ability to make a difference when he used fentanyl with his brother the day Peter showed up at the Villa. We'd had a vision and we'd lost it.

The cars were starting to move. I saw and heard sirens and lights. Royal-Lee and I got back in the Lincoln. Royal-Lee was quiet in the passenger seat, knees hugged tight against her chest. I turned the ignition and backed up. The body that had been pinned to the wall collapsed. I drove the wrong way up the shoulder just as emergency vehicles were arriving and the cars moved to the left lanes. Then I turned us around on the shoulder and pulled over and we watched the traffic.

At first it had stayed at a standstill, the cars out of their lanes, disorderly but peaceful, like a movie set in some world where cars get left scattered across the freeway. Then the vehicles began to find three paths, little rivers forming new channels, as more cars came and then police on motorcycles arrived with their lights flashing, weaving across lanes, back and forth in red and blue, so the cars could only drive in the HOV lane. Other cop vehicles arrived, watching over those still alive in the cars that had taken fire. Dozens were hit and bleeding. Traffic moved slowly, and an ambulance came, and fire trucks. A van arrived and raised its antennae as a reporter and her camera crew got out. Everyone was together in society in pantomime.

Above, the sky held the last minutes of sunset. Helicopters came. A pink heart-shape settled low in the sky amid rivers of purple and orange and pinker strands of clouds like colored smoke. The smell of gunpowder hung in the air. Sooner or later, I would be on the news. There would be plenty of questions about the body, what it meant, and why it had been placed in and out of the Continental. We were in shock and just watched for maybe thirty minutes or an hour. I eventually turned the key a click in the ignition and the FM radio played. The music was just being interrupted. "We apologize for this interruption, but we now turn our attention to a breaking emergency report from the 405N. There has been a shooting, with multiple casualties reported, and many more injured in cars that have taken fire during what is being reported as a second mass shooting today for the Los Angeles area. It is unclear if the shooter or shooters were politically motivated, or linked to the earlier shooting that took place near a voting station in Azusa. Several voting centers in the greater Los Angeles area have been locked down in response, and while there is no clear winner for this election, it seems already there are grave consequences to this Election Day. Connected to the election, a gruesome killing has been reported, occurring at a private masked Election Day ball hosted at the estate of pharmaceutical mogul Richard Sickler. It appears and . . . please . . . parental discretion is advised for this story . . . Richard Sickler is dead, victim of . . ." I turned the dial to a different station. His head had been cut off. I got out and took a deep breath. I lay down on the hood of the car, the warm metal under my back. I listened to the music and watched the gradient of the sky fade toward dark.

I took out my phone and flipped it to selfie mode and then put it away. What did it all mean? Why had I met Phil? What now? There was no sense hating life, or trying to figure it out, or wishing upon a star for purer causes or fuller understandings. You had to take whatever was coming to you, and use it. That was God. You couldn't control the world, or fate, or figure out the big mystery all at once. You could only play with it, like a kite in the breeze, ready to soar. Like an artist. Like me. At least that's how I felt. I felt like an artist. Now I make art out of the events of the day, choosing my victims to sculpt in their funeral beds, in the caskets, reproducing the victims of war and poverty and industry and refashioning their images and final resting places into designs that speak to the deaths and their causes.

What would I say to the police when I went to them and told them I had killed the shooters, and placed the body of my old teacher, Phil Krolik, on the freeway? Time would tell, but I wasn't going to say anything until I was lawyered up, and sober. Richard Sickler was dead. Dad would be happy. The sky was turning purple. I looked back through the windshield. The Church, my mother, my dad, Faia, everyone would have a story. Faia and I would make up, after she got all the money. My dad had helped Dick amend his will in time.

Royal-Lee got out of the car. She had been sitting silently in shock.

"Are you okay?" I asked Royal-Lee.

Royal-Lee nodded. They were okay, I saw. The future was coming. It was in the air. Something better, different, more awake to the dawning of the millennium, only sixteen years too late. Shit was going to get crazy.

"Are you okay?" Royal-Lee asked me.

"I'm good," I said, and nodded. I watched Royal-Lee leave and walk along the blacktop, then jog up into the night, east and away from it all. Royal-Lee had ten grand in one pocket. That was enough to get you anywhere.

I unzipped my jumpsuit a little and pulled it down across my shoulders, and pressed my upper back against the hood. A breeze was blowing, and I wanted to feel a little of the late fall air on my skin, cool wind whooshing down from Bel-Air, through the Los Angeles cemetery, over the freeway, mixing with the smoke of flares and the exhaust and lifting my hair and dropping it back down onto the black steel hood.

Special Thanks

To **Ottessa Moshfegh**, my great love, who sharpened the knife—without whom this book wouldn't and couldn't exist.

To **Carl Steven Goebel**, the inspiration, my only brother, and my blood. Thank you for being with me in KILL DICK, I miss you every day.

To **Steven C. Goebel**, my father, who read this book more than anyone, perhaps. To **Liz Marie Eiting**, my loving mother, who forgives. To my sister, **Marie Elizabeth Eiting Saldivar**, who makes life worth living. To her daughter **Delia Saldivar**, the next generation and our hopes and dreams—may the world be better when you are our ages. To my perfect agent, **Bill Clegg**, for reading the book fifteen times. To **Kate Gale** for believing. To Red Hen Press and all who work there. To **Mark Cull**. To my editor and steadfast companion, **Marc Merrill Gumbin**. To my copyeditor, **Carrie Cooperider**. To my master publicist, **Michael Lawson**—both on this novel and *Eileen* the film. To **Alex Israel** for the amazing artwork he gave for the cover, and for friendship and advice.

To my beloved grandparents, now deceased—**Marie Elizabeth Redmond Eiting** and **John (Jack) Ralph Eiting**—you are my entire heart. You saved me from the streets. To everyone who worked at PSI. To every counselor, lawyer, rehab administrator, judge, and ass in a seat in meetings, mental institutions, and rehabs who helped me find my way. To my entire extended family—my heart—especially **John Carl Eiting** and family, Carrie Eiting and family, Trish Eiting and family, Kate Eiting, and all my cousins. To my priests. To my generous blurb providers: Lidia Yuknavitch, Melissa Broder, Matthew Specktor,

Anna Delvey, Scott McClanahan, Giancarlo DiTrapano, Anna Dorn, Lukas Gage, Kimberly King Parsons, and Harriet Armstrong. To my stars: Joaquin Phoenix, Rooney Mara, Anne Hathaway, Thomasin McKenzie, Shea Whigham, Jennifer Lawrence, Brian Tyree Henry, Steff and Chuck Roven, Anthony Bregman. To Ken Kesey for talking to me at age 12, and all my friends who believed in me while I was crazy. Thank you, Alex Merto for cover design, Nikhil Melnechuk for images, Lianna Gualberti for playing Susie Vogelman, Daniel Hamaj for photography, Veronica Kelegian as Faia Sickler, and Alexa St. Von as Royal-Lee. Matthew Johnson of Tyrant Books and Fat Possum Records. Lydia Sviatoslavsky, Ben Crisp, and also Erica Barry of UTA.

And to my angel of Skid Row, **Theresa**—who showed me around her world, introduced me to the street bosses, and fought her whole life for prison reform and social justice in and out of prisons and on Skid Row until she died. The fight rages on. To all the radicals and artists. Most of all, thank you to everyone who made me believe in art as an act of survival—and to those who didn't, for giving me something to prove.

And to Dick—wherever you are—thanks for dying so beautifully on the page.

You rotten piece of shit.

Biographical Note

Luke B. Goebel is an acclaimed author and screenwriter. A recipient of the Ronald Sukenick Innovative Fiction Prize and the Joan Scott Memorial Fiction Award, his debut novel, *Fourteen Stories, None of Them Are Yours*, garnered critical acclaim. Goebel also co-wrote the major motion pictures *Eileen* and *Causeway.*